THIS IS THE WAY THE WORLD IS . . .

Jake had a lot of news. He says there were floods in Glens Falls last month, eleven people dead; there's a new provisional state government in Rensselaer, which makes at least three that we know of; the governor in Rensselaer wants to send a delegation next year to an American Jubilee at Mount Weather, in order to celebrate the President's next birthday; and there's been no word from an expedition that set out six months ago from Schenectady, bound for the atomic power plant at Indian Point to see if it could be made useful again.

The party is presumed dead. . . .

BRAD FERGUSON

THE WORLD NEXT DOOR

TOR®

A TOM DOHERTY ASSOCIATES BOOK
NEW YORK

THE WORLD NEXT DOOR

A Tor Book
Published by Tom Doherty Associates, Inc.
49 West 24th Street
New York, N.Y. 10010

Cover art by David Mattingly

ISBN: 0-812-53795-5

First edition: October 1990

Printed in the United States of America

0 9 8 7 6 5 4 3 2 1

For Virginia Kidd,
with thanks and appreciation

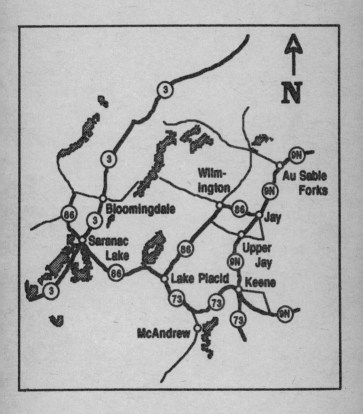

PROLOGUE

MOUNTAINS ARE NOT FOREVER, BUT ONLY IF YOU'RE
God or a geologist. If you're neither, then mountains
will do until forever comes along.

These particular mountains were mere molehills in
the cosmic, God-sense of things, even though they had
stood, tall and proud, for many millions of years. They
knew of no other mountains, and so they considered
themselves to be young ones. It was certainly true that
the smug, self-assured vigor of the young, the kind
that knows no end, ran through them . . . but it was
not their own vigor. There are things older than mountains.

The mountains unknowingly drew their strength
from the ancient yet ageless rock upon which they
stood. It was rock so old that it had never been seen;
it had formed and been buried deeply long, long before anything with eyes had evolved. Now that was
respectably old, even in the jaundiced opinion of God.

The rock was so old and so quiet, so undemanding,

that the mountains above it were ignorant of its presence. In their happy arrogance, the mountains had come to believe that they themselves were responsible for their own making and that they determined their own fate. Those beliefs did not annoy the underlying rock; indeed, they supplied a gentle and most welcome amusement that expressed itself in low laughter that rumbled, unheard, for millennia.

There was more besides the mountains and the rock. There were also scampering things, incredibly active and tragically ephemeral things, that lived on the very skin of the mountains. The scampering things were as unaware of the true nature of the mountains as the mountains were of the true nature of the rock.

The rock was old enough for its initially subtle awareness to have grown enough to cast itself around the planet and extend across the chasm of possibility into alternative probability. The rock was everywhere and anywhen. It knew, as the mountains could not, that without the scampering things, the mountains and the rock together would be barren, useless and without further purpose. It was the instinct of the rock to protect the scampering things and permit them to live and grow.

Some of the scampering things carried within them a compulsion to categorize and characterize their world by bestowing names upon small bits of it. They had given the mountains the name of Adirondack, which meant merely "they of the great rocks." The scampering things had not even bothered to name the mountains for the mountains themselves, but for the inconsequential fellow things that lived upon them. This infuriated the mountains and added greatly to the slow amusement of the rock, which knew everything and understood all of it.

In the last eyeblink of time, the rock had suddenly realized that there were far fewer scampering things living upon the mountains, and that even the mountains themselves had somehow been terribly damaged. The rock did not hesitate. It supplied its strength unstintingly to the mountains, but the rock soon realized that even all its vast resources would not be enough to permit survival, let alone recovery. The scampering things would soon die, and all purpose would end.

That could not be and would not be permitted. The rock thought about it and, being very old and very wise, quickly found a solution. The rock would realize hope from the promise of doom.

It had to. After all, the rock knew that a planet only four billion years old has just barely gotten started.

CHAPTER 1

HE HAD A HEADACHE, AND THE NEWS FROM EUROPE *was pretty goddamn awful and it wasn't making much sense to him anyway, so he turned off the cheap bedside radio. He thought things had been bad enough last night when he'd left to do the gig, but at least both sides had been talking about compromising and reconciliating and accommodating. This morning, though, the Russians were rolling along the autobahns just as nice as you please in their shiny new tanks, bringing a whole new meaning to German reunification.*

He didn't know why America should give a rat's ass about what happened to a bunch of stupid bastards over in Europe, but it did, and so there it was. To nuke or not to nuke, that was the question—and here was the world, hanging on the edge and waiting for the answer. He thought he ought to leave town like most other people, but he had two shows tonight, and if he no-showed, he wouldn't get his check for the week.

He reluctantly decided that he'd stick at least through tonight, telling himself that they hadn't blown up the world all those other times. He went to see if there was any aspirin left in his bag. It turned out there wasn't. He settled for washing his face with the trickle of tepid water from the cracked motel sink and turning in. Despite the constant blare from the highway just outside his window, he stayed awake for only a few minutes more. He was used to sleeping days.

Jake Garfield awoke blinking. He sneezed once and looked around blearily. The only thing he saw was a squirrel that was watching him from about thirty feet away. The sun was just coming up; it looked to be about six or so.

"Hey, Prosper?" he called.

"Back here, man," came a voice from the woods. "Nature's callin' me pretty damn loud this mornin'."

Jake climbed out of his bedroll and stood slowly, easing his muscles into motion. Jake's hip had found a rock under the bedroll sometime during the night, and so he had the beginnings of a bruise. He rubbed it, frowning. Sleeping on the ground was not the way Jake preferred to take his rest, but he'd seen no building he trusted on the road from Saranac Lake before night had fallen. As it was, his night's rest hadn't done him much good; he felt as if he'd turned in just a few moments before awakening.

The structures he and Prosper had found along Route 86 to Lake Placid were uninhabited and in ruins. Once, long ago, those outlying buildings had represented the forward guard of Lake Placid's growth. Now the forest was busy taking the buildings, the road and everything else made by man back into itself. New growth was sprouting everywhere, without human intervention to inhibit or direct it. In a few centuries, perhaps much less than that, the whole area would be as wild as it had ever been before the white man had come. The new forest would have spread into all the towns and eaten everything everywhere. It was something to think about.

"What do you want to do about breakfast?" Jake called.

"There any leftover rabbit?"

"Nope. Picked clean."

"Blueberries, then, I guess," Prosper called back. "There's some bushes back here. I'll get 'em."

"Thanks a lot."

Jake stretched and began his exercises. His sore muscles began to yield to deep knee bends and other calisthenics. His partner Prosper reappeared just as he was finishing; he'd gathered several handfuls of blueberries and was carrying them in his hat.

They divvied the haul and began eating. "Sweet," Jake said.

"Pretty good," Prosper allowed. "Berries been good all summer—good as I can remember, anyway. How'd you sleep?"

Jake shrugged. "Okay for a while, and then I'd wake up for some reason," he said. "On and off all night."

"You havin' nightmares?" Prosper asked.

Jake shook his head. "No. At least, I don't think so. I was busking somewhere. That's all I remember. Why?"

"I had nightmares, man," said Prosper. "Don't remember anythin', except I was real scared about somethin', you know?"

"What?"

"Don't know," Prosper said. Then he smiled. "Maybe I was scared of 'nother berry breakfast, man." They both laughed.

After eating, Jake sat on the ground and closely inspected his feet. His increasingly ragged shoes were doing less and less to protect them, and he had not yet been able to find serviceable replacements. He gave close attention to a developing sore spot on his right instep; it promised to be big trouble.

He had to be able to walk far and walk fast. Wanderin' Jake Garfield and Prosper Cross were buskers—traveling tellers of tales and strolling singers of songs. They were minstrels. Singing for their supper is what the two men did for a living, and their continuing survival proved they were reasonably good at it. They lived by their wits and their ability to entertain isolated people emotionally starved for something fresh, something from outside. These days, that was everybody.

Jake glanced over at Prosper, who winked back and grinned, his teeth flashing white. Nothing ever seemed to bother Prosper. It was amazing.

"Let's get going," Jake said, and they did, setting off again on old Route 86. "Lake Placid, here we come."

"Not far 'til Placid now," Prosper said. "We'll find people there, I know it. Used to be a big place, man—says so right there on that map of yours. Maybe it still is."

"I hope you're right," Jack sighed. "Prosper, I've got to do something about these shoes. I think I'm getting another blister."

"Want to stop?"

"Not yet. In town will be soon enough."

"Where there's people, there'll be shoes," Prosper said. "We'll sing you up some shoes in Placid, don't worry. Now if that sore spot gets worse, you let me know. We'll take a rest, get a fire going, sterilize a needle, pop that li'l sucker. Okay?"

"Okay," Jake said. "I just wish we'd see somebody."

"So do I, man."

"I never expected Saranac Lake to be empty," said Jake. "Hell, it used to be the center of everything in these mountains. It was even bigger than Lake Placid.''

"Well, there's people around here somewhere," said Prosper. "I can almost see them wavin' to us already, no foolin'.''

They walked on, talking when it suited them and simply enjoying the beautiful September morning when it did not. The hours passed and the sun climbed high.

"There's a sign," Prosper said at last, pointing. "What's it say?''

Jake read it to him.

WELCOME TO LAKE PLACID
SITE OF THE 1932
WINTER OLYMPIC GAMES

Underneath this was a simple design of five interlocked rings that meant nothing to either of them.

"What were 'Winter Olympic Games'?'' Prosper asked.

Jake shrugged. "I'm not sure," he said. "They were sports. That's about all I know.''

"What kind of sports?''

"Skiing, ice skating. Things like that.''

"Those are sports?''

"I guess they were, once.''

"Sounds silly. Might as well make fishing a sport.''

"Might as well. Prosper, I don't see anybody.''

"I know, man. That's bad. How long since you were here with your papa?''

"Fifteen years.''

"That's a long time, man.''

"Yeah.''

The last time Jake had been here, Lake Placid had been full of people and in excellent repair. Now the town, like Saranac Lake and most of the others they'd passed through, was deserted, and many of its buildings had fallen into ruin.

Jake had had several big Adirondack towns specifically in mind to visit and had been badly disappointed, and not a little bit scared, to find every one of them empty. He and Prosper had found the town of Blue Mountain Lake abandoned. They'd then continued north to Long Lake and Tupper Lake, only to find that the two villages and the forest between them had burned perhaps a decade before. After that, they had gone to Saranac Lake, and now they were in Lake Placid.

Jake and Prosper made their way slowly and carefully, making at least a cursory inspection of the houses and stores they passed. They kept an eye out for something useful, but there seemed to be nothing left for them to take; the bones of Lake Placid had long since been picked clean by others who had come this way. They were also on the lookout for dangerous animals—most likely wild dogs—that might have taken over the buildings for their own use. If there were any, though, they were keeping themselves quiet and well hidden at the sight of humans, and for that Jake was grateful.

"No go, man," Prosper said at last. "This place is as dead as Saranac Lake was."

"I'm afraid so," Jake said. "It's hard to believe."

"Flu?" Prosper asked.

"Probably," Jake replied. "It must have run through here like wildfire." He glanced at the sun. "Look, let's give the place a once-over-lightly."

"You sure? Looks like the locusts already came through."

"It can't hurt," Jake said. "Worth the chance, anyway; others might have figured it that way and skipped a search. You go that way and check out those houses; I'll head down there to those stores. Meet you at the bend of the road up there in, um, about an hour."

"Think it's safe to split up?"

Jake nodded. "This place is dead," he said.

"Well, okay," Prosper said, a note of reluctance in his voice. "Anythin' happens, though, you give me a shout."

"Don't worry about it—and watch out for those monster rats."

"Tryin' to make me laugh?" Prosper called over his shoulder as he walked away.

Jake thought it wouldn't take even an hour to inspect the buildings in this end of town. He noticed with a practiced eye that none of the storefronts had any glass in their windows, but that there was little if any broken glass mixed with the debris on the sidewalks or in the streets. He concluded that someone had carefully salvaged the window glass . . . and that the job had been done years before, because the empty store interiors were in terrible condition from long-term exposure to the weather.

Jake took a closer look at the interior of a Rexall drugstore. As his eyes adjusted to the dimness, he spotted something sitting in plain sight on an otherwise empty shelf near the back of the store. After checking carefully for spoor and scent, he crept inside the store through the empty windowframe.

The object proved to be an electric light bulb, miraculously intact. The bulb was nestled in a small pile of rags that may or may not have been arranged at random; in any case, the rags had kept the bulb from being rolled off the shelf by the wind. Jake picked the bulb up carefully and wiped the thick dust off it with his hand. GENERAL ELECTRIC SEVENTY-FIVE WATT was stamped in black on the nose of the bulb, and there were some mysterious numbers and letters as well.

Jake remembered electric light, but just barely. He had a fleeting memory of once reaching 'way up to flip a switch and having a room—the bathroom?—

explode with bright, white light. Now the bulb that had once made such a miraculous thing possible had become so useless that no one bothered to take it . . . and, Jake reflected, no one had dared to smash it, either. Well, neither would he. Jake replaced the bulb just as he'd found it, slapped the dust off his hands, and left the premises.

Just two blocks farther along, Jake came across a hardware store. He was always on the lookout for small hand tools to replace those he'd had to leave behind in Rensselaer. Not only were such tools useful in and of themselves, but they made excellent trading goods and were easy for a traveling man to carry. He entered with his usual caution.

As it happened, Jake did not find any hand tools this time. He found something better.

He was rummaging around on his hands and knees when he came across a small, filth-covered plastic chest hidden under a bolted-down workbench in the back of the store. The top of the red chest was almost completely covered with something lumpy, brown and gruesomely dry; it looked to Jake as if something had crawled on top of it long ago and died. That did not stop Jake from removing the lid, which came away easily enough. Whatever lay on top of the chest fell away and off to the side, creating a little mound of debris.

Inside the chest were six cans of Coca-Cola wrapped in a cardboard carrier.

Jake's eyes widened. He knew what Coca-Cola was, but not from direct experience. If he'd ever had any, he couldn't remember it, but the older folks talked about Coca-Cola the way they talked about oranges and coffee and cigarettes and all the other things they missed the most. They'd trade *big* for this, too. Jake had long since come to realize that people were willing to pay the most for those things they needed the least, and he couldn't imagine anyone *needing* something like Coca-Cola.

Jake promptly forgot how heavy his knapsack had become. He quickly shrugged its straps off his shoulders, dropped it to the floor and crouched to move things around inside it so that the Coca-Cola would fit. The word *six-pack* came into his mind from somewhere. Jake knew that it was important that this *six-pack* be left intact; it would somehow be worth more that way, although the reason why escaped him.

Jake guessed from the scanty evidence before him that the chest was about five years' worth of filthy and had not been moved or touched in at least that long. He could not understand how the chest had remained undiscovered by other scavengers. *Maybe hardly anyone's around anymore to check things out,* Jake suddenly thought, and he again felt a chill. It seemed more and more likely to him that none of the big Adirondack towns had survived. He hoped that the smaller, more isolated ones had done better.

Jake wondered if McAndrew, a small town only a few miles down the road from Lake Placid, was still all right. He had liked McAndrew a great deal on his last trip through. The people were friendly, and there'd been a girl there. He would like to see her again, assuming she was alive. The world being the way it was, of course, chances were reasonably good that she no longer lived . . . but she had been something special.

Jake also wondered if Hiram LeClerc and his son, traders he remembered well, were still around and doing business in McAndrew. He hoped so, because suddenly Jake and Prosper were rich, thanks to the Coca-Cola. They might even be worth something in gold. Jake grinned in disbelief at the thought of he and Prosper actually being *rich*. That didn't stop him from looking for more goodies, though, and after a patient search of the cracks between the warped floorboards, Jake found two wire nails and a thin screw about three inches long. He put them in his knapsack, secured it and, whistling softly, left the store.

A little farther on, just short of the bend in the road, Jake found the town's public library. The small white structure sat on the edge of the road that bordered the lake itself. There was a sign tacked neatly behind the still-intact glass face of the bulletin box just beside the front door. The sign had been hand-lettered in black marker on heavy yellow construction paper. Jake thought the librarian must have done it, because he knew librarians and their ways, and the lettering on the notice was precise and orderly, even though it cried doom.

Wednesday, June 19, 1985
TOWN COUNCIL
LAKE PLACID, N.Y.

———

FLU!!!
AVOID CONTACT WITH OTHERS
REPORT ANY VAGRANTS TO A PATROLMAN
STAY WARM AND EAT RIGHT
COVER ALL SNEEZES AND COUGHS
BOIL ALL KITCHENWARE
DON'T SHARE CUPS AND GLASSES
MAY GOD KEEP US
AMEN

Too bad He hadn't, thought Jake. He scratched his beard and thought. The flu notice confirmed his suspicions about what had happened here—and in Saranac Lake, too. An epidemic of Fidel's flu had been enough to kill the towns. He didn't think that everyone in Lake Placid had died from the flu, any more than he believed everyone in Saranac Lake had. The population of both towns had simply been too big to die off completely. The flu took four out of five of those who caught it, and that was a lot of people, but it wasn't *everybody*.

So where had they gone?

Jake entered the library after checking for spoor. As he'd feared, the inside was a disaster. The roof was gone, and animals had ravaged the books for nesting materials. Jake heard a number of somethings skitter away as he entered.

There was more than enough light inside to see by. Looking around, Jake saw that the library's shelves contained nothing but ruined books, all of which had been chewed or pulped by water. He saw no books still in usable shape, but he noticed that the shelves were nearly three-quarters empty. The library had been scavenged both inside and out, but probably not until the roof had gone; Jake doubted anyone would want to move thousands of books until they absolutely had to be moved.

Jake heard a sound and, slowly, he turned.

The person hiding just outside the library apparently didn't realize that he was casting a shadow across the doorway; Jake spotted it easily from across the room. An honest citizen would have hailed Jake by now; if the library had been an active place, Jake might even have had some quick explaining to do. Jake hoped whoever was outside was alone.

Jake quietly left the library through one of the windows. He placed his feet carefully, avoiding the shards of glass on the broken strip of pebbly concrete running around the building. He crouched low and hurried away, heading toward the lake.

Jake heard footsteps coming up quickly behind him, and he took a quick look back. He saw a *big* man with wild hair and a dark, tangled beard. He was shabbily dressed and carrying a well-honed hunting knife that glinted like gold in the sun. The man had killer's eyes. Jake didn't know whether his attacker had rape, murder, cannibalism or just a simple holdup on his mind;

it looked as if all four could be likely. He decided to assume it was so, because it helped keep him running.

The man was gaining on him. Jake didn't think twice. He undid the straps of his knapsack and let it fall behind him, hoping that his pursuer would stop to pick it up and perhaps even examine it. That would let Jake gain a lot of ground. It might even allow him to get away, circle back, find Prosper—if the man hadn't found him first—and get the hell out of town. He hoped Prosper was all right.

The big man came upon the knapsack. He didn't stop. Jake tried to run faster.

Pursuer and pursued were racing down an overgrown path that led to some wooden ruins by the side of the lake—a boathouse, Jake thought, or maybe just a fancy dock. It was a dead end, though, unless he wanted to go into the lake . . . and Jake had no hope of fighting him off in the water. It looked to Jake as if he was going to have to make a stand. *Might as well pick my own spot,* he thought. *Here will do.*

Jake wheeled and pulled his fighting knife from the sheath at his hip.

The big man stopped and frowned. "Gimme," he grated. He held out his free hand.

"Give you what?"

"All you got," he said, pointing with his own knife. "Mebbe your ass, too." He pointed again and grinned, exposing yellowed, broken teeth and purple gums. "Like me, honey? My name's John."

Jake crouched, knife extended. "I'll pass, thanks. Let me go on my way, John."

"Can't do that, sweetheart. Why don't you lose that shiv?"

"Not likely."

"Okay," John shrugged. "Forget it." He stood up straight. Then, in a flash, he threw the knife.

It wasn't a throwing knife, but it did its job of distracting Jake for a precious fraction of a second as it went by his head, tumbling badly. John produced a second knife, and he lunged at Jake. Jake cursed himself for an amateur and set himself to face his attacker. The other man's knife just missed opening Jake's guts; Jake seized the big man's wrist and held on. John plowed his free fist into Jake's stomach. Jake cried out at the blow but did not let go.

John then kneed Jake in the groin; Jake broke away, gasping, stumbling and sprawling. It was only then that Jake thought he might die.

Panting heavily, looking around quickly, Jake spotted a fist-sized rock close to hand. Jake flipped his knife to his left hand and ducked to seize the rock with his right. He chucked the rock at John, putting everything he had into it. It hit John hard in the stomach just below the breastbone and doubled him over. The knife flew out of his hand and fell within reach of Jake's foot. Jake kicked it away into the brush.

John was on all fours, drinking in air. "Just get away from me, all right?" Jake said, wheezing. "Go on, get the hell out of here!"

"Whatever you say, girlie," John said. Then he sprang, grabbing Jake and bearing him down to the ground. The big man got both of his huge hands around Jake's throat and began to squeeze. He was grinning a broken, foul grin. The man's breath was loathsome; it drenched Jake's face. He ground his hips against Jake.

"Kiss me, baby," John crooned.

The big man had apparently forgotten all about Jake's knife. He remembered it, though, when it tore through his guts four times. "Shit," John sighed. Then he went limp.

A moment later, Jake rolled John off him and got to his knees, gasping. He was covered from neck to knees with John's blood. His attacker was still breathing, but faintly; with all the blood on the ground, Jake knew John would not last much longer. Jake looked around carefully. No one else was coming.

"I don't feel a thing," John said matter-of-factly. "I been hurt before, but this is different. Help me up, honey, okay?" The big man's eyes were open; what they were seeing was not certain.

"Where's my friend?" Jake asked.

"Huh? I'm your friend, darlin'."

"My friend," Jake repeated. "The black man."

"Didn't see nobody like that. Only you, honey."

"You'd better rest."

"Mebbe so. Where is everybody, anyway?"

"Not far."

"Good. I was worried." John blinked hard for a moment. "Sorry I roughed you up, sweetheart. I just missed you, thassall. You were away for so long. I took good care of the kids while you were gone." He smiled without malice; a thin river of blood spilled from the left corner of his mouth.

"I know you did," Jake said. "Don't worry about it."

"Hey," John frowned, "I'm not a faggot, y'know. Don't you go thinking I am, either."

"I know," Jake said.

"Well, you better believe me, because I'm not. I'm a man, goddammit." Then John sighed and died.

If John had had friends, Jake knew they would have made an appearance by now. He was safe, and in the distance he could hear Prosper coming. He stood and checked himself over for slashes and broken bones. He was cut and bruised here and there, but not seriously, although he judged that the bruises would look pretty awful by the next day. He also checked himself to see if John's knee had done him any real harm. It hadn't, but he was tender down there.

"Jesus," came a familiar voice. "I'm glad I saw you before I saw *this*."

"Hello, Prosper," called Jake. "Find anything?"

"You mean just now, or before?"

"Before."

"Couple nails, three books of matches. They'll light. My God, Jake, there's blood all over the place. I just got to the bend in the road and thought I heard something down here, so I come to take a look. Who *is* this?"

"His name's John," Jake said. "Thief, obviously. Crazy, too, I think. I'm going to go wash. Look him over, will you?"

"Yeah. Uh, where's your knapsack, man?"

"Up the trail a piece."

"I'll go get it."

Jake walked down a short, steep slope to the edge of the lake, took off his clothes, and waded in. The water was summer-warm and comforting; it soothed his aches. Jake paddled back and forth, passively letting John's blood float away from his body. The encounter with the man mystified him. In his travels, Jake had often enough met men who preferred other men, and John was not at all like them. John was a killer.

Prosper returned. "You got a few new scratches on those stripes of yours," he called.

"Nothing to talk about."

"Must have been some fight."

"Was, I guess."

"Wish I'd been here to help."

Jake laughed. "Come to think of it, so do I."

"I *told* you, man. Next time, yell."

"I will, don't worry. You find anything on our friend there yet?"

"Boots," Prosper said. "Good ones."

"Boots?" Jake stopped paddling and stood up in the water.

"Look close to your size, too," Prosper said. "His pants look like they'll fit me. Shirt's useless, except as rags. Two more knives. Nothing else.'' Prosper began stripping the body.

"Sounds like plenty," Jake called. He emerged from the lake and, crouching by the bank, began to rinse out his clothes. They were bulky and hard to clean, but Jake rinsed them repeatedly until they at least no longer ran red. His clothing remained stained with blood, though—a little bit of his and a lot of John's. He wished for the five thousandth time that he had some soap.

Jake wrung out his clothing and dressed. His clothes would dry just as well if he was wearing them, and the warm afternoon promised that he would not catch a chill. He walked over to John's body and picked up one of the boots Prosper had set aside. It looked fine. He saw that the uppers had been hand-stitched together from the tanned skins of different small animals, and that the soles had been cut from the tread of an automobile tire. The boots showed careful craftsmanship and no small amount of skill.

"I wish we could get a look at the place where this guy lived," Prosper said.

"Well, so do I—but I'm beginning to feel like a vulture."

"Might be full of trade goods," Prosper continued. "Those boots, these pants—nice stuff. No tellin' where he got 'em from. Think he got friends around here somewhere?"

Jake shook his head. "Didn't strike me that he had people. Maybe he did, once, but not now."

"How do you know?"

"Just something he said, that's all."

Jake found that John's boots were a little too big for him, but that made them perfect for hiking, with his feet as swollen and touchy as they were. He sat down, pulled the boots and stood. He wiggled his toes and, despite the circumstances, grinned. Jake's decrepit shoes were beyond any hope of salvage, so he chucked them into the lake and listened with great satisfaction to the double splash they made.

"Congratulations," Prosper said. "Now what do we do with the late owner?"

"My problem," Jake said, looking down at John's body. Jake felt that it would not be quite decent to leave John sprawled where he lay, but neither would he take the trouble to bury a man who'd just tried to kill him. Giving John to the lake seemed a good compromise. Jake used his newly shod feet to set John's corpse sliding and rolling down the slope and into the lake. The body fell into the water heavily. It then floated free and, slowly, away.

"Poor bastard," Jake said. "God rest his soul. I don't think he was responsible for what he did."

"Amen," replied Prosper.

"I want to get out of here," Jake said suddenly. He retrieved his knapsack and put it on, hissing slightly as the straps found a fresh cut here and there. "We'll stop a little early today, get us a roof or a good tree over our heads for the night, take it easy. We'll make McAndrew sometime tomorrow."

"Right behind you," replied Prosper.

Tired as they were, the two buskers began trotting as they reached the bend in the road and headed out of town.

CHAPTER 2

A FEW MILES AWAY, DIGGER DIGBY TOOK ANOTHER look through the 'scope, squinting and still not quite believing his luck. The whitetail buck he was watching through the crosshairs went on placidly worrying the bark of a birch tree.

Digger licked his dry lower lip and scratched his full, graying beard. *Son of a bitch!* he thought again. *What a piece of meat! He's filled out, too—three, maybe four feet tall. Two hundred pounds on him, easy—and look at those antlers! A six-pointer! Jesus! Where does he get off, being so big?*

It would be nearly a hundred yard shot, well within Digger's range of competence with the rifle. He sincerely hoped his bullets were good. Digger made it a habit always to carry two of them on his trips, just in case he met something worth shooting. The ammunition had looked all right when he'd traded for it during a fit of personal prosperity three years before. There hadn't been a bit of corrosion on either of the bullets, and they had made just the right sound when he'd rung them against the worn wooden countertop at LeClerc's, one after the other—but a customer never knew for sure about bullets. Dick LeClerc never did, either, so as a matter of policy the town storekeeper refused to guarantee ammunition.

Digger already knew the rifle would work. It was his own. He'd had it since he was a boy, and he'd always taken good care of it. It was only a .22, a young boy's rifle, but light as it was, Digger felt certain that it was the most reliable firearm anywhere near McAndrew. To make up for the weapon's lack of punch, Digger dum-dummed his bullets. The lead slugs tended to spread on impact in any case, and the crosses Digger cut in their noses made sure of it. Whether Digger could still hit what he aimed at was another matter entirely; in five years, he hadn't done more than dry-fire the rifle after stripping and cleaning it. In all that time, Digger had spotted no game worth the price of a bullet, and he wasn't one to squander ammunition on target practice.

Digger was a stubborn and powerful little man who had always lived in the woods and loved them deeply. One of the reasons he loved them so was because his father had brought him here when he was very young, and his finest memories were of the good times he'd had here with his father. Another reason was that the forest was as full as it could be of birch, elm and oak, as well as what seemed like seventy-five kinds of good Adirondack pine, and so it served as a loud cry of life in the face of death.

Digger had been overjoyed that spring, as everyone else had been, to note the presence of substantial new growth after more than three decades of continuing dieback; plants and trees were shooting up all over the place. The woods were clearly on the rebound, and if anything bigger than critter-size was ever going to come his way again, Digger knew it would do so on a beautiful late summer day just like this one, so he always walked through the forest carefully and watchfully.

By sheer dumb luck, Digger had approached the deer from downwind. He'd been on his way home, having already emptied and reset his critter traps for the rabbits, woodchucks and squirrels that trotted obediently through the runs he usually worked. Digger's haul, a pretty fair one today, lay still in the heavily stained canvas mailbag at his feet.

Like everyone else, Digger had thought that the deer were all gone from this part of the mountains, hunted out or otherwise dead long ago; he hadn't seen one, or even the spoor of one, for many years. Now at least one was back, by God, and this one looked healthy. The buck had good weight, well-formed antlers and no bald spots. In short, there was nothing obviously wrong with him. This buck seemed to be traveling all by himself; Digger had been watching him for more than five minutes, but none of the buck's friends had shown up. A lone buck hadn't been an unusual sight in the old days, though, and he knew that this particular specimen easily could have wandered fifty miles or more in just the past week.

There were still a few weeks to go before mating season began, or so Digger recalled. He saw the thin, golden velvet still covering the deer's antlers. Soon enough, the velvet and his hormones would begin to itch at the buck, and he'd take care of scratching both his itches then . . . assuming he could find a doe, that is.

Digger had a sudden thought. *What if this is the last one? I need him bad and no mistake, but what if this is the* very *last one? I wish some of his pals would show up; I'd feel better about this, I swear to God I would.* He licked his lower lip again and kept his mind on Annie and Justin, waiting for him back in the cabin. None of them was going hungry, not this year . . . but a growing boy like Justin could always use some honest-to-God venison and broth. Digger could find a hundred uses for that deerskin, too, and venison would trade very well; Dick LeClerc would jump at the chance to handle venison, and Digger could retire at least some of his not-insignificant debt with the store-keeper.

Digger turned his Red Sox cap around so that the brim faced backward. He always did that for luck when he was about to use the rifle. It had been his father's cap.

A breeze came up and caressed Digger's face with cool, pine-scented air. He heard the wind gently rustle the branches of the trees around him. He watched as the deer sniffed at the leaves hanging nearest his head and began chewing them almost daintily.

For all his experience at survival and all the hard and mean things that the years had done to him, Digger felt a slight pang of regret as he drew a breath, held it, and squeezed the trigger. There was an answering puff of mist in just about the right spot on the deer. The buck, staggering against the blow, threw his head up. Digger saw his eyes widen with fear and shock and, perhaps, realization.

The deer seemed to see Digger at last, but too late. The buck's legs crumbled beneath him; he crouched, and then fell gracelessly at the base of the tree. He lay quivering.

The cartridge in his rifle was spent, but Digger engaged the safety anyway and quickly ran to the deer. As he drew closer, Digger could see that the buck was still breathing shallowly, his flanks working hard. With a slight movement of his head at the approaching sound of the man's footfalls, the deer's soft brown eyes found Digger's hard blue ones and held them. There was blood at the deer's mouth and nostrils, and there was also the pathetic sound of panting. The deer's tongue lolled.

Lung shot after all, dammit, Digger thought angrily. *Sloppy, just goddamn sloppy!* He had tried for the heart and had missed, and he was furious with himself. He could not abide cruelty.

Digger looked deeper into those dying eyes. *Sweet Jesus,* he thought. *I think he wants me to fix him up, I swear he does. I wonder if he's ever seen a people before?*

"All right, fella," Digger mumbled. "Go to sleep, now." He drew his hunting knife and, holding the deer's jaw steady with his left hand, gave mercy with one quick, firm stroke. He held on firmly as the buck tried to throw his head back and forth. Blood showered from the gaping slash in the deer's throat and spattered on Digger's worn and patched dungarees.

It was over in seconds. The pooled blood of the deer drained slowly into the ground as Digger wiped the knife on the leg of his Levi's and sheathed it. He then took a deep breath and found the air filled with the coppery tang of fresh blood and new death. He sighed and wiped a bloody hand across his brow.

Now Digger had to get the deer home. It would be three miles or more, but he thought he could handle the load. He never considered spilling the deer's innards then and there to save hauling their weight; there was too much value hiding inside the buck to leave it for the bugs and beasties. He would take it all with him.

Digger checked the sun. It was two o'clock, near enough. If he could make a mile an hour, he'd be home about an hour before dark, and he and Annie could get a good start on taking apart the deer. There was already plenty of salt at home for preserving; Digger had made a trip to the lick just two weeks before and had brought home nearly fifty pounds.

Digger set about constructing a travois. Building the primitive sled required green, springy wood that was less likely to break under strain. He quickly found a likely birch and, with his hand axe, chopped off three thick and reasonably straight branches and trimmed them.

It took Digger an hour of reasonably hard work to make the travois. When he was finished, he picked it up, shook it roughly, and banged it hard against the ground a few times. He then looked it over carefully for damage, found nothing obvious, and pronounced the job a good one.

By main force, Digger got the deer's body onto the travois. He lashed the carcass down on its side with some more vines and, bending, tested the crude sled by grabbing its nose and heaving it quickly against the deer's weight. The travois held together and the deer stayed in place, but Digger knew that the sled would never last through a three-mile drag—not without on-the-spot repairs, anyway. There was no help for that, though; Digger knew that he would just have to keep fixing the travois as he went along. He gathered some more vines and wrapped them around his waist.

Digger set the critter bag next to the buck's belly and tied it down. The rifle went over his shoulder, next to his bow. Digger bent and, with a grunt, again lifted the nose of the travois—slowly, this time. It creaked, but not badly, as it bent slightly under the weight of the deer.

Digger stood and turned his baseball cap around, peak forward. Facing ahead, he maintained a powerful grip on the nose of the travois and took a few steps. The heavy sticks that formed the runners of the sled made deep ruts as they cut through the soil of the forest floor. After a moment, though, the deer's bulk seemed merely difficult instead of impossible to bear.

Digger hadn't lost an arm-wrestling contest in many

years; now he'd see whether that kind of strength really meant anything. He was grimly determined not to lose this deer or any part of him. The deer was *his*. He took another look at the sun, oriented himself, and set out for home, where Annie and Justin were waiting.

CHAPTER 3

HE WAS STANDING AT THE COUNTER AND TAKING his time in deciding whether to have the Big Mac or the Quarter-Pounder with Cheese or the Chicken McNuggets or the Mac-Kebob. He would have been distressed to notice that, behind him, the line had grown long and was growing longer, and people were beginning to stir impatiently while muttering hateful remarks that he could not hear.

Looking again at the backlighted menu hanging on the wall behind the counter, he slowly realized that he had not had a Big Mac in a couple of weeks. He thought he might like to have one of those, since Big Macs were his favorite, and he suddenly decided to splurge on a small container of fries as well. After all, this would be his only real meal of the day. He finally gave his order to the Broom girl, who entered it into her console. Each time she touched one of the zero-travel keys on the console pad, there was a short, sharp peep, and words and numbers would appear on *the display facing him. The writing was too small and disappeared too quickly for him to read.*

The total, however, was displayed in big numerals and was designed to linger on the screen. His bill came to seven dollars and twelve cents. That was more than he had expected to pay, surely, but he took some pride in knowing that it was not more money than he had on him. He could pay his way.

As he began carefully counting out the amount—all in change, and much of it in pennies—the Broom girl stepped to the big food warmer behind her to get his burger, and then to the deep fat cooker to scoop up his fries.

The Broom girl placed the items in a white bag and came back to the counter to add a few more things to it from an unseen repository somewhere at her feet. She then placed the bag in front of him, folded its top neatly closed, and waited to be paid.

His hands were shaking because he was old and tired and more than a little hungry, and so he dropped the coins as he was handing them to her. The coins rang and rattled loudly onto the countertop, and several of them bounced high and fell to the floor behind the counter, rolling for no little distance before they came to a clattering halt against the warmer and the fryer and the big machine that shat vanilla and chocolate ice cream in alternation. People's heads swung around at the commotion.

He expected the Broom girl to say something mean to him and would not have blamed her if she had, but she smiled at him nicely, quickly gathered up all the money and counted it out without any hint of complaint. He tried to thank her as kindly as he knew how, but it came out only as an embarrassed verbal stumbling.

As he turned to leave, he saw some of the people in line behind him giving him dirty looks. Some others were smirking. He could not bring himself to meet their eyes.

The Broom girl had bagged the meal to go because she knew he usually wanted it that way, but on impulse he decided to eat inside the restaurant today. He hoped the manager wouldn't mind. The weather was nice enough, but he'd been at the roadside stand all day, and he'd still be out there come sunset. He wanted—he needed—to sit inside somewhere for just a few minutes, like a civilized man, away from the road and the dust. He needed to take his ease, and he needed not to be at the stand just then. He knew he would not be missing much. What he'd just spent on his simple meal was more than double his entire morning's take.

He took a Ronald McDonald disposable tray from a stack next to the napkin and straw dispensers, and walked slowly to one of the small two-person tables near the large front windows of the restaurant. He wanted to watch the world pass by from a place that wasn't his roadside stand. Despite everything, he liked watching people.

He looked around the restaurant first. The place was half empty but, judging from all the activity behind the counter, business was good nevertheless. Most of the customers were staying in their cars and buying their lunches at the drive-thru window around to the side; from where he was, he could see that the kids in the drive-thru crew were very busy. Only a few travelers, all of them parents with young kids, had chosen to eat inside. The swinging doors leading to the bathrooms in the back were getting quite a workout.

As he looked here and there, he noticed that some of the adults were staring back at him with expressions of pity or distaste. Well, he knew he wasn't the neatest and cleanest man in town, not by a long shot, but he wasn't a bum, either. He made a living, meager as it was, thanks to Social Security and whatever he could pull in from the roadside stand. He didn't want any

*welfare, or whatever they were calling it these days
. . . and if he took a drink or two at the end of a long,
hard day—well, so what? He pulled his own weight
and didn't take a dime from anyone.*

*He looked out the window at the cars passing by
on 73. Traffic was heavy, which was unusual for this
time of year. The summer season had been over for
a couple of weeks, and city people wouldn't be coming up to look at the leaves turning color for nearly
another month. He thought that 9N might have been
closed again, blocked by some spill of poisons or a
collapsed bridge or something, and so 73 and 86
were being used as a long detour between Keene and
Jay. That kind of thing happened once in a while.*

*He looked inside the bag. As usual, the Broom girl
had given him several packets of ketchup to go with
the fries. He had never told her that he didn't use
ketchup, because he did not want to seem ungrateful
for her kindness in including so much of it. Even more
kindly, she had given him a large fries instead of the
small one he'd ordered, and she'd included a cup of
fizzy water without his having asked for it. He removed
the cover from the cup and took a sip.*

*As usual, while the fries were reasonably hot, the
hamburger was barely warm, but he cared no more
about that than most other diners at McDonald's did.
He tore the ends off two of the salt packets the Broom
girl had also thrown into the bag for him and sprinkled
their contents onto the fries. He tried one, and it was
perfect. The timers and temperature regulators in the
frying machines made sure the fries were always individually and collectively perfect. He had come to
rely on the perfection of fast food as the only finely
done thing in his world.*

*He bit into the Big Mac, the sharp tang of the spe-
cial sauce making his jaws wince. It was wonderful.
He finished his meal slowly, being careful of his teeth.*

* * *

Jess Harper was gently rocking back and forth, back and forth, dozing lightly on his porch in the gentle, reddening light of the afternoon sun and smacking his lips. His big, black dog, Eisenhower, was sleeping soundly at his master's feet, his tail just outside the cruising range of the rockers on Jess's chair.

The small, neat house Jess shared with his wife sat right at the intersection of McAndrew Road and Route 73, and once upon a time that had been a noisy inconvenience. In those days, Jess and his wife had sold cukes, corn and peaches they grew out back to passing motorists for a cheap price. The cash money had never quite made up for the constant racket and bother, but it had helped, and they would have suffered from the highway noise in any case. Now things were a lot different, of course. They were much quieter, for one thing.

Jess was more than old enough to remember clearly the way the world used to be, and he considered himself to be the last of the great capitalist entrepreneurs. He made drinkin' likker—Jess always called it *product*—and sold it at a fair price that made it inconvenient for other folks to go to the trouble of brewing their own.

Jess did this in sufficient quantity to make a good living. His product was highly desirable, and Jess could have sold it under any circumstances, but he never took advantage of his position by sacrificing quality or gouging his customers. That common-sense attitude had kept Jess Harper alive through the worst times. His customers thought of him as a friend, and he was. Product was considered so vital that, even though the Harper place was within the town limits, the Harpers and the workers on their farm were exempt from common work—that is, work assigned to each citizen of McAndrew for the benefit of the town, over and above whatever work the person usually did.

Common work was a lot like what taxes used to be, which was exactly why Jess was happy to avoid it.

Jess also made methanol, otherwise known as wood alcohol. Unlike product, there was no art to cooking up methanol, and for that reason Jess did not enjoy the process—but the town needed methanol, and so he made it. Jess also knew that, if he didn't make methanol, someone would build his own still out of an old boiler or something and start making it himself. After that, it wouldn't be long before Jess had competition in the product-making business, and he saw no earthly reason why he should encourage competition. Things were just fine the way they were, thank you.

Jess considered that he'd done all right for a lazy man. He'd once heard that the laziest man in history was the one who'd invented the wheel, and he found he agreed with that—but he also took it to mean that the lazy man should not be ignored, because he could always surprise you. Jess had made it his business to surprise the town of McAndrew with his unlikely success, and he had done so long since. His little place by the road had grown as the property around his lot had been abandoned by its owners. Now it was a thriving farm and had been for a long time, and no one gave Jess's prosperity a second's worth of attention. Jess Harper's success was like the presence of Big Slide Mountain south of town, across Serpent Lake: ever-present and unarguable. His place among his people was secure. He provided product at an unbeatable price, and he provided security at McAndrew's northern approach.

Jess's chief assistant in his endeavors was his faithful Betsy. He couldn't imagine life without her. He was realistic enough to know that, without Betsy, he'd have been dead from starvation or worse long ago. As it was, Betsy had kept him housed, fed and clothed through the bad times, and comfortable through the good ones.

Jess used to make product with Betsy in the old days, too, but much more privately and not nearly so much of it. There were Treasury agents and sheriffs forever nosing around back then, so Jess would make product in a place 'way back in the woods, where Betsy used to be. Jess had never been greedy and, mostly because of that, he'd never been caught. It hadn't taken Jess long—maybe just a day or two after Kingdom Come—for him to realize that, as the only by-God moonshiner anywhere in or near the town of McAndrew, he had a product that people would line up to buy, once the many liquor stores in the nearby big towns of Saranac Lake and Lake Placid had been emptied. Jess had been right, too; the liquor stores had quickly been looted out, and his mastery of moonshining had long since made him the IBM of his town and the General Motors of these mountains. Making product had become legal, if only because no one was around anymore who cared to say that it wasn't.

Betsy, once hidden away deep in the woods for fear of the law, was now proudly planted in his front yard, and the still had been sitting there for many years. She was as good a producer of wealth as any oil well or gold mine had ever been, what with the way the world had shrunk. Betsy produced more than enough for Jess to be able to hire people to work his farm and tend his animals, and to keep the Harpers' bellies full and their lives sweet. That was rich, in Jess Harper's world. It was as rich as Henry Ford had been once, even with all his mansions and cars and the rest of it.

Jess roused suddenly, his eyes opening. Had that been a shot, way off? He didn't know; perhaps he'd dreamed it. Jess now heard only the uninterrupted clatter of kitchen stuff. His wife, Samuella, apparently hadn't heard anything and was still preparing dinner.

But Eisenhower's ears were up. "Hear somethin', Ike?" Jess asked the dog. "Where was it, boy?" Ike was looking up 73, to the west. The dog was curious but not tense; clearly, he sensed no trouble coming, and Jess had learned to trust him on such questions.

In any case, Jess's inner sense of timing was informing him that the mash cooking up in the barn was ready, and mash would not wait. The sun told him that it was past three, and that was a little late in the day for starting a product run, but the time didn't worry Jess. He liked working in the afternoon and evening, for no good reason other than it pleased him to work that way. Jess liked to sleep late in the morning, and he'd happily work into the night if he had to, just so he could sleep in.

He got up from his rocking chair and noticed again that, when standing, he could no longer see his feet. He was uncommonly happy about that. He'd gained thirty pounds since the winter, and it was the first time since Kingdom Come that he could remember having anything even approaching a weight problem. Sammie had fleshed out, too. It had been a good year, all right. Everyone had gotten so used to being hungry all the time that finally having *enough* seemed like a miracle.

"On guard, Ike," Jess ordered, and the dog took his accustomed position at the top of the porch stairs. There Ike sat and there he would remain until Jess ordered him to do something else or until Ike died of old age.

Jess didn't like needing help to run a load; making the product was *his* thing, his supreme talent, and he enjoyed doing it all by himself. Nowadays, though, Jess needed a little help and, on the Harper farm, help came in pairs.

Jess found the Simpson brothers dozing in the shade of the barn, which was pretty much where he'd expected to find them. "C'mon, boys," he called. "Up and at 'em. Let's do 'er."

Ralph Simpson roused and blinked. Seeing Jess, he rose quickly and kicked his sleeping brother's leg. "Umph!" Greg grunted. "Why the hell don't you watch where you're going, you shithead—!"

"Boss, Greg," his older brother said softly. "Cork it."

"Oh-oh. Right." Greg rose and greeted Jess. "H'lo, Mr. Harper—"

"Clean the barn out yet, boys?" Jess inquired.

"Uh, just gettin' to it, Mr. Harper," Ralph answered.

Jess sighed, shaking his head. "Boys, boys," he said wearily. "Why does everything take you guys forever to do? Ralph, you spent all morning just going into town to deliver a note to Ed Pearson and run a couple of fool errands, and none of your chores got done. Now here you both are, goofing off again."

The Simpsons looked very contrite.

"You know I don't tolerate a filthy barn, boys," Jess continued. "Want the animals to get sick? How much do I have to dock you two before you learn how to keep a barn?"

Jess waved a hand in mock weariness as the Simpson boys began to make their ritual assurances about how they would thenceforth mend their errant ways. "Never mind, never mind—get it done by sundown and I'll let it ride. This time. You're both more'n twenty now; it's time you boys grew up."

The Simpsons nodded together in relief. "Yes, *sir*!" Greg said. "Thank *you*, Mr. Harper!"

Jess waved his hand again, this time in dismissal. "Time to check the mash," he said. Ralph wrinkled his nose; Jess saw him do it, and he chuckled. "Boys," he said, "I've been dealing with mash barrels for longer'n you've been on this earth—twice as long, I guess. Anyway, hasn't hurt me any. Hold your nose, Ralphie, if you've got a third hand. Let's go." Jess strolled around the corner in his habitual slow, rolling walk; the Simpsons followed at a respectful distance.

Jess opened the side door of the barn and entered its cool dimness. As his eyes adjusted, he saw green gleams of reflected light over in the far corner, where the digging tools were hanging. "Hello there, kitties," he called, and there was a faint rustle in answer as the barn cats shifted drowsily. The cats were good hunters who kept the farm free of mice and rats, which cut Jess's losses from vermin. The cats demanded little or nothing from Jess in the way of payment except, rarely, when one or two of them would trot over to the house to demand a show of affection. Barn cats were, in Jess's eyes, perfect animals—and, besides, Sammie loved cats, which was in itself enough reason for Jess to want to have them around.

There was another point to having cats. Keeping the farm free of rodents tended to keep it free of snakes as well. Jess never wanted to see another snake in his lifetime. They'd proven valuable enough during the really bad times when everyone was starving and snake meat had come to be considered a delicacy, but that was then and this was now. It was bad enough that the rodent population seemed to be picking up again; the cats had been pretty busy lately.

Despite Jess's carping at the Simpsons, the barn was reasonably clean. The bad smell wasn't due to filth. The wooden mash barrel placed smack in the center of the barn was supplying more than enough stink for anyone's taste. Jess cared as little about the smell as the barn cats did, though, because to Jess the barrel— and, more particularly, what surrounded it—smelled like nothing but money.

The mash barrel sat proudly in manure, great heaps of it, that had been gathered from elsewhere in the barn, Jess's cow pasture, the goat pen, the paddock and the Harper privy. Even the barn cats had contributed their fair share to the pile. The manure was treated as the precious substance it indeed was. As the manure decomposed, it threw off two things: a high smell and a low heat. The gentle unseen glow of that heat was what drove the working of the mash.

Jess's main talent lay in deciding just when the slow-cooked mash was ready for the still. If he left it in the barrel for too long, all the cracked corn, scraps of potato and other things would cook up into nothing but vinegar. Jess knew there was a market for vinegar—Dick LeClerc used barrels of it for his pickling, and Sammie used a lot of it in the dressing for the salads she was forever making—but vinegar didn't pay nearly as well as product. In any case, Jess was more than happy to buy his vinegar from other folks. Doing so spread the wealth around a little, and that sort of thing kept people happy. Besides, unlike product, vinegar stunk horribly even after you finished making it.

—*Heinz ketchup*—

Jess blinked. Now where had *that* come from? Yes, ketchup; he remembered it well enough. You needed a lot of tomatoes to make it—it was red as the devil, Jess recalled—so there wasn't any ketchup to be had now, of course. Nobody around McAndrew grew tomatoes because there wasn't any viable seed to be had. Jess seemed to remember that there was vinegar in ketchup, too; maybe his thinking of vinegar was what had reminded him of it. Jess had never been a ketchup man. Heinz 57, though; he remembered that. Heinz made fifty-seven kinds of things—ketchup, pickles, vinegar, maybe even soup. The "57" was on all the labels. Funny how the thought had bubbled up like that. Jess was sure he'd never before given a thought to the Heinz Company, although he was certain he was using some of Mr. Heinz's old bottles and jars to distribute Betsy's best. *I guess that makes it fifty-eight varieties, then, doesn't it, Mr. Heinz?* Jess thought, and chuckled.

Jess put on the only pair of overalls hanging on a

nail by the door, and pointed at the shovels hanging in the corner. "Hop to, fellas," he ordered. "Try not to get too much of that shit there on you. Nice 'n neat, now, that's the way."

The Simpsons each took a shovel and walked over to the barrel. They began clearing the manure from around it, removing it to a distance of about two feet and scraping the boarded floor as clean as possible. While Ralph touched up the floor, Greg shoveled a path through the mound so that Jess could approach the barrel.

It was done quickly. "Thank you, boys," Jess said. He went to the barrel, removed the top, and sniffed at the mash. Its gentle warmth rose and caressed Jess's round, pink face, and he smiled. It was perfect. Jess once again reflected on the sheer neatness of the natural process that brought a salable commodity like product from the crap lying around his place. It was another sign that God was good and that, when He takes away, He also gives back.

Jess set the lid on top of the barrel and thumped it firmly back into place. "Ralph?" he said. "It's ready. Get the dolly."

"Yes, Mr. Harper." Ralph walked to the corner of the barn and retrieved the dolly from its position against the wall. He pushed it easily back to the barrel, maneuvering it through the path Greg had shoveled for Jess, so as not to foul its wheels unnecessarily. Together, Ralph and Greg managed to seat the barrel onto the shelf of the dolly. Ralph made sure the weight of the barrel was centered and then he leaned the dolly back, quickly finding its balancing point and holding it there. Walking backward, he wheeled the barrel through the path in the manure pile and brought it outside, his head twisted around so he could see where he was going. Greg walked along to his right and kept a strong arm on the barrel to steady it against ruts. Jess followed at a distance of three paces, supervising.

Ralph began to whistle through his teeth as he maneuvered the dolly toward Betsy. Jess could not place the tune, but it made him think of kids and—television. Television?

"Ralph?" Jess called. The Simpsons stopped and Ralph looked inquiringly at him; the dolly wobbled. "No, no," Jess continued, waving them on a bit impatiently. "Keep going. I just wanted to ask you something."

"What's that, Mr. Harper?" Ralph asked as he turned back to his task.

"That song you were whistling. Where did you hear it?"

Ralph thought about it a moment. "Gee, I don't know, Mr. Harper," he said. "Thought I'd made it up, I guess."

"You must have heard it somewhere."

"I don't think so, Mr. Harper."

"Hmmm. Ever heard of *Leave It to Beaver*?"

"Huh, Mr. Harper?" Ralph looked puzzled. "Sure I've heard of beavers. Leave one what?"

"Never mind. You're too young. By the way, did you boys hear a shot before?"

"A shot? No, Mr. Harper, we sure didn't," Greg said.

"How about you, Ralph?"

"No, Mr. Harper." Ralph shot his brother a quick, mystified glance, and then continued in silence toward the still.

"Well, maybe you were snoring too loud to hear it."

"Gee, Mr. Harper—" both Simpsons began.

"Forget it," Jess said, waving them on again.

Right after Kingdom Come, Jess had figured he'd be able to get ample supplies of anything he might need if he could supply product in return, and he'd turned out to be right about that. He'd also figured he wouldn't be able to get copper after a while, no matter what, and he'd been right about that, too. While everyone else in the mountains had been running around looting the stores empty, Jess had calmly gutted every abandoned automobile and house he could find of its copper piping and tubing, or he had paid others to do it for him. Some people had continued to take cash money even months after the attack, thinking that cash was still worth something or soon would be again. Jess had known instinctively that the attack had knocked the value of cash money down somewhere below the value of spit, but he hadn't *cheated* anyone, not exactly. In every case, the scavenger had set his own price—almost always a ridiculously high one, and Jess had paid it with little or no haggling. Jess frequently congratulated himself on having had the foresight to lay in a good supply of copper; his stockpile had allowed him to keep Betsy patched and producing for more than thirty years.

Jess swung open the top of the kettle and motioned the Simpsons to proceed. The brothers picked up the barrel of mash and, with a great deal of groaning, carefully dumped its weighty contents into the kettle without losing so much as a kernel of corn. The mash dropped wetly into the kettle with loud splashing noises. Jess then sealed the top of the kettle shut with screws and wing nuts, giving each an extra twist.

Jess stooped to inspect the fat, green wood laid under the kettle, checking its distance from the bottom and the way it had been banked. He nodded in satisfaction. The Simpsons had done a good job in setting it up; it had once taken seemingly forever to teach them how to do it right.

Jess rummaged in his pants pockets for his flint and steel. Crouching, he patiently struck sparks and blew on them until the straw and thinly shaved kindling under the kettle caught. Jess watched patiently for a few minutes, encouraging the fire with an expertly placed puff of breath or the wave of a hand. The Simpsons remained silent behind him, standing by, waiting.

Finally Jess was satisfied. The fire was burning low but steadily. "That's it, boys," he said, rising and brushing the knees of his overalls free of dirt. "Clean out that barrel there and take the crap out of the barn. You can throw it into the fallow field. You can take care of cleaning out the rest of that filthy barn, too, while you're at it."

"Yes, Mr. Harper," they answered together.

"Now, Greg, you bring my chair over from the porch, please. Ralph, get started in the barn."

"Yes, Mr. Harper."

Greg was back with Jess's chair almost immediately; Jess had him set it about ten feet upwind from Betsy. "Thank you, Greg," Jess said as he settled himself. "You get along now and help Ralph. The product will make itself from here on out."

"Right, Mr. Harper." Ralph hurried away, and Jess settled down in his chair to resume his nap. He had almost drifted off again when Ike began barking. It was his intruder's bark.

"Ralph! Greg!" Jess called. "Yellow alert!" There were three hunting rifles and a precious box of ammunition hidden in the barn, and the Simpsons knew how to shoot. Jess had taught them how, just as he'd taught Sammie. He would have happily paid the cost of the ammunition himself, because learning to shoot straight was cheap insurance, but the town had assumed the expense. The straighter Jess Harper and his people could shoot, the safer the town was from an incursion from the north.

Jess got up and hurried around the side of the house. Ike was standing at the bottom of the porch steps, looking west and barking loudly.

"Good job, Ike, good dog," Jess said, reaching down and stroking the dog's head. "Easy, boy. Hush, now. Down, boy." The dog fell silent but continued to sniff the air. Jess felt the light breeze from the west on his face.

Soon enough Jess could see a man approaching. He appeared to be dragging something behind him; it was hard to see exactly, with the sun getting so low. *Who's that, I wonder? Oh, the way he's dressed, it's gotta be Dan Digby. I can see the cap. Yep, that's him.*

"Halloo, Digger!" Jess called, cupping his mouth. The figure stopped and waved an arm, acknowledging the hail.

"It's okay, boys," Jess called toward the barn; the Simpsons emerged, holding their rifles at the ready. "It's Digger, and he's alone; you can stand down. Looks like he got himself something big today. Ralph, why don't you go run up there and see if Digger needs any help getting it home? Greg can put the rifles away."

"Uh, what about finishing up in the barn, Mr. Harper?" Greg asked.

"I expect that whatever doesn't get done today will keep until first thing tomorrow morning," Jess said. "But first thing, mind."

"Yes, Mr. Harper," they both answered. Ralph trotted away.

The screen door behind Jess squeaked open. Sure enough, it was Sammie; she was holding one of Jess's two old .45 automatics from Korea. She was exactly as tall and round as Jess was. Sammie looked easygoing and kind, but it was clear that there was steel not far under that seemingly soft exterior. That, too, was just like Jess.

"Everything okay, dear?" she asked.

"Sure, honey. It's just Digger Digby."

"Oh, that's nice," Sammie said. She flipped the safety of the .45 on and dropped the weapon in the pocket of her apron. "I'll go put on some water for tea."

"You do that; I'll bet Digger's had a day for himself. Thanks.'' Jess sat down on the porch steps and commenced waiting; Ike trotted over and sat on his haunches by his master. Jess passed the time by scratching Ike behind his ears and telling him how good the mash looked this time. The dog, as always, proved to be an excellent listener.

Ralph and Digger arrived at the house about ten minutes later. Both men were dragging the travois, but only Ralph was puffing. Jess's eyes widened when he spotted the deer; he whistled. Digger looked tired.

"My Lord, Digger,'' Jess said, astonished. He walked over and inspected the carcass closely. "He's a beauty, all right,'' Jess said at length. "No wonder Ike was all excited; he must have got wind of it. Haven't seen a deer in many years, much less a fine specimen like that.''

"Not since the seventies, that's for sure,'' Digger agreed. "The deer were hunted out pretty quick.'' He let the travois down and shook Jess's hand. "Thanks for your consideration in sending out Ralph.''

"Happy to do you a good turn.''

Digger turned to Ralph, who was studying the red marks left on his left hand by the travois. "Ralph,'' he said, "I'd be pleased if you'd accept a piece of this gentleman for your help, right after I'm done taking him apart. I think your mom could make good use of the venison.''

Ralph's face lighted up. "Gee, Mr. Digby! She'll be real happy about that. Thanks a lot! Well, I gotta go help my brother now—''

"Fine, Ralph,'' Jess said. "Thanks again.'' Ralph headed for the barn.

"Hey, hi, Ike!'' Digger said, kneeling. The dog woofed. "How's the world's best dog, eh? Good boy!'' He rubbed Ike's head and stroked his flank; the dog responded by panting heavily and making happy little sounds deep in his throat.

"How have you been, Digger?'' Jess asked.

"Not too bad," Digger replied, giving Ike a final rub on his head. He rose and brushed the dirt from his knee. "Yourself? And how's Sammie?"

"We're both fine. You look a little done in, though."

Digger nodded. "I've been dragging this fella for more'n a mile. It's taking three times longer to get him home than I hoped it would. That road just keeps tearing up the travois; I can't go more than a quarter-mile without it falling apart. I was trying to make it home before dark."

"I don't think you will," Jess said.

"I know I won't," Digger said. "I was thinking of trying to carry the deer—you know, a fireman's carry."

Jess nodded. "Might work. Say, Digger, I could cut you a good deal on that handsome fella. What do you think?"

Digger shook his head. "Sorry, Jess, but I really need the deer. Some of him's going to go to Dick LeClerc to settle some debt. I could sell you some of the venison, though. Make you a good price, if you let me leave him here overnight. I'm all in, no lie." He sat on the topmost porch step and sighed.

Jess sat down next to him and scratched his chin. He studied Digger. "I'll be straight with you, Digger," he said after a moment. "I can get more for that fellow with the hat rack on him than you can—from Dick LeClerc or from anybody. Heck, I bet you I can even sell the head to somebody, not that anybody really needs a trophy. I'll even bet you that Dick will take it for himself, for that big living room wall of his."

"No bet," Digger said, nodding his head and smiling. "It's likely enough, that's for sure."

"I don't need the skin, either," Jess offered, and Digger nodded. Jess knew he could easily find a buyer for the skin, or keep it himself—it was a beautiful one—but he also knew instinctively that Digger would not give it up. "Let's just talk about the meat," he said.

"That sounds fine," Digger said, nodding again.

"How much of him were you planning to give to Dick?" Jess asked.

"I don't really know," Digger replied, shrugging. "I don't know what Dick gets for venison; I don't think it's ever come up before. I figured I might have to give him almost all of it. We owe him quite a bit. What the hell—pardon me, Sammie. I mean, just how much is deer meat worth, anyway?"

"Beats me," Jess said, "but here's my proposition. We become partners on the deer. You take, say a quarter of the meat—a back quarter—home with you, free and clear. That looks to be, um, thirty-five pounds or more. Take all the skin, too, but leave me the head intact; I can work around that slash there on the neck, no problem. I also take the rest of the deer, keep what I can and do the deal with Dick, and I retire your debt with him."

"The whole debt?" Digger asked, surprised.

"The whole debt," Jess said firmly.

"You know how much that is?"

"Digger, it's my business to know everything Dick LeClerc does. Don't worry, your debt's not much—at least, nothing I can't make our antlered friend here cover and more. You get a quarter, Dick gets enough from me to pay off your debt with him, and I get what's left of the deer. Deal?"

"You going to want the innards?"

"Yep," Jess replied firmly. "Dick can make pemmican and sausage, or he can get someone to do it for him. Hey, he could hire Annie to do it, I bet. You know, I could make it part of the deal—?"

Digger nodded, smiled, and extended a hand. "Deal." They shook on it.

"Want the Simpsons to quarter him?" Jess asked.

"That'll be fine," Digger replied, nodding. "It'll

be a relief for me not to have to carry all of him home.''

As if on cue, Sammie emerged from the house with her prized tea service; there was also a small but welcome platter of buttered corn cakes. "Hello, Digger," she smiled. "How have you been, and how's the family?" She handed the tea service and plate to Jess, who placed it between himself and Digger.

"Been well, thanks," Digger said. "Annie and the kid are fine, too. No real news. Nice to see you again, Sammie."

"We don't see either of you very much anymore," she scolded him. She seated herself next to Jess but one step down, facing Digger.

"I'll try to do better about that," Digger said. "I'd like to send Annie around, too. She doesn't get out nearly enough."

"No, she doesn't," Sammie said. "She's always welcome here, of course, as is your boy."

"Well, thanks, Sammie," Digger said. "I'll pass that along."

It was getting late, but Digger was glad of the chance to rest, and he would not have turned down Harper hospitality in any case. "Mmmm," he said, looking at the platter. "Corn cakes. How *do* you do it, Sammie? These are wonderful."

"Why, thank you, Digger," Samuella replied, pleased.

"There's another way to take your corn," Jess pointed out, "but you've never been a drinkin' man."

"Nope." Digger said around a mouthful of corn cake. "Couldn't afford it."

Jess laughed. "That's a good reason not to drink. Me, I don't drink—much—because Samuella here would operate on my brains with something dull and rusty if I did."

"No, dear," Sammie said. "I'd make it quick for you. I owe you that much."

"Thanks, honey," Jess said. "I love you, too. By the way, Digger, how soon do you want your share of the meat?"

"I expect I could pick it up tomorrow? Say, in the early afternoon?"

"Unless you want to wait," Jess said. "I could have the boys cut him up for you now."

Digger shook his head. "No, thanks, Jess," he said, glancing again at the sun. "I think I'd like to get going. It's getting pretty late, and Annie'll be worried. Uh, could you make sure for me that Ralph Simpson gets his hunk? A couple of pounds off my end should do it."

Jess nodded and stood. "Will do," he said, brushing his hands against his overalls. "Wish you could stay for dinner, but we understand. But maybe you and yours can make it to supper here come Saturday? I can almost guarantee you that it'll be venison."

"We'd like that," Digger said. "Thank you. Um, what's today?"

"Wednesday," Sammie said. "It's hard to keep it straight, I know."

Digger shook hands with Jess again and kissed Sammie on the cheek. "Thanks for everything, Jess, Sammie," he said, as he grasped the carrying strap on his mailbag. "Thanks especially for those corn cakes."

"You keep quiet there, Daniel Digby," Sammie said. "We'll see you on Saturday. There'll be more corn cakes."

"Saturday, then," Jess said.

"Right. Bye." Digger bent to rub Eisenhower's ears in farewell, and the dog snarfled with pleasure. Then Digger set the mailbag strap on his shoulder and, with a last wave, headed on along 73 toward home.

Jess turned away and walked over to the barn to see just how the Simpsons had chosen to goof off this time. He supposed that a reasonable man would have long since fired the Simpsons and gotten someone else to do the work that needed doing around the place, but Jess saw the Simpsons as—well, not family, but something close . . . and Jess had never been the kind who would fire family.

CHAPTER 4

HE HOPED THEY WOULDN'T GET INTO TROUBLE *again, but his brother was pretty much daring Miss Gordon to do her worst. Now Joey was covertly engaged in shooting rubber bands and spitballs at everyone around him. On the scale of exaggerated culpability by which adults measure the misbehavior of children, Joey was a gap-toothed menace who, on a scale of ten, merited a score no lower than nine-point-seven.*

Miss Gordon had once told their mama in a parent-teacher conference that while she always knew boys would be boys, she hadn't known that twin boys were worse and seven-year-old twin boys in the same class were worse yet. Mama had come home and asked them to take it easy on poor Miss Gordon, who was a good and kind young woman, and he himself had, mostly. Joey, however, didn't care to take it easy on anybody, and he also didn't care what punish lessons Miss Gordon gave out. Joey knew from his dad what real pun-

ishment was—and so, for that matter, did he. He didn't much care what Joey did, except that he himself would come in for some measure of blame for it. That's how things were between twins, even if they sat two rows and three seats apart. Both always got blamed for whatever either did. Maybe he'd be in trouble because Joey was eighteen minutes younger than he was, and that made him automatically responsible for him. He was, after all, the older one.

Miss Gordon put down her book and looked up to find Joey sitting quietly in his seat, his hands folded and his eyes wide with innocence. She'd missed him firing a salvo of seven rubber bands and three spitballs across the room. She did not miss the expressions of disgust on the faces of Joey's female targets but, lacking direct proof, she did no more than glare warningly at Joey.

He watched as Miss Gordon finally looked away from Joey and stood up to address the class. "I hope you've all thought about things in the extra time you've spent here today," she said. "I hope it won't be necessary to keep you all after school again because some of you refuse to behave yourselves while the rest of us try to watch Faces and Places in the News *on television."*

A paper ball—dry, this time—landed on top of his desk and nearly skittered over the side before he clapped a hand over it. It was a note; he unfolded it and read it. It said, THIS IS BULLSHIT. *He looked up to find Joey making a monster face at him.*

"Ahem," Miss Gordon said. He looked up to find her standing right in front of him. He looked at the teacher with as innocent an expression as he could manage.

"Justin?" she asked. "What have you got there?"

"Uh, nothing, Miss Gordon," he said.

"Isn't that a note?"

"Uh, what note?" I can't let her see it! *he thought frantically.* It's got *shit* written on it!

Miss Gordon held out her hand. "Let me see it," she demanded.

He glanced across the room. Even the usually un-flappable Joey was looking a little worried. He could think of nothing else to do, so after a moment he balled up the note and chewed it, just like the spies did in the movies.

"Justin?" his mother called. "You awake yet, honey?"

The boy roused and rubbed his eyes. "I'm up, Mama," he said. He blinked and turned his head to see his mother crouching at the hearth, building a fire. The light from outside had grown orange and weak. "Is Digger home yet?" he asked.

"Not yet," his mother said. She was frowning, but Justin knew it to be her worry frown and not her mad frown. "He'll be home soon, though. Better clean up for supper."

"Yes, Mama," Justin said.

Digger hurried east along 73 and, just as the sun was setting, he hit the short, concealed trail that led past the family cabin. "It's me," he called when he got within fifty feet of home, just so no one inside would think the cabin was being stalked. The cabin itself was not on the trail, but was hidden behind some trees a few yards west of it. Annie and her first husband had moved into it ten years ago, having found the place abandoned and in an advanced state of disrepair. It had fallen to Digger, though, to make the place livable after his own marriage to Annie five years later.

Digger moved through the concealing growth and, suddenly, the cabin was in front of him and the door was opening. Annie was standing there, scowling.

Justin was standing just behind her, rubbing the sleep from his eyes and smiling. "Hi, Digger!" he called.

"Hello, Justin," Digger said as he drew near. "How's the boy?" He took off his Red Sox cap and put it on his stepson's head. It dropped over the boy's eyes, and Justin giggled.

"Hi, dear," Digger said to his wife.

"You're late," Annie said. She looked pointedly at the red glow to the west. "Three hours and more."

"I had a good day."

"Hmph."

Digger dropped the critter bag onto the cabin floor near the table and crouched to hug the boy. "Hi, kiddo," he said. "Miss me?"

"Sure!" Justin said. "Mama was worried."

"Hush, Justin," Annie said.

"Were *you* worried?" Digger asked Justin.

The boy looked serious; his dark eyes were huge in Digger's. "You were late, and it was getting dark out, and it's not safe to be alone outside," he said seriously.

"I'm sorry," Digger said. "I didn't expect to be out so late, but something happened. I'm sorry you two were worried about me, but it was a special emergency." He looked up at Annie. "I got us a deer."

His wife's jaw dropped. "You got us a what?"

Quickly, he told her about it. "Jess is going to settle our debt at the store," he finished, "and we'll get about thirty-five or forty pounds of venison and a deerskin out of it—not to mention a ton of goodwill from both Jess Harper and Dick LeClerc, which isn't too bad. And *you're* going to turn that deer's innards into sausage for Dick LeClerc for store credit—if you want to, that is."

"A job?" Annie grinned, and Digger thought it was a fine thing indeed to see her smile like that. "*Credit* at the store? Great! Hey, champ, are we getting rich, or what?"

"Me mighty hunter," Digger grunted. "Bring-um home heap big game." He beat his chest with a fist and coughed. That was something his father used to do to get a laugh, and it still did.

"What's a deer?" Justin wanted to know.

"A deer is a big forest animal," Digger said. "I'll show you a picture of one in my dad's mountain book a little later."

"Okay," Justin said. The boy ran into the cabin. Digger picked up the mailbag, and he and Annie followed him.

"We're going to have to do something about preserving all that meat," Annie said, thinking out loud. "Salt, of course, and tannin for the hide. I've got more than enough salt on hand for that much meat, but I just don't remember how much tannin I'm going to need for that big a skin. I've only got a little on hand. Oh, bother it; me and Justin will just round up a ton of acorns tomorrow and boil 'em up."

"I can see we're going to be up to here in acorn bread again," Digger said ruefully.

"Now listen to Mr. Picky," Annie said. "Lord above, I haven't had to worry about a big kill in a good long time." She smiled. "I just can't believe your luck."

Digger smiled back. "I wish I knew where that big old deer came from. Heck, honey, I remember seeing 'em from a distance on vacations, when I was a boy and my dad would take me up here. Beautiful creatures. I tell you, I almost hated taking that one today." He dropped the bag on the table; it thumped heavily. "In here is the usual assortment of critters, but it's a good haul. I would have considered today a real plus, even without the deer. Oh, by the way, we're having dinner with the Harpers come Saturday."

"Really?" Annie said cautiously. "What about Justin?"

"He's invited, too."

"That's not what I mean," Annie said.

"Justin'll be fine," Digger said firmly.

"We'll talk about it later," said Annie.

"All right."

Annie smiled again and undid the hitches on the mailbag. "Pretty good haul, champ," she said, giving a quick look inside.

"I'll help you with the critters," Digger said.

"No need," she said. "Hey, three rabbits!" She examined them closely. "Healthy little buggers. They look fine, Digger."

"I thought so, too," Digger said. "Let's eat pretty soon, okay? We can clean the rest of the take after dinner."

"I can clean a rabbit quick enough," Annie said, nodding. She put the butcher block on the kitchen table. "How about you get the fire ready?" she asked. "It's a little high for cooking rabbit."

"Right." Digger rummaged in the fireplace with a poker, spreading ash around carefully to bring the fire down without smothering it. Annie cleaned the rabbits quickly and efficiently, salvaging everything worth keeping. She then salted the meat and, after a thought, sprinkled some rosemary on it.

"Justin?" Annie called over her shoulder. "There's still enough light. Get me some dandy greens and a bucket of your blueberries for dessert, dear, all right?"

"Right!" the boy cried, excited and happy to be given something important to do. He ducked under the kitchen table to retrieve his small wooden berry bucket, and then he ran outside to the blueberry bushes nearest the cabin. All the bushes were bearing well this year. The ones closest to home were considered to be Justin's personal property, and so he was in charge of harvesting them and worrying about them. Annie watched him pick for a minute. In his enthusiasm, the boy would probably pick too many berries and some would be wasted, but it didn't matter very much. There were plenty of blueberries now. Dandelions were all over the place, too, and the boy could quickly gather enough of them for a nice salad.

"He had a bad time during his nap," Annie said, keeping her eyes on her work. "It was just before you got home."

Digger looked up quickly. "He did?" he asked apprehensively. "Is he sick?"

"No, no," Annie reassured him. "He had a dream, it looked like. That's all. Tossing and turning. He mumbled some, too."

"Oh. Could you make it out?"

"No, not really." Annie arranged the rabbits on the cast-iron grill. "Just gibberish."

"Did he say what the dream was about?"

Annie shook her head. "He never mentioned it after he woke up. I guess he forgot about it."

Digger nodded. "Just so long as he's not sick."

Annie bent and set the grill on the fire; the flames hissed and grew yellow. "I've been watching him ever since he woke up," she said, wiggling the grill into a more precise position. "He's fine, I guess . . . but I don't think he should go to the Harpers on Saturday."

"Okay." Digger put an arm around his wife and squeezed. "I'll make our excuses to Jess and Sammie when I see them tomorrow. Let's try not to worry too much; Justin's been healthy for a good long time now. God's been good to us so far. Let's hope He continues."

"Amen." They rose together from the fireplace, just as Justin came back inside with half a bucket of berries. "I didn't think we needed any more," the boy said.

Digger was pleased. "You're right, son," he said, smiling and putting a hand on the boy's small shoulder. "We sure don't. That's just enough for the three of us."

"I didn't want to waste anything," Justin said.

"You're a real good berry-picker," Digger said, ruffling the boy's hair and making him laugh.

The rabbits cooked quickly, and Annie lost no time in getting them to the table. They held hands and bowed their heads as Digger recited the Catholic grace he'd learned long ago from his refugee Boston Irish father. "Thank you, Lord," he added. "It's a fine meal. We're grateful."

"Amen," his wife and stepson chorused, and they all dug in.

It was indeed a wonderful meal, and they ate it quickly. In celebration of Digger having bagged the deer and the paid work Annie expected to get from Dick LeClerc, they were using their least chipped and most presentable fancy dishes, the ones they usually saved for holidays. Happiness and contentment added sauce and spice to the meal, and the family's worries went wherever worries go when faced with laughter.

Toward the end of the meal Justin asked, "Digger? What happened to our television set?"

"Television set? We don't have one, Justin."

"People in town do, don't they? Everybody does. Mama said so once."

"Yes, some people still have televisions," Digger said, "but they don't work. They're just left over from the old times. Most people never got rid of them, that's all. Televisions need 'lectricity to work, and then someone has to send pictures into them."

"Huh?"

Digger shrugged and smiled. "I'm just telling you what my dad told me when I asked him the same question. I can't remember ever seeing a television set work, but I know what they were supposed to do. Must have been really something. Anyway, there was never a television here in the cabin. There's no wires for 'lectricity, either."

"Televisions were like little theaters," Annie said.

"I remember seeing one work once, when I was just a little girl."

"I watched television today," Justin said.

"You did what?" Digger asked.

"I watched TV, and it was fun! But it was scary, too. I was in school and we were watching TV."

"You were?" Digger was puzzled.

"His dream, maybe?" Annie suggested.

Digger shrugged. "Beats me. Justin, was all this in your dream today?"

"It wasn't a dream," Justin insisted. "It was real. The teacher was nice."

"Miss Neary is always nice," Digger said.

"It wasn't Miss Neary," Justin replied. "It was Miss Gordon."

"Miss Gordon?" Annie asked. "Who's Miss Gordon?"

Justin shrugged. "I dunno," he mumbled, suddenly cautious in the face of adult inquiry. "Just Miss Gordon, that's all."

"Only Miss Gordon I know is Connie Gordon," Annie said, "and she's been Connie Matthews for seven years now."

"Wait a minute, love," Digger said to Annie, holding up a hand. "Justin, what was on the, uh, TV?"

"I forget," Justin said, eating his blueberries. "It was boring. But Joey passed me a note and we got caught. Miss Gordon yelled at us for it. She scared me, but not Joey. Then I woke up. Are you mad that I ate the note?"

Digger shot a look at his wife and saw her face turn pale. "Easy, hon," he said, holding her hand. He was shaken himself. "No, we're not mad, son," Digger said, wondering what it was all about. "Everything's all right."

"Joey looks just like me," the boy said. "How come?"

Annie quietly put down her fork and left the table. Digger led Justin to speak of other things.

After the boy had been tucked into his small bed in the corner of the room and had fallen asleep, Annie finally said something to Digger. Her tone was hushed. "What's all this about Joey all of a sudden?" she demanded of her husband. "Have you been talking about him to Justin lately?"

"No, I haven't," Digger answered. "Why should I? Not that I know much, but Justin never asks me anything about him."

"Sure he didn't," Annie said bitterly, turning from him. "He picked it up from our dinner conversation, right? We talk about poor little Joey every damn day, don't we?"

"Easy there, Annie," Digger said, reaching for her to comfort her. "No one's done any wrong here."

Annie stepped away from him. "He says they *look* like each other," she said after a moment. "Jesus!"

"It's just a dream, honey. That's all. People dream all sorts of things."

"Sure they do."

"Yes, they do. Why, Doc'll tell you the same thing. Justin isn't dreaming about Joey at all. He's probably dreaming all about himself, I bet, and he puts the name Joey to it because he's heard it from us before."

Annie was still frowning. "Then what's all this stuff about school and television?"

"You're asking me like I knew, honey," Digger returned. "I don't know, all right? Maybe the boy *wants* to go to school, so he dreams about it. He's heard about television sets, seen pictures of 'em in the magazines you taught him to read from. Who knows how a kid's mind works? Maybe he's dreaming all this because he's lonesome. Lord knows he doesn't see many people except us."

"How can he go to school?" Annie said heatedly.

"If he gets hurt, he doesn't heal right. If he catches cold, he nearly dies. He gets sicknesses for no reason at all."

"He hasn't been sick like that in years," Digger said. "Doc thinks he's over it—"

"You going to guarantee that?" Annie said heatedly. Her eyes filled. "I'm always so scared I'm going to lose him."

"He needs to be with other kids, Annie."

"You mean over at the school?" she asked him. "Put him in that town school and I *will* lose him, just like I lost the other. All those kids with their runny noses and horseplay!"

"You've always been a good teacher to the boy," Digger said. "I've never said otherwise. He reads fast and well, and he figures arithmetic like a whip. I just think he needs more."

Annie looked at her husband wanly and then walked over to him. He held her close. "That poor little baby," she said into his shoulder. "I fought so hard . . ."

"I know," he said. "I wish I'd been around then. I wish I could have helped." She hugged him tightly.

Across the room, Justin suddenly began mumbling in his sleep.

Annie gasped. Justin was talking to Joey.

CHAPTER 5

IT WAS GETTING LATE, AND MOST OF THE PEOPLE IN the town of McAndrew were beginning to think about turning in.

Not so Randy LeClerc. His chores done and dinner eaten, Randy sat at the small desk in the bedroom he shared with his brother. A stumpy candle was set next to his math homework to hold back the night. The candle didn't shed very much light, and Randy's eyes were beginning to get tired from looking at the closely set print in the old mathematics textbook. His note-paper was covered with figures; Miss Neary had laid the homework on pretty thick today, all right, even though the school year had just started a couple of weeks ago, and the harvest break was coming up. First he'd had geography, then he'd had to memorize that stupid poem for English, and now there was this dumb arithmetic. He'd gone through the regular assignment quickly enough, but the bonus problem at the end of the chapter was a tough one.

Randy was ten, and ten was the very last chance that a boy had to be a boy. Things started happening at eleven or so, and there was always the certainty of work, work and more work, forever and ever, amen, once you got too old to be a kid anymore. Randy's brother Bobby was sixteen, and all he ever got for it was trouble. Bobby was still outside working; he hadn't managed to finish *his* chores before dinner and, looking out the window, Randy could see the light of a lantern dodging here and there inside the barn.

Randy liked being ten. *So why am I wasting my time here, doing this stupid homework?* he wondered. *I've got other things to do!*

The boy brushed back his red hair with a small hand, sighed, and looked at the bonus problem in the textbook again. The bonus problem was the last one he had to do that night.

Randy gave it a try. He licked the point of his pencil—something his dad always did at the store when he was about to begin figuring the books—and stared at the page. It didn't take long for the boy to realize that he had absolutely no idea how to solve the problem.

Who gives a shit? Randy suddenly wondered. *Doesn't mean anything! Who gives a shit? I sure don't!* The boy smiled at the audacity of the thought. *I don't give a shit!* he told himself. It was something his father sometimes said under his breath when he was weary and thought his sons weren't within hearing. Randy felt grand about daring to think a grown-up thought. Making the decision not to give a shit made Randy feel strong and independent, like an adult, especially since shit was one of the words he wasn't even supposed to know yet. Randy had never felt quite that way before, not even when he was assured by his dad that the tedious chores he was assigned to do were vitally important to the survival of the entire family. No kid had ever really believed that feeding some skinny chickens or sweeping out a stall was all that big a deal. Randy said *I don't give a shit!* to himself once again, this time with great force and greater glee, and he slammed the textbook shut so hard that a cloudy sort of smell rose from it. *I don't give a shit! Yeah!*

"Randy?" came his mom's voice from downstairs. "Stop fooling around up there and finish that homework, you hear me? And don't you hurt that schoolbook!"

"Yes'm," Randy answered, loudly enough for his mother to hear through the closed door. The boy put his book and paper to one side of the desk and left the candle burning. He got up from his chair and bent low to retrieve a shallow box from under his bed. It was heavy and densely packed; Randy needed both hands to slide it out.

Inside the box were his greatest treasures, the things he guarded and regarded above all others: his comic books. Actually, they were his father's, back from when his father was a kid. Bobby had never cared much about them, so they'd fallen to Randy.

With care, Randy extracted one of them and studied its cover by the dim light of the candle. It was a Superman. Nope, he wasn't in the mood for that, as much as he liked Superman; he placed it back into the box and dug deeper. Maybe this Green Lantern would do, or that Batman there—or perhaps a Fantastic Four, or an Incredible Hulk? No, no. He was looking for something special . . . and there it was, buried under a copy of the Flash: a Captain Cobalt. Captain Cobalt was Randy's absolute favorite superhero, and he hadn't re-read this particular issue in quite a while. It was the one with Dr. Heavey in it. Randy loved that story. He straightened up, went back to his desk and sat down.

The garish cover of the comic book showed Captain Cobalt, in his blue and white form-fitting uniform, strapped onto a laboratory table. The balding, cadaverous Dr. Heavey, wearing his black-as-evil laboratory coat, was off to one side, manipulating the dial-festooned controls of a bright red machine that was shining a blue ray on the hero. Captain Cobalt's sweating face was twisted with pain, and his bulging muscles were taut with suffering. The evil Dr. Heavey was gloating in Comicbook, that strange written language of light and bold capital letters in which every declarative sentence ends with an exclamation point. **"HA! HA!"** Dr. Heavey was saying. **"YOU'LL SOON BE DEAD, CAPTAIN COBALT! YOU'LL NEVER ESCAPE MY HEAVEYITE RAY!"**

Heaveyite, Randy knew from his previous research on the subject, was a mysterious substance invented by Dr. Heavey himself in his secret lab under the streets of Manhattan. Randy knew that radiation from blue heaveyite affected Captain Cobalt pretty much as green kryptonite was said to affect Superman. Heaveyite neutralized Captain Cobalt's atomic powers, and it could kill him if he was exposed to it for long enough.

Randy knew for an absolute fact that Captain Cobalt had been a real person, and it was a discovery he was proud to have made independently. Superman and most of the rest were said to have lived in places like Metropolis and Gotham City. Randy knew those cities were fakes because he'd long ago looked for them on the big United States map in the classroom and had not found them, careful as he'd been. Just to make sure, he'd asked Miss Neary about them in a round-about way, and she'd told him there was no Metropolis and no Gotham City and never had been. Captain Cobalt had lived in New York, though, which used to be a real place, and that was good enough for Randy. In fact, the size of New York's name on the classroom map showed it had once been the biggest place of all, so it had certainly been an appropriate place for a superhero to ply his trade. The Fantastic Four and some other superpeople had lived there, too, but Randy assumed the bombs had gotten them all. Only Captain Cobalt could have survived an atomic explosion—in the comics Randy had read, he'd survived several without harm—so Randy had figured it out for himself that the Russians had gotten him with heaveyite. The Russians must have been scared of Captain Cobalt, all right, so it made sense that they'd want to kill him off. They had probably assassinated him by sneaking up on him from behind and letting him have it with a blue heaveyite bullet, just like that actor guy had gotten Abe Lincoln. Otherwise, Captain Cobalt would still be around, helping to fix the world and set it aright.

Randy carefully opened his comic book in the middle, skipping the lead-in and going directly to the real story—Dr. Heavey's capture of Captain Cobalt. The conniving scientist had lured the Captain into a trap by kidnapping Captain Cobalt's girlfriend, actress Claudia Cloud, and threatening to kill her. When Captain Cobalt had, inevitably, shown up to rescue the hapless Claudia, Dr. Heavey had zapped him with the heaveyite ray. He'd then had his hulking, dimwitted assistant, a mutant named Fred, strap the helpless Captain to a laboratory table. The scene on the cover followed from there.

Randy avidly re-read the long-since memorized story of how Captain Cobalt, by summoning every erg of his remaining atomic power, had used his neutronic vision to melt a key connection in the heaveyite ray projector, causing it to malfunction. At this point, Dr. Heavey and Fred had cravenly and predictably run away. Quickly recovering his strength, Captain Cobalt had then burst his bonds and rescued Claudia from the cell in which Dr. Heavey had imprisoned her. The Captain knew that the damaged projector was going to explode at any moment, so he manfully chose to fly Claudia away from the lab rather than try to capture the fleeing Dr. Heavey and Fred. Indeed, the projector did blow up just as Captain Cobalt removed Claudia to the relative safety of the Manhattan streets. The blast utterly destroyed the underground lab, and presumably, Dr. Heavey and Fred.

Of course, Randy was wise to the ways of the comic book world, and he knew that Dr. Heavey and the faithful Fred had not really died in the explosion. Inevitably, they would have shown up again a few issues later—**THE RETURN OF DR. HEAVEY!!!**—except for the fact that the issue Randy was reading was number 143, dated November 1962. Randy's dad had told him once that comic books had always come out a little earlier than the cover date. The November issue had probably come out sometime in October, and so this one hundred and forty-third issue of Captain Cobalt had been the last.

Randy had turned back to the beginning of the comic and was preparing to read it all the way through when the doorknob rattled. Quickly, he grabbed his math textbook and placed it over the comic just as the door opened.

It was Bobby. "Hi, stupid," he greeted his brother. "What're you doing?" He closed the door.

"Homework," Randy answered, staring into the math book.

Bobby spotted an edge of the comic sticking out from under the textbook. "Not unless old lady Neary's teaching the history of comic books, you're not," he grinned. "Better not let 'em find you wasting a candle on a comic book, keed. Sure death." He drew a thumb across his throat and made a sound like a death rattle.

"I know," Randy said, surrendering. "I was about finished, anyway." He closed the textbook and, rising, replaced the comic in the box. He slid the box back under his bed as quietly as he could.

"You're running pretty late tonight," Randy said.

"Had to finish up something in the barn for Dad," Bobby said. "Common work kept me late. Harvest's coming soon, and there won't be time to do much else while that's going on."

"How much work did you draw?"

Bobby frowned. "Three hours a day of maintenance detail until next week—and that's after the hours I keep at the store," he said. "We'll be patching and whitewashing every day until it's too dark out to see." He frowned. "Then I've got more to do here when I get home. Seems to me I could be spared some of it."

"I wouldn't mind working at the store," Randy said. "I could spell you."

"You'll have to, soon enough," his older brother answered. "Don't be in a rush to do it, though. It doesn't pay, believe me. Besides, you've got your own chores to do here. I'm going to be run pretty ragged, and I'm counting on you to help me out. Okay?"

"Sure!" Randy said.

The pitcher on the dresser the boys shared was still half filled with water. Bobby poured some of it into the washbasin, took off his shirt, and began washing without bothering to use soap.

"You boys about ready for bed?" their mother called. "It's getting late."

"Yeah, Mom," Bobby answered. "I'm just helping Randy with his homework." He grinned at his younger brother, who returned it. Grinning made them look even more alike.

"Well, you tell him to put it away," their father said. "It's time for bed."

"Right, Dad," Bobby said. "G'night."

"And don't forget to wash," their mother called. "Use soap."

"Right, Mom," said Bobby.

"G'night, Mom, Dad," Randy added.

"G'night, boys," their mother answered.

"Sleep tight," added their father.

Bobby ignored the folded towel next to the wash-bowl and dried himself with his shirt. He took another from the dresser, put it on and walked across the room to his bed. He added the soiled shirt to some other dirty laundry and wadded it under his blankets so that it would look as if someone were sleeping.

"You going out again tonight?" Randy asked.

"Sure am," Bobby said. He began rearranging the clothing into a new and, he hoped, more Bobby-like lump.

"Oh," Randy said. "I was kinda hoping we could talk."

"Talk?" Bobby asked. He straightened up, study-ing his handiwork; his back was to Randy. "Talk about what?" he asked, as he began rearranging the blan-kets for a third time.

"Oh, just stuff," Randy said, sitting up. "We never talk anymore, Bobby."

"What do you want to talk about?"

"Oh, I dunno," Randy said, shrugging with a ca-sualness he did not feel. "Uh, how's Stephanie?"

"Stef's great," Bobby said absently. He gave the blankets one last push and tuck, nodded, and then walked to the window. He opened it as quietly as he could. "See you later," Bobby said over his shoulder.

"See you later," Randy echoed, trying to keep the disappointment out of his voice.

Bobby climbed out the window and stood on the narrow porch overhang, making sure of his balance. He stretched out an arm and got a good grasp on the drainpipe that ran down the side of the house about three feet from the window. Holding on, Bobby lithely swung onto the trellis and climbed down quickly. He reached the ground and disappeared into the night.

Randy got up, blew out the candle and looked out the window and into the deep dark for a while, listen-ing to the crickets and watching the few lights in town still burning begin to disappear like stars being snuffed out by the breath of God. Soon enough, Randy closed the window, undressed, and climbed under the covers.

Waiting for sleep to come, Randy wondered again what it would be like to be able to fly through the air like Captain Cobalt. He often dreamed that he could.

Downstairs in the living room, Dick and Millie LeClerc were sitting quietly together on the sofa opposite the hearth, watching the fire and holding hands in the utterly comfortable way that a thoroughly married couple watches fires and holds hands. Nothing at all seemed to be happening anywhere in the entire world when there suddenly came a gentle series of thumpings and scrapings against the outside wall of the house.

"Bobby's going out again," Dick told his wife.

"I hear him clear enough," Millie replied drily, shaking her head. The firelight accented the red in her hair in a way that Dick always took pleasure in noticing. He squeezed his wife's hand, and she smiled.

"Don't worry about it," he said.

"Does he really think he's fooling us?" Millie asked.

"Sure he does," Dick said. "The boy needs to think so, too. It's good for him to think he's putting one over on us. A boy needs that." He suddenly grinned. "He's going to have to 'fess up soon, anyway. How's he going to keep on sneaking out on us after I close the upstairs for the winter?"

"I don't know if I like that Stephanie Crane," Millie said.

"I don't know if I do, either," Dick said, "but she's a tough little number."

"She's a little schemer, is what *she* is. I just have to believe he can do better."

"Maybe he can, but maybe she's also just what he needs; Bobby could do with a bit of taming. Actually, in some ways I hope they catch."

"Bite your tongue."

"It's time Bobby started thinking about settling down," Dick insisted. "He's sixteen, after all."

"But that's so *young*, Dick."

Dick shrugged. "No, it's not. I was his age when we got married. Remember?" He smiled.

"But that was different!" Millie said, noticing that when her husband smiled in firelight, she really couldn't tell that he wasn't sixteen anymore.

"Different?" He gave his wife's hand another squeeze. "Let's turn in. You can remind me."

Stephanie was waiting for Bobby in the visitors' dugout at the field next to the school. She'd been sitting on the bench for about an hour, watching the rise of the full moon, fat and bright and beautiful. There was a wind stirring the crops growing on what had once been the baseball diamond, and it made an eternal rustle. The nights were getting cooler now, too; Stephanie felt a chill and wrapped herself in the blanket she'd brought along with her.

Stephanie had moved aside some of the farming tools stored in the dugout in order to make a narrow place for her and Bobby. She'd spent the time thinking about him and what a good catch he was and how they'd done it on this very spot just three nights before for the first time and how she was still a little sore from it but so what and wasn't that bright thing up there in the southeastern sky old Jupe himself? Yes, it was. Must be.

There had been three bright shooters already, all to the south, as well as a handful of lesser streaks elsewhere in the sky. It was such a clear night that Stephanie could easily make out the Milky Way. She had always wondered why people called it that, since it had never looked like milk to her; it always looked more like smoke getting ready to thin out and disappear, or maybe like a spring morning's mist out on Serpent Lake.

She was starting to think that Bobby had somehow forgotten all about her when there came a slight noise from close at hand, and suddenly he was standing right there in front of her. "Hi, Steffie," he said.

"Hi yourself," she answered. "I was beginning to get worried about you." They came together and kissed sloppily, their lips parted and their tongues moving much too quickly. They had not quite gotten the hang of the thing yet—everything they knew was out of an old book or two, or based on bad advice from equally ignorant friends—but what they lacked in skill they more than made up for in enthusiasm. Eventually they stopped to come up for air and wipe their chins, but they never let go of each other.

"School okay?" he asked her.

"The usual," Stephanie answered. "Tons of homework. I can't wait 'til next year. You're lucky to be out."

"I don't know about that," Bobby said. Stephanie could see him smile in the moonlight. "I could do with a few days back in old lady Neary's classroom," he added. "Too much damn work to do outside of it."

"Well, you've got a big place. Your dad's rich."

Bobby shrugged. "Doesn't make any difference," he said. "I've got to handle everything at the farm in the mornings while he goes into town and runs the store. Then I go into town and do the store's deliveries in the afternoon. After that, I've got to pull some time for the town. Now it's worse, because Dad won't hire more than one or two extra hands, even at harvest time, and we have a lot to do." The boy sighed tiredly. "Maybe that's why he's so rich," he said. "He holds onto what he's got pretty good."

"All the better for you, then," Stephanie said. "It'll be yours someday, you know."

"No," Bobby said, "that's not the point—and I

shouldn't have said what I did. Dad's no cheapskate. I'm just in a bitch of a mood, I guess.''

"Shhh," Stephanie said. "Maybe I can help with that.''

"Maybe you can, at that.''

Arms curled around each other, they went to the dugout bench and seated themselves. Stephanie untied her long, blonde hair, letting it fall free; Bobby lifted his hand to stroke it. "Maybe I'm rich right now," he said.

She rubbed his hand with her cheek. "Maybe so," she smiled. They kissed again.

"I've been thinking about you a lot," Bobby said after a while.

"Same here. Um, wait a second. I brought a blanket this time.''

"I saw it," he said. "Good idea."

Stephanie spread the blanket as best she could on the floorboards in the space she'd cleared between the players' bench and the lip of the dugout. "Grab your end?" she asked.

"Huh? Oh, sure." Bobby fumbled around in the dark for a second or two, found the end of the blanket, and yanked it. "How's that?"

"Fine." On hands and knees now, they crawled through the short distance that remained between them. Still kneeling, they held each other closely.

"These have been the three longest days of my life," Bobby finally said.

"Oh, I don't know about that," Stephanie answered softly.

"You didn't miss me?" He sounded distressed.

Stephanie laughed. "Silly! Of course I did. I only walked past your place six or seven times, trying to get a look at you on your way out of the barn or something. Didn't you see me?''

" 'Fraid not. Wish I had.''

"Me, too." She fell silent as, together, they lay down side by side, fumbling a bit in the dark.

"The blanket was a good idea, Stef," said Bobby. He held her close to him.

"I hope to shout it is," she answered. "Comfortable?"

"Yeah, I'm comfortable."

They kissed again as Bobby began unbuttoning Stephanie's shirt. It was a big and bulky plaid thing made of thick fabric, a hand-me-down from one of her grandfathers. The buttons refused to be undone with one hand, though, particularly an inexperienced one; Stephanie finally took over and, temporarily letting go of Bobby, undid them herself. Bobby felt badly about not having been able to do the job himself but said nothing, hoping Stephanie would let it pass without comment. He sat up, pulled his own shirt over his head, and chucked it somewhere nearby.

Stephanie threw her shirt after Bobby's. A gentle breeze came up against her back, chilling it and raising goosebumps. Stephanie had not taken off her shirt the first time; the new sensation of feeling the wind against her bare skin made her feel daring and very adult. The old paperback novels she'd found in the trunk of her father's attic almost always made a point of mentioning the huge, round breasts of the ladies in the stories, particularly the ladies the hero—usually a detective or a soldier or someone like that—was doing it with or wanted to do it with. Stephanie's breasts were not large, but after careful study she had concluded they were round enough, and at least they were both the same size, unlike Sarah Broom's. Dull old Sarah was a little bit lopsided topside. The first and only time Stephanie had seen Sarah naked was at an impromptu skinny-dip party in Serpent Lake the summer before, and *Jesus!* had Sarah caught hell from her crazy mother about it when she'd found out. Sarah was a frog, all right, but not even a frog deserved a crazy woman like Mrs. Broom for a mother—although if she thought her stupid crush on Bobby made any difference *now,* well . . .

She stopped thinking about it as Bobby reached out and very gently, almost tentatively, stroked her shoulder. His hand wandered down and soon found her left breast. She hissed slightly as the palm of his hand grazed her nipple, which was already taut with the chill in the air; she felt it crinkle even further. It was a wonder to her that his touching her up here would cause her to feel something so strongly down *there.* When Bobby did it, though, it felt very different from when she did it to herself. She hadn't quite figured it all out yet.

Stephanie was certain that Bobby had no complaints. She thought he loved her already, but she still wasn't quite sure. It would suit her just fine if he did, of course. If he didn't, well, she would work on it; there was plenty of time. True, he was good-looking enough, but the important thing was that he would inherit his father's business. Bobby could have looked like Injun Joe the Mountain Monster, and it wouldn't have made any difference; he'd still have been the best catch in town. All the other girls knew it, too, but none of the others had managed to get Bobby to notice them. Stephanie had decided that Bobby was pretty dense about girls and more than a little shy around them, so she had acted accordingly. She'd bluntly offered herself to Bobby on their second walk together, three nights before, and things had worked out pretty well.

"I love looking at you in the moonlight," Bobby whispered.

"I love looking at you, too," she said, wondering if that was an awful thing for a girl to say. Apparently it wasn't, because he began kissing her again.

There was so much she didn't know. She had never had The Talk with her father. She knew that he probably would have been awkward about it, anyway. Doing it was a constant topic of conversation among McAndrew's girls, but the amount of misinformation in circulation was simply astonishing. Apparently even girls with mothers didn't talk together much about doing it, either.

As it was, neither Stephanie nor Bobby had ever done it before until they'd done it together, and each of them had been convinced that they'd done it completely wrong, although they'd each kept quiet about that conviction to the other. For her part, Stephanie had found that the paperback novels in her father's attic failed to cover the essentials. Bobby had just seemed so impossibly *big*, much too much so to fit in there—and as for climaxes, Stephanie had not heard bells ring (*A Fire in Dixie*), cannon go off (*The Valiant Vixens of Valley Forge*) or fireworks explode (*Blue Sky Over Red China*). Nothing much had seemed to happen for her at all, except for some pain and continuing soreness. Bobby, however, *had* finished; despite her inexperience, Stephanie could tell that much, and she'd found direct evidence of it later, upon inspection . . . and that somewhat surprising discovery had thrilled her more than a little bit. But the whole thing had been nothing like when she'd watched one of Jess Harper's stallions mount a filly, and thank the Lord for it. Now *that* thing had been *big*—!

"Maybe we could bring a lantern next time," Bobby said.

"Hmmm?"

"I said, maybe we could bring a lantern next time. To see better, I mean." Bobby suddenly sounded embarrassed.

"Oh. Oh, sure. Sorry, I was thinking. Actually, I'd like to find a better place for us to go. This dugout isn't much."

"Okay," he said. "What about one of the old houses?"

"Yuck! For-*get* it! Bugs and rats!"

"Well, then, what do you suggest?" he said.

"We'll talk about it later." She reached for him and drew him to her. As she touched him, she suddenly wanted him inside her again very badly, despite the pain she expected and the embarrassing doubts about how well they might be doing it. In that moment, there wasn't a bit of cold calculation in Stephanie anywhere, and it surprised her. She had suddenly discovered that, sometimes, doing it wasn't really a matter of choice.

They quickly took off the rest of their clothes and lay back together on the rough blanket. Bobby settled on top of Stephanie, settling his upper weight on his elbows, just as Stephanie had asked him to do before. They wasted precious little time on preliminaries; Stephanie reached down, took Bobby in hand and guided him inside her. His breath became loud in her ear as she clutched him to her.

It was an event of passing wonder to Stephanie that, this time, it only hurt her a little bit. At the end, as Bobby cried out, Stephanie was beginning to feel something wonderful, something that she'd glimpsed only the ghost of before.

It was almost getting *good,* it really *was*! Amazing!

Stephanie wished Bobby would go on just a little longer, but she could tell that it was getting soft and, anyway, he seemed to have fallen asleep—and right on top of her, too. *Well,* she thought with some annoyance, *so long as I can breathe and nothing's being pinched, it's okay, I guess*. With her free arm, she found a corner of the blanket and tossed a flap of it over the both of them.

Lying there, she had time to think. She certainly did not wish Bobby LeClerc any ill, but she wished for the thousandth time that she could truly love the one she was doing it with, like most of the women in those books. When your father was dying and you had no one else to turn to, though, just what were you supposed to do? Hit the road and starve? Un-*like*-ly!

She held her man to her and, soon, she drifted off with him.

The members of Team Tango had been carefully trained to come away fully at even the slightest strange sound, and so they had all been awakened by one of their number, a PFC, crying out in distress. Now Lieutenant Banks was reading the soldier the riot act.

"Having a nightmare, baby boy?" the lieutenant said scornfully. "You going to let a big, bad dream get your throat cut some night, Private?"

"No, *sir*!"

"Do you expect the rest of the team to make up for your inadequacies, Private?"

"No, *sir*!"

"You looking for the comfort of your mama, Private?"

"No, *sir*!"

"You going to begin exerting some goddamn *self-control*, Private?"

"Yes, *sir*!"

"Get down and give me a hundred."

The soldier immediately dropped and began to do push-ups. "One, *sir*, two, *sir*, three, *sir*—" he counted. When he finished, he was barely breathing heavily.

"Get back to sleep," the lieutenant ordered.

CHAPTER 6

HE WAS IN A CAR HEADING GENERALLY NORTHEAST, *and everything he owned that was worth taking was packed in the trunk and the backseat. He'd been driving through very heavy traffic, and the number of accidents he'd seen was almost beyond counting. He'd thought the latest gasoline shortage might keep some people at home. Well, it hadn't, any more than the pleas from the governor had.*

It was past dawn now. He'd been on the road since midnight, right after his second show at the club, but he hadn't gotten very far out of Syracuse; he hadn't averaged more than five miles an hour all night. He could still see the city in his rearview mirror, and every so often he imagined an unimaginably bright flash replacing it for a split second. Somebody on the radio had said that the car itself might offer some protection from a nearby blast, if you turned the engine off, ducked down in the front seat and held on. He did not want to have to put the idea to the test.

He was passing by yet another smash-up in the two rightmost lanes—five cars, this time. The first one had been rear-ended by the second, and the others had crashed into that one. The cars themselves weren't in very bad shape, but a lot of their windows were either gone or webbed with cracks surrounding small holes where heads had impacted upon safety glass. Usually, he felt little sympathy for people who got hurt in accidents because they refused to wear seat belts, but seat belts had not been designed for the use of eight or ten people stuffed into a compact car.

He saw that state troopers had arrived on the scene. They were talking to the survivors and scribbling down whatever they said in their brown leather notepads. Everyone seemed to be waiting for the ambulances to cut through the traffic somehow. It's going to be a long wait, *he thought.* Even the shoulders are packed.

He saw nine bodies had been dragged onto the grass bordering the shoulder of the road. They were all female; one was young and had been rather pretty. Nothing covered the bodies; he presumed that, with all the accidents, the police had run out of sheets and body bags. The bodies were each dressed in similar dark clothing; he wondered if the women had been nuns.

Then, as he drew closer, he saw the bullet wounds and, with what little shock remained to him, he realized what had happened. It had been a small accident, all right—a rear-ender, perhaps. It was no big deal, except that the driver of one of the cars involved had decided to kill the people he felt were responsible for causing the problem.

He saw a man sitting on the hood of his car and weeping uncontrollably. Another was crouching with his back to traffic; he was shuddering with the force of his vomiting. Everyone else was still sitting inside their cars; he thought that some of them might be dead. A little farther on, he saw a man's body sprawled on the road. The troopers had not yet picked up the assault rifle near the body, nor had they covered the gaping wound in the man's head. There was no knowing if the troopers had killed him, or if he'd done the job himself.

There were pebbly greenish chunks of shattered safety glass all over the road; he heard it crunching under his tires as he passed over it. He hoped none of his tires would blow; he'd already used his spare and hadn't stopped to get the flat fixed. His gas was okay; the tank was half full, and there were two five-gallon cans in the trunk, which was another three-quarters of a tank—and, Christ, he could really use some coffee, but his Thermos was empty and he didn't dare stop for a refill because he was scared to death that he might never get back onto the highway.

He glanced at the dashboard clock. It was just a few seconds shy of seven o'clock. He turned on the AM radio and thumbed the middle button he'd preset back in Albany for the hourly network news. He was still close enough to town that reception wasn't a problem.

The newscast was a little encouraging. Things seemed to be a little better, according to the first story, but it was hard to tell. Every story was based on sources saying and officials opinionating, all anonymously. Ambassadors were meeting, but nothing much had really changed. Troops were still moving toward borders and threats were still being made, but sources on both sides said an accommodation might still be reached. There was talk of a cease-fire.

Most important, though, no one had yet punched the button marked APOCALYPSE. There was no guarantee that they would not do it today or tomorrow or the next day, though, and he thought the woman reading the news sounded a little worried. He didn't blame her much, because all those newscasts came out of New York City. There must be six dozen goddamn warheads aimed at the Empire State Building, *he thought*. Take *that*, King Kong.

He listened to the news and the commercials until the anchorwoman got to the dumb story at the end that was supposed to be funny but usually wasn't, and then he turned the radio off. Traffic was beginning to pick up a bit, and he gave all his attention to the road. He thought that, with a little luck, he just might make the mountains by nightfall. He hoped that would be soon enough.

God, *he thought,* please just let me get there.

Jake had slept like a dead man, but the rest had not been enough; he felt logy and not quite himself. He hoped they'd find a place to stay soon, get something going.

"Mornin'," Prosper said. "Your turn for breakfast, man."

"I remember."

"Berries?"

"Berries."

Prosper grimaced. "Oh, good," he said. "Somethin' different."

A few hours later and a few miles away, over at the school in McAndrew, Priscilla Neary wasn't feeling very well. She'd had some pain overnight, and it had made her just uncomfortable enough to keep her from getting any real rest. Instead of sleeping, Miss Neary had spent most of the night in her father's den, wrapped in his robe and sitting in his chair, reading by dim lamplight for as long as her eyes could stand it. She'd coughed some, too, and she'd even found some spots of blood in her handkerchief after one particularly bad bout. She'd finally turned in around three-thirty by the grandfather clock, with her head full of Ibsen and her insides finally quiet enough for her to drift off into a tense, uncomfortable sleep. She'd almost slept through the ringing of her treasured Baby Ben alarm clock three hours later.

Miss Neary was still hurting, but not nearly as much. She was more tired than anything else—*just plain pooped out*, as she thought of it—and, as a result, her day was proceeding at a slow crawl. The Lord wasn't making it easy for her today, that was for sure.

She glanced again at the Baby Ben, now sitting in front of her on the desk. It was a bit past noon, which meant she was late in dismissing the children for lunch. Well, it couldn't be helped; she had to finish the fourth grade's recitation first.

One of Miss Neary's less endearing traits, as far as her students were concerned, was her habit of assigning poetry to be memorized. Her fourth grade was struggling with Henry van Dyke's "America for Me." Miss Neary thought the piece was jingoistic trash, but it nevertheless had a good rhythm to it, and its utter lack of deep significance had made it so harmless that it had once been part of the standard repertoire of almost every grammar school English class in America. In any case, the poem was in the textbook, and Miss Neary believed in following the textbook.

"Now," Miss Neary began, "can any of you explain what Henry van Dyke was trying to say? Scott, what do you think he was saying?"

"I don't know, ma'am," Scotty Mahler shrugged. "He sounds proud. He sure—"

"Surely."

"—surely likes America, doesn't he?"

"Yes, he does," Miss Neary agreed. "What do you think he likes about America the most? Randy?"

Shit! Randy thought as he got to his feet. "I think he's homesick," he said, after thinking for a second. "He's away somewhere, maybe in Europe, and he's talking about all the nice things he remembers in America. I think he likes being free, too. He says it's blessed that there's room enough here. Was it crowded in America when he wrote that, Miss Neary?''

The teacher shook her head. "No, it wasn't, not very. The poet published that piece thirty years ago or so, when there weren't very many people living in America.''

"You mean like now?'' Randy asked.

"No,'' Miss Neary said, shaking her head. "There were many more people in America then—but it wasn't crowded, not at all.''

"Then I think he means freedom,'' Randy said. "He means that there's room enough to do anything or be anything you want.''

"The land of opportunity,'' Miss Neary said, almost to herself.

Randy looked puzzled. "Excuse me, ma'am?'' he asked.

"Before your time,'' Miss Neary said absently.

It was a nice day, there was good easy-listening music on his little portable radio (tuned to WIRD, the Voice of Lake Placid and one of the few AM signals you could get in the mountains because it was there already), and there was even a little business getting done. He'd already taken in more than ten bucks, most of it from a big family with a taste for fresh cukes. He wished he felt better, but he was so goddamn hung over that it wasn't funny. A drink would fix things up fast, but he'd run out the night before. All he had to drink was the cup of black Maxim he'd just made with his immersion heater. The heater was plugged into thirty-five feet of frayed extension cord that ran from his ruin of a house to the roadside stand. The extension cord supplied power to his little radio as well. He liked the kind of music the station played. There were frequent interruptions for commercials and news, but he would turn down the radio when anything that wasn't music was on.

There was a liquor store, Casey's, about half a mile up the road toward Lake Placid. Just as he decided to abandon the stand and head up there for a pint of rye, a car headed toward Keene pulled up, and two boys and three girls piled out. "Hi, Pop," the driver called. He was young, blond and looked athletic. "How far to the Northway?"

"Not far," he replied, clearing his throat. With a shaking hand, he pointed down the road in the direction they'd been going. "Go Keeneward on 73 until you hit 9N, then head for Elizabethtown and go on through. By then you should be seeing signs for the Northway. Just stay on 9N. Where you kids from?"

"Syracuse," one of the boys said.

"The school?" he asked. "That's a good school."

"Nah. Just Syracuse. Hey, whatcha sellin' here?"

"Cukes, apples and nuts. The price is right, and everything's fresh. Want something?" He wiped his dry lips with his fingers. Having a few more bucks in his pocket wouldn't hurt when he was in Casey's.

"Nah, don't want any of that shit." The boy looked up and down the road; there was some traffic, but not much. "Just your money oughta do it."

"My what?" he said dully, not getting it. He wished again for a drink. He always wished for a drink.

"C'mon!" The kid pulled a knife and flipped it open.

Now his rheumy eyes widened with sudden under-standing and fear. The kid's entourage stood around the two of them closely so as to block any view from the road. "Gimme the fucking money, you old faggot! Now!" The youth knocked the little radio off the coun-tertop and stamped on it, shattering its brittle plastic case. Its stubborn electronics played on tinnily until the kid crushed the speaker with his heel.

He could not move, much as he wanted to. The knife came closer, and he whimpered.

Mercifully, the rest of it was a blank, but when the deputies finally arrived, he was dimly aware that his money was all gone, his stand was smashed and his stock ruined, and that he'd nearly bled to death in the bargain.

Eisenhower was barking his head off again. It was just past noon, and Jess was in his chair on the porch, trying to catch a few winks. He hadn't slept well the night before, and his nap just now had done him no better.

Jess had been pretty tired after his exertions with Betsy. Last night's run had produced product with a thicker than normal scum floating on top of it. Usually, running a load through again took care of the problem, but Jess had had to run this load twice more before the product was clear and clean enough to suit him, and he had not finished until very late. Then he'd had the oddest damn dream about something or other, and it had prevented him from getting any real rest. On top of it all, Digger Digby had come by early that morning to pick up his share of the deer; Jess had roused himself for that, too, just to make sure everybody was happy with the division.

Now his nap was ruined, too . . . but he came awake realizing that Ike's barking had rescued him from a nightmare. He thought it was odd that he couldn't remember any of the details—well, there was one. There'd been a knife in it, right at the end. Ugh.

"Jess?" Sammie called from inside the house. "What is it?"

"Ike's at it again," Jess said, rubbing his eyes. "He's smelling something from the west. Yellow alert, hon."

"Right," Sammie said.

Jess raised his voice so it could be heard from inside the barn. "Boys?" he called. "Yellow alert. Someone's coming in from Lake Placid way."

"Yes, Mr. Harper," chorused the Simpsons. He heard their shovels and rakes clatter to the boards of the barn floor as they hurried to get the rifles.

Jess stood, hitched up his overalls and waddled inside the house. He felt a little strange—almost scared, but it had nothing to do with whatever it was Ike was so excited about. Jess had been through yellow alerts often enough before. The fear was—he didn't know. Whatever it was from, whatever had created it, it was fading fast from his mind.

Sammie was in the kitchen preparing lunch. "Welcome back to the world, m'dear," he said.

"See anybody yet," she asked, pecking him on the cheek.

"Nope."

"Get any sleep?"

"Just a little." He yawned. "Then Ike started in. Wish I had a cup of coffee."

His wife pointed to a big jar on the counter. "There's some right there," she said. "Go ahead and make some."

"No, I mean real coffee, not acorn coffee. You know, I mean the good-to-the-last-drop kind. I swore I could smell some just before I woke up."

"*Coffee* coffee?" Sammie said. "You *must* have been dreaming."

"I suppose I was."

Sammie frowned. "I wish you were sleeping better, honey," she said. "You were pretty restless last night, tossing and turning. And I heard you moan just now, just before you woke up from your nap. Are you hurting anywhere?"

"I moaned?" he said, surprised. "I feel all right, hon. I'm just a tad tired, is all. Bad dream, too, but that's all."

"Really?"

"Really," he said positively. "Daymares can be the worst kind."

"Well, if you say so," Sammie said.

"Don't worry," Jess said, turning to look out the window. "Got your gun?" he added casually. "I see a couple of people comin' up the road."

"Right here," she answered, patting her apron pocket. "Yours is still in the drawer."

Jess walked over to the dining table and opened the hidden drawer where folks were supposed to keep their silverware. He retrieved the household's other .45 automatic, checked the clip and worked the action. "Okay," he said, satisfied. "I'm going back outside."

"You be careful, now."

"Of course. Hell, honey, it's probably just Digger coming back for something. Maybe he and Annie decided it'd be okay for them to come by on Saturday after all."

"Maybe so," she said, "but if it's Digger, he's coming from the wrong direction and he's brought a friend nobody knows about."

Jess shrugged. "Then it's somebody else."

"I hope it's not John Meyers again."

"We'll see," Jess said. He walked out onto the porch and looked up the road. There were two people, all right; they were coming at walking speed and were still quite a ways off. That gave Jess plenty of time to check the barn. He walked over to it as quickly as he could manage and entered its dimness. His eyes adjusted quickly and he saw the boys hunkered down behind a pile of hay, rifles at the ready. They were near the barn door and had a perfect view of the road in both directions.

"We're ready, Mr. Harper," Ralph and Greg called in unison.

"Fine, boys," Jess returned. "This kind of thing keeps up, we won't ever get anything done around here. Speaking of which, you get that paddock cleaned out yet, Greg?"

"Yes, Mr. Harper. We're just about finished the barn, too."

"That's right, Mr. Harper," Ralph chimed in.

"So you are," Jess said approvingly, looking around. "Well, then, let's see who we've got coming." Jess seated himself in his rocker and waited. The distant figures grew closer, and the Simpsons tracked them carefully with their rifles.

"I can see them clear now, Mr. Harper," Ralph called after a moment. "They're strangers, all right."

"Don't know 'em at all, Mr. Harper," Greg confirmed. "Hey, one of 'em looks pretty strange, even for a stranger. He's dark, like."

Jess had to trust the Simpsons' eyesight; his own distance vision had gone with his hair. "Does either of them look like Big John Meyers?"

"No, sir, Mr. Harper," Greg said, "neither of them sure does. They're both too small." Ralph grunted his agreement.

Well, that was a relief. "Okay, then," Jess said crisply. "They're strangers. Red alert. Boys, if I get attacked or give you the signal, you let them both have it."

"Yes, sir, Mr. Harper," the Simpsons said together.

"Keep me covered," Jess said as he walked out of the barn and up to his front gate.

All the while, the figures drew nearer. Jess waited.

The first important thing Jake noticed was that Jess Harper, who was indeed still alive and in fine shape to boot, had a handgun leveled at his belly and a big, black dog standing guard by his side. The dog was growling softly. Jake also saw a barn door gaping open, and he could only guess at who and how many might be in there, pointing other weapons at them from the darkness.

"We'll be okay," Jake told Prosper.

"You sure?" Prosper replied nervously. "Looks bad."

"It's all right. I knew that man."

"Right there will be fine," Jess called when the two buskers came to within twenty feet of the gate. "Hands up, please."

They stopped and raised their hands. "Hello, Mr. Harper," Jake said. He smiled.

"Do I know you?" Jess said, a little surprised.

"I'm Jake Garfield. I was last through—"

"—fifteen years ago," Jess finished for him. "I remember you. Hello, Jake. It's been a long time. Who's your friend there?"

"My partner, Prosper Cross. He's new to these parts."

Jess nodded a greeting. "Hello, Prosper. Good to meet you."

"Uh, likewise, sir."

"Jake, as I recall, you came through here last with your dad."

"He's passed on since."

"Sorry to hear it. Now, you two planning on coming into town, son?"

"Yes, sir," Jake said.

"Okay, then," Jess said, nodding. "Here's how it works. Move slow, now. Drop those packs and then step away from them at least five good-sized paces. Then I want you both to sit right down on the road while we wait for the doctor. Don't do anything else— not *anything*, unless I tell you. Got all that?"

They both nodded. Jake unslung his guitar and placed it gently on the dusty road surface; his knapsack followed, and Prosper placed his own things next to it. They then moved away and sat down, keeping their hands visible at all times. It was not the first time they'd been through this kind of routine.

"Good enough," Jess said. He did not relax. "Ralph!" he called over his shoulder.

"Yes, Mr. Harper?" came Ralph's voice from the barn.

"You get Tony and go fetch Doc, fast as you can. Tell him we're at red alert, but there's been no trouble and no one's hurt. Party of two arriving."

"Right away, Mr. Harper." Just a minute or two later, Ralph and Tony, Jess's own horse, were heading down McAndrew Road toward town at the horse's best speed.

"He shouldn't be too long," Jess said. "Doc Hock lives right in town."

"Fine, sir," Jake said. "Say, I see Betsy over there is in fine shape."

"Why, thanks," Jess replied. "I try to keep her stuck together." Jess looked at the two men carefully. "As I recall, Jake, you're a recovered."

"That's right, I am," Jake replied, nodding. "I caught Fidel's flu when I was a boy."

"Your mother died from it, is that right?"

"Yes, sir."

"I remember," Jess said. "You and your dad came through not long after that. Prosper, how about you? Ever had the flu?"

"No, sir, I haven't."

Jess frowned. "Oh."

"He's clear, Mr. Harper," Jake said quickly.

Jess shrugged. "We'll see what the doctor says." Then he smiled and added, "Well, you two might as well catch me up on your news while we're waiting—and do me a favor, please."

"What's that, sir?" Prosper asked.

"Call me Jess. Now, Jake, how about you start things off by telling me where you got those fine-looking boots of yours?"

The twenty-three pupils of McAndrew School were in the schoolyard, killing their lunch hour until Miss Neary declared a merciful end to it. Running and ball-playing weren't allowed, so it was usually a pretty dull hour during which the boys did little but talk and watch the girls skip rope.

It would be different today.

"Hey, *look*!" Scotty Mahler said, pointing toward Main Street. "Somebody riding a horse!" Even some of the high school kids were standing and looking.

"It's Ralph Simpson and Tony," Mickey Tree said, peering; he had the best distance vision of anyone there. "Must be a red alert."

"Yeah, that's right," one of the other kids agreed. "Someone's come by, and they're getting Doc."

As Ralph galloped by the schoolyard, Johnny Palmer shouted, "Hey, Simpson! What's the hurry?"

"Buskers!" Ralph yelled back as he sped by. "Two of 'em!"

"Did he say 'busker'?" someone asked.

"No, he said 'buskers,' " Randy pointed out. "Two buskers, he said."

"You mean those guys who sing and dance and all that crap?"

"Yeah," another fourth grader said. "Gee, we haven't had a real busker here since I was a kid!"

"Wow!" someone else shouted. "Let's go see!"

"Miss Neary'll hide us if we do," Mickey Tree cautioned.

"Nah! She wouldn't!"

"Yes, she would," came a voice from behind them. They all turned, slowly. Miss Neary was standing there, holding her brass school bell.

"Uh, hello, Miss Neary," said Scotty Mahler. "Uh, there's buskers, ma'am. Two of 'em. Just arrived."

"So I gather; I heard Ralph shout the news as he passed by. We'll find out all about the buskers later. Don't worry."

"Can we go run up and see, Miss Neary?" Johnny Palmer asked. "Please?"

"Young man, you're all in my charge, and I am not walking three miles up that road to meet people who are going to come trotting down that very same road at their leisure, happy as cats in a cask of cream. We'll wait for them to come to us—assuming Doctor Hochman allows them through, of course."

"Doc *couldn't* turn 'em away!" Randy LeClerc said, horrified.

"Yes, he could, as he has before," Miss Neary answered. "Always better to be safe than sorry. Time for class now; let's go inside."

Ed Pearson's place was within earshot of the school, and on his days off he always knew when it was time for his lunch because he could hear the children begin to raise hell down by the schoolyard.

He was finishing a skimpy meal of acorn bread and goat cheese when he heard hoofbeats coming toward his house. He hurried to the front window and saw Ralph Simpson aboard Tony. Ed had shouted the obvious question, and Ralph had shouted back the surprising answer. Then they were gone, heading toward Doc's place farther along Elm Street.

Ed scratched his ribs and thought for a moment. He then went to the shelving above the desk in his living room, where he kept the town's archives. The archives were a set of binders, nearly three dozen of them, that contained a usually meticulous, almost daily record of what had happened in McAndrew since Kingdom Come. Maintaining the archives was the last visible sign of Ed's late career as a newspaperman—in fact, he saw his career as unbroken because of it—and while he still used his old office typewriter to write the dailies, the ribbon situation, as he called it, was becoming impossible. The damn thing was gray-dry and worn through in too many places. Ed received little compensation for being the town archivist but, in the old phrase, he wasn't doing it for the money; his record keeping scratched an ancient and ever present itch, and he was happy to do it. Having to backspace and retype every other letter because the key had hit another hole in the ribbon was a pain in the ass, though, and it had been going on for much too long.

Ed took down the binder for three years before and opened it at about the halfway point. He began going through his collection of daily reports, one day per page, and quickly found the one he was looking for. The last busker had indeed come through during the summer of that year, just as Ed remembered; it had been a long time since they'd had visitors.

Once buskers, preachers, traders and even settlers had visited McAndrew and other central Adirondack towns on a regular and frequent basis. Sometimes McAndrew would see a fresh face as often as once per month, even as out of the way as the town was, but that was true no longer. The arrival of a stranger was always an important occasion.

Ed felt the old newsman's juices beginning to flow, and he suddenly decided to climb aboard his bicycle and get himself up the road to Jess's place. After all, the arrival of buskers was something pretty special, even if Doc didn't pass them on through.

Ed kept his bike in his living room behind his couch, so as to keep it out of the weather. Jesus, he wasn't looking forward to having his ass beaten up again by that worn-out bicycle seat. The condition of McAndrew Road, which had never been too good to begin with even in the old days, got worse every year despite the efforts of the Road Committee to keep it clear and patched. Ed reflected that the same could be said about his rear end: Every year, despite his best efforts, it got worse.

He wheeled the bike outside the house and across the street, and opened the kickstand with his right foot. Settling the bike so it would stand, he cupped his hands around his mouth and hollered. "Yo, Ben!

Connie!'' he shouted toward the house just across from his on Elm Street.

A bald head stuck itself through the curtains of the living room window. ''Hi, Ed,'' Mayor Benjamin Gordon called back. ''We heard the Simpson boy riding by. I *did* hear him say the word 'buskers,' didn't I?''

''Sure did.''

''I take it you're heading up there now?''

''Sure am.''

''Wait a moment,'' Ben said. ''We'll be right out.'' The mayor's head disappeared from the window, and the front door of the house opened not more than thirty seconds later. Ben and his daughter Constance Matthews hurried out, Connie securing the door behind them. Ben had obviously been napping; his face was still a bit swollen from sleep as he walked over to greet Ed.

''Well, this is sure turning out to be an exciting day,'' Ben said.

''It's unusual enough already, that's for sure,'' Ed replied. ''Hi, Connie.''

''Hello, Ed,'' Connie smiled. ''You men have fun, now.''

''You're not coming along?'' Ed asked, a little surprised.

''No,'' Connie said. ''I've got some things to do in Neary Square. I'll catch up to the buskers when they come into town. If they do.''

''Besides,'' Ben said, ''she's not real good on a bike.''

''Thanks for pointing that out, Daddy.''

''No problem, honey,'' Ben said. ''See you later.''

''Right.'' She kissed her father on the cheek, smiled at Ed again, and walked quickly down Elm Street toward the center of town.

''Let's get going,'' Ben said.

The two men walked around the front of the Gordon

house to the small attached garage. Ben stooped to work the latch on the door; it yielded easily and rolled up into its housing with a familiar and annoying clatter. Ben stepped inside, took his bicycle, and walked it over to where Ed's bike was parked.

"The mayor should rate a horse," Ben insisted.

"If you say so, Mr. Mayor. Pass a goddamn law."

"The town archivist should rate a horse, too."

"Oh. Running for re-election, are we?"

"Hell, Ed, I'm a Democrat," Ben grinned. "Horses for everybody!"

"Anybody tell the stallions about this? They ought to enjoy it."

"Typically ineffective Republican comeback," Ben sneered. Then, laughing, the two old friends mounted their bicycles and set off.

Ralph and Doc caught up to and passed Ben and Ed while they were still about ten minutes from the farm. Unlike the mayor or the archivist, the doctor was deemed important enough for the town to support a horse for him, particularly as the doctor had a bad leg. Doc's horse was named Ambulance—an even-tempered old fellow whom everyone in the area, especially the kids, loved. Ambulance's slow-going style suited Doc, who was never in a rush to get anywhere unless someone had severed an artery or was about to unload a baby. Ralph had relayed the word that there was no reason to rush, so Doc had taken his time. He would not risk Ambulance's aged bones on that miserable road for anything less than a real emergency.

Doc dismounted, petted and talked to Ambulance briefly, and retrieved his small medical bag from where he'd lashed it, right behind the cantle of his saddle. Doc then handed the reins to Ralph, who led Ambulance and Tony to the barn.

Ed got off his bicycle, parked it near where Doc was standing and, grimacing, put a hand to the small of his back. Doc grinned, and Ed mouthed a rude phrase at him. Ben parked his bike next to Ed's. The three men walked toward the place where Jess was sitting.

"My God, Ben," Ed said. "One of them's a Negro."

"So he is. Been a long time since we've seen one of those."

While they were still at some distance, Doc hooked a thumb at the strangers, who were still sitting patiently in the dust of the road. "The white one looks vaguely familiar, even from here," Doc told them. "Can't quite place him, though."

"I don't recognize him," Ed said. "His beard's kind of wild, like the one Gabby Hayes had. Gets in the way of his face. The Negro's beard is better."

"I can't make them out at all," Ben said. "They're too far away for seeing, even if I squint. They look okay, Doc?"

Doc shrugged. "Hard to tell from here. They look like they wash often enough, though. That's always a good sign."

"Well, be careful," Ben said. "We've seen some mean ones in our time, clean or dirty."

"Right." Doc walked on ahead, favoring his leg, and stopped next to Jess. "Hello, Jess," he said. "How's those sugar beets coming?"

"H'lo, Doc," the farmer said. "They're fine. Thanks for asking."

"Good to hear, good to hear."

Jess gestured toward the white stranger with his free hand. "This here is Wanderin' Jake Garfield," he said.

"Oh-ho," Ed said as Ben frowned.

"He came through here with his late dad, many years ago," Jess continued. "The other fellow is Jake's friend and partner, Prosper Cross. Jake, Prosper, this is our town doctor, Doc Hock. The other two gentlemen over there are our mayor, Benjamin Gordon, and Ed Pearson. Ed's our historian, more or less.''

"Usually less," said Ed. "Hello, Prosper. Jake, welcome back. How've you been?''

"Fine, thanks," said Jake. "Good to see you again, Mr. Pearson, Mr. Gordon.''

"Same," Ben said. "Prosper, welcome to our town—or the town limits, anyway.''

"Thank you," said Prosper.

"You're Doctor Hochman, aren't you?" Jake asked. "From over in Bloomingdale? The veterinarian?''

"Now *that's* a word I haven't heard in quite a while," Doc said, grinning. "Well, now I'm a doctor to everybody around here, four legs or two. There isn't a lot of difference, when you get right down to it.''

"I imagine old Doctor Gene is gone by now," Jake said.

"Yes, he is," Doc replied. "Um, we'll catch up later, Jake. Right now, I've got to examine you two.''

"I've had the flu," said Jake.

"There's other things to look for," Doc said. "We'll start with you, though. Stand up and take off everything above your waist, please.''

"Uh, wait a second," Jess interrupted. "Prosper, please scoot over a bit there, enough away from Jake so Doc—that's good. Thank you. Go ahead, Doc.''

Doc began looking Jake over from a distance. "Man, you're a little banged up, aren't you?" he said. "Whip marks, fresh bruises, some cuts. What happened?''

"He ran into John Meyers yesterday," Jess said, interrupting. "We talked some about it.''

"Oh, Christ," Doc said. "What happened to Big John, Jake?''

"He's dead," Jake said simply. "I had to kill him.''

"Jesus," said Doc, and Ben sighed. "Where did it happen?" Ed asked.

Jake saw the pain in all their eyes. "Over in Lake Placid," he said. "He jumped me, tried to do worse. I offered him every chance to leave me alone—"

Doc nodded sadly. "I know. Hold your arms out to your sides. Okay, turn. Slowly, now—good. Now drop your dungarees, please—oops, sorry."

"I haven't been able to find any shorts lately, Doc."

"Well, this'll only take a minute. Turn around again, please. Okay. So far, so good. You don't look too bad, considering. Do you hurt anywhere?"

"Not any more than I'd expect the morning after a good fight."

"Okay, then." Doc walked over to Jake as Jess kept Prosper covered. "Now we'll do the stuff you do close-up," Doc said. "Cough, please. Fine. Again. Okay, you can hitch up your pants." Doc took a pine stick from his pocket. "Let's see your teeth and gums."

As Doc looked in Jake's mouth, he began talking. "John Meyers was a good man," he said. "Had a wife and two kids, lived 'way back in the woods, came into town once in a while. Friendly guy. Made shoes and boots for us. Then one day, about a month ago, one of his kids went foraging and brought in some yams."

"Sweet potatoes?" Jake asked.

"No, yams; they're bigger. Keep your mouth open, please. Anyway, the yams looked fine—I saw a couple of 'em myself—but John's family died overnight. Judging from the way the bodies looked, they didn't go easy. The yams didn't kill John, but they got to him. He went crazy—or maybe he didn't eat any god-damn yams at all, and it was watching his wife and kids die that way that did it. Maybe it was a little of both. There's no way of knowing, because he was in no shape to say. Okay, you can close your mouth now."

Jake licked his lips to rid them of the piney taste of the stick. "What happened then?" he asked.

Doc took Jake's chin in his right hand and turned his head to one side and then the other so he could look inside Jake's ears. "He charged into town and we had to lasso him," Doc said. "Even at that, he beat up five men really bad. Sweet Jesus, I thought he'd gotten rabies, but it was only the yams. We put yams on the forbidden list after that because there was no way in hell to tell the bad from the good. I mean, who expected bad yams? Yams used to be dependable. Hell, we survived on yams." Doc palpated Jake's neck briefly.

"What happened to John after you caught him, Doc?" Jake asked.

"We exiled him as a danger to the community."

"That means we threw him the hell out of town," Ed said.

Doc stooped to get the stethoscope from his medical bag. "Breathe deeply," he ordered. Jake flinched a little as Doc placed the instrument's cold pickup here and there on his chest and ribs. After a bit, Doc motioned Jake to turn around so he could listen to his lungs from the back.

"He came back, so we had to beat him up and send him away again," Jess said.

"Should have hanged him," said Doc. "It would have been kinder. Cough, please. Again. That's fine."

"Maybe so," Ben said, "but I never want to see another hanging in this town, I swear to God."

"Unless we really *have* to hang somebody," Ed said.

"Amen," added Doc. "Jake, where'd you get these whip marks?"

"Down in Rensselaer. We were held prisoner for a few days."

"Oh?" Ben said.

Jess held up his free hand. "We talked a little about that, too, Ben. Hear them out first."

"Never any harm in taking a listen," Ben said agreeably.

Doc finished with the stethoscope and put it back into his bag. "Jake," he said, "you check out fine. No sign of flu, no bloodpox, no sign of infection, no nothing. Those whip marks of yours are almost healed, and the fresh wounds from yesterday are slight. You should eat more, but that's about it."

"It's hard for me to gain weight, Doc."

"Try," said Doc. "All right, Jake, please sit down over there somewhere. Your turn now, Prosper. Take your jacket and shirt off, please."

"They whipped you, too," Doc said after a bit.

"Started with me," Prosper said quietly. "Jake got whupped when he tried to stop 'em."

"Them?" Ben asked. "Who, for heaven's sake?"

"Governor's men," replied Prosper. "Briscom's guards, I mean." His expression turned ugly. "I guess you could say we was rude to the governor."

"We refused the governor's invitation to the execution of one of his wives for treason," Jake said.

"Christ," Ed said. "Things *can* get worse."

"There any proof of all this?" Ben asked.

"Can it wait until I finish with this man here, for heaven's sake?" Doc asked.

"Certainly," Ben said.

"I have a flyer over there in my knapsack," Jake said. "It announces the execution—come one, come all. That's about the best I can do."

Suddenly Doc finished and said, "Thank you, Prosper. Gentlemen, I'm happy to say that you both pass. Mr. Mayor?"

Ben Gordon stepped forward, and Jake rose. "Anybody following you two?" asked Ben.

"No, sir," Jake said. "It's been weeks. We've seen

no sign of anyone, and we took care to cover our tracks.''

"Well, then," Ben said, "that'll do for now." He extended his hand. "Welcome to McAndrew."

"Glad to be here, Mr. Gordon," Jake replied. They all shook hands.

Jess holstered his gun as he, Ben and Ed walked over to offer their own welcome. "Ike!" Jess called. "Friends here, boy! Say hello."

The dog trotted over to Jake, sniffed his clothing, and then ran a wet tongue over the back of his hand. Jake got down on one knee and got well acquainted with Eisenhower, rubbing his flanks and letting Ike wash his face. "Hello, Ike," Jake said softly, over and over again. "Hello, boy. *Good* dog, *good* Ike." The dog made happy doggy sounds deep in his throat.

"He likes you," Jess said unnecessarily.

"I like him," Jake said. "I haven't seen a dog in a good long time." After another moment Jake rose, and Ike went to inspect Prosper.

Jess smiled. "I found Ike six years ago, when he was just a pup. His mama—wild, I guess—wasn't anywhere around and never showed up again; I expect something got her while she was hunting. Anyway, there were three puppies, all sick to death. My wife and I took 'em in, and we pulled this one through." Jess bent to rub Ike's head; the dog responded with a wide open canine grin.

"You're a lucky man to have a dog," Jake said.

"I am that," Jess said.

"Are you thinking of staying for any length of time?" Ben asked.

"We'd like to, Mr. Mayor," Jake said.

"Call me Ben. Do you two do anything besides sing and dance? Manual labor, for instance? Jake, I seem to recall that you did some carpentry as a sideline when you came through last."

"That's right," Jake said. "I also do white-smithing. Prosper helps."

"Really?" Doc asked. "Shoot, I've got some real work you two could do right now. The last person we had around here who had any real knack for such work died seven—no, eight—years ago."

"Ready and willing," Jake said, and Prosper nodded.

"You two ought to make out fine around here," Ed said. "Good luck to you both."

Jess turned and started heading back to the house. "Come on inside, everybody," he called over his shoulder. "I believe this happy occasion calls for a small taste of the product—oh, wait a second."

The farmer stopped and turned toward the barn. *"Get back to work!"* he shouted.

"Yes, Mr. Harper," came two distant voices.

CHAPTER 7

JESS RAISED HIS GLASS. "TO YOUR HEALTH," HE said, and all the men sitting around the kitchen table saluted their host with their glasses. Sammie, who never drank, was standing at the kitchen counter, throwing together a big bowl of salad.

Jake took a sip of his drink. "My God, that's good," he said, a note of surprise in his voice. He felt the warmth of the product travel down his gullet and into his belly, numbing as it went. He held his glass up to the sunlight coming in from the window; the product looked clear and clean as water. "Smoothest moon I've ever had," he said.

"You got that right," Prosper agreed.

"I let it mellow for three full weeks," Jess said. "I never heard of anyone else who bothered to let product hang around longer than overnight. Drinking product right out of the still is stupid."

"Up to your usual standards, sir," Ed said, saluting

him with his glass. "Maybe even a touch better than that."

"Prosper, you and Jake could cut yours with some apple cider if you like," said Sammie, still busy with the salad. "We've got a jug or two of it in here." She tapped the door of the cupboard under the sink with her foot as her hands tore greens and stirred spices.

"Thanks anyway, Mrs. Harper," Prosper replied, "but I'll pass. This, uh, product's just fine plain. Best I've ever had."

Jess saluted Prosper with his glass and drained it of the little that was left in it. "I could go another," he said. "Anyone want theirs freshened?"

Jake held out his glass and Jess poured another inch of product into it. "Say, Jess?" Jake asked. "These glasses are pretty tough, aren't they? I mean, they've lasted. Hardly a chip."

"Jelly jars, son," Jess replied. "People always used them for drinking glasses because they came free and lasted forever. Hell, we had quite a few stashed away—"

"More than three dozen," Sammie said. "Welch's were best. I was always a packrat, Jake."

"—and we've still got more'n twenty-five of them, even after all this time. Tough sons of guns. Anybody else want a refill?" It turned out that all the rest of them did.

"So, Wanderin' Jake Garfield," Ed said at last, "why don't you and your friend there tell us a little bit about what you've learned in all your wanderin'?"

Jake grinned. "Sure. Want to hear about Briscom first?"

"You read my mind." Ed took a piece of paper and a stub of pencil from his shirt pocket. "I'll be taking some notes," he said briefly. "It's an old habit."

"You, too?" Jake's knapsack was at his feet; he bent to retrieve several scraps of paper and a hunk of cardboard from a pocket on its side. Ed could see that each piece was covered on both sides with closely-set writing in pencil.

"Now there's a man after my own heart," Ed said. "A compulsive note-taker." He wrote *9/18, lunchtime. Jess's place. Busker (JG) likes to take notes. Other one (PC), the strong, silent type. Negro.*

"I'll tell you what I know in as close to chronological order as I can," Jake said. "I've already mentioned some of this stuff to Jess while we were waiting for Doc to show up."

"They've been all over the place, Ed," said Jess. "All over this part of the country."

"Really?" Ben asked. "There's a lot I'd like to know."

"We'll get to it," Ed said. "First order of business, though, is Brother Jimmy Briscom. What's his story?"

"It's hard to say," Jake said. "You know his background?"

"Some," Ed replied. "He's a preacher who claims to have been the state's assistant secretary of commerce when the war broke out."

"That's right," said Jake. "Briscom says he's the logical successor to, uh, what's his name, I wrote it down here somewhere, wait a minute—"

"Nelson Rockefeller," Ed supplied.

"That's the guy," Jake said. "Rockefeller was governor when the war happened, although no one knows exactly where he was when the bombs started to go off. Anyway, no one's ever seen him since."

Ed nodded. "Rocky was always either in New York City or Albany," he said. "Either way, you can write him off. We'd have heard from him long before this, if he was around to be heard from. In any case, he'd be ninety or so by now, unless he got his ass shot off by a jealous husband first—pardon me, Sammie."

"Hmph," Ben said. "At least he wasn't a member of *my* party, him carrying on with that divorcée and all."

"Right, Ben," Ed shot back, "and *your* party's man down there in Mount Weather is a real saint, isn't he?"

Jess held up a hand. "Come on, fellas," he said tiredly. "We've heard all this about a jillion times. Can we get on with the news?"

"Well, hell, sure," Ben groused as Ed smirked. "Give the old fart the last word, go right on ahead."

"Actually, we've met him," Prosper said.

"Hmmm?" Ed said. "You've met whom?"

"The President. We've met him. He wasn't so bad as you say."

There was a stunned silence, and then the questions flew fast and furiously until Jake held up a hand. "I gather you'd like us to start by telling you about our visit to Mount Weather and not what happened to us in Rensselaer?"

Ben grinned. "I'd say that was a fair statement, son."

"Jesus, you actually *met* the son of a bitch?" Ed asked. "When, for heaven's sake?"

"Now, Ed," Ben said patiently. "I swear, it's like throwing bloody meat to a lion."

"We met him two years ago last July," Jake said. "We were inside the mountain for a few days."

"What's it like in there?" asked Ben. "I heard it was just like the old days inside."

"I guess it is," said Jake. "It's a little underground city with streets and some stores and other things. They even have restaurants. There were street lights, too. The mountain has its own electric power, all anybody could want. We weren't told, but I think there must have been an atomic reactor somewhere around."

"Street lights," Ben said. "I remember."

"There was even a lake," Prosper said. "You couldn't swim in it, though. I guess they didn't want for it to get dirty."

"There were a few electric cars and trucks going here and there," Jake said, "and there were people on the streets—not a lot of people, but some. All the important buildings were made of reinforced concrete and stood on springs as tall as I was, so they could wobble back and forth if a bomb was dropped up above."

"Sounds crazy," Ed said.

Jake smiled wryly. "Seemed that way to me, too. Anyway, after we got there, we were taken to see the President in the Oval Office, which was in one of the central buildings. He wanted to meet us right away. His whole Cabinet was there with him, too."

"The Oval Office?" Doc asked. "That was in the White House, wasn't it?"

"They told us it was a scaled-down duplicate," Jake said. "It was pretty fancy for all that, though—paintings on the walls and everything. There was even a stuffed eagle on a bookshelf. They had lights banked around the outsides of the windows so that, when the curtains were drawn, you couldn't even tell you were underground."

"There was air-conditioning, too," Prosper added. "Man, I've never been anywhere else like that, before or since."

"Tell me about the President," asked Ben. "How did he look? Was he well?"

"The President seemed okay to me, I guess," Jake said. "He was gracious, made us feel welcome. He looked pretty old, though—not like the pictures I've seen."

"Oh, I don't know," Ed said mildly. "I expect he had a right to look a little bit old, having killed the country and all."

"Now, Ed," said Ben.

"Let's not start, now," Sammie warned. "I run a peaceful kitchen."

"Okay," Ed said agreeably. "Say, Jake, just how many mistresses *does* the old bastard have down there in that mountain of his, anyway?"

"Ed!" Ben cried, as Sammie began laughing. "That's positively indecent!"

"You'll have to forgive our mayor," Ed told Jake. "Ben met the President once, back when he bothered to run for office, and he's never gotten over it."

Ben Gordon winced. "I don't have to be a supporter of the President to be able to recognize a malicious and unpatriotic attack on him when I hear one—"

"Don't you go doubting *my* patriotism, sir!" Ed shot back.

"All *I* doubt, sir, is your common sense!"

"You guys are friends?" Prosper wondered, his eyes wide.

Ed turned toward him. "Never doubt it." He looked at Jake. "Tell me exactly what happened in the Oval Office. What was it like in there?"

"It was more than a little pitiful," the busker replied. "The President kept rocking back and forth in his special chair, talking about how it wouldn't be much longer now before a new Congress would be elected and brought together to re-ratify the Constitution and like that. He repeated himself a lot. The other people in the office kept nodding and smiling, agreeing with every single thing he said. It was like a revival meeting, only much quieter."

"What about the President's family?"

"His wife and daughter are gone, but he's still got one of his brothers and two sons," said Jake. "There's even a granddaughter."

"Oh? Did you meet Bobby?"

"Yes," Jake said. "He was at that Cabinet meeting, and we saw him around a lot after that." Jake grinned. "Bobby sang with us a couple of times."

"How did you and Prosper happen to come upon Mount Weather, Jake?" Ed asked.

"Pure luck. We had come down into Maryland and were heading south into West Virginia when we started running into people who asked us if we were heading for Mount Weather. So we decided to go there."

"Isn't the location supposed to be a secret?" asked Ed.

"I guess so," Jake replied, shrugging. "Seems, though, that everyone for fifty miles around the mountain knows what it is, where it is and who's inside it, so it can't be much of a secret anymore. I can't say we went out of our way looking for it, but once we knew the mountain was there, we headed straight for it with no trouble."

"I wanted to meet the President," Prosper said. "Always have. My folks, they voted for him. I remember that they used to talk about him all the time. They liked him a lot."

"Anyway," Jake continued, "the mountain is near a little town called Upperville, about sixty miles west of where Washington was. The area's protected by other mountains around there, so it's pretty intact. I guess the Russians couldn't get in close enough to bomb it directly."

"Maybe they didn't even know about it," Ben observed. "I don't remember ever hearing about Mount Weather before the war, and I used to read pretty widely. Do you recall anything about it, Ed?"

"Nope," Ed replied, "and I wouldn't have believed it if I had."

"There was a secret mountain for the military people, too," Jake said. "It was north of Washington. That mountain was closed down long ago, though, along with a few other—what did they call them, Prosper? I keep forgetting."

"Relocation centers."

"—relocation centers, right, and everything was consolidated at Mount Weather. I got the impression it was tough enough for them to keep the operation at Mount Weather going.''

''I didn't know about the other facilities at all,'' Ben said, surprised. ''You ever hear of that military mountain before, Ed?''

The archivist shrugged. ''Nope. Everyone knew about the underground SAC command center in Omaha, though. I don't remember if the Cheyenne Mountain underground base for NORAD was operational at the time of the war, but I'd heard about that one, too,''

''So there's no United States military command?'' Ben asked.

Jake shook his head. ''Mr. Gordon, there's a few of what they're still calling U.S. Army troops to guard the mountain, and there's also a small civilian police force in Upperville. That's all there is. I expect that, sometime sooner rather than later, somebody or other is going to walk inside that mountain and take over, and that'll be the end of it forever.''

''Really?'' Ben asked.

''I think so,'' Jake said. ''Fact is, it hasn't happened yet only because there's nothing down there that's really worth taking.''

Ben Gordon looked sad. ''I suspected that the federal government was in trouble,'' he mused, ''but I never knew it was this bad.''

''It sounds like it's made up of a bunch of guys from thirty-five years ago who still haven't learned when to give up,'' said Ed. ''I'm not a whole lot surprised, either. We've never heard directly from the feds, not since the war. It's all been bits of news and rumor from buskers and travelers—mostly unfounded, I see now.''

''Looks that way,'' Ben agreed. ''Damn, the idea takes a little getting used to.''

''So all the stories we've heard about reconstruction

and reconstitution are bunk, right?'' Sammie asked, turning to Jake. ''There's really nothing going on in that direction? You haven't seen anything for yourselves?''

''That's right,'' Jake said. ''There's no sign that the federal government is doing anything at all. Mount Weather issues proclamations and announces emergency regulations, and no one more than five miles from the mountain pays attention to any of it.''

''And that's all there is?'' Ben asked almost desperately.

''That's all,'' Jake said. ''One of the Cabinet people told me on the sly that the United States was now pretty much the size of Manhattan Island, because that's all the area the federal government could control—and most of that is unpopulated farmland devoted to feeding the people inside the mountain and the troops stationed around it.''

''Amazing,'' Jess said. ''I really thought things were going to get put back together one day. Time we woke up, I suppose.''

''The President gave us both souvenirs before we left,'' Prosper said. ''Jake swapped his for supplies once we got out of the area, but I kept mine for luck. It'll go when it has to, though.'' He stood up from the table, reached into the pocket of his jeans, and quickly found and withdrew what he was looking for. He showed it to them all, cupped in the palm of his hand. It was a small thing that glittered gold.

''It's a tie clip,'' Ed said, shaking his head. ''Jesus, I can't imagine anything more useless. The man must be crazy.''

''There's a little boat on it,'' Sammie said.

''It's not just a boat,'' Ben said, pointing out a detail. ''Look closer. See? It's PT-109.''

''Nobody really knows if Brother Jimmy Briscom really had a state job or not before Kingdom Come,''

Jake explained later, "or even if that means he had a right to be governor, but nobody's questioning it. Any criticism of Briscom is considered treason in time of war, and you can get yourself hanged for that."

"I see," Ed said. "Yeah, that fits. It's good to know all this, Jake. You have to realize we're really out of the way here—three miles off the only highway in the area and surrounded by woods. We're not even marked on most of the old gas-station maps. Shoot, that's probably why we've lasted so long. Hardly anybody ever noticed us, even in the old days."

"I don't doubt it," Jake said. "We saw enough empty towns on our way here to last us a lifetime—"

"Empty towns?" Ben asked. "Which ones, exactly?"

"Can we get to that later?" Ed interrupted. "I'd like to get some sense of Briscom. Does he have an army or a police force that might be interested in us?"

"Briscom's got police," Jake said. "They're local. There's something he calls a National Guard, too, that patrols the general area."

"The National Guard?" Jess asked. "Is it still around?"

"Those guys'd be pretty old by now," Ben said. "Hell, *I* was in the National Guard."

"Guess it's not much of a threat, then," Ed said.

"Very funny."

"What are all these police and troops doing besides living off the sweat of the taxpayers?" Doc asked. "I'm morbidly curious."

Jake shrugged. "They keep people in line," he said. "That's about all they have to do to earn their keep. Briscom will stay in power just as long as the thugs who work for him keep making a profit. Now, want some more news?"

"Lay it on us," Ed said. "Can't imagine what comes next, after all this."

"I expect you'll love this, Ed," Jake told him. "Governor Briscom wants to send a state delegation to Mount Weather next May to attend what's being called the American Jubilee."

"Huh? What's that?"

"It's a big bash to honor the President on the occasion of his next birthday," said Jake.

"*Big* bash," Prosper added.

"*What?!*" Ed barked. "Is he kidding? What kind of idiot *is* this Briscom, anyway?"

"Now, Ed," Ben said mildly. "Don't start."

"I wish I still had the goddamn paper just so I could attack the stupid son of a bitch in it," Ed continued. "What a jackass!"

"I think the Jubilee sounds like a fine idea," Ben said calmly. "Although we might not wish to participate in any expedition sponsored by Briscom, we should try to find out more about the celebration itself. Ed, you're going on about it like they're trying to *make* us send someone."

"Just what we need," said Ed. "A pointless pseudo-patriotic pageant. Christ!"

"Nice alliteration," Ben observed.

"A Jubilee for any reason strikes me as a waste of time and effort," Jess said, and Doc nodded agreement.

Ben humphed loudly. "We'll take up the matter at the next monthly town meeting," he said. "It won't be decided here and now, that's for sure."

Ed grinned. "Get ready to lose, Your Honor," he said happily, rubbing his hands together. "I can't imagine the town going for it. Oh, I *am* going to enjoy this one! Anything else, you two? You've made my day."

"Nothing too dramatic," Jake assured him. He looked over his notes. "Where was I? Oh, yeah. This next item's pretty recent. A group of scientists from

Schenectady set out six months or so ago to check on the atomic power plant at Indian Point.''

"Where's that?'' Doc asked.

"Down in Westchester County,'' Jake said. "Indian Point had just begun full operation when the war happened. There was word that the plant was still intact, so a party went to see.''

"Schenectady?'' Ben wondered. "Why from Schenectady? Why not one of the so-called state capitals?''

"GE was in Schenectady, I think,'' Jess said. "I don't really remember, but that seems right. That doesn't mean GE has anything to do with it, though. Jake, do you know anything more about it?''

"Afraid not,'' the busker said. "Just the basics, that's all.'' He took another swallow from his glass. "The party was supposed to see if the plant could be made useful again, maybe supply the state's entire power needs—what's left of the state, anyway.''

"Good luck,'' Ed said, frowning. "I doubt there's an intact power line left between here and there.''

"Doesn't matter much,'' Jake shrugged. "The expedition hasn't been heard from since a month after it left Schenectady. Suspicion is that some Hudson Valley bandits got 'em for their camping equipment— mostly pre-war and very, very nice stuff, thank you. There's also cannibals in the Valley these days, or so I hear.''

"Oh,'' said Ed.

"There was a flood in Glens Falls just last month,'' Jake continued. "Eleven dead. The town was trying to make a comeback, but that finished it.''

"That's terrible,'' Sammie said, not looking up from her salad making. Jake saw that she was energetically tossing the salad with two big wooden forks.

"Really too bad,'' Ben added. "I remember Glens Falls from the old days. Nice town, good people.''

"Tell us about the empty towns now,'' said Ben.

"Okay," Jake replied. "I came here from Canandaigua—"

"Where's that?" Ed asked.

"It's the town at the northernmost point of the westernmost Finger Lake. I always thought that was kind of poetic."

"Oh, right," Sammie said, suddenly remembering. "Canandaigua. Were you born there, Jake?"

"No," said Jake. "I was born just outside Albany, right before the war started."

Jake Garfield was a second-generation busker. His parents, Dan and Rosalyn, had turned to busking sometime shortly after Kingdom Come. Dan had been an advertising salesman and Rosalyn a housewife before the war. When magazines suddenly disappeared, busking seemed a natural vocation for a salesman and his pretty young wife to turn to.

Jake, their only surviving child, had turned out to be a natural at busking. He joined his parents' act, known then simply as The Garfields, as a babe in arms. He became his father's full partner at the age of nine, after his mother died in a little town called Beerston. Jake didn't remember where Beerston was. All he remembered about it was that a nice old lady there had sat him in her kitchen and fed him milk and fresh biscuits while his father went down the road a piece to dig the grave.

The new act, Garfield & Son, ran for the next eighteen years on a circuit that ran through the Adirondacks, down through New York State and Pennsylvania, and well into the safe parts of central Ohio. The act closed when his father suddenly dropped dead at the end of a long day on the road. That had happened just outside the Finger Lakes town of Canandaigua. Jake buried him there and stayed on with a nice old farm couple, the Franklins. Winter was coming, so Jake had needed a place to stay, and the Franklins had needed a handyman. They had quickly come to be a family. He called them Ma and Pa; it came naturally, and it had felt pretty good. He wound up staying for more than three years.

The Franklins died within a week of each other during a particularly harsh winter. The town ignored the will the Franklins had written leaving the farm to Jake and seized it under an emergency provision enacted just that week for that very purpose. The farm was good land, and the town council owed some favors around.

Jake hit the road again. He hated the town for reminding him that he was an outsider, to be cheated and swindled with impunity, and he knew he could no longer stay there. Jake had spent most of his life singing for his supper. He knew he could do it again.

Jake had also developed sidelines. He preached the Gospel when it suited him, not because he was a religious man, but because he was good at preaching and people generally thought better of him for doing it. Sometimes he taught school, too—Sunday and otherwise—if there was a need . . . but there weren't many children around these days and, even in the best of circumstances, most towns found it uneconomical to maintain a school.

Jake was also good with tools. He was not a jack-of-all-trades, but whatever he fixed stayed fixed, and that was good enough to keep him housed and fed when the initial welcome won by his busking began to wear a bit thin.

Good as the road had been to him, things got better after he met Prosper Cross.

Prosper was born near Detroit, the only son of Elwood and Janine Cross. He was orphaned at five and was thereupon drafted onto a government farm elsewhere in Michigan, back when there still were such things as government farms and enforceable emergency regulations that allowed *de facto* slavery. The boy spent three years on the farm before managing to escape.

Prosper walked the roads and did odd jobs. He found he had some skill in singing and dancing, and he had a winning personality. He also found, quite unexpectedly, that his black skin made him an object of intense interest to white folks who hadn't seen a Negro in years. It was certainly true that, while there were few enough white people around, he hardly ever met someone of his own race on the road.

Prosper had met Jake in an Appalachian town eight years before, when they each arrived within a day of each other to work the place. Instead of hissing and spitting to defend their territory, the two men took to each other instantly and formed an act on the spur of the moment. Prosper was a better singer and dancer, but Jake could juggle, do magic and play the guitar. Their combined act was greater than the sum of its parts, and they did well. From the outset, their split was fifty-fifty.

Prosper had developed a few sidelines of his own, although his main strength lay in assisting Jake in whatever it was that Jake happened to be doing. Prosper was strong and willing to work hard at whatever came his way, unless it had something to do with farming. Prosper was good at farming, and he was particularly good at handling farm animals, but he avoided all such work if he possibly could. The boy inside him remembered.

"You'll stay with us tonight, of course," Ben said. "Visitors always lodge with the mayor on their first night. It's our custom."

"It also lets us pick your brains for longer than if we let you sleep in the woods," Ed grinned. "Besides, I don't think you'd mind trading a night on the ground for one in a couple of soft beds, with a hot meal in the morning thrown in."

"You've got *that* right," Jake said, and Prosper nodded, grinning.

"The salad's ready," Sammie called, "and the drink of choice is well water. I won't have the taste of my special salad dressing blunted." She put a huge bowl of tossed greens on the table. "Jess, you'll find plates and silverware in the usual places."

"The boss speaks," Jess said in mock resignation as he rose. He went to the cupboard and began gathering dishes, taking his time. He was careful not to chip any; the dishes barely clinked together as he stacked them. "After lunch," he said over his shoulder, "you two might like to come into town with me. I've got to pay a call on Dick LeClerc."

"LeClerc?" Jake asked. "That's the storekeeper, right?"

"I think you knew his father Hiram better; Hiram was the owner when you were through last. He's passed on since, and his son Dick's got the business. Dick sells his own stock and keeps account of all the supplies we hold in common."

"We'll be glad to come along," Jake said. "I remember Dick, all right. Matter of fact, he might be interested in some of what we've got with us."

Jess turned, half a dozen dishes in his hands. "Depends on what it is," he said casually.

"Oh, just some stuff," Jake said. "Want to see?"

"Sure," Jess said, and the rest of them echoed it. Jess put the dishes on the table, and Ed began passing them around.

"Just make sure you eat all your salad, everyone." Sammie called. "Food's not to waste."

"Yes, dear," Jess said, sitting down. "Jake," he went on, "I see some clear space right next to you on that tabletop."

"Well, then," the busker replied, "I guess I'll use it for display purposes." Jake bent to open his knapsack and rummaged around for a minute while Sammie, sitting next to him, put some salad on his plate. Jake soon reappeared with a few items of Indian handiwork in hand; he placed them on the table. There were several beaded purses, a brilliantly executed and beautifully tooled leather knife scabbard, and a rolled-up bath towel marked HOLIDAY INN.

"What's that?" Doc asked wryly around a mouthful of salad. "Someone making hotel towels again?"

"It's what's inside that counts," Jake said. He unrolled the towel carefully to reveal a doll.

"Indian handicraft," Ben sighed, looking at it. "God, it's gorgeous work. You know, I miss those people."

"They're gone from the mountains?" Jake asked.

"There weren't very many here to begin with," Ben said. "We haven't seen an Indian since forever, it seems like. May I?" he added, pointing at the doll.

"Sure," Jake said. The mayor wiped his hands on his shirt and picked up the figure, treating it gently. The doll seemed to fit his fingers perfectly. The entire body of the figure was carved from wood and dressed in the fashion of an unmarried girl of the Mohawks. The doll's features were beautifully wrought and highlighted by the barest touch of stain. There was some ornamentation on the dress, but not very much; the dress derived its beauty not from glitter but from the perfection of its cut and the closeness of its stitching. The dress looked like buckskin, but it could have been any hide patiently scraped and worked and stained to look like it.

"This is one hell of a piece of work," Ben said, admiration clear in his voice. "I haven't seen anything nearly this fine in quite a while."

"Can I take a look at it next?" Sammie asked Jake. He nodded, and Ben carefully handed the doll to her. She smiled the same sort of smile she used to give to her Raggedy Ann doll, some sixty years before.

"There are quite a few Indians settled around the

Finger Lakes,'' Jake said. ''Whites and Indians are trading again. Basically, we get along now. The Indians have a long memory, though, and trust comes hard for them.''

''Can't blame 'em much,'' Ed said.

''This thing is art,'' Sammie said positively, still smiling. ''This is no souvenir. This here doll was made with skill and love. I think it was made by a real artist for his little daughter.''

''Could have been,'' Jake said, ''but the truth is that the artist was making dolls for trade. I chopped wood for it in Blue Mountain Lake, on the way here.''

''Oh,'' Sammie said. With a hint of reluctance, she handed Jake the doll. He rewrapped it in the Holiday Inn towel and put it back in his knapsack.

Jake then produced a sealed box, opened it and poured out some bits of hardware, including the few pieces he'd found in the Lake Placid Rexall. Several dozen nails, screws and bolts rang and rattled on the tabletop. There were two brass hinges and a sixteenth-inch drill bit with a quarter-inch shank. Jake set down the box, reached into his knapsack, and produced a pair of needle-nosed pliers with blue rubber handles.

''Jake?'' Jess asked. ''Have you two been in the cities? That's pretty good hardware for country folks.''

''We haven't gone anywhere near a city,'' Jake replied. ''Nobody with any brains does. There's a couple of items here—like the doll—that we traded for, but we scavenged all the rest of it from empty towns.''

''Jesus,'' Doc said. ''You're the next best thing to being rich.''

Jake smiled, went back into his knapsack, and produced a small hammer.

''Very nice,'' Doc said.

Jake held up a finger. He then twisted the head of the hammer, which came away to reveal the shaft of a flathead screwdriver attached to what had been the handle of the hammer.

"Wow!" Ed said, impressed. "Got any more, Jake?"

In answer, Jake set the hammer down and twisted the etched knob set into the end of the screwdriver handle. It came off and out dropped another, smaller screwdriver. There were three additional screwdrivers hidden away in the tool, each one hidden within the next larger screwdriver. The smallest of the screwdrivers was about an inch and a half long from end to end. Ed picked it up between thumb and forefinger and examined it closely to see if there might be yet another screwdriver in there somewhere.

"I think I remember these hammer sets," Ed said, still peering at the tiniest screwdriver, "but I didn't think I'd ever see one again. Jake, there are people here who'd trade big for a good set of screwdrivers, and never mind the hammer." Ed handed the screwdriver back to Jake, who quickly reassembled the tool.

"We plan to rent them out," Jake said. "The pliers, too."

"That's right," Jess said, nodding. "Never sell outright what you can rent to people. Renting is cheaper than buying for your customers, you'll make more money in the end, and your inventory won't be going to waste inside someone's drawer, so you'll be doing more good with it than otherwise. You guys are doing okay, Jake."

"Do you have anything else, Jake?" Ben asked.

"Just one more thing," the busker replied. He ducked down, quickly reappeared with the six-pack of Coca-Cola, and set it on the table next to the big bowl of salad.

There was a stunned silence. Everyone stopped eating. Ben dropped his fork.

"Oh, my," Ed said after a moment. The rest remained speechless.

"I gather you folks don't see Coca-Cola very often," Jake said.

"I haven't seen a Coke since just after Kingdom Come," Ben said, shaking his head. "Jesus God, I used to drink a gallon of it every day, seems like. I still miss it."

"I don't believe this," Jess said, shaking his head. "Incredible."

"Coca-Cola hits the spot, twelve full ounces, that's a lot," Doc sang softly. "Damn."

"I think that was something else," Ed said absently. "Jake, where did you get this?"

"Found it in a store in Lake Placid."

"That close to home?" Ed said, surprised. "I wonder how we managed to miss it?"

"Takes real talent to skip over something like that," Ben said. "Must have been your search team, Ed."

"Operating under your instructions, Mr. Mayor."

Jess looked at Jake closely. "Son, do you have any idea what you have here?"

"Yes, I do," Jake said. "I know you older folks put a lot of stock into things like Coca-Cola. I mean, Doc even remembers a song about it, even after all this time, so I figure it's got some value."

Jess shrugged. "It does and it doesn't, Jake."

"Eh?"

"It's worth *too* much," Jess said flatly. "What you have there is quite probably the last Coke in the world. It's easily worth half my farm, including Betsy out there, and I can't afford to indulge myself like that."

"*I* would, if I had the goods," Ben said. "I loved that stuff."

"But you don't have the goods," Jess said, "and I doubt you'd be saying something like that if you did. Jake, if I bought that Coke from you with an eye toward making a profit on it—what I'd call speculation— who would I trade it to? Ed over there? Ben? Doc? Some trader like yourself? What would they do with it, except drink it or trade it? And who would they trade it back to—*me*? No, I'm afraid those Cokes aren't trade goods; they're just too rare. There isn't enough of value around here to cover their worth. Better you hide them somewhere and wait for circumstances to change.''

"We're all mighty impressed that you found them, though,'' Ben said. "It's nice to see that kind of thing again.''

"That's for sure,'' Ed said. "Keep 'em safe, Jake. Hide 'em somewhere. Despite what Jess says, you never know when you might run into a sucker with half a farm to trade. Hell, maybe you can charge Ben over there to sneak a peek at 'em once every week.'' Everyone but Ben laughed.

"No doubt you'll eventually find a sucker,'' Jess said. "There's one born every minute, according to old P.T., and I think he underestimated the frequency of the event.''

Jake looked disappointed. "I really thought we had something here,'' he said. Prosper looked sad.

"You do, son,'' Jess said kindly. "Indeed you do, and no mistake. But you could have come in here with a big fat diamond, and I'd have had to tell you the same thing. Tell you what—why don't you show that six-pack to Dick LeClerc this afternoon, and see what *he* says about it? At minimum, you'll make his eyes pop out, and a man owes it to himself to get as much fun out of life as he can for free.''

"Okay, Jess,'' said Jake.

"You can see Dick right after I show him my deer,'' Jess said, with perfect timing.

"Deer?'' everyone asked, and Jess grinned the same, slow way he grinned whenever he showed a winning hand at poker.

CHAPTER 8

MISS NEARY DECIDED TO GIVE UP TRYING TO TEACH that day. Her pupils clearly had their minds on things like buskers and not on their English or mathematics. She bore no grudge against her students for this; it was true enough that today was a special day, and Lord knew that special days were rare enough in McAndrew. The afternoon had been a long one, too, and her chest had been bothering her more and more as the day had worn on. It was nearly three o'clock, according to her Baby Ben, so she decided to dismiss the class after she finished passing back the math homework she'd corrected during lunch.

Miss Neary rose from her seat and handed the pile of homework papers to Susanna White, the girl who sat in the front row of the fourth grade, directly in front of her desk. The White girl was forever trying to curry favor with her.

"Start passing these back, please," the teacher said. "All grades." Susanna smiled what she thought was a winning smile as Miss Neary returned to her chair. *Horrible child*, Miss Neary thought. *Just like her mother. At least she's good at passing out papers.*

The homework papers rustled as they went from hand to hand. She heard a little *tsk* from the fourth-grade seats; Randy LeClerc was scratching his head and looking disappointed. Miss Neary smiled inside, where no one could see. *He's so used to getting all his math homework right,* she thought. *It's rare for him to get a problem wrong, that's for sure.*

"All right, everyone," Miss Neary said as the last of the papers was distributed. "I'm quite aware that we have a couple of visitors to our town today—"

There was a buzzing from the students; Miss Neary raised a hand, and they fell silent.

"—and that means your minds probably aren't on your schoolwork."

There was a bit of muttering at that, and a stifled giggle or two. She ignored the hubbub because, if she didn't, she'd have to keep the children after school for raising a ruckus, and she was becoming desperate to send them home. She badly needed to rest. *Just a short nap,* she thought. *Please.*

Miss Neary went on. "I expect that, by now, it's been decided whether the buskers will be staying with us or not and, if they are, I'd further expect that they'll be arriving in town soon." She put on her sternest, don't-fool-with-me look. "If any of you expect to be heading up McAndrew Road after school today to see the buskers, well, forget it. You'll wait for them to come here, assuming they do."

There was a collective groan of disappointment from all corners of the classroom. Miss Neary held up a hand, and the sound ceased. "There'll be plenty of chances to see the buskers, assuming Doctor Hochman passes them through," she said. "That will have to do. I won't have anyone getting hurt on that road because he or she couldn't show a little patience." She looked around the room. "All right?" she asked.

"Yes, Miss Neary," the students chorused.

"Very good," she said. She knew that, despite all she said, most of the children would head up the road anyway, but she'd done her best. She knew that her only alternative was to keep them after three o'clock, or have them all thrown into the lone jail cell over in Town Hall.

"Just one other thing," Miss Neary said. "Does anyone need more blank homework paper?"

Two of the high schoolers raised their hands. "Very well," Miss Neary said. "Come by my desk on your way out, and I'll give you each a clean sheet—but I don't want you coming back to me for more until the end of next week, hear? Make it last. Write smaller."

"Yes'm," the two students said.

"All right, then," she said. "All of you get home safely." The students rose and filed out quietly, according to her standing instructions.

Alone now, Miss Neary winced as another painful twinge blipped through her chest. It surprised another cough out of her, and she fought to keep it from going out of control. If the buskers were allowed to come into town, there would almost certainly be a gathering in the square tonight, even if it wasn't Saturday. She would want to be there for it, but there'd be no way she could make it without a nap and a couple of long swallows from one of Jess Harper's jars. She was beginning to hurt just a little too much.

She gathered her things quickly and left the classroom for home.

Almost all of Miss Neary's pupils—all of them except for the two or three like Susanna White who always did *everything* the teacher said, and who would be sure to inform on the others the next morning—

wasted no time in sprinting up McAndrew Road to see what might have happened about the buskers. The fastest of them, the older boys, met Jake, Prosper, Ed, Ben, Jess and one of the Simpsons about a mile from town, coming the other way. Ed and Ben were walking their bicycles. Jess was in the back of the group supervising Ralph Simpson as he carried the Harper portion of Digger's deer in a wheelbarrow; the butchered carcass was covered with a tarpaulin in order to protect it against flies.

The boys stared without apology at the strangers. Theirs were the first new faces they'd seen in three years, and already Jake and Prosper were making a difference. Most McAndrew men shaved as cleanly as they could at least once a week with honed hunting knives, while the rest kept their growth trimmed; Jake and Prosper sported full, untrimmed beards. One of the older high school boys thoughtfully scratched the stubble on his chin.

"Ah," Ed said, "I see the high school contingent has arrived."

"Hello, everybody," Jake said, smiling broadly. "I'm Jake Garfield. This is my partner, Prosper Cross. We're very glad to meet you."

"Glad to meet you, too, Mr. Garfield, Mr. Cross," one of the boys called.

"Oh, call us Jake and Prosper. Mr. Garfield was my father." That brought a quick laugh.

"Anyone want to help us with these bikes?" Ben asked. "We've been pushing 'em for more than two miles now, and I don't mind telling you I'm a little sick of it."

"I'll take yours, Mr. Gordon," said Reggie Bowman.

"Thanks, son," Ben said. "I owe you one."

One of the other boys, Albert Walls, took Ed's bicycle from him without saying anything. "Thank you,

Albert,'' Ed said, and the boy nodded. ''You can ride it on in, if you like.'' Albert shook his head.

Reggie spoke up. ''If it's all the same to you, Mr. Pearson, we'd rather walk along with all of you.'' Albert nodded his head energetically at that.

''We appreciate your company,'' Jake said. ''Thank you.''

''Where you from, Jake?'' one of the boys asked.

''I was born down in Albany, but I've also lived near a town on one of the Finger Lakes. Know where they are?''

''Sure,'' all the boys said.

''Are you from America, Prosper?'' asked one of the younger boys.

''Yes, I am,'' he replied. ''I was born right near the city of Detroit. Know where that is?''

''Sure, but I thought maybe you were from Africa or somewhere like that.''

''No, but my ancestors were taken from there hundreds of years ago. You might have read about that in school.''

''What's it like in all the different places you been?'' inquired another.

''Different,'' Prosper said, drawing a laugh. They were all still staring at him, but he was a little more comfortable with that now. The crowd was clearly friendly and no worse than curious.

''Can you juggle?'' someone asked.

''Sure,'' Jake said. ''Anybody got an apple?'' The group produced three among them; all were left over from their lunches. Jake cast the apples into a simple fountain. He kept on walking as he juggled.

''Jeez,'' the same boy said, ''I wish I could do that. Can you teach me, maybe?''

Jake smiled. ''Maybe,'' he said, still juggling. ''We'll see.''

''Thanks! That'd be great!''

"What do you hear about the Russians?" another boy asked.

"I haven't heard a thing about the Russians," Jake said. "I haven't even heard a good rumor about them in years. Haven't met anyone else who has, either."

"Know any magic tricks?"

In answer, Jake caused one and then another apple to disappear. Grinning, he threw the remaining apple up and down a few times all by itself. The boys watched in fascination as the missing apples suddenly reappeared and the fountain formed again.

The boys were open-mouthed. One put his foot in a pothole and stumbled, nearly twisting his ankle.

"Doesn't anybody want to know about this here deer I've got?" Jess called out, pointing at the wheel-barrow.

"Deer?"

"Who's got a deer?"

"You mean that thing in the 'barrow? All I see is a tarp. Hey, Ralphie, what you got in there?"

"Deer."

"Somebody's got a deer?"

"Jake and Prosper brought in a *deer*? Wow! Whatta couple of guys!"

Jess gave up.

The questions for Jake and Prosper kept coming, and the buskers did their best to answer them all. They were still doing so when the group met the main body of Miss Neary's students about half a mile from town. The schoolkids were accompanied by some of McAndrew's adults. Jake smiled broadly when he saw several young mothers with babes in arms or toddlers waltzing behind them, their chubby little arms instinctively extended for best balance. There were not many children, but there were more than a few. It comforted him.

It wasn't until the arrival of these latecomers that

Jake and Prosper got *really* busy. They talked and sang and greeted and recited and whistled and juggled and magicked and joked and grinned, grinned, grinned the rest of the way down the worn blacktop of Mc-Andrew Road with half a hundred people in tow and more coming to meet them every minute.

McAndrew Road ended abruptly at the foot of Main Street, where the thick growth of trees ahead suddenly thinned to nothing and revealed the town. All the people, more than a hundred by now, were singing a marching song Jake had learned as a boy. He'd heard it once, long ago, from another busker the Garfields had met on the road and traveled with for a week or so. It was a simple song—and simple-minded, too. It could be memorized by just about anyone after no more than one hearing, and it was unforgettable forever afterward.

> *Around the corner*
> *And under a tree*
> (tramp, tramp)
> *The sergeant-major*
> *Said to me,*
> *Now who the heck would want to marry you?*
> *For I should like to know.*
> *Every time I look at your face*
> *You make me want to go*
> *Around the corner*
> *And under a tree . . .*

The happy group had endured forty-seven repetitions of it so far, by Jake's count, and no one showed any sign of tiring of it. *Wait until I introduce them to ''A Hundred Bottles of Beer,''* Jake thought.

The group continued down Main Street, still whooping and hollering. People came out of their homes to stand on the sidewalks and marvel at the strangers who'd suddenly arrived in their midst. Jake and Prosper called out greetings to everyone, and they all responded in the same way. Most of the people they passed joined the parade.

Jake saw that many of the homes they passed were intact and inhabited, and all of those had been kept clean and in good repair by their people. However, no one maintained a lawn; all the front yards of the homes on Main Street were planted in garden crops. Even abandoned houses had gardens in their yards, and Jake suspected that the people living nearest to those houses were tending those plots as well as their own, because that was what people did in other places.

Jake sidled over to Prosper. "Looks good," he muttered. "Looks real good."

"It does," Prosper replied. He was smiling. "Damn, it feels fine to see some people again."

"You said it."

Mayor Gordon led Jake and Prosper to the town square that opened up off Main Street. Neary Square was McAndrew's business district. Most of the stores had been boarded up since after Kingdom Come, but some—mostly on the southern and western sides of the square—were still open and doing business. Jake looked across at the north side of the square and saw that the large Protestant church he remembered from his last trip through was still standing and in good repair.

Main Street ran along the square's south side, and Jake and the gathering crowd passed by the open repair bay of a service station. A sign reading BLACKSMITH hung right under the winged horse of the station's old corporate logo, but the smithy seemed abandoned. Jake also passed by a store with a big, peeling MILK sign above the door, but it was closed and padlocked. The store seemed to be nothing but a warehouse for milk bottles.

As he walked on, Jake saw a number of other storefronts that seemed to be used only for warehousing or not at all. He noted a shop with a CARPENTRY sign, but that one, too, was closed and empty.

There was a small bandstand in excellent repair in the center of Neary Square, right where any self-respecting bandstand belonged. A small cannon and a pyramid of cannonballs sat in the northeast corner of the square; a bronze plaque dated 1901 proclaimed that the cannon was a memorial to McAndrew's honored dead in the Spanish-American War, and it gave the names of a corporal and two privates. Park benches in good repair were set here and there along the paths in the square's grounds, which were devoted entirely to grass and flowers; the grass was trimmed and the flower beds weeded. Jake saw no foodstuffs growing in the square; the place had been kept as a garden for the eye.

A patched but clean fifty-star American flag flew from a tall staff set atop what Jake knew to be McAndrew's town hall. The flag was the old three-color one, not the altered flag that had found favor with many people since Kingdom Come. That one, the war flag, substituted dead black for the red and blue.

Neary Square was beautiful, and the maintenance of its beauty required no little effort. Jake remembered that the square was indeed a special and highly prized place in McAndrew. He looked for and spotted the painstakingly carved wooden marker set in a grassy area next to the bandstand, well out of the way of foot traffic.

BARTON MITCHELL **NEARY** 1891–1968	**ANNETTE GIBSON** **NEARY** 1904–1968

It had been a long time, and the mounds had weathered to nothing. Jake knew from his previous trips that

Judge Neary, with the absolutely necessary assistance of his wife, had been leader of the community from the time of the war until his death nearly six years later, and was credited by those who remembered him as the man most responsible for bringing the town through the many crises caused by the war. The Nearys' only daughter still taught school here, according to what the kids had told him on the way into town.

"Show time," Prosper said quietly, bringing Jake out of his reverie.

"Right," said Jake. "Let's knock 'em dead."

The buskers jumped nimbly onto the bandstand, swinging themselves up and over the railing. Jake held up his hands to quiet the cheering crowd. It had become quite a sizable one. About three-quarters of McAndrew's population of four hundred people had turned out to greet the buskers. Try as he might, Jake could not quiet them; they had been too long without someone such as him and Prosper. For once, Jake felt *welcome*, and that was something he'd not felt since he'd met the Franklins. He found that he'd missed it terribly.

The cheering and applause died away of its own accord after a moment or two.

"Friends," Jake said, "for those of you we haven't met yet, my name is Wanderin' Jake Garfield, and I'm an Albany boy—"

"You're welcome here anyway!" someone called, and there was a general laugh.

"—thank you, sir, and I busk for a living, such as it is. Let me introduce my friend and partner here— Prosper Cross. Prosper?"

There were more cheers, and Prosper waved and grinned.

"As some of you know, I've been here before," Jake continued. "I'm happy to be back; it's been a long time. You folks are even more friendly than I remembered.''

"You shouldn't have left the last time, cutie!'' a woman called, and the crowd laughed.

"Then I wouldn't be having such a happy home-coming this time, now, would I?'' Jake unslung his guitar and picked at it a little, coming up with something brief but twangingly hillbillyish. The crowd applauded wildly as he played.

"Any requests?'' Jake asked.

Ben Gordon spoke up. "Uh, Jake, we usually begin town gatherings by singing the Banner.''

"Oh, of course,'' Jake said. "It'd be a privilege.'' He took off his hat and set it on the railing in front of him. The crowd fell silent. Jake played a few soft introductory chords for the song he and they probably knew the best of all. Jake launched into the national anthem by himself, but Prosper soon joined him in harmony, and the crowd did not leave them out there alone for long. They all sang it together, and afterward the people cheered. Jake then struck up "There Is a Tavern in the Town,'' and everyone who knew it— which was just about everyone—joined in, Prosper beating time on his bongos.

Jess Harper was standing at the edge of the crowd with Ralph Simpson and the wheelbarrow, looking for someone. "Wait here a minute, Ralph,'' he said suddenly. "I see Dick LeClerc; I'm going to go get him.''

"Yes, sir, Mr. Harper,'' Ralph said. "I'll be right here waiting.''

For all his bulk, Jess eased himself through the crowd and quickly reached the general store owner. Dick was standing there with his wife and two sons, arms around them all and singing along. Jess tapped Dick on the shoulder, and Dick craned his neck to look behind him. "Well, hi, Jess,'' Dick said. "Big day, eh?''

"It sure is," Jess agreed. "Got a minute for a little business?"

"I've always got a minute for that," Dick said. He mumbled something briefly to his wife and sons, and then went back through the crowd, with Jess leading the way. Dick spotted Ralph and the wheelbarrow and grew curious instantly.

"Well," Dick said, "whatever it is, it's big enough."

"Let's go on over to the store, Dick," Jess said.

"Oh-*ho*," Dick said. "That big, eh? Well, sure."

The three of them walked around the edge of the crowd toward Dick's store on the west side of the square. A big white pre-war sign with black lettering said LeCLERC'S with no further description "and no goddamn soda-pop cap on it, either," as Dick's father, Hiram, had often put it. Hiram had been the best and most loyal Republican in McAndrew, and he had wanted to make it perfectly clear to everyone that he himself, and not some goddamn soda-pop company, had paid for the sign over his store.

Puffing, Ralph pulled and bumped and wrestled the wheelbarrow up the flight of wooden stairs at the entrance to the store as Dick opened the padlock on the front door, threw the hasp aside, and opened up for the second time that day.

The store was dim but not dark inside; the store windows, still intact and kept clean, allowed plenty of daylight in. The first impression the place made was of pickles; the sharp and tangy smell of vinegar permeated everything in the store. Cucumbers, peppers, cauliflower, cabbage and onions in transition soaked in the same barrels Dick's grandfather had used for pickling at the turn of the last century. Now, despite all that had happened and everything that had come undone, Dick was using the very same pickle barrels at the turn of the next.

Most of the store shelves, particularly the ones in

the back, were empty; what stock Dick had was kept in the front, where the light was better. There was cloth and preserves, all produced locally. Special items, like old hardware, were kept under the counter.

"Okay, here we are," Dick said, closing the door behind them. He left the CLOSED side of the sign facing out into the street. "What've you got?"

In answer, Jess drew aside the tarp and exposed what was left of Digger's kill—about eighty pounds of meat, which was what was left over after Jess had taken his own share. The hide was gone, too, except for that on the head and neck.

"My God," Dick breathed. "Where the *hell* did you get this boy, Jess?"

"I didn't. Digger Digby got him, and he brought him to me. Now I'm bringing it to you. You get the innards, too, by the way. They're back at my place."

"What's Digger's interest?"

"None; I've already settled with him. Now, do you want this young fella, or do I have to lug him back up the road?"

Dick grinned. "We'll deal," he said. "Don't worry."

Jess grinned back. "Ralph, you can go outside—but stay close enough that you can hear me when I shout."

"Yes, Mr. Harper. Goodbye, Mr. LeClerc."

"Take care, Ralphie," Dick said. As the front door swung closed, Dick bent to inspect the deer. "He's a beauty," he said. "I can tell, even without his suit on. What happened to the hide?"

"Digger took it," Jess said. "No way he wasn't going to. I don't think anyone's lost his taste for venison, though; there's plenty of mileage left in this gent."

"That's for sure," Dick agreed. "Okay, what do you want for him?"

Jess smiled in anticipation. "Now we get down to it, old buddy."

They bargained for more than an hour, mostly to settle on a fair price but also partly for the sheer joy of bargaining. Then, the deal done, they went back outside to enjoy the rest of Jake's performance.

Jake and Prosper sang together and separately for more than two hours. They were still singing even after the sun had set, with Venus already behind the mountains to the west, and Mars just about ready to join her there. Despite the late hour, few if any of the people of McAndrew had left for home. Many had returned home briefly to collect a few items of food from their pantries, and now more than half the town was holding an impromptu picnic on the grounds of Neary Square. Some folks had even brought lamps and torches.

The crowd remained wildly enthusiastic and, with that kind of encouragement, the buskers found it easy to keep on going. Jake's sense of showmanship, however, warned him that two hours was enough, so he finished off with "Be Kind to Your Web-Footed Friends" and answered the disappointment of the crowd with the promise that he and Prosper would be around for some time to come.

Jake noticed one thirtyish woman up in front. He winked at her, and she smiled. He finished the song with a flourish, waved at the applauding and cheering crowd, and jumped down from the bandstand.

He walked over to the woman. "Hi," he said, extending his hand. "I'm Jake Garfield."

"Constance Matthews," she said, shaking it. "Pleased to meet you, Mr. Garfield—or should I just call you Wanderin' for short?"

"The pleasure's mutual, and you can call me anything you want. Uh, we *did* meet the last time I was through, didn't we?"

"We did indeed," she said. "Once or twice in particular."

"I thought so," he said. "You haven't changed much, except you turned from pretty to beautiful. Pretty's easy. Beautiful's harder."

"Why, thank you, sir."

"Your hair's a lot different," he said. "Longer. I think that's what threw me."

"Well?" she teased.

"I like it, I *like* it," he added hastily. "And your dad's the mayor now. Damn, I thought he looked pretty familiar—"

"Yes," Connie said, trying not to laugh and not succeeding very well. "I guess he must have, at that."

"He also seemed a little distant."

"I guess he was," Connie said. "You know fathers."

"Not as well as I ought to." Jake saw no ring on Connie's finger, but that didn't necessarily mean anything in a world where something such as a wedding ring was a precious heirloom item, not to be worn casually.

Connie caught him looking. "My husband died four years ago," she said.

"I'm sorry."

"I'm over it now," she said. "Ken caught himself a bad-kind tumor and went into the woods one day. He never came back."

Jake nodded; it wasn't an unusual story. They both stood there as they were for a moment, quiet but together, as the crowd began to cluster around them to bid Jake welcome.

"I take it you and your partner are staying with us tonight," Connie said. "I guess we should be going; it's getting a little late."

"Suits me," Jake said. "Thanks. Just let me take a minute to introduce myself and Prosper to Mr.

LeClerc over there, all right? I've got something to show him.''

''I'll wait,'' she replied.

After the crowd broke up, Ed Pearson went home, lighted a candle on his desk with a coal from the fireplace and sat down in front of his typewriter. He retrieved the notes he'd taken at Jess Harper's from his shirt pocket and unfolded them, going over them as he did so.

He rolled a sheet of paper into the typewriter, thought for a moment, and then began typing, gathering steam as he went.

JOURNAL ENTRY
September 18

Two buskers named Wanderin' Jake Garfield and Prosper Cross arrived at Jess Harper's today and were cleared by Doc to come into town. Jake's an Albany native who's come to us from the Finger Lakes area and has been through here once before with his father Dan, now deceased. Prosper's new to us.

They brought a lot of news with them, which I'll file on a separate sheet.

Jake and Prosper led a community sing in the square until well after sunset tonight, and we all had a good time. I was there for most of it, breaking away only to post a summary of Jake's news on the Town Hall chalkboard. Some folks turned the sing into a picnic, even though there isn't much on hand yet to picnic with, and there won't be until we get the crops in. That won't happen until maybe late October, and only then if we're lucky and there's been no rain from the south.

Digger Digby shot a deer yesterday and let

Jess Harper handle dealing with Dick LeClerc about it. I haven't seen Digger since then, and neither Jess nor Dick is talking details. I trust Jess got the better of the bargain, whatever it was. I believe we saw our last deer around here in 1973, but I haven't bothered to look it up. I'm not the only one around here hoping that the deer's a good omen.

—E.P.

CHAPTER 9

FOR WHAT IT WAS WORTH, HE HAD HIMSELF A *splendid place from which to watch the death of the city.*

He was in his offices just across Sixth Avenue from Rockefeller Center, twenty-two stories up in the Time-Warner Building. He had spent the night on the couch, tossing and turning fitfully, unable to do more than doze. Now, dressed only in his designer underwear and with his bare feet up on his desk, he leaned back in his expensive, orthopedically correct Swedish chair and watched a thousand tall columns of ugly, black smoke spiraling brokenly skyward into the heavy air from downtown Manhattan and over in Brooklyn. Not long before, he'd seen an NYPD ultralight fly rather close by. It had been heading north, toward Harlem. He couldn't see in that direction, but he knew what it must be like up there this morning. After all, he'd grown up in a place much like it.

The sound of sirens and explosions and, occasion-

ally, screaming had filtered through his double-glassed windows all night long. Now it was finally sunrise. Despite everything, the electricity was still on, and so he had set his air conditioner to sighing chilled and filtered air at a leisurely rate perfectly suited to the beginning of an unseasonably hot and muggy September day. He didn't think it wise to turn on the room lights, though, because they might attract attention. He could see precious few lights on, no matter where he looked. He wished desperately for some coffee, but he had run out of it during the long night, and either the maker wasn't working or he wasn't using it right. His number-three secretary always took care of things like making the coffee.

Suddenly he heard the quick electronic yelping of a police siren, nearby and coming closer. He clambered out of his chair and, standing by the window, looked directly down at Sixth Avenue.

A blue-and-white NYPD car had run up onto the sidewalk in front of the Exxon Building next door. Its front bumper was hard up against the gray stone of the decorative fountain in the plaza, blocking the path of a man carrying a large cardboard box. The fountain was off, but he could see that some of the water had not drained; an appreciable amount of trash was bobbing in it.

The rooflights of the police car spun and flashed a bright chord of red, white and yellow as two cops jumped out of the unit and lowered their Police Specials on the man.

He could see that the box was perhaps large enough to contain a ghetto blaster or a portable television set. He noticed almost without thinking that the cops were white and the man with the box was black. The cops were doing a great deal of shouting; some of it percolated indistinctly through the window. He watched as one of the cops, the one who'd gotten out of the police car on the passenger side, popped the trunk of the vehicle open. The black man walked over to the car, put the box in the trunk, and slammed it shut. The other cop then used his gun to gesture to the man to sit on the rim of the fountain. The man did so, lacing his fingers over his head like a fourth wise monkey, a think-no-evil monkey.

The second cop then quickly stepped in front of the man and fired. The man's head exploded, and his body was flung backward into the stagnant water of the fountain. There was a heavy red stain that spread slowly, like ink.

The first cop said something to the second, who shrugged, holstered his weapon and got back into the car. After a moment, the other cop joined him, and then the car backed off the sidewalk and onto the avenue, and proceeded uptown at a leisurely pace.

He continued watching the floating body until the pigeons and sparrows came, which didn't take very long at all. He imagined that rats would follow soon. He returned to his desk, sat in his chair and closed his eyes.

He'd followed his instincts the day before and closed the office early, sending everyone home and telling them not to come in again until further notice. There hadn't been a hotel room to be had in Manhattan, so he had chosen to stay on his office couch overnight rather than take the chance of going home to Long Island.

He thought that, now, he might like some news, so he tuned his desktop stereo to one of the city's two all-news stations. The radio said that there had been scores, perhaps hundreds, of riot-related deaths in the city since the previous sunset. Mobs had stormed hospitals for drugs, grocery stores for food, electronics shops for gadgets and toys, video stores for pornography, and liquor stores for consolation. Poor and desperate people had swarmed out of their ghettoes, across the social and economic borderlands, and into *the wealthier neighborhoods. There, they had wreaked havoc. The NYPD had quickly given up trying to control the situation and had busied itself guarding city officials and its own precinct houses; apparently, some cops had busied themselves by doing a bit of looting. The state's National Guard was unavailable. It had been federalized the week before and sent to Florida as part of the general mobilization.*

New York City might not be the enemy's number-one target, but it could be no worse than third on the list. However, not everyone who had somewhere to go and could afford to get there had fled the city. Like himself, they had decided to stay on until the bright and bitter end, if it indeed came. Until this morning, he had thought it would not happen, that people weren't crazy. Now he knew better.

The radio announcer was reporting that many of the luxury apartment buildings along Central Park West had been invaded by mobs. One particularly vicious mob had swarmed through the Dakota around midnight. The Dakota was the venerable and celebrity-riddled nineteenth-century apartment building in front of which John Lennon had been murdered nearly twenty years before; now it was famous again. People had forced their way into many of the building's huge apartments, murdering everyone they could find. One very famous actress had been found dead in her fine old Dakota bathroom, her bloodied, naked body hanging from the shower head. She'd been raped and sodomized repeatedly before she'd been hanged with a pair of pantyhose—her own, apparently. The news report noted that her hands had been tied behind her back with a man's belt, size thirty-four; her feet, however, had not been secured in any way, and so they were badly lacerated from her having banged them helplessly against the tub's faucets and spout as she strangled. Her husband had been found in the adjoining bedroom with a cracked skull and a hole hacked into his chest. His heart was missing. So were his genitals.

After an hour or so of wild celebration and at least four unsuccessful attempts to torch the Dakota, the mob had departed. The cops and reporters had not gotten there until an hour or so before dawn. The mayor, safe and secure in his emergency control center, was quoted as deploring the violence and urging people to stay home and remain calm.

The more he listened, the more he worried. His top recording artist and finest friend lived in the Dakota. He had talked to her on the phone just the day before. She'd said that she was going to weather the crisis right there at home, with a remote control in one hand and a Chinese take-out menu in the other, and that she would be just fine and that he should not worry about her. He tried calling her now, but he found that his phone was dead. After a moment, he gently replaced the receiver on its cradle for what he knew was a final time.

She'd long ago given him her first Grammy citation, the one for "All the World for You." That had been their breakthrough single; he'd borrowed heavily to make the video, but it had paid off. He gazed at the citation for a long time, until the glare of the rising sun rose high enough to be reflected by the facing glass in the frame, turning it into a blur of dazzling, molten gold.

He knew he had to leave. He had to go over to the Dakota, if only so he could be sure about what had happened to her. He did not think he would live through the trip, but that was all right. He had to try. He had no one, really, except her.

Prosper stirred as the light of the rising sun struck his closed eyes. He opened them against the growing brightness and, with a pleasant shock, realized that it had all been only a dream, merely the latest in a recent series of nightmares, and that it was over now. He was already forgetting the details.

"C'mon, Jake," he called to the mound of blankets in the other bed. "Time to rise and shine."

A hand appeared and made waving motions at him. "Go 'way," came a mumbled voice.

"C'mon. Greet the new day. I smell breakfast."

There was a pause. "Breakfast?"

"Breakfast. I also smell somethin' that'll do for coffee."

"Coffee?" The lump made some sniffing noises. "Smells like roasted acorns. C'mon, lemme sleep."

"You gotta get up, man," Prosper said. "Sun's been up for ages. Nice day out, but it's gettin' old pretty damn fast."

"Can't be later than seven," the lump said. "G'back t'sleep."

"C'mon, man." Prosper sat up in his bed. He grabbed a pillow and tossed it at the lump; it made a solid *thump*, and the mound began to shift slowly.

"Almost there," Prosper said. "All you gotta do now is sit up."

The mound groaned. "Okay, okay. All right. Just gimme a count."

"One, two, one, two, three *and*—" Prosper said, and Jake pushed the blankets away and sat up, wiping grit from the inside corners of his eyes with thumb and forefinger. "Cripes," he said. "I feel like I've been asleep for a week, but it didn't do any good. Nightmares all night."

"I had me a bad night, too," Prosper said. "They happen, man. It's just your brains workin' things out, that's all."

"Hey, is there an outhouse, or do we have to use the woods?"

"Luxury 'pon luxury," Prosper said, hooking a thumb toward the bedroom door. "Bathroom's in the hallway just outside. Flush bucket's right next to the toilet."

"Jesus," Jake said, yawning. "That's right. Ben showed us. I remember now. An indoor outhouse." He paused. "Think this is a good town?"

"Yeah, I think so," Prosper said. "Feels good."

"Sure does."

"Um," Prosper said. "I guess you've got first crack at the john, because I just can't bring myself to get out of this bed yet. Damn, it feels good."

"Suits me," said Jake. "There's a lady in the house, though. I ought to get dressed first."

"Just don't confuse the sink with the pot," Prosper said. "I'd like for us to be able to stay here a while."

Jake laughed as he climbed out of bed and stood, scratching and stretching. Then he ducked and dragged his knapsack from under the bed. He opened the top flap, pulled out a pair of shorts and a shirt, shoved the pack under the bed again, and put them on quickly. He then retrieved his jeans from the bedside chair he'd tossed them onto the night before, put them on, and cinched the frayed rope he used as a belt around his slim waist.

"Presentable," Jake proclaimed, "but my feet still hurt."

"You gonna use that john *today*, maybe?" Prosper asked. "This bed gets less and less comfortable the more my back teeth start to float."

"Should only be about an hour or so," Jake said as he shut the bedroom door behind him.

"Very goddamn funny," Prosper called after him, and Jake hooted.

Downstairs, Connie had already set four places at the big kitchen table. "Daddy?" she called into the living room. "They're up."

"I hear 'em," Ben said, getting up from the couch. "Quiet, aren't they?"

"I don't mind. It's nice to see a couple of new faces."

"That it is," her father agreed. "Breakfast about ready?"

"Ready. Come and get it anytime."

A big pot of boiled oats with just enough in it for four people sat on the wood-burning stove, and Connie had perked a pot of acorn coffee. She took the steaming coffeepot off the stovetop and set it on the ceramic Je T'aime Montreal stand in the middle of the kitchen table. Connie thought for a moment and opened the breadbox to find two reasonably fresh corn muffins left over from the previous Sunday. There was also a jar that still contained a trace of blueberry preserves, but there wasn't nearly enough for four and, in any case, she didn't want to serve preserves with corn muffins. Connie reached into the cooler that sat on the sill of the kitchen window and, moving aside the tent of wet cheesecloth that covered the cooler, took out a half-empty pint bottle of milk and a quarter-pound chunk of butter. She then replenished the evaporated water in the cooler with a couple of dipperfuls from the covered bucket next to the sink and replaced the cheesecloth, arranging it so that its edges trailed in the water.

Connie carefully poured the contents of the milk bottle into a cup so as to separate the milk from the shot of cream that floated on top of it; she intended the cream to go onto the oats and the milk into the coffee, although her guests would please themselves on that score. Her mother's old china bowl yielded only a small clump of maple sugar, which was all that was left.

"A veritable feast," Ben said as he came in.

"I do my best," Connie replied. She kissed him on the cheek. "Good morning, Daddy."

"G'morning, hon," he said. "How'd you sleep?"

She almost laughed. "Terribly," she said. "How about you?"

"Same," he answered. "It's getting to be a habit, isn't it?"

Connie went to the stove and began stirring the oats. "What happened in your dream last night?" she asked quietly, not looking at him.

"You came over from your apartment in Lake Placid to visit," her father said, pouring himself a cup of acorn coffee. "We were worried about whether the ceasefire was going to hold, and we all wanted to be together if it didn't. The President—some other President, I mean—made a speech on TV and said that if we stayed the course, whatever *that* means, everything was going to be all right. I don't think I believed him."

Connie nodded. "I remember all that," she said. "There were reports of riots in some of the cities, too. I think I just wanted to be home here with you and Mama, whatever came."

"You stayed over, too, and we all got to sleep pretty late," Ben said, sitting down at his place at the table. "We just stayed up talking about your work and the war in Europe and all."

"The school," she said, remembering suddenly. "That's right. I teach second grade over at the school, and I finally went to bed because I knew I was going to have to get up for work. My God, Daddy—there's hundreds and hundreds of kids over there!"

"That there are," Ben agreed. "Quite a few—and of all ages, too, just like there used to be."

"You've told me about that before," Connie said, "but I've always found it hard to believe. It's hard to imagine that many kids being in the world."

"I know," her father said, "but the world was once nothing but kids, or so it seemed."

"The dreams, Daddy," Connie said suddenly. "They *mean* something, don't they? They're not just some fantasy. What's in the dreams is coming clearer, too. I remember and understand more and more about them, each night that goes by.''

Ben nodded. "Same here," he agreed. "Damn it all, I wish Doc would listen to me about this," he said. "This has been going on for weeks. How can a man be so *stubborn*?''

"What's happening to us, Daddy?" Connie asked. "What's going on?"

"I don't know, honey. I really don't." He put an arm around his daughter's waist and squeezed. "But we'll get through it. Lord knows we've been through worse.''

"We sure have," she said. "I just wish we could make it stop." Suddenly she was all business. "Daddy, be a honey and start handing me those bowls on the table, will you?''

"Sure," he said and, as he did so, Connie ladled a helping of oats into each. "Smells good," he said as he placed two of the filled bowls on the table.

"Just so they don't burn," she said. "Burned oats. Ugh.''

Her father suddenly grew thoughtful. "You know what?" he said quietly. "I think the dreams will stop, and very soon now.''

His daughter smiled wanly as she handed him the other two bowls. "Is that a promise?''

"No, just a feeling," he replied as he put down the other two bowls. He heard a footfall at the bottom of the stairs. "Perfect timing." he said.

"Good morning, Mr. Mayor," Jake said to Ben as he walked into the room. He smiled at Connie. "Good morning.''

"Good morning to you, too, Jake.''

"Need any help with breakfast?" asked Jake.

"All done," Connie said. "Just grab yourself a chair. No, Daddy, you sit down; I'll get the oatmeal myself. Hi, there, Prosper.''

"Good day, everyone," Prosper said as he came in. "How is everybody this fine morning?"

"Everybody's just fine, Prosper," Ben said, smiling back despite his worries. Prosper's good humor was catching.

"Mmmm," Prosper said, sniffing. "I *thought* I smelled oats."

"Sit yourself down," Connie said. "Sorry there's not much to dress it up with, but we were caught a little short."

"No problem here," Prosper said. "Just a splash of cream and a little bit of that maple sugar over there, and I'll be just fine, thanks. This is a whole lot more than we're used to."

"I'll take mine straight," Jake said. "Might pass me the milk for the coffee, though."

Connie handed Jake the cup of milk. "Thanks," he said. Jake splashed some into the acorn coffee, stirred it and sipped. He nodded. "Good coffee," he said.

"Your politeness is appreciated," Connie said in a kidding tone. "The only thing good about acorn coffee is that it's hot."

"There's two good things about it," Jake said around a mouthful of oats. "It's hot and it's here. Good enough for me, anyway. Prosper and I have had enough mornings without it, and that's for sure."

"Amen," said Prosper.

"We could dress this up with some blueberries," Connie offered. "There's a couple of bushes out back."

"Uh, no, I'm fine, thanks," Prosper said. "Coffee's all I need."

"Damn, I miss coffee," Ben said, almost absently. "It's getting so that I keep dreaming about it."

Prosper looked at him. "You do? So do I."

"Funny." Ben said. "You don't look old enough to remember coffee."

Prosper shook his head. "Not from before," he

said. "I had some at Mount Weather for the first time when we saw the big man. Never had any since. But, Lord, I miss it right now, like I was used to having it whenever I wanted, and now I can't." He stifled a yawn. "Sorry," he said. "Long day yesterday, and I'm still not over it. Reminds me, though—wasn't coffee supposed to be good for waking you up?"

"That it was," Ben said. "It had caffeine in it. That was a drug, a sort of picker-upper. Coffee was hot, too, if you wanted it that way, and a hot drink will bring up your internal temperature and get you going just about as quickly."

"Another one of Dad's theories," Connie said.

"Fact," retorted Ben.

"It doesn't account for warm milk helping people to go to sleep," his daughter replied. "Now there's a hot drink that doesn't get you going."

"Warm milk never put me to sleep in my life," Ben said positively. "Besides, the milk's warm, not hot. Warm milk's bad enough. Hot milk's worse." He made a face, but then he blinked. "I forgot about cocoa. Cocoa was great."

"Cocoa?" Connie asked.

"You put chocolate in the milk and got cocoa," Ben said, remembering. "You could thin it with water, but you'd be crazy to do it. I'd clean forgotten about cocoa."

Connie shook her head, still smiling. "Chocolate," she said. "Now there's one of those magic words again, like oranges and television, all gone forever and never to be seen again."

"Ever had an orange?" Jake asked.

"No, I haven't," Connie said. "Once, when I was a kid, I ran a bad fever and they gave me two aspirins they said were flavored like oranges. Tasted like sour berries, though. Ugh."

"It was the last aspirin in town," Ben put in, "and it just happened to be children's aspirin. St. John's, I think it was called. I didn't think you remembered that, honey. Aspirins never did have much acquaintance with oranges. Oranges tasted much better than that.''

There was a shout from the other side of the front door. "All right if I come in?" called Ed Pearson.

"Sure," Ben called, and Ed came in through the living room and entered the kitchen. He was carrying a pencil, some paper and his carefully folded and maintained National Geographic map in his left hand. "Hi, everyone," Ed said. "Don't let me interrupt breakfast.''

"What can I get for you, Ed?" Connie asked.

"I already ate, thanks," he replied. "A cup of coffee would be nice, though.''

"Well," said Ben, "we let you two off the hook last night, but now seems like a good time for you to catch us up. I'll turn things over to our town archivist here.''

"Just so you understand," Ed told Jake and Prosper, "I keep our town history. I keep a record—a diary, more or less—of what's gone on around here during just about every day since Kingdom Come. I used to be the editor of the daily newspaper that served this area before the war, so keeping the town archives comes naturally to me.''

Prosper nodded, interested. "I don't think we ever met anyone else who keeps that kind of record," he said. "I can't remember many towns that keep any records at all—even for births, deaths or weddings, anything like that.''

"Not many people we've met can read and write—people born after Kingdom Come, that is," Jake added. "The ones who do know how generally don't bother keeping it up. They're too busy scratching out a living.''

"Everyone in McAndrew is literate, including the young people," Ben said, not without pride. "They can do figures, too. Our school is still functioning. Every kid in town can read and write at least a little bit, and some are really good at it. We've got a superb teacher.''

"Priscilla Neary," Jake said. "I remember her. She lent me a copy of *Great Expectations* the last time I was here with my dad, and I read it right through because I couldn't take it with me.''

"If the kids can't read and write and cipher," Ed said, "then we figure civilization's all over with and finished. We don't want that to happen, so we have the school, and the town supports the teacher at public expense.''

"I haven't seen much evidence that public education's being kept up elsewhere, like you folks are doing," Jake said.

"We're honoring a promise we made a long time ago," Ben said. "We were in deep trouble right after the war, what with people from the cities running around crazy and our crops dying from the big freeze. Judge Neary became our mayor then, and to tell it short, he showed us all how we could stay alive, mostly by using our heads and working together. Before the judge died, one of the things he urged us to do was to keep the school open, because maintaining public education was a powerful statement that we were still civilized. We voted it in as official policy at the town meeting we held just a day or two before the judge passed on. We've always considered it a deathbed promise, so we've kept to it.''

"Sounds good," Prosper said. "I've wished for a long time that I could read and write.''

"Stick around long enough, Prosper, and we'll teach you," Ed said. "Now, how about a quick tell of where you two have been? Jess said you still had a surprise or two for us. Was he kidding?''

Jake nodded. "Let's clear the table so you can spread out that map, and we'll show you," he said.

They all handed their plates to Connie, who salvaged scraps and put the dishes in the sink; Ben would draw another bucket of water and wash them later. After Connie wiped down and dried the table, Ed opened the map carefully; the map grew more fragile with each passing year, and he feared damaging it further. It had already torn badly along some of its folds, and there was no longer such a thing as scotch tape in the world.

The map was a picture of America at its height. It showed thousands of place names attached like tails to more thousands of dots—big and small dots, solid and hollow dots, each one indicating a place where hundreds or thousands or even millions of people lived . . . and, in the end, where most of them had died, some quickly and some not.

Jake pointed here and there on the map, indicating the circuit he and Prosper traveled. "You've seen a lot of the country," Ed said.

"We've seen maybe too much of it," Jake replied.

Ben nodded. "Prosper, how about you?"

"I stayed in Appalachia, mostly, until I met Jake. There's parts of the mountains you can't live in because they're still hot, but there's other parts that are just fine."

"What about cities, now?" asked Ed.

Some of the cities on the map, mostly in the northeast, were X'd over, circled or both. Ed had never had much reliable information about cities outside their own area. Cities he knew to be destroyed were X'd out; possibles were circled. Here and there, a city bore an X in a circle because it had first been listed as a possible and, later, confirmed destroyed—or, at least, Ed had become convinced of its destruction by his interviews with later travelers. He recalled that Pittsburgh had been like that. He'd wondered about Pittsburgh for years, until he'd talked to that Mennonite family on their way through to Vermont nearly twenty years ago.

Jake studied the map for a moment and then silently began pointing here and there east of the Mississippi, extinguishing cities with a finger. Ed put an X over each city as Jake pointed to it.

"You're confirming all of my possibles," Ed muttered.

"No help for it," Jake said quietly. "Some we know from what we've seen, and the rest of it we got from the people at Mount Weather, so I guess you can consider it official."

He began pointing again, this time at Ohio. "Akron, Cleveland, Youngstown and Columbus for sure," he said. "I heard Cincinnati, too, but I've never been out that way. I don't remember them saying anything about it at Mount Weather."

"You can add Toledo," Prosper put in, "but I'm not sure about Cincinnati, either."

"Cincinnati's a possible, then," Ed said, circling it.

"Over in Illinois, you can confirm Chicago," Jake said. "I don't know about anyplace else in Illinois."

"Up here, put Milwaukee," Prosper said. "You don't have Detroit yet, either—um, everything around there, too. Um, down around that way, you've got Des Moines, Omaha and Lincoln. That's all I remember from around there."

"Little Rock," said Jake. "And, over here, Memphis and Knoxville."

"What about Texas?" Ben asked. "We've never heard anything about Texas at all, good or bad."

"If it's in Texas, it got hit," Jake said. He pointed and pointed and pointed.

"Jesus," Ed breathed, making marks.

"El Paso, too," said Prosper. "Don't forget El Paso."

"Right."

"New Orleans," Jake said, finding the Mississippi. He began heading upriver. "Memphis, St. Louis and Kansas City. Wichita and Topeka, too. 'Way up there, Minneapolis and St. Paul, both together."

"I forgot Florida," Prosper said. "Mark down Miami, Tampa, Jacksonville, Tallahassee, Orlando and, uh, Cape Canaveral over here."

"This is all from missiles?" Ben asked, almost dazed. "I didn't think there were that many."

"The Mount Weather people said a lot of it came from missiles aboard submarines just a few miles out to sea," Jake told him. "Bombers got some more cities in the second wave. There wasn't any third wave."

"I knew it was bad," Ben said, staring at the map, "but this is . . . incredible. I guess I was hoping for the best, despite everything."

"It's worse on you older folks," Prosper said. "Us, we never knew anything else."

"I know what you mean," Connie said, "but sometimes I have a hard time with it, anyway."

"Atlanta and Columbus are all I know about for sure in Georgia," Jake said, continuing. Then, almost impatiently, he suddenly shifted his attention to the west coast, quickly obliterating most of California and annihilating the Pacific Northwest.

"Don't forget Tacoma," said Prosper. "And Butte, too."

Jake and Prosper continued to tick off city after city after city in a syncopated rhythm of horror. Ed began to wish more and more desperately that they would stop, but they did not run out of cities for quite a while . . . and, even at that, they admitted that they must have forgotten quite a few.

CHAPTER 10

IT WAS A PERSONAL BEST, ALL RIGHT. SO FAR, HIS score stood at five people dead and three thousand in ready cash warming his pocket. Not bad.

Three of his dead were women. One of them had begged him to kill her before very long and he'd obliged her, although he'd taken his time about it.

He smiled.

He was driving his sixth stolen car of the week. He'd stayed on back roads, even though he doubted anyone was bothering to look for him. Any other time, he'd be a real story, all right—FIVE DEAD IN UPSTATE SPREE—but today people were worrying too much about other things to care about him.

He smiled.

Under other circumstances, he might resent such a lack of attention, but not today. It left him free—free to do whatever he wanted to whomever he wanted with little or no fear of retribution. Even if they caught him, there wouldn't be time for them to do anything to him.

He was freer than he'd ever known. It was his kind of world, and he would miss it when it went—FIVE BIL-LION DEAD IN SUPERPOWER SPREE—and it was too bad, really.

He thought he might last a little longer up in the mountains, away from the cities, and so he was headed there. He was making very good time. There was little traffic on the sometimes unmapped two-laners he was taking. He'd been going all night, though, and he was getting tired. The thrill of the kill could take him only so far, and the sun was almost up. He had taken to hiding out during the day. He was now, more than ever, a creature of the night. Even tigers rest, he thought.

He rounded a bend and saw a farmhouse up ahead. The lights were on.

He smiled.

Lieutenant Banks awakened feeling content, and that was not good. He needed his edge. Soon enough, his accustomed anger resurfaced, and he felt better. Angry people stayed alive.

Team Tango was now three weeks out of Rensse-laer. Brother Jimmy Briscom didn't like it when pris-oners accused of a capital crime ran away. It made him look foolish, and people who made Brother Jimmy Briscom look foolish were, in turn, made to die. The escape of the buskers had finally prompted Governor Briscom to send a National Guard team not only to capture and return them for trial and execution, but to scout around to see if there was any territory worth the governor's attention. The trail of the buskers had led to the Adirondacks, and no one from Rensselaer had been up that way since the last flu epidemics.

As nearly as Banks could figure, the buskers were about two weeks ahead of Team Tango, and they were that far in front only because Banks was taking his time about surveying the territory through which they were passing, stopping to *savor* parts of it. The best savoring so far had been in a town called Raquette Lake, where there'd lately been a set of teenaged identical twin girls. He had wanted to bring the girls along for a few days of fun, but they had proven to be too much trouble, so Banks had had Sergeant Wigg shoot them the morning after Team Tango had left town.

The loot from the trip had been minimal so far. There hadn't been any gold or jewelry to be found. All the big towns in the mountains were dead and had long since been stripped of anything valuable. Some of the small towns had survived, but not many, and most had not done well. Team Tango had not come across a settlement with more than fifty people in it since leaving Rensselaer. Usually there were many fewer.

The buskers were leaving a trail that a blind man could follow. There was no rush to get after them. Team Tango would stay on their trail . . . and *savor* whatever it passed as it pursued them.

Banks snarled and snapped at his men, getting them ready for another day's march. The old maps said that the town of Blue Mountain Lake lay a day or so ahead of them on Route 28.

They might get lucky again.

At about the same time, many miles away in McAndrew, Stephanie was just arriving home after spending most of another night with Bobby.

Her father was sitting on the living room couch. One of Jess Harper's jars was in his hand; there was about an inch of product left in it. "Hello, Daddy," she said.

"Hello," Mike Crane mumbled. "Kinda late, ain't it?"

"Sorry," she said. "I hope you weren't worried. Daddy, are you hurting? That jar was full when I left last night."

"Yeah, I'm hurting a little," he said. He held up the jar. "This is seconds."

"Why didn't you call the neighbors over?" Stephanie fretted. "I'll go over and get Doc Hock right away."

"No, don't bother," her father slurred. "I been dealing with it okay. I'm fine. How're you?"

She came over and put a hand on his forehead. "I really don't want you drinking any more product tonight, Daddy. I think you should get some sleep, if you can."

"Actually, I can't feel too much no more," Mike said, "so maybe I will. How was your date with Dick LeClerc's boy?"

"It was all right."

"He gonna marry you?"

"I think so."

"Good," Mike said, nodding dreamily. "That takes care of *that*, then." He was silent for a few minutes. "Some father I am," he finally said.

"You've always been a good father," Stephanie said quickly, hugging him hard. "The best."

"Nah," he said. "Look at what you gotta do because I can't leave you nothing. No goods, house falling the hell apart. You gotta get what you need from Bobby LeClerc. That stinks. *I* stink."

"Daddy, please don't say that," Stephanie said. Her eyes filled. "You're wonderful, Daddy."

He looked at her and tenderly caressed her cheek with a shaking hand. "I wish to God I could save you from all the troubles in the world, honey," he said. "I'm so damn worried about you, what you'll do afterward."

"I'll be fine. Don't you worry."

He managed a grin. "You're tough, all right—just like your mom was, rest her soul. Just don't forget to show folks your sweet side, too. Your mom had trouble with that part—showing the sweet side, I mean."

"I'll try, Daddy."

"Sweet side's why I married her." He yawned. "I'm pretty tired now, hon. I think I'll turn in."

"I'll help you upstairs."

A few hours later, Sarah Broom was sitting in the swing on her patio. She had an hour for her knitting, and it would likely be the only quiet time she would have all day. Her mother was out.

Truth to tell, Sarah had not expected to miss school as much as she did. She had not realized at the time how important school had been to her, although she had come to love Miss Neary and still dared to hope that the teacher felt a little affection for her in return. Sarah had soon discovered that the best thing about school had been the wonderful fact that her mother had not been there with her. Sarah had also suddenly realized—and not without a great deal of guilt—that she loved, but did not like, her mother.

Then she had turned sixteen and, with that, school had ended. Sixteen was when most girls had either found husbands or were close to it. Instead of having a husband herself, though, Sarah had her mother and her plain looks and, because of all that, she had her knitting and her quiet time.

It was a plain and simple fact that no boy in town would have Amanda Broom as his mother-in-law. It was also a plain and simple fact that there were five fewer boys than girls her age in town. Now that part didn't matter too much to her, because that was just statistics. What did matter was that, long ago, she had picked out her man, and he did not even know that she was alive because he had been taken by another. *That* was the part that was killing her.

She heard a rattling sound coming from down the street and, as she did every day at this time, she briefly considered running inside the house. She never did, though, and she did not today.

Sarah sat calmly in the swing, knitting, as Bobby LeClerc came slowly up the street on his delivery bicycle, the one with the big basket between the handlebars. She watched Bobby approach out of the corner of her eye, even though he was still so far away that he seemed little more than a blur to her.

God, it hurt. It hurt a lot.

"Hi, Sarah," Bobby called as he coasted up to the house.

"Hello, Bobby," Sarah replied, putting down her knitting. "How are you today?"

"Just fine. Yourself?"

"Fine, thank you. Did my mother give you an order to deliver?"

"Yep, just a few groceries. Here they are." Bobby reached into the delivery basket, pulled out a small burlap sack and handed it to her. "You got the sack from the last time?" he asked. "I'd bring this inside for you, but you know your mom doesn't want anybody inside the house—"

"I know. I'll go get the old sack."

"Thanks," he said.

Once inside, Sarah's eyes filled. *Can't he see?* she wondered. *What's the matter with me?* She called herself ugly and stupid and twenty other bad things as she dropped the groceries on the counter. She retrieved the sack from the last delivery from the storage space under the sink.

Sarah wished she could hate Stephanie Crane, but it was not in her to hate anyone. Sarah knew that Stephanie had set her cap for Bobby long ago, and that there was nothing she or anyone could do about it. Lord knew she had tried, though. She had done something awful and yet exciting just that summer, in a last-ditch effort to get Bobby to notice her. A few of the girls had decided to sneak off to a remote part of Serpent Lake one hot day for a little innocent skinny-dipping; Sarah had decided to tag along, which completely surprised the other girls because Sarah did not usually do things such as skinny-dip. What none of the other girls knew, though, was that some of the boys were going to follow them to the lake and spy on them. Sarah knew it only because she'd overheard two of them talking about it, and she also knew that one of the boys in the group would be Bobby LeClerc. Bobby would see her without her clothes on and watch her for a while, and then he'd fall in love with her. It would be that simple.

To Sarah's despair, a laughing Stephanie had showed up at the lake about five minutes after everyone else had plunged in. A few minutes after that, the boys had come howling out of the woods, causing most of the girls to shriek and giggle. Sarah had gathered up the shreds and tatters of her dignity, waded out of the lake, and dressed. She left unnoticed.

The story about what had happened at the lake did not take long to get around town. Amanda Broom had found out about it instantly and given Sarah a good licking, but by that point Sarah had not cared much at all.

"Sarah?" Bobby called. "Did you find it?"

"Uh, yes. Yes, I have." Sarah left the kitchen and returned to the porch. "Here it is," she said. "Thank you, Bobby."

"No problem," he said. "See you around." He got on his bicycle and pedaled away. She watched him go.

After a while she sat down again and resumed her knitting until she started crying.

School was over for the day and Miss Neary was sitting at her desk, grading papers. She might have done the job at home, but there was all that beautiful afternoon light coming through the window to sit in and enjoy, and she'd found herself feeling pretty chipper when three o'clock had come. There would be time enough for a nap later.

There was a soft knock on the open classroom door. Miss Neary turned to see Prosper Cross standing there.

"Ma'am?" he asked. "Are you busy? I could come back another time."

"Why, Mr. Cross," she said. "No, I'm not busy. Please come in. May I help you with something?"

"Thank you, ma'am."

"Would you like to sit?"

"No, ma'am, I'm just fine. Uh, Miz Neary—"

"Yes?"

"I was wonderin' if you could teach grown-ups to read like you teach kids."

Miss Neary smiled. "There's nothing I like better than teaching folks of all ages how to read, Mr. Cross. Would you like to learn?"

Prosper nodded his head. "Yes, ma'am, I sure would."

"Can you read at all now?"

"I can read numbers," said Prosper. "I learned that much from road signs. I never got the hang of putting a whole lot of letters in a row and having them make any sense, though. Ma'am, is it true that when you read something proper, it's like a little voice in your head telling you what's right there on the paper?"

"Some people hear that little voice," Miss Neary said. "Other people just read right along without it. Mr. Cross, I think I can help you, but how much we can do together depends on how long you and Mr. Garfield are going to stay in town."

"Jake and me think we'll be sticking around for a while," Prosper said. "You folks are giving us a lot of repair work and other odd jobs and, anyway, we like it here. We'll be staying a few more weeks, anyway."

"That's enough time for us to make a good start," Miss Neary said. "Why don't you come here after school hours? If you can't make it on any particular day because you've got work, just send word."

"Yes, ma'am," Prosper said, grinning. "That sounds fine to me. I expect we can work out how you get paid."

"There's plenty of time for that," Miss Neary said. "All right, why don't we start? You can sit right there in front."

"Yes, ma'am."

Miss Neary went over to the bookshelf, extracted a slim volume, and set it in front of Prosper. "Have you ever heard of Dr. Seuss?" she asked.

"No, ma'am, I haven't." Prosper looked at the cover. "Is that drawing there supposed to be a cat?"

"Yes, it is, and he's wearing a hat." She pointed to the words in the title of the book. "Now I'll show you a trick. See how the letters here and here match, just as the sounds of the words do?"

CHAPTER 11

JAKE GARFIELD DROPPED THE LOAD OF WOOD HE was carrying into the Gordons' bin and sighed wearily. For someone who'd practically made a career of being painfully skinny, he was beginning to feel an embarrassing tautness in his arms and legs, almost as if he were developing muscles. The fact didn't displease him and, in fact, he felt better than he'd been feeling for a long, long time. Jake looked around to see if anyone was watching, and then crooked his right arm to make a muscle. The stringy thing there was turning into a discernible bump, all right. He felt it again and was impressed with himself. It showed what rest, exercise and good food could do for a person. Doc had been right, after all.

Jake and Prosper had been working on a for-hire basis since their arrival in McAndrew two weeks before. Prosper had been out since early that morning on a fence-repair job in the south part of town, just off Logger's Trail. As it had turned out, Jess Harper had been absolutely right about the Cokes. Everyone had wanted to gawk at the six-pack and touch the slick, painted steel of the cans, but no one had wanted to buy the thing. When Jake would invite a prospect to make an offer, the man would laugh and shake his head and, sometimes, pat him on the shoulder. Jake had finally hidden the Cokes away and gone to work. Work, at least, had real, usable value.

Jake and Prosper had begun by singing for their supper for the first few days. Just about everyone, from the mayor on down, desired the company of the buskers. The buskers knew, however, that nothing got older faster than the act of a couple of guys who didn't know when to stop singing long enough to do some honest work. Jake had begun cutting firewood for people, using an axe, a maul and a set of wedges he'd rented from Dick LeClerc. Prosper did odd jobs for pay and, in a gesture the town had appreciated, he'd volunteered for five hours of community service per week to pay for the schooling he was getting from Miss Neary, who'd refused direct payment.

A great deal of hard work later, Jake and Prosper held a comfortable number of the IOUs that served as currency in McAndrew. The partners still busked— but only on Saturday night and Sunday afternoons, and only when there wasn't something else for them to do. They stood to earn a pile from folks who, with the sudden availability of skilled and dependable labor, found themselves unwilling or unable to cut their own wood or do other chores to prepare for the coming winter . . . and it didn't hurt any that Jake and Prosper always threw in a little extra cut wood beyond the cord or two contracted for. Jake knew that, for his part, his woodchopping would soon win him real carpentry jobs—small ones at first, and then jobs requiring more skill. He was beginning to think that he and Prosper might winter in McAndrew. It was a good town; they liked it, and it liked them.

He and Prosper were living in an abandoned house on Elm Street, not far from where Ed Pearson and the Gordons lived. There hadn't been much time to straighten up the place, but it had at least been swept out and fixed up enough to keep out the weather.

"Uh, hello, Mr. Garfield," came a shy voice. He turned to find a short, thin, brunette girl of sixteen or so standing near him. She was holding a small sack. Her hair was in braids, and she was rather plain; Jake thought she would look much prettier if she dared to smile. She seemed nervous.

"Hi," Jake said. "I don't believe we've met—?"

"I'm Sarah Broom," she said. She could not look him in the eye; she seemed to be staring at Jake's left shoulder. "I live not too far from here. With my mother, I mean."

"Hello, Sarah. Glad to meet you. I'm Jake Garfield."

"Uh, this is for you, Mr. Garfield." She held out the sack, still looking anywhere and everywhere but at him. "It's, uh, something for you to eat. Lunch. I, uh, made it for you. Special, that is."

"Why, thank you," Jake said, trying to sound pleased. He put down his axe and donned his shirt. "I appreciate it very much."

"It's only a little bread and cheese," Sarah said. "Cow cheese, I mean."

"Very thoughtful of you," Jake said. "Want to share some with me?"

"Uh, no," Sarah said, blushing. She was almost mumbling now. "No, thank you. It's all for you. All of it, every bit. I have to go. Really, I do. 'Bye!" She began to hurry away.

"Hey, hold it a minute," he called, and she stopped dead in her tracks. "Sarah?"

She turned. "Yes, Mr. Garfield?"

"Call me Jake. Sarah, what's the matter?"

"Uh, what makes you think something's the matter?"

"Have I offended you or something?"

"Uh, no! Of course not, uh, Jake. I'm sorry if you thought so."

"Come on, sit down. We'll talk."

"Uh, all right." She seated herself across from him, and he handed her one of the squares of cheese she'd brought with her. "Thanks."

He chewed on the acorn bread—not bad—and waited for Sarah to say something. Finally, she did.

"It was my mom's idea," Sarah began. "The lunch, I mean."

"Oh, I see."

"It was suppose to get you to notice me," she said. Then she giggled, and Jake realized he'd been right. Sarah had a grand smile.

"Well, you've been noticed. Pleased to meet you, Sarah."

"Pleasure's mine. Jake, can I ask you a question? Uh, they say you're a preacher sometimes, and the last preacher that came through answered people's questions."

"I'll answer if I can," said Jake. "Shoot."

About half an hour later, Jake watched as Sarah walked down Elm Street. Before she disappeared around a bend, she turned to give him a big wave. He waved back.

"Care for something to drink?" asked Connie Matthews. She was walking around the corner of the house and toward him, bearing a small tray with two glasses of apple cider.

"Thanks," Jake said, taking one. "This is thirsty work."

"I know it is," Connie replied. "I appreciate your doing it, too. Otherwise Dad would have—and he really shouldn't, not at his age. Looks like you're about finished."

"Yep," Jake replied. "Two more armfuls ought to fill that bin of yours." He sipped at his cider, and his eyes widened. "Say, this is very good."

"Made it myself," Connie said. "We have a cider press in the garage."

"I thought I smelled something good."

"You going to eat the rest of that lunch Sarah brought?"

"Just the bread, I guess," he said. "I'm not hungry enough to eat cheese. Matter of fact, I hate cheese. Would you like it?" He held out the sack.

"Thanks," she said, taking it. "Poor Sarah. I'll bet you anything that coming over here to give this to you wasn't her idea."

"No, it wasn't," said Jake. "She told me so. Wherever I go, mothers are forever trying to match me up with their daughters—more so after my father died. I spent most of my time in Canandaigua avoiding predatory mothers. It got really bad whenever I'd busk at a wedding."

"Ever wind up getting married?" Connie asked.

"Nope."

"Big mistake."

"I don't think so," Jake said. "I wasn't ready for it."

"And now you are?"

"Maybe, maybe not."

"Do women you've never met before often try to feed you food you can't eat?" Connie asked wryly.

"It happens," Jake said, shrugging. "Actually, Sarah's the fifth one in two days who's come by wherever I was working. They always bring something for me to eat. Usually they find me down at our own house. Sarah said she went over there first, but then heard me chopping wood over here."

"I like Sarah a lot," Connie said. "She's a good

and kind person. She was very helpful to us when my mom died a couple of months back. It's that mother of hers, Amanda. She just can't leave the poor little thing alone.''

"I know the type," Jake said. "Sarah's good people, though. She had a little problem she wanted to talk about, is all.''

"Boy problem?"

"Yes. How'd you know?"

"The whole town knows she's sweet on Bobby LeClerc, and that she doesn't have a chance with that Stephanie Crane around.''

He nodded. "It's a shame. I guess it's not telling tales to tell you that she really loves him, you know.''

Connie nodded. "Everybody knows. It's almost tragic.''

"Do you know she's never talked to Bobby about it?"

Connie was surprised. "She hasn't? Not once?''

"Too shy.''

"What'd you tell her?"

"I advised her to try as hard as she could," said Jake. "She says she'll talk to him at the first opportunity.''

"Well, I hope she's subtle about it," Connie said. "Bobby will just plain run away if she's too direct, and Stephanie will feed her to the fish.''

"Oh, I don't know," Jake said, grinning. "I think more of Bobby and less of Stephanie than *that*." He looked up at the sun. "Looks like it's about time for me to quit and go home. I've got some work to do there before it gets too dark. I can finish cutting the wood here in the morning, if that's all right with you.''

"That'll be fine. How's that place of yours coming along, anyway?"

"Pretty well, I think," Jake said. "It's good enough right now to present to Dick LeClerc for supplies when Prosper and I are ready to leave. He can turn it over to a couple that's willing to pay for a place that's already been reclaimed."

"Sounds all right," said Connie. "All the work you two are doing must be wearing you both a little thin, though."

Jake shook his head. "No, the work's not bad," he said. "We're glad to have it."

"You could still be busking, though," Connie said. "It'd be easier on you, right?"

"It's always easier to plunk your ass on a chair and sing." He shrugged and, finishing the cider, put the glass carefully on the tray Connie was holding. "We want to fit in here, so I chop a little wood, and Prosper moves some furniture and does a few chores. Besides, I like chopping wood; it gives me a chance to think."

"Think about what?" Connie asked.

"Oh, you know. Things."

"What things?" she persisted.

"Just things," Jake said, shrugging. "Nothing important."

"Long-ago things?"

"Maybe."

"Oh," Connie said. "By the way, are you going to the town meeting this afternoon?"

"Wouldn't miss it," Jake assured her. "Every time I go into LeClerc's, people are standing around arguing whether we should send somebody to Mount Weather for the President's birthday or not. I'd like to get the matter settled, if only so we can start talking about something else."

"What do you think about sending somebody?" asked Connie.

"Me, I wouldn't go," Jake said. "I've been there." He drained his glass and placed it on the tray. "Thanks for the cider."

"I added some spice."

"I could tell."

* * *

Most of the four hundred people who lived in and around McAndrew had crowded into the First Methodist Church on Neary Square for the regular monthly town meeting. Jake arrived about ten minutes early and, not finding a seat, circulated among the people standing along the aisles and in the back.

It was a big church for a mountain town. There were two sections of polished mahogany pews running from front to back, with aisles up the middle and down the sides. Jake counted the pews quickly and guessed that the church could seat perhaps a hundred people. Every seat had long since been taken.

The church was well-maintained, and its many stained-glass windows were remarkably intact. Missing stained glass had been replaced with thin boards carefully cut to match the twisting leading of the window. The boards were colored red, pink or white to match the surrounding glass, so as not to jar the eye too badly.

Jake looked around. He spotted Ed Pearson and waved. The town archivist was standing against the east wall, next to a stained-glass window that depicted a lamb with a halo; the lamb was hunkered down next to an open book. Ed smiled and waved Jake over.

"Hello, Ed," Jake said. They shook hands. "Quite a turnout."

"The town meeting usually draws well," Ed said. He held up a few sheets of folded blank paper. "Priscilla Neary lets me raid her stores for two or three extra sheets of paper every month, just so's I can get it all down." He grinned. "Doesn't take me but an extra sheet; I save out the rest. Don't tell Pris."

"The teacher keeps all the paper?"

"Sure," Ed said. "She's in charge of it. There's a ton of blank paper over at the school, and it's all in fine shape. It all belonged to the county school system, I guess. Pris Neary acts for the town and issues the paper piece by piece as needed; most of it goes to the kids at the school.''

"What are you going to do when it runs out?'' Jake asked.

Ed shrugged. "Learn to make paper ourselves, I guess—or we'll write on birch bark. The colonials used to do that. Maybe somebody from outside will be in a position to sell us some paper by then. That'd be good. Hi, Priscilla!''

Jake looked around to see Miss Neary standing there. "Hello, Ed,'' she said. "Good evening, Mr. Garfield. Mr. Garfield, where is Mr. Cross? I waited for him at the school today, but he never came by for his Saturday class, and I don't see him with you.''

"I haven't seen him since this morning, ma'am,'' Jake said. "He was doing a repair job on the south end of town. He should have been finished long ago, or else sent word that he couldn't make it today. I certainly apologize for him.''

"Makes no nevermind,'' Miss Neary said. "I graded some papers while I was waiting. I'll expect him Monday after school, though.''

"Certainly, ma'am.''

"Good night, then. Enjoy the meeting, Mr. Garfield. They tend to be lively.''

"Yes, ma'am.''

"Excuse me,'' came a voice from behind him. "You must be Jake Garfield, because you're the only guy here I don't know.''

Jake turned to see a short, bearded and powerfully built man standing in front of him. He was holding a baseball cap in his left hand. "Howdy, stranger,'' Ed said, shaking hands with the new arrival. "Long time no see. Jake, this is Digger Digby.''

"Hello,'' Jake said, offering his hand. "Glad to meet you.''

"Nice to see you, too,'' Digger said, shaking it.

"Now I'm not the only one in town who's got a wild man's beard."

"I've heard of you," Jake said. "You're the guy who bagged the deer the day before my friend and I got here. Congratulations."

"That's me," Digger replied. "My one claim to fame. I remember you and your dad from last time. I heard he's gone. I'm sorry."

"Thanks."

"Where's your partner? Haven't met him yet."

"He's not around right now, but I think he'd like to meet you, too. Um, Digger, you keep by yourself most of the time, don't you? Or so I hear."

Digger shrugged. "Yeah, I'm a loner, but that doesn't make me a bad person."

Ed laughed and clapped Digger on the shoulder. "Digger's okay, Jake," he said. "He's a family man who comes into town as often as he can. He and his wife Annie have a seven-year-old son named Justin."

"Justin was a sickly little baby," Digger said. "Annie still worries the boy'll pick up some horrible disease, so we tend to keep to ourselves. Actually, I'm Justin's stepfather, not his father. I married Annie when he was two and he had a little trouble getting used to me. He'd get colds and rashes; Annie pretty near gave up on having me around before Justin stopped reacting to me."

"Lucky," Jake said.

"It was," Digger replied. "Doc Hock once said he thought Justin might have been suffering from allergies to other people, but now he thinks Justin's over it, now that he's older. Ever hear about anything like that in your travels, Jake?"

Jake shook his head. "No, I haven't. Was Justin's condition due to Kingdom Come?"

The little man shrugged again. "There's no way to tell. Maybe it was, and maybe it wasn't. It could have also been some damn birth defect that has nothing to do with the war, but who knows? We just watch the boy carefully, and that's all we can do—that, and pray.''

''Speaking of which,'' Jake said, ''I think I must have met just about everyone in town, but I haven't met the pastor of this church. Where is he?''

''Pastor?'' Ed said, surprised. ''Shoot, Jake, I haven't even thought about him in years. He died during the long winter right after the war.''

''He did? Then who's in charge of this place?''

''The town is, through a committee,'' said Ed. ''We use the church mostly for town meetings, but we also use it for community sings and such when the weather's bad and we can't use the square. Anyone can come in here anytime for worship, too. Whenever we get a preacher through town—not often—we let him use the church all he wants. Heck, it's the only suitable building in town big enough for everybody to get together indoors, and there's plenty of seats. You preach, don't you?''

''Now and then,'' Jake said. ''I'm not ordained. I've just got a touch for it.''

''Maybe you'd want to give it a try here some Sunday. Up to you, of course.''

''Maybe I will,'' Jake said. ''I've never preached in a church before. I usually do it out in some field somewhere. It's a beautiful church, sure enough.''

''The committee does a nice job of keeping it up,'' Ed said. ''Notice the fresh coat of whitewash? A squad of kids just finished it.''

''The church looks fine,'' Jake said. ''The whole town's been kept up—at least, the parts that folks live in have.''

''That's so,'' Ed confirmed. ''Too bad the church bells don't work, but they're not really bells. They're some sort of electric chimes, and they don't work at all. They sounded pretty good, as I recall. The old pastor raised the money for them from the summer crowd. He installed the sound system just before the war, so we never got to hear 'em much.''

"What about the theater down the street?" Jake asked. "The, uh, the Trans-Lux? It's bigger, isn't it? Why not use it for meetings instead of the church?"

"Ever been inside a movie theater, son?" Ed asked.

"Uh, no, not that I remember."

"Well, then, you might not know that movies had to be shown in the dark," Ed said. "Otherwise, you couldn't see what was happening on the screen. There are plenty of seats in the Trans-Lux, all right, but there aren't any windows for sunlight, and we can't bring in candles or torches because there's no ventilation to speak of. We don't bother with the Trans-Lux at all; we never even bothered to seal it against animals. Christ alone knows what's living inside there now. I'd say burn it down, except that whatever's living in there would run out of it and into people's homes.''

"I snuck inside the Trans-Lux once, when I was a kid," Digger said. "First thing I did, I looked behind a busted-up glass counter and saw a whole nest of baby rats. Boy, I got out *fast*. Gotta be careful about rabies, y'know—and mama rats bite hard if you go anywhere near their babies.''

"Well, no more teasing baby rats for *me*—" Jake began.

"Attention!" came a loud voice from the front of the church. Jake looked around and saw Ben Gordon up in the pulpit, waving his arms. "Can I have your attention, please?" Here and there, people began shushing their neighbors and calling for quiet. The gathering fell silent in less than half a minute.

"Thanks, friends," Ben said. "It's now the appointed hour so, as mayor, I'm calling our regular monthly meeting to order. Please rise for the singing of our national anthem." They sang it loudly and lustily, and when it was over they applauded.

"All right," Ben said. "First order of business is the reading of the minutes of the last meeting."

"Move they be accepted as if read," Ed called. "Besides, I forgot to bring 'em with me."

Ben sighed. "Well, there's no help for it," he said. "Second?"

"I second," came a voice from somewhere.

"All in favor say aye the ayes have it," said Ben. "If anyone really wants to look at the minutes for last month, go see Ed Pearson after the meeting and set something up with him. I'm sure he'll be happy to oblige." Ben cast a withering look at Ed, who sent it back and added a grin.

"Next order of business is old business," Ben said. "Any old business?" Ed raised his hand, and Ben pointed at him. "The chair recognizes Mr. Ed Pearson, our town archivist."

"Thanks, Mr. Chairman," Ed said. "What about my new typewriter ribbon?"

"What about it?" Ben rejoined. "Didn't you bring this up last time? I'd remember better if I could refer to the minutes, of course."

"I'll refresh your memory, Mr. Chairman," Ed said. "You want the archives and everything else typed because you say keeping archives is civilization and so is typewriting, and I agree—but the ribbon I'm using has been in use for more than ten years and it's not good for much now, even if I re-ink it. It's full of holes and you can't type on holes, to belabor the obvious. I need a new ribbon. I should add that I'm just about out of ink for the re-inking, too. Heck, if I could make a ribbon, I would, just so I could stop bothering you and everybody else about it."

Ed blinked at him. "So what do you suggest we do, Mr. Pearson?"

"I suggest we look for a new ribbon for me and, preferably, more than one. Right away, too."

"Where do you think we should look?" Ben demanded. "I think we've scavenged just about every-where within range. If a ribbon had turned up, you'd have it."

Ed shook his head. "Not everywhere, Mr. Chair-man. I suggest that a party be sent to the Tupper Lake area."

"That's pretty far afield, isn't it?" Ben asked. "About forty miles, if you head south on Logger's Trail. Besides, it's burned out."

"Might be worth it," Ed said. "We've never gone through there like I know we could."

"Others have probably stripped it bare by now."

"Maybe so, maybe not," Ed said. "There may still be plenty of things for us to find; you never can tell. Remember, Jake Garfield found that six-pack of Cokes over in Lake Placid, right under our noses." That brought a rumble from the audience. Jake looked around and saw that some of the young men in the crowd had begun engaging each other in animated conversation. He suspected that, at least in some quar-ters, the notion of going exploring was a popular one.

"Jake also met Big John Meyers," Ben pointed out, and that brought a different kind of rumble from the crowd. "It's not secure out there."

"Heck, Ben, it's not secure anywhere. Send enough people along and the bandits will stay away. I say we go."

"Ed," Ben said, "I wish I could oblige you, but I don't think it'd be responsible. We have the harvest coming on, and we have to start getting ready for win-ter. Look, can't this wait a while?"

Ed shrugged. "If I'm going to be town archivist, I have got to have something to archive with. It's not life or death, no. It's just civilization, that's all."

"Point taken," Ben said. "Have you made a mo-tion, Ed? I can't tell."

"Want me to?"

"No, don't bother; the matter's on record. We'll

take it up at a meeting during the winter and talk about setting up a party for a spring departure, right after planting. How's that suit you?''

"Suits me fine," Ed said. "I can wait that long. Thank you, Mr. Chairman.''

"You're welcome. All right, then. Anyone else? No? Then the next item on the agenda is committee reports.''

The onslaught began, and eventually the agenda wound its way to new buisness. As it turned out, everyone wanted to talk about the American Jubilee and nothing else.

"Okay, okay," Ben said, holding his hands palms out in front of him as if to ward off the crowd, "I get the idea. All right, let's hash this out about the Jubilee. Just so we're chewing over the same version of things, the deal is that Governor Briscom down in Rensselaer wants to send an official delegation to a celebration of the President's birthday—the so-called American Jubilee—down in Mount Weather next May. I suggest that there are three alternatives. We can contact Briscom and send people to join his delegation, or we can send our own delegation, or we can decide to ignore the whole thing. That sound right to you?''

There was a rumble of approval from the crowd.

"Fine, then," Ben said. "The chair recognizes Priscilla Neary.''

"Thank you, Mr. Chairman," she said, rising. "Friends—''

"Louder!" shouted someone in the back.

"This is as loud as I get," Miss Neary said primly. "Friends, I'll keep it short. Do we want to start playing these political games and, in particular, do we want to start playing them with an apparent madman such as this Brother Jimmy Briscom person? I don't believe we do. Let's just stay home and mind our own business. We've been all right so far by doing just that. If we truly want to celebrate the President's birthday, we can do so right here. Thank you.'' Miss Neary seated herself to a round of applause.

''The chair recognizes Ezra Hamilton,'' Ben said.

An old man sitting near the back rose. ''Thanks, Ben. I just wanted to say we should be very careful, whatever we do—and that I agree with Miss Priscilla Neary. We've stayed all right by minding our own business.''

''Thank you, Ezra.''

Hands shot up again amid cries of ''Mr. Chairman!''

''Anyone mind if I recognize my daughter?'' Ben asked, and no one did. Connie rose from her seat in a pew near the front of the church.

''Mr. Chairman,'' she said in a voice that carried well, ''I'm second to none in my respect and affection for Priscilla Neary, but I'm sorry to say that I think, in this case, she's mistaken. Certainly we've been safe, tucked away here in McAndrew ever since Kingdom Come . . . but the kingdom came many years ago. I think it's about time we got on with our lives and the life of this community. I think it's about time we stopped hiding out. I think it's about time we rejoined the rest of the human race. We younger people never knew the world you, our parents did. If this state is finally beginning to get itself reorganized, we ought to be a part of it. Let us build a new world—one for ourselves.'' There was a great deal of applause as Connie sat down.

Ed was fuming. ''Jake, I know you like her—'' he said.

''Like her?'' Jake asked. ''Who?''

''Her,'' Ed said, pointing. ''Connie Matthews. But she's absolutely crazy.''

''I do? She is?''

Ed turned from him and, waving his arms, yelled ''MISTER CHAIRMAN!!!'' so loudly that it made Jake wince.

"Ed Pearson?" Ben Gordon said in a mock surprise. "Do you have something to say, perhaps?"

"I sure do," Ed called back. "I think this American Jubilee thing is the most ill-conceived notion that's been advanced inside this building in the past thirty-five years, and that's saying a lot."

Ben Gordon cleared his throat. "Priscilla, will you please take the chair? Ed, come on up here."

Digger nudged Jake in the ribs and winked as the room fell nearly silent. Jake turned to Digger and whispered, "People got pretty quiet all of a sudden, didn't they?"

The little man was grinning. "They sure did," Digger answered in a low voice. "Everybody already knows where Ben Gordon stands on the Jubilee. Aside from his being a Democrat, he's been talking it up all over town to whoever'd stay in one spot long enough to listen. Ed's a Republican from 'way back and never did have much use for the President anyway, so he's just naturally against it."

"So they're going to argue about it?"

"As sure as God shaves without a mirror every morning," Digger said. "Ben and Ed will hash the thing out pretty well in as little time as possible and then, if it's still necessary, we'll pick up the question again at the next meeting. By then, all the people in town will have chewed the matter over for themselves and discussed it and picked what side they want to be on, and there won't be a need for any more speechmaking about it. Then we'll vote. Sometimes Ed and Ben settle something so thoroughly at first crack that it's never even brought up again."

"Aren't Ed and Ben good friends, though?" Jake asked.

"The best," Digger said. "But what's friendship got to do with it? Look—Ben's got that expression on his face again. Now we'll cut through the crap. You just wait and see."

There was some applause and a few loud cries of approval and derision from supporters of one position or the other as Ed took his place at the front of the church. He stood next to Ben, clasped his hands behind his back and kept his expression carefully bland.

"I think it's simple," the mayor began. "You all heard my daughter, and I can't add much to what she said. It's been a long time since the war. Let's put our fear aside and rejoin the rest of the world. What better excuse could there be than this Jubilee? I say we find out more about this patriotic festival, with an eye to a representative party from our town attending it. I agree, though, that we don't want to have anything to do with this Governor Briscom."

There was applause and a murmur of dissent from the audience; Ben held up his hand for silence and continued.

"We sing the national anthem and recite the Pledge of Allegiance every chance we get," Ben said. "That's altogether right and proper, but there's much more to being a citizen than just singing a song and reciting some poetry. There's some responsibility involved, too." The mayor paused for a moment, looking here and there around the room, letting his words sink in. When he continued, his tone was more solemn and his words more measured. "We, all of us, are citizens not only of McAndrew, not only of Warren County, and not only of New York. We are, always and forever, first and foremost, citizens of the United States of America."

He said the words again, more slowly and softly, his voice caressing them: "The United States of America." Ben waited to let the proud phrase roll around the room, and watched as it found targets everywhere. The mayor sensed that he had the crowd now, as if the mere name of the nation were itself an incantation to garner support for it. *Well*, he reflected, *maybe it is, at that. We had magic going for us in those days—just not enough of it, that's all.* Ben let the powerful words work into the minds of his audience for a moment more before he concluded his remarks.

"Let's plan to join in the Jubilee and be fully American once again," he finished. "It's been too long, much too long. Thank you."

There was prolonged applause, which faded only as Ben held up his hand again for quiet so that Ed might begin.

Ed cleared his throat. "I can't add much to what I said just a minute or two ago, folks," he began. "No one is as proud to be an American as I am. No one loves singing the Banner and pledging his allegiance to the flag more than I do. However, my own strong sense of patriotism doesn't keep me from realizing that this whole idea of an American Jubilee is self-serving twaddle."

Ed began pacing back and forth, as he always did when making a speech or lecturing a class over at the school. "Let's look at it from a practical point of view, shall we?" he continued. "There's a man in Rensselaer who says he's the governor of the state, and apparently he's terrorized a bunch of folks down his way into agreeing with him. Let's ignore the information we have that he's a loony. Let's forget that his stooges whipped our friends Jake Garfield and Prosper Cross for no damn reason other than that they objected to Briscom killing off one of his wives. Let's just assume that Briscom is a wonderful guy."

Ed looked around the room. "Okay, then," he continued. "Say we go to Rensselaer and present ourselves. What happens then? Do we simply go to Mount Weather, come back, and that's that? I doubt it most sincerely. Briscom will know we're here. Will the governor want us to pay taxes to him? Probably, because the nature of government is to grab other people's money—remember? Briscom will want a piece of our crops and goods, all right—but how much? We're just getting our feet under us again; do we want some *stranger* taking away ten, twenty or thirty percent of what we've worked so hard to get? I don't think so, and I don't think *you* think so.''

The audience began murmuring again, and Ed took heart from it. ''What else is this governor going to want?'' he continued. ''Will he want to draft our young men for his army? Does he plan to go to war against some other state or what's left of the federal government? Do we want to get involved in all that? I don't think so.

''I also don't know what this fear is that people are talking about,'' Ed said. ''We're not hiding out here because we're cowards, but because we're cautious. We've lived through a bad war and an even worse aftermath. Now things are better. You heard the reports a little earlier, and you've seen the fields outside of town with your own eyes. The game's starting to come back, too. As you all know, Digger over there got himself a deer a couple of weeks back, and we've all been looking out for another one ever since.'' That brought some knowing laughter.

''I'm not saying we should stay here forever,'' Ed went on, ''but is this Jubilee thing any reason to come out of hiding? I think we need a better reason than that. All we're hearing here is that some nut down in Rensselaer wants to drag a bunch of us down to Mount Weather to help the President blow out the candles on his birthday cake. It's not worth it, believe me. Let's not confuse the President with the country. Let's not confuse celebrating the President's birthday with the celebration of America. Most important, let's not forget to use our heads.''

Ed began ticking off points with the fingers of his right hand. ''We're still our own boss; let's stay that way. We're finally running a surplus on our crops; let's hold onto it. We've been doing a good job of keeping to ourselves, nice and quiet, in these mountains; let's keep on doing so." He took a breath. "I guess that's enough," he said. "Thanks for listening."

As the applause mounted, Miss Neary moved to adjourn, Jake seconded, and Ben put the question. After a chorus of ayes, everyone began heading for the doors.

"What about my nightmares?" called old Warren McAdoo, to no effect. "Can't we talk about my nightmares?"

"See what I mean?" Digger said to Jake as they were swept up in the crush. "Now we'll figure out what to do."

"I guess we will at that," Jake said.

Jake and Prosper had set themselves up rather comfortably in the small and easily heated living room of the Elm Street house they'd claimed for their own. They'd picked up mattresses, pillows and blankets from Dick LeClerc, and while the purchase had eaten considerably into their initial balance with the store, it was worth it; they'd had quite enough of sleeping on floors and alongside roads. For his part, Jake had never before in his life owned any bedding, although he felt as if he'd owned the bed he'd used at the Franklin place. His father used to say that home was where you hanged your hat, but that wasn't true at all; you could hang your hat any-damn-where. Home was where you kept your bed.

It was going to be a chilly night. He set the wood in the stone fireplace to burning and sat in front of it, watching the fat logs char and catch. There was something comforting about a fire, something that went beyond the physical world; he imagined that his most distant ancestors had felt precisely the same way about it. Perhaps its holding back the night was enough. Fire slew the dragons lurking in the dark.

"Hi," came a soft voice.

Jake spun around, almost sprawling. He was startled, and the brightness of the fire left him blind in the dark. "Who's there?" he called.

There was a gentle laugh. "How soon they forget. It's Connie." She walked forward into the firelight, unbuttoning her jacket. "Hi, Wanderin'."

Jake let out his breath and smiled. "Oh. Hi, Connie. Sorry, but you startled me. Uh, welcome to our humble home. To what do I owe the pleasure of this visit?"

"I just needed to talk for a while." She dropped her jacket, crouched and sat on the floor next to Jake. She looked into the fire. "Is that all right?"

"Sure."

"Prosper around?"

"No. I guess he's staying somewhere else tonight."

"The grapevine says he hasn't exactly been lacking for female companionship since you two arrived in town," Connie said.

"I guess he's considered exotic or something. That happens in most places we're in."

"Lucky Prosper. What about you, Wanderin'?"

"Me? I'm about as exotic as ragweed."

They were silent for a few minutes, doing nothing but look into the fire.

"You *do* remember, don't you?" Connie asked.

"Of course I remember."

Connie sighed. "Good," she said. "For a while there, I was worried." She laughed softly.

"I always regretted leaving," he said.

"I know that you had to go off with your dad."

"No," he said. "No, I didn't—not if I'd made a stand, but I didn't."

"I could have gone off with you, too, you know."

Jake shook his head. "No, you couldn't have. The road's no life for a woman."

"Oh, really?" she said.

"Really," he replied. "Hell, it's no life for a man, either."

Connie looked into the fire for another moment. "I got pregnant, you know."

Jake's head snapped around. "You got *what*?"

"Pregnant. We made a baby, Jake. A little wanderer."

"Jesus! What happened?"

"I miscarried. Fourth month."

"Oh. Oh, hell." Jake looked into the fire again for a long while. "Connie," he said finally, "I'm so sorry. If I'd known, I'd never have left, no matter what. Please know that." He put his arm around her. When he heard her sniffle, he looked at her again and saw the tears slowly trailing down her cheeks.

"I didn't even know by the time you left," she said thickly. "Mama and Daddy were wonderful. No hysterics, just support and love. I needed that from them; I felt so *alone* without you around. For shit's sake, you'd think people'd love a baby no matter how it got here, they're so rare—but all a lot of people here cared about was that I had a bastard in me, and that's all they needed to know. There's three old biddies in this town who I'll never forgive because of what they put me through back then."

"Point 'em out to me."

She snaked an arm behind him and held him close. "Never mind—but thanks for being angry for my sake, Jake; it makes you seem gallant. I kinda like it."

"I should have done more," he said. "I should have stayed."

"You didn't know," she said, squeezing him. "That was the only time I was ever pregnant, Jake. I kept trying with Ken. When we didn't catch, he figured it was his fault and so I tried with a few others. Ken knew all about it, of course. I didn't catch with them, either."

"Maybe we were just incredibly lucky," he said.

"Maybe," Connie said. "Doc thinks I'm border-line sterile, but he admits that's only a guess. Even at that, I'm better off than a lot of other women. Ever make any babies on the road, Jake?" She sniffed and wiped her face dry of tears with the sleeve of her shirt.

"None that I know of," he said, "but I was never in one place except Canandaigua long enough to find out, and I don't think I left anything behind there. Or anybody, I should say."

"It's been a long time," she said. "Us, I mean."

"Yes, it has."

"I wish you'd get rid of that beard. Scraggly."

"I will," he said. "Tomorrow morning. First thing."

"You going to leave me again?"

He suddenly made a decision, and he knew it was the right one. "No," he said. "Never."

"This isn't just because I want to have a baby."

"I know."

They looked at each other then in the light from the fire, and he could not think of anything other than how beautiful she was when lit in subtle gold. After a long time, he lifted a hand and touched her long, dark hair, brushing it back softly with his fingers. She smiled and, rising, walked the few steps to his mattress, unbuttoning her blouse as she went.

CHAPTER 12

IT JUST GETS WORSE AND WORSE, *HE THOUGHT AS he skimmed the incoming hourly news summary from the Associated Press. The text whizzed across the face of the screen as copy flowed into the newsroom computer at twelve kilobits per second over the line from the AP's big computer down in New York.*

As was his habit, he tried to read each story as it raced out of his terminal's paltry eight kilobytes of temporary storage. The bulletins and urgents had been hitting once every ten or twenty seconds. Since his terminal could store only eight such stories at a time, fresh news only a minute or so old kept falling out of queue. It was insane. He wished again for the long-gone days of teletype machines that punched rather than chattered copy into paper. He missed linotype machines that clattered and tinkled the body of a story into type with sturdy brass fonts, and he missed the heavy Ludlow machines that formed headlines from fat ingots of lead. He missed the smell of copiers that used alcohol to burn a brownish copy into specially treated paper. Things happened more slowly in the old days, but you could touch them and feel them as they were getting done. Now everything whizzed by in a glowing amber blur, like a radioactive Road Runner screaming BEEP FUCKING BEEP at all the aging coyotes trying to keep up with him.

He was the only one left at the paper who still used a by-God typewriter to write on and, since he was boss, he was the only one who could get away with it. The truth was, though, that no one else at the paper wanted to bother with a typewriter at all. For the life of him, he couldn't force himself to write anything of substance on his terminal—he found it impossible to "think through" the machine—so he continued to use the same battered Royal portable that had been serving him well since his college days. It fell to Gracie, the office secretary, to key his copy into the system on her own terminal so it could be dealt with by the production people. Gracie didn't seem to mind.

It was yet another late night at the paper. Everyone on the editorial and production staffs had stuck, despite the sad fact that, because of shortfalls in advertising revenue, he could no longer afford to pay overtime rates to his people. No one but his most loyal accounts wanted to advertise in the paper anymore, and selling the marginal accounts was taking up more and more of his time. Most everyone else spent their ad money with WIRD or bought smaller but more effective ads in the Albany paper that circulated a regional edition in the mountains. His little daily was on its last legs, crushed between the rock of WIRD and the hard place of the Albany Times-Union—and his paper's imminent demise was a fact he admitted only to himself. He'd given the paper thirty-nine years of his life—it would have been forty come next February—and it had all been for naught. He and Emma had nothing put aside for their retirement, either. The *paper had eaten everything. He wondered if it might be possible to get some sort of a job at his age. He'd always supposed he could get a job teaching at SUNY, but he'd never put the idea to the test, and he didn't know anybody there.*

He sighed; he was tired of worrying about the whole thing. He still had a paper to get out sometime tonight, and there was little for him to do now except watch the wire and keep an eye on CNN. All the broadcast networks and many of the cable outlets were running news all night that night, but he preferred CNN. It seemed to him that it was fastest at getting a story on the air, and they almost always had pictures first.

He had three pasted-up newspaper pages—the two center pages and the back page—before him on his desk. A fourth, the front page, was still back in the production room, waiting for a headline and the lead story. All but these four pages for tomorrow's paper had already been delivered to the printer over in Saranac Lake. These four pages made up one printing plate, and he was holding them back as long as he could, in case there was a major break. He had until about two a.m., which was well past dawn in Europe, before the pages had to go to the printer for the paper to be out on time in the morning. That was about forty minutes from now. Something certainly should have happened by then.

He was watching CNN with the sound turned down; the graphics that popped up from time to time behind the anchor weren't telling him anything he really needed to know. There was the map of Europe again, with the little red arrows arcing from Poland and Czechoslovakia into Germany and Austria, and on into Denmark and the Netherlands.

He had hoped he'd never see anything such as those arrows. He was one of those people who, just ten years or so before, had watched the Berlin Wall come down—a sight he remembered as perhaps the most moving thing he had ever seen on television. He had watched gleeful Berliners attack the Wall with sledge-hammers, pickaxes and even their fists, and he and Emma had cried a little at the incredible sight of young, drunken Germans dancing the night away atop the Wall.

That very night he had begun daring to hope that Gorbachev's policy of glasnost *and the concomitant decline of totalitarianism in Eastern Europe signaled the beginning of a new era of at least relative peace. A new kind of world had seemed so close, so possible . . . until Gorbachev was replaced soon after the Baltic states declared their independence of the Soviet Union, and the two Germanies had proclaimed their reunification and withdrawal from both NATO and the Warsaw Pact.*

With the hardliners back in power, the Soviets had reverted to type. The dissenters were back in the government loony bins, and the world had suddenly become a much more dangerous place. Now the Soviets had moved west, on the laughable pretext that the Germans were about to deploy their own tactical nuclear weapons. It was absurd nonsense. The Soviets had moved simply because they had not known what else to do. Their only hope was to create a new status quo, one with their former satellites back in the fold, and with a new and stronger Iron Curtain that enclosed as much western territory as their advancing forces could manage. The invasion was the last gasp of the Soviet old guard, and it was a gasp that might destroy the world.

Soviet forces had swept through Germany quickly enough, but reliable supply lines could not be established; the German Army was still a largely intact fighting force. Berlin's official call for a ceasefire had had little or no effect on German field commanders. The Soviets could have pulled back and dealt with their problems behind the lines, but the orders from Moscow remained unchanged: Advance.

They were advancing, for whatever good it might do them. The CNN map disappeared and was replaced by excellent video of the previous day's fighting in Amsterdam, before NATO ground forces had been forced to withdraw from the city. He was just old enough to remember the Nazi invasion of the Netherlands, and he remembered how those people had suffered under the Nazi heel, and how bravely they'd resisted the invader. He suspected that a new and equally courageous underground was already doing a brisk business in the Netherlands.

There was a knock on his door. It opened, and Jim Neumann stuck his head in. "How much longer, Chief?"

"Not long," he replied. "We'll know one way or another real soon now. Is everybody sticking?"

"Sure," Jim said. "What else?" The door closed, and it was quiet again.

He and Emma had gone to Amsterdam sometime in the early '70s. One night, when Emma was feeling a little ill from three weeks of traveling, she'd sent him out by himself to see the sights while she rested.

He'd had quite a time. He found that he liked the city's vibrant, freewheeling atmosphere, even though it had been created largely by people a generation younger than he. He'd found hippies, even by then an endangered species, smoking marijuana and hashish without restraint in the four or five restaurants and coffee houses in the city where it was de facto legal to do so. He'd eaten a ton of Chinese and Polynesian food at one of the many cheap and good restaurants located in the city's formerly Jewish and now Asian ghetto. He'd gone to the Rijksmuseum to see the Rembrandts, and he'd also gone to the Van Gogh Museum, where a smiling con artist had tried to sell him one of the paintings on exhibit. He'd been to the Anne Frank

House, and he'd watched pretty girls eating herring they'd just bought from street vendors. He'd gone sightseeing in the harbor, too; the boat ride had been conducted by a tour guide who'd kept up a constant monologue in four different languages.

He'd walked through the city's safe and clean redlight district in something pretty close to amazement. Prostitution was completely legal in the small houses that ran along the narrow, twisting streets of the area. He'd seen tired-looking young women of every description sitting on low chairs in shop windows rimmed with red or orange fluorescent lights. Some of the women had been sitting in the windows with their knees wide apart, staring dully at the men passing by. Others were dozing. Men skulked in and out of the buildings. If he'd been even slightly tempted to indulge himself, the furtive look of the johns had dissuaded him. He found that he much preferred to play tourist.

There was even a church in the middle of the district and, appropriately, the cross atop its spire was lighted in red. He'd entered and found the building to be no longer a church, but the headquarters of a group determined to preserve the distinctive look of Amsterdam in the face of a plague of American-style construction. Long afterward, it struck him as funny that the only building he'd entered in Amsterdam's red-light district had been a church, but Emma had laughed and said that it just showed the world how thoroughly square he was.

He sighed. He expected that the Amsterdam he remembered so well was gone. The fierce fighting must have put a swift end to all those well-meaning efforts at preservation. The red-light district must be history, too, blasted into rubble. That probably made no difference, either. He most sincerely doubted that the thousands of Soviet paratroopers now in control of the city were being very picky about where and with whom they indulged themselves.

He wondered if the Rembrandts and Van Goghs had survived, or was some son of a bitch Red general packing what remained of them off to the Kremlin even now? And was what happened to the paintings really all that important anymore, when the world looked about ready to blow itself up?

The NATO line had collapsed. That was the fact, no matter how Brussels HQ or Downing Street or the White House might try to interpret the story for the benefit of the local citizenry. He knew that, somewhere, someone in Washington must be deciding whether to use nuclear weapons on the ever-advancing Soviet forces in Europe.

He was afraid that he knew what that decision would be . . . so he was rather surprised a moment later when the bulletins and urgents began arriving with word of a Soviet offer of a ceasefire in place, and Jim came crashing into his office to tell him they only had thirty-one minutes left to get the new front page pasted up and over to the printer.

He picked up the phone. He would take one of those minutes to call Emma.

Jesus, Ed thought as he suddenly came awake. *Another goddamn nightmare.* His heart was pounding, but he was beginning to feel the unique kind of relief that comes from realizing that it was, after all, just a dream. He couldn't even remember what had been in it, not exactly. He only knew that it had been a bad one.

It was still dark, and he knew from the residual fear in his gut that, dream or not, he'd be up for a while. He got up and went to the window, scratching his ass through the thin material of his ragged pajama bottoms. He looked toward the east. The quarter-moon was about an hour past rising; that made it two in the morning, near enough.

Moving carefully in the dim light, he paddled to the

bathroom and, finding the base of the throne with his feet, positioned himself to take a leak. He didn't flush, of course. He never flushed more often than once a day, except when company was coming. In a world where water had to be hauled from wells and a full flush took six gallons of it, the decision whether or not to flush was not a trivial one. Six gallons of water weighed about fifty pounds, and that was a lot to haul around simply for the sake of aesthetics. Ed could have paid one of the kids in town to haul the water for him—many people in McAndrew did—but he couldn't see spending his credit that way.

I was about to call Emma.

He blinked in surprise at the thought. He remembered a bit of his dream now. He'd been about to make a phone call. He'd been sitting at his desk at the paper, and he'd been about to call Emma at home. Here, that is.

My God, he suddenly realized. *I even remember the phone number I was going to call. I know it like my own name. It's 623-2621—a long number, like in the cities. It's all numbers, though; no letters in it at all. No CYpress or CHelsea or CEntre or SPring. There was PEnnsylvania 6-5000, too—that was a Glenn Miller song, wasn't it?*

Ed felt his way downstairs and, finding a candle on the living room shelf, stooped to light a stick of wood from the still-glowing embers in the fireplace. He used the stick to light the candle, and then he walked over to the small vanity table next to the couch.

The phone was still there. He had never bothered to disconnect it or move it out of the way. He hadn't dusted it in quite a while, though; it was more gray than black. He wiped a finger across the round number plate in the middle of the dial and read what he already knew was there: MC 21, his old phone number. *Their* old phone number. Phone numbers had once been so goddamn important.

There'd been an operator once, a nice old lady named Sally Jane. If you wanted to make a call, you'd have to wait for her to give you a line so you could dial out, or she would dial the number for you. If you wanted someone else in town, you couldn't dial it yourself; you had to tell Sally who you wanted, and she'd connect you. If she was off duty, you couldn't make a regular call, but Sally would have rigged her board so that you could call the sheriff's office just by picking up and hitting the whatchamacallits, the little stubby things that were held down by the receiver when you hung up. He remembered Sally Jane well, although he had not thought of her in a long time. She'd been dead for almost thirty years.

Ed picked up the phone for the hell of it and held it to his ear. It was dead, dead as ever, dead as the phone company, dead as the world. He put a finger in one of the holes in the dial—the one with TUV 8 printed in red and black on the plate behind it—and brought it around to the stop. Then he let it go. The dial returned automatically to its position of rest, making that still utterly familiar rasping, clicking sound as it revolved counterclockwise at the urging of some hidden spring. He dialed TUV 8 again, smiling a little at the familiarity of the motion. Dialing a phone was something he'd done a hundred thousand times in his life before Kingdom Come. It felt *right*, even though he hadn't done it in thirty-five years or so. It felt as right as, oh, say, striking a match.

Ed suddenly saw a bobbing light out of the corner of his eye. It had come from outside. He looked out the window and saw Ben Gordon moving across his living room, toward his couch, a lighted lantern in his hand. He looked to be settling in for either a good read or a long think.

Ed didn't think Ben would mind some company. He went upstairs and dressed. Just before he left the house, though, he remembered that he had a mostly full jar of Jess Harper's product under the kitchen sink, so he fetched it along.

Bobby LeClerc was finally beginning to catch his breath. Stephanie remained lying where she was, her head resting on his stomach. She could hear his gut making small bubbly sounds, and she thought that was cute. She kissed his belly lightly, and he sighed.

It had been quite a night. Stephanie had read that short, turgid passage in *Two Against Tokyo* over and over again, trying to decide if what she'd inferred from its carefully obscure wording was actually what the writer had meant to say. It had seemed incredible . . . but so had French kissing when she'd first learned about it, and *this* seemed to be nothing more than a rather dramatic escalation of *that*. When she'd brought the subject up obliquely with one or two of her girl-friends, they'd reacted with surprise and something very near disgust.

She hadn't really known if it would work, either, and she'd been scared to try it. Well, it had worked just fine. Boy, had it ever. She thought Bobby had been going to croak.

"Wow," Bobby said at last. He rose up on his elbows; Stephanie turned her head around to look at him. She could just make out his dark eyes in the moonlight.

"Is that all you have to say?" she grinned.

He laughed. "I guess so," he said, shaking his head. "Where the *hell* did you learn how to do that?"

"Just a natural talent, I guess," she said.

"You're wonderful," he said, settling back.

"So are you." She changed her position to lie next to him, and she snuggled closely to his warmth. He pulled a blanket over them both, and they kissed, their lips apart. They went slowly now, having discovered on their own how to kiss deeply and well. She wondered if he could taste himself as he kissed her and, if so, what he might think about that.

They had not returned to the dugout in the ballfield since that time two weeks before. Bobby had looked around for a nicer rendezvous for them in what little spare time he had, and he'd found a likely house just short of where Spruce Street came to a dead end east of McAndrew. Nobody else had ever claimed the house, nor had anyone ever looted or salvaged it; it was possible that the town salvage committee had targeted the house for later work. No one was living in the neighborhood presently.

There was no indication of what might have happened to the people who had once lived in the house. Bobby had found its roof and windows intact and so the furniture, even if terribly dusty, had at least been kept out of the weather. Bobby's careful exploration of the place had turned up no sign of animals or pests, but some long-undisturbed tracks in the dust and the rumpled condition of the big bed in the house's one bedroom told Bobby that he and Stephanie would not be the first couple to use the house, although they would be the first in something like their own lifetimes.

The bed was in excellent shape. Although the cotton sheets had turned fragile and the foam in the pillows had grown brittle, the blankets were of a bulky synthetic that was of no interest to moths. Bobby had scrounged some additional bedding from his parents' attic—nothing that would be missed, or at least not right away—and had set up a nest for himself and Stephanie.

For her part, Stephanie liked the house very much, and already thought of it as their place. She hoped Bobby would suggest before too long that they file a formal claim on it over at Town Hall. That would not only get them the house free and clear, but it would also make Bobby-and-Steffie an official fact; filing on the house would be exactly equivalent to announcing their engagement. It was a tricky thing, though. She had to wait for Bobby to come up with the idea; suggesting it herself might drive him away.

She was supposed to have gotten her period by now, but there was no sign of it.

Stephanie could imagine her and Bobby homesteading the house, and their friends moving into other houses in the neighborhood as they, too, paired off and got married. She and Bobby would be the first on this end of Spruce Street, though. Nobody had lived around there in quite some time, but it was far away enough from the section of town where almost everyone else lived to make it attractive to the new generation.

On some fronts, things between Bobby and Stephanie were going well. For instance, Bobby had come to feel so secure that he had not bothered to sneak out his bedroom window that night. He had simply said good night to his parents, told them he'd be back to do his morning chores, and left the LeClerc home through the front door. Stephanie thought the world of Bobby for having had the balls to do that, because it brought Bobby-and-Steffie even closer to reality. She also knew it would help reassure Mike.

Stephanie remembered the time Maria Tirello had finally surrendered her cherry to her long-time boyfriend, Sam Barnaby. Maria's father had found out about it almost immediately, and he'd gone absolutely rabies. The old man had hauled out the family shotgun, and Sam and Maria had gotten married right away. That was what Maria had wanted all along—as had her father, because Sam's father was a successful fisherman who maintained crews on Serpent Lake and the Ausable River. Sam would inherit the business, and that meant Maria was set for life. Stephanie thought it was too bad that Mike wasn't the kind to brandish a shotgun. It would make things so much simpler.

To tell the truth, Stephanie was bored. The first wild rush of heat between her and Bobby had passed long ago, to be replaced by a pallid sort of sameness. They met almost every night to do it and it felt good, but five minutes later there seemed to be nothing. Was that supposed to be the way things were supposed to be for the next forty years? Why was it that, five minutes after doing it with Bobby, she felt like going for a long walk by herself?

Bobby suddenly snored, as he usually did when he dozed off on his back. Half-asleep herself, Stephanie nudged him, and he stirred. "TV's nothing but news," he slurred.

"Huh?"

"See if MTV's on, okay?"

"Bobby?"

He started and came fully awake. "What—? Oh, Stef. Hi. Sorry. I dozed off, I guess."

"What were you talking about?"

"I was talking about something?"

"About, um, TV, I think you said. Television?"

He looked at her. "Yeah," he said, barely remembering. "I was dreaming that I was watching a television." He blinked. "What I wanted to see wasn't there, though. It wasn't *on*, I mean. At least, I don't think it was. Funny."

"Hmmm? What's funny?"

"The TV. The picture on it was flat, like a photograph in a magazine. It moved, all right, but it was flat as cow flop."

"So?"

She felt him shrug. "So I always thought a TV was like a little theater—you know, like a stage you could look *into* instead of *at*. If you saw a room, it was really a room—maybe a tiny one, but just like a room all the same, and you could see everything that was going on in it. Know what I mean?''

She thought about it. ''You mean like looking inside a dollhouse?'' she asked.

''Yeah, that's what I mean,'' he said, gesturing. ''Deepness. There wasn't any deepness to it.''

''Who were you talking to in your dream?'' she asked.

''My mom,'' he said, suddenly remembering. ''I was talking to my mom. We were in the living room. Jesus, that's funny, too.''

''What is?''

''The room,'' he said. ''The lights were on—the old electrical ones, I mean. You know, with the glass bulbs and all?''

''That's quite a dream you had,'' Stephanie said.

''I guess it was,'' Bobby said, ''but it's not real important right now.'' He put an arm around her and she snuggled against him, suddenly feeling closer to him. After a moment, she kissed him quickly on his chest and, laughing, flipped onto her back, pulling the blanket off them both. When he rolled on top of her, she put her hands on his shoulders and gently urged him down her body.

''My turn now,'' she said.

Ben answered his door quickly. ''Good evening, sir,'' he said to Ed. ''I thought it might be you. C'mon in and make yourself comfortable.''

''I brought a friend,'' Ed said, holding up the jar.

''Any friend of yours is a friend of mine,'' Ben said, and Ed noticed a bit of strain in his voice. Ben went on ahead into the living room and, crouching to light a taper from the glowing coals in the hearth, lighted several fat candles here and there around the room. Together, the individually flickering candles provided a low but steady light.

Ed looked around. ''Is Connie up, too?''

Ben's lips tightened. "Connie's not here tonight."

"Oh."

"She's a grown woman."

"She's a good one, too—and I think she knows what she's doing."

"I hope so," Ben said. "If he leaves her again, I'll kill him."

"He didn't know the last time, Ben—and he had to go off with his father. He's a fine man. Everybody in town thinks the world of him."

"I think I've been real patient with him."

"You've been a goddamn saint," Ed said.

They stood together for a moment in the deepening silence of night.

"Look out the window," Ben said softly. "I was watching before you got here. Look toward the center of town."

Ed did. Lights were burning throughout Mc-Andrew. He saw two more appear even as he watched. "It must be two-thirty in the morning," he almost whispered. "What the hell is going on?"

"I'm not sure," Ben said. "I'm not sure at all but, whatever it is, it's waking everybody up." He paused. "Why are *you* up, Ed?"

Ed shrugged. "I had a bad dream and couldn't get back to sleep, that's all."

"So did I. Ed?"

"Hmmm?" He was still looking out the window, thinking.

"Let me give you a word, and don't you go thinking I'm crazy."

"A word?"

"A proper noun. The name of a place. The word is 'Amsterdam.' "

Ed swung around. "What?"

" 'Amsterdam,' " Ben repeated. "It means something to you, doesn't it, Ed? That was what your dream was about. The attack on Amsterdam."

Ed could only nod.

"Something very odd is happening," Ben said. "Why don't you unscrew the cap of that jar there, and we'll talk about it a little."

"Suits me just fine." They sat in two comfortable chairs near the fireplace.

"You want a glass?" Ben asked.

"Hell with it," Ed said, and handed the jar to Ben for the first gulp.

Priscilla Neary was up again, alone as ever with her pain, sitting next to the fire, her Ibsen open facedown on the arm of her chair, just where she'd left it when she'd retired for the night. She picked it up again and began to read.

Miss Neary had been awakened a little while before by a vivid dream about something. It had been about some kind of war with tanks and parachutists and Russians in it, but she was fast forgetting the details. She thought the war was happening somewhere in Holland, a place she'd only read about.

It had been a strong dream, strong enough to awaken her and send her sitting by the fireside. It hadn't been a bad dream, though, not really. That was because, in it, she wasn't hurting even a little bit. In her dream, she didn't have cancer.

"You were nowhere around, Digger," Annie whispered. "It was *him*."

"Him? You mean Freddie?"

"Him. The bastard was watching TV and drinking a bottle of beer. He drank and belched and farted and drank some more. He smelled bad, too. I wanted to watch the news, but Freddie wouldn't let me. I remember I had a big purple mark on my arm. He'd given it to me a few days ago, and it still hurt a lot. I don't know where the boys were. Maybe they were hiding from him. He kept yelling for them to come on out.''

''Did they?''

Annie shuddered. ''I don't know,'' she said. ''Digger, I didn't feel like I could do anything to stop him. I was just waiting for him to hit me or the boys again. It was like—it was like it was before you came. What was your dream like?''

''I don't know exactly where I was, either,'' Digger said, ''but I was in bed in a room, and it was noisy outside. There were lights coming through the window, too—red, green, blue, you name it. I didn't like it at all. I was just lying there in the dark, alone, waiting for sleep to come. I didn't even know you existed.'' He reached out and brushed her tangled hair away from her brow. ''It was just a nightmare, that's all,'' he said. ''It was just a couple of nightmares.''

There was a muffled sound from across the room, where Justin was bedded down. He was beginning to moan in his sleep.

Jess Harper came awake slowly. He'd just had the most boring dream about lying somewhere and not doing anything but stare at a ceiling. He couldn't see very well in the dream, and he'd felt awful. There'd been strange mechanical sounds all around him, and the echoing sounds of the voices of strangers. The presence of sound struck him as strange; he couldn't remember ever dreaming sounds before.

The bedroom was dimly lighted by the rising moon. Jess looked across at the other twin bed and saw Sammie on her side, sleeping peacefully. He felt much better seeing her there. He turned over and went back to sleep himself.

''You were watching TV?'' Connie whispered. ''So was I. But I don't know where I was.''

''I was in a motel room somewhere,'' Jake said. ''I

think it might even have been somewhere around here. The motel had cable, so I was watching the news.''

''They had what?''

''Cable,'' he said, not really knowing what it meant himself. ''It had cable. I was watching the news about Amsterdam.''

''So was I,'' she said. ''I was watching with my parents at the house. It seemed so *real*. It still does.'' Clutching one of the blankets against her, she sat up in order to look out the window. ''Jake, what's happening?'' she asked. ''The whole town seems to be up. There's lights going on all over. Jake, *what is going on?*''

''I don't know.'' He sat up with her and held her close to him, feeling her fear. It was no greater than his.

''The television was working again, and I was sitting in the living room with Bobby and watching it,'' Millie LeClerc told her husband. ''There was a man down in New York City talking about a war. Then the phone rang, just like when we were kids, and I was talking to somebody.'' She sounded very positive about it.

''Thass innersting,'' Dick said groggily. ''Can we go back t'sleep now?'' He turned over, away from her. ''Put the candle out, okay?''

''But it seemed so *real*!'' she insisted. ''And there was something else wrong, too, but I can't quite put my finger on it.''

''Thass innersting, too. Can we talk about it inna mornin'? Please?'' He burrowed deeper into his pillow.

''I never saw such an uncurious man in all my life,'' Millie said to his back. ''That was the oddest dream I ever had, and you're totally ignoring it.''

''G'night, Millie,'' he mumbled in reply. ''I love

you.'' He made kissy sounds into the depths of his pillow.

''I love you, too,'' she said, and she bent to kiss the back of his neck. She left their bed as quietly as she could and, taking the candle, went across the hall to check on the boys—on Randy, she corrected herself.

Millie opened the door and peered into the boys' bedroom. She frowned at the sight of Bobby's empty bed, but that was a sight she apparently was going to have to get used to. She watched the sleeping form of her younger son in the other bed. If Randy had been at all disturbed, the moment had passed. He was sleeping soundly and easily; his breathing was regular and steady.

She smiled and began to shut the door—until she suddenly remembered just what the man on the phone had told her.

CHAPTER 13

THE NEXT MORNING, STANDING IN THE PULPIT OF the First Methodist Church, Jake Garfield looked out over the congregation. He hoped his nervousness didn't show. Preaching was a lot different from singing. Jake felt that, when he was singing, God wasn't looking over his shoulder quite so closely.

The church was more than half filled, which Jake took as a good sign. He knew that the church attracted far fewer people on a typical Sunday. Jake's friends had come today, of course, and apparently the mere prospect of something new and different had been enough to draw a number of the curious.

Jake scratched his bare chin. The pale man he'd seen in the mirror that morning had looked like a stranger . . . and, yet, strangely like his father, too. Connie said getting rid of his beard had emphasized his eyes. She liked his eyes—and there she was now, front pew center, looking into them.

Jake saw that some of the other people in the church

were nudging each other and muttering. Some wore knowing smiles. He supposed that his shaving was as good as announcing his intention to stay in town and marry Connie, which was fine with him—but he worried about what Prosper might think. His partner still hadn't arrived home by the time he and Connie had had to leave for church, and it appeared that he wouldn't be on time for the service, either.

In front of him on the lectern was his Bible, which was a very old and battered one. What was left of the gold debossing on its tattered brown cover said that it had once been placed by the Gideons, whoever they might have been. Jake had seen a few other such Bibles. Apparently the Gideon family had caused so many Bibles to be placed that a number of them had survived Armageddon. Now *that* was impressive.

Although it was Sunday and this was at least nominally a Christian church, there had been no preliminary singing of hymns, nor had Jake led any prayers. Jake's plans called for the congregation to simply sit together for awhile, in peace, while he talked to them. Unfortunately, he wasn't thinking much about his sermon. He was thinking about Connie and the possibility of financing a lease on the old carpentry shop in Neary Square with some of those IOUs he'd collected.

He felt as if he finally belonged somewhere again.

"Good morning, everyone," he began. "Thank you for asking me to share your service with you today. I don't see this opportunity you've given me as a chance for me to lecture you on your responsibilities to God. That would be pretty arrogant on my part, considering I don't know anything about that. Instead, I see this as another way we can get to know each other in, I hope, a spirit of fellowship. A church is a pretty good setting for that, but so is a songfest in Neary Square, or a quiet walk along the shore of Serpent Lake on a cool, clear evening. But here we are.

"I don't know or care much about religion," he

went on. "Faith's one thing; religion's another. My father and mother were of different religions, and I wasn't raised in one at all. I've read the Bible, though. There's things in it that comfort me, and there's other things that scare me half to death. Here's one of the scary things, from Isaiah, chapter one, verse seven: *'Your country is desolate, your cities are burned with fire: your land, strangers devour it in your presence, and it is desolate, as overthrown by strangers.'*

"Here's verse nine, just a little below that: *'Except the Lord of hosts had left unto us a very small remnant, we should have been as Sodom, and we should have been like unto Gomorrah.'*

"And then there's chapter twenty-four, verse three: *'The land shall be utterly emptied, and utterly spoiled: for the Lord hath spoken this word.'*

"And verse six, same chapter: *'Therefore hath the curse devoured the earth, and they that dwell therein are desolate: therefore the inhabitants of the earth are burned, and few men left.'* "

Jake paused. "I guess we know what Bible prophecy looks like from the inside, don't we?" he said, and he saw them nod in sad agreement. "Our cities were burned with fire; we are indeed a very small remnant; and our land is the next best thing to being utterly empty and spoiled. I guess the only thing we've missed out on are those invaders devouring our land, but that's only because *their* cities got burned and all the rest of it, too. As far as anyone knows, we never even attempted to invade each other. We just destroyed ourselves with fire, and let it go at that." He paused. "We are left to wonder how it happened that we came to do it."

He looked around the room. "I see that many of you here are old enough to remember for yourselves the outbreak of Kingdom Come," he continued. "I do, too, but I was very young and didn't understand. My father told me that, when the war became inevitable, some religious people believed that it was a *good* thing, because it would usher in the Millennium. Jesus would appear, prevent the outbreak of hostilities at the last minute, and rule the Earth for a thousand years through a perfect government based in Jerusalem.''

Jake shook his head. ''It didn't happen that way, of course, even though most folks I've met still refer to the war as Kingdom Come, just as a kind of shorthand. So do I. Many of the same people who used to talk about the Millennium now say that it's still coming, but it won't get here anytime soon. It won't come, they say, until a long, long time from now, after the world has been repopulated and rebuilt, and humanity faces a similar or even worse crisis than we did back in 1962.''

He paused. ''If you thought these were the end times, they're not. The prophecy of another Kingdom Come is not entirely pessimistic—not at all. It carries the conviction that humanity has a long and prosperous future ahead of it, maybe even enough of a future to climb back up to where we were. Maybe even beyond.''

Jake shook his head and sighed. ''I think it's possible, even probable, that we will not be able to do that,'' he said. ''We have hurt ourselves and our world too badly to be sure of what might happen to us next. We have few children to carry on for us. Even the animals bear very few young. We all seem to be dying in little pieces, and we're taking a long time to do it.''

He let them think about that for a moment, and then he went on. ''We still haven't taken full responsibility for what we did to ourselves,'' he said. ''Some of us still blame God for having let such an awful thing like Kingdom Come happen. We're like the drunk who steals a horse, gets into an accident, and then blames the man who owns the horse for making it so available.

''We have to say it plainly, and we have to believe

it in our hearts," Jake continued. "God didn't cause the war. We did. We acted according to our free will and we dropped the bombs, or else we paid the taxes that allowed those bombs to be built. We put the guns in the hands of the people who pulled the triggers. Even those of us too young to have had anything to do with the war, except to be its continuing victims, have to share some of the blame for it if we fail to recognize where the responsibility for the war lies. The war is not an issue for my generation, no—but the same evil that prompted the war is in us, too.

"It's we who say that an omnipotent God should have been powerful enough to prevent the war," he said, "and it's we who then turn around and blame God for not having done anything to stop it. Well, we're dead wrong on both those points. *God has limits.* He may indeed be able to make a rock so heavy that He himself can't lift it, as the philosophers used to argue, but there is something He cannot do: He cannot overcome the free will of humanity. He may be bound by nothing else except that, but make no mistake: *He is bound by that.* It is not that God would not stop the bombs from falling; it is that He could not. If we decide to do wrong, God is as helpless as we are when a hot rain takes our crops or a fire destroys our homes. About all He can do is mitigate the consequences . . . but there are so many, many consequences to our actions that perhaps not even God can keep up. We killed the beautiful Earth even as we killed ourselves."

Jake grew thoughtful. "I sometimes wonder how the people who my dad said used to blame God for letting Hiroshima and Nagasaki happen would feel these days. Would they still think God is just as bad as He ever was . . . or would they think He's a hundred million times worse?"

* * *

"Not bad, Reverend," Connie told him outside, after the service.

"You can't kid me," Jake said mournfully. "I was awful. And I'm no reverend, either. I'm more of an irreverend."

"Far from it," Connie said. "Really, Jake. You made me think about some things I'd never bothered to think about before."

He smiled. "You're good for me, you know that?"

"I try."

Someone tapped Jake insistently on his shoulder, and he turned. It was Amanda Broom and her daughter, Sarah. Mother and daughter were dressed nearly identically, and in a way that looked too matronly for Sarah and much too virginal for her mother.

"Hello, Mrs. Broom, Sarah," Jake said politely. "Thank you for coming."

"I wouldn't have missed your little talk for the world," Amanda said positively. "Neither would my Sarah. Would you, darling?"

"I liked your sermon very much," the girl began shyly. "I especially liked the part about—"

"Well, then," Amanda said briskly. "When are you going to favor us again, Mr. Garfield?"

"I don't know, Mrs. Broom. I suppose I will whenever they'll have me."

"That will be soon, I trust." Amanda turned to her daughter. "Say goodbye now, Sarah. We must get along home. Mr. Garfield, perhaps you might drop by for dinner one of these evenings? My Sarah is quite a cook."

"Yes," Jake said. "We'll have to do that. Uh, Sarah, have you—"

"Uh, no," Sarah said. "No, I haven't. I will."

"Eh?" Amanda said. "Will what?"

"No time like the present," Jake told Sarah, ignoring her mother.

"Sarah, follow me," Mrs. Broom said. "We have

others of our dear friends to see. Good morning to you, Mr. Garfield.'' Amanda left with Sarah in tow. The girl glanced back at Jake, who nodded and smiled at her and gave her a little wave that he hoped was encouraging.

"What am I, cow flop?'' Connie said. "I was standing *right here*, and she completely ignored me! Jesus, that woman burns my butt.''

"I guess she sees you as competition for Sarah,'' Jake said.

"Or herself,'' Connie suggested. "C'mon, Rev. There's others of your dear friends waiting to bend your ear.''

Sarah Broom suddenly spotted Bobby LeClerc standing with his brother and parents near the steps of the church. Apparently his father was waiting for a chance to talk to Jake. More important, Bobby was not with Stephanie.

"Excuse me, Mother,'' Sarah said. "I'll just be a minute.''

"What's the matter?'' Amanda asked. "We have to see the Mahlers. They're standing right over there.''

"I, uh, I have to give a message to the LeClercs.''

"What? What kind of a message?''

"It's for Bobby, Mother. It won't take long. I'll be right back.''

"We have to say hello to the Mahlers,'' Amanda said stubbornly. "It just wouldn't do if we didn't.''

"I'll be right back, Mother.'' Without stopping to think another second about it, Sarah walked away quickly. She could hear her mother burble in studied outrage, but what Sarah had to do was important— important enough for her to be willing to face the bullying displeasure of her mother and, even worse, the humiliation she might receive from Bobby. It didn't matter, though. Sarah knew that Jake was right, that if she didn't get what she had to say to Bobby said, it would stay with her and worry at her innards for the rest of her life.

"Hello, Mr. LeClerc, Mrs. LeClerc," Sarah said. "Hi, Bobby, Randy."

"Hello, Sarah," Millie said. Sarah thought she looked tired and upset. "How are you, and how's your mother?"

"We're fine, thank you. Uh, Bobby, could I talk to you a second?"

"Sure," the boy shrugged. "Mom, Dad? Excuse us?"

"Surely," Dick said. "We'll say hello to Jake for you."

"Thanks. Come on, Sarah."

They walked across the street and into Neary Square. "What is it, Sarah?" Bobby asked.

Sarah had never been so nervous in her whole life. "I'm afraid you'll think I'm stupid," she said.

"No, I won't."

"I needed to know something, that's all."

"What?"

She paused for a moment and then blurted, "Why didn't we ever see each other again after we went to that picnic last spring? I thought we had a pretty good time, didn't we?"

"We had a good time," he said, shrugging. "Look, Sarah, that's ancient history."

"Is it?" she asked.

"Uh, yeah. Yes, it is."

"Because you're seeing Stephanie?"

"That's part of it."

She looked down at the ground. "Bobby, I have to tell you something."

"Hmmm?"

They stopped walking. "I wanted you to know something," she said, looking into his eyes. "If you ever want me or need me to be there for you, I will be. I'm not looking for a piece of your father's store,

I'm not looking to inherit your house, and I'm not looking to be the first girl on my block to get a husband so all my friends can envy me and some man can take care of me.''

''Now wait a minute—''

''No, Bobby,'' Sarah said, holding up a hand. ''I need to say this. I love you, and I have for a long time. What I wanted to tell you was that if you ever want me, you can be sure of me. Lead me and I'll follow you anywhere, no questions asked and no grudges held.''

Bobby looked at her, and tears sprang into Sarah's eyes. ''I'm going to hate myself in five minutes for having told you any of this,'' she continued. ''I'm going to feel really ugly and stupid, but I had to tell you. It'd be worse for me if I didn't. I'll go now, Bobby. I'm sorry I ever bothered you.''

''Sarah, wait—''

''Gotta go,'' she said in a choked voice. She ran off.

Bobby watched her go. He wished she'd given him the chance to tell her that he did not think she was either ugly or stupid. He did not quite know what to think at that moment, but he certainly was not thinking anything like that. He rejoined his family in front of the church, still puzzled.

Late in the day, some of the men were sitting on boxes and crates around one of the pickle barrels at LeClerc's.

Doc was leaning back, comfortably balanced on the rear legs of a sturdy cane chair. He took a big bite out of a sour pickle that was crisp and dripping with juice. ''I say it's wish fulfillment, and I say the hell with it,'' he said, his mouth full. He waved the stump of pickle at his black bag, which was resting on Dick's countertop. ''I've seen three semi-hysterical people already this morning,'' he added. ''They think they're going crazy or catching some sort of dreaming disease the Russians let loose. How am I supposed to deal with all that?''

"I've been dreaming right along," Ed said, "and all the dreams are about the same goddamn thing. I started out having dreams about little things like working at the newspaper and watching color TV at home and going for a drive in a car and like that, and now I've got these huge, bothersome dreams about wars and everything. It's like dreaming in whatchamacallit— in Technicolor or something.'' He spread his arms wide. "I mean, it's like one of those movies they used to show on a really wide screen. Remember *Spartacus*? It's like that. Anyway, every time I sleep— napping or overnight—I have to watch more of this goddamn epic in my head, and I can't leave the theater. And I *want* to leave the theater, believe me.''

"Me, too," Ben chimed in. "I'm not sleeping very well at all, and it's getting worse.''

"Coincidence," Doc said around another mouthful of pickle. He waved the stump of it at the mayor. "Ben, what happens is that you tell Ed about your dream, and the next night he follows up on it with his own version. Guess what happens? You both wind up having the 'same' dream, except that it's not.''

"That's not the way it happened, Doc," Ben said. "Ed and I dreamed the same exact details. We sat up all night discussing it.''

Doc shook his head. "While passing a jar back and forth, I'll bet.''

"So?''

"So I'm near enough right so as not to matter," he said. "Look, Ben, you're worried about Connie. Ed, you're probably worried about something, too—''

"No, I'm not," Ed said stubbornly. "I'm not worried about a goddamn thing.''

"—but even if you weren't, I'd have to say that this whole dream thing is just a crazy coincidence. The subconscious is a wild and woolly place, and this American Jubilee thing has stirred up a lot of old feelings on one side or the other. People are going to work it out in their heads somehow—and don't you ever underestimate the power of suggestion. There's one good thing about all this, though."

"What's that?" Ben asked.

"All the talk about dreaming has driven that nonsense about going down to the Jubilee out of the public mind," Doc said, grinning. "It's becoming a dead issue."

"It's not dead," Ben insisted stubbornly. "It's only dozing for a while. We've got plenty of time to settle it."

"No one's interested anymore," Doc said. "Forget it."

"Thank God," said Ed. "But I don't buy all this mass-hysteria bullshit you're trying to serve up, Doc."

"I don't know," Dick said, "Doc could be right; the Jubilee sure stirred up a lot of old feelings. That certainly might account for all this dream talk. Me, I'd been having dreams, too, but I slept like a baby last night. This'll pass."

"I don't buy it," Ed said. "People all over town are dreaming about the *same things*. It's just not natural."

"Seems natural enough to me, under the circumstances," Doc said. "People are dreaming about some war, and they're helping each other fill in the details without realizing it."

"They're not dreaming about any kind of war I ever heard of," Ed said.

"Oh, really?" Doc replied. "You've got Russians invading Holland, for example. Now, doesn't an invasion of Holland sound the least little bit familiar? Think back to 1940."

"Those were Germans," Ed said patiently, as if explaining things to an idiot. "These are Russians."

"So what?" Doc said. "You've substituted Russians for Germans, but there they are, taking over Amsterdam just like the Germans did. No difference."

"But everything's so *real*, Doc," Ben said. "I can even tell you the name of the guy who's on the news program I've been watching."

"Tom Brokaw," Ed supplied. "Gray-haired guy, right?"

"Right," Ben said, nodding, "except that I think he's beginning to dye it."

Ed nodded. "I watch Brokaw, too, just like Ben does—except when I'm watching CNN, that is."

"See?" Ben said, nodding quickly. "Now, I like Brokaw better than that new guy who's on CBS—" Suddenly Ben stopped. He looked a bit puzzled.

"What the hell are you talking about?" Doc asked.

Ben scratched his head. "I'm not sure," he said, "but whatever it is, it's rattling around in there somewhere, and it wants to get out."

"Because Ed or somebody else put it there," Doc insisted. "Look, gents, Ed says he likes Tom Broker and you two get together without even realizing it and embellish the whole thing with details about Broker, having gray hair and liking some other guy a little less. Hell, I remember ABC myself; I used to watch Lawrence Welk on it every Saturday night. But I never heard of any Tom Broker."

"I know what I know," Ben insisted.

"So do I," Ed said.

"The whole town's going crazy," Dick sighed.

"It'll pass," Doc said, taking another bite of his pickle.

He was wrong.

JOURNAL ENTRY
October 5

No news, unless you count mostly everyone going a little bit nuts from anxiety and lack of sleep.

Personal: I had another one of those weird dreams last night. I feel a little guilty about using up ribbon and paper recording things like dreams, but I've come to think it's important, no matter what Doc and some of the others say. This time I wrote down what I could remember of it before I forgot, but I couldn't remember much, anyway. I was back at the paper again and there were a lot of people around, people I'd known for years—although, remembering back, I couldn't tell you who even one of them was. Not one. There were electric lights, too, and they were all on, and most of the desks had little TVs on them, except the TVs didn't show pictures, but words that you typed on a keyboard wired into the TV . . . little amber words glowing on a dead black screen.

Crazy, just crazy. I wish I understood.

—E.P.

CHAPTER 14

IT WAS FULL LIGHT NOW, BUT BOBBY LECLERC WAS still sleeping. Stephanie left their bed and, naked, paddled across the chilly floor and out into the dim hallway to the bathroom.

She closed the door and stood in front of the sink. There was a big mirror over it, and the frosted window admitted enough of the morning light for her to see her reflection pretty well. She turned sideways to the mirror and stared. Nothing showed, of course, but that didn't stop her from looking.

Maybe it wouldn't show much. Some girls—*women*, she corrected herself—some *women* never showed much at all. Others swelled up like crazy, and some of them stayed swelled up forever. Well, *she* certainly wouldn't do *that* . . . but she suddenly wondered what she would look like with stretch marks, and she frowned. She hadn't thought of that before.

Maybe there was just a *little* bit of a bulge . . . but

she really didn't think so. It was 'way too early for that.

God, he's such a jerk, she realized. She was committed now, though, and there was little else she could have done in the first place. After all, her daddy was dying. *Why did it have to be like this?* she wondered sadly. She had the vaguest memory of a place where it wasn't like this, not at all, and she desperately wished that she knew how to get there.

The bathroom door suddenly opened. "Oops," Bobby said, sticking his head in. "Sorry. Didn't know you were in here."

"Don't you even know enough to knock on a closed bathroom door?" she blazed. "Where were you raised, in a goddamn *barn* or something?"

"Doesn't seem to me you're doing anything that requires knocking," Bobby said sourly. "You're just looking at yourself in the mirror again."

"No, I wasn't!"

"C'mon, Stef. The lid's still down."

"Whatever I do in here is *my* business, and don't forget it!"

"Really?" he said. "Jesus, we're getting pretty particular, aren't we? *Last* week you wanted me to watch when—"

"Just shut up and get the fuck out of here!"

"My pleasure," he said. "Just tell me one thing."

She waited, scowling, her arms crossed under her breasts.

"Just tell me," he continued, "why you've become such a total witch. Just tell me that, okay?"

"Bastard!" she screamed, kicking the door closed. Bobby pulled back before it could hit him.

Standing there, she listened as his footsteps receded down the hall. After just barely enough time had gone by for someone to pull on a shirt and a pair of pants and slip on a pair of moccasins, she heard the front door open and then slam shut.

Stephanie sat naked on the cold toilet lid and, after a quiet moment, she hugged her knees to her chest and began crying softly in the way a young girl cries when she hears that someone who is a stranger to her has died, yet she is moved nonetheless.

Bobby was more than an hour overdue at the store and he knew that, by now, his father must have gone absolutely rabies about it. Bobby was all done with that, though. The knapsack he was wearing said so. He had, finally, had enough. He was done with reacting. Now he would act.

It wasn't hard for Bobby to guess that she would be in or near her house, because that was where she usually was . . . and, indeed, he found her sitting on the patio swing and knitting something warm and practical while humming a sweet song he didn't recognize. It was precisely the way he had expected to find her.

"Sarah?" he called quietly.

She looked up from her knitting. The bright sun made her squint. "Hello, Bobby," she said. She did not seem the least bit surprised to see him or his knapsack.

"Your mom home?"

"She went down to your dad's store. She won't be back for a couple of hours."

"Good. Mind if I come on up?"

"Please," she said. "Sit yourself down here." She scrunched over on the swing to make room for him. He slid his arms from the straps of the knapsack and let it fall to the porch floorboards a foot or two in front of the swing.

They were both quiet for the first few minutes.

"How's Stephanie?" Sarah asked at last, her eyes still carefully on her knitting.

"Who cares?" he shrugged, looking here and there and everywhere but at her.

She dropped a stitch. "Oh," she said.

They were both silent after that for a fairly long time, neither one quite daring to put into words the next and most necessary thing. Finally, though, it was he who said, "You made me an offer yesterday. Outside the church, I mean."

Sarah put down her knitting and looked him in the eye. "Yes, I did."

"Mean it?" he asked.

She didn't hesitate. "Yes."

"Okay, then," he said. He sounded relieved. "I want to leave town right now."

"All right," she said quietly. "There are some things I want to bring with me, though."

"No problem, so long as we travel light."

"Fine," she said. "Come on inside, then. While I'm packing, you can tell me where we're going. Uh, just one thing."

"What's that?"

Sarah hesitated, and then took the plunge. "I want us to stop first at Jake Garfield's place down the street," she said. "He's home now; I heard him working over there."

It took Bobby a moment to realize what she intended. "Um, Sarah," he said, "we could probably find a preacher on the road somewhere. Jake's not really ordained, you know. Your mom's going to have enough trouble with all of this—"

"That's not important," she said briskly. "Jake Garfield knows the words, and he's a good and special man, and that's more than enough for *me*. Besides, we wouldn't find any sort of preacher on the road before tonight, now, would we?"

"No," he said, and then he smiled. "No, we wouldn't, would we? Okay."

"So that's settled," she said, smiling back. "Now let's get me packed and us both on our way. All right?"

"All right." Bobby suddenly noticed that Sarah had

a beautiful smile. They kissed almost chastely, and then they went inside to gather Sarah's things.

Priscilla Neary closed the front door behind her, shutting out the sun. She leaned back against the door and sighed, closing her eyes and surrendering at last to the pain. A sudden, bad twinge turned her sigh into a gasp and then into a small moan. Then it passed.

Still leaning against the door, the teacher unbuttoned her father's rough denim jacket. She did not bother to take it off. She would not be home for very long.

One of the children had anonymously left an apple, of all things, on her desk that morning, and had even taken the trouble to shine it with mayonnaise. It gleamed as if it had been waxed. Miss Neary put the apple and the rest of her things on the table just inside the front door and went into the living room.

Miss Neary had nothing left in her to give. In the past month, she had come to understand with a grudging acceptance the inevitability of her condition. She had held on because, despite everything, she had remained reluctant to take that final walk in the woods. Miss Neary had always been a practical sort who found the unknown intolerable . . . and death was the biggest unknown of them all. Pain was a known thing and could be borne, but only up to a point, and she had now passed that point. She had lost more than eight pounds in the past week. It had become very hard for her even to breathe, and she was feverish more often than not. She imagined that the organs inside her chest must be turning into something like wet cardboard, ready to burst and fall apart should she cough too hard or inhale too deeply.

She had sent the children home early that day, although she had taken care to let none of them guess exactly what was wrong. She would also have to skip Prosper's reading lesson that afternoon. Her pupils no doubt suspected something was up, but they certainly expected to return to class the next day. There would be no school and no lesson for Prosper tomorrow, however, because Miss Neary would not be there to teach it . . . and there might never be school again, either, because she had no one to take things over for her. The town had long ago decided that while it was happy to have Miss Neary, it would not support a second teacher. Miss Neary had often thought that Connie Matthews would have done well as her assistant and eventual successor, but it was not to be.

The town might well decide to make an attempt to keep things going, but Miss Neary knew that the school would soon die. This was not a world friendly to things like schools and learning. Those parents who objected to mandatory school attendance because they wanted their children to stay home and work would soon enough win their point, without her around to fight them. The town would seize upon the opportunity to expand the number of work hours school-age children owed the town, without her to raise Cain about it. Without her around, the town would repeal its truancy laws, and that would be the beginning of McAndrew's long-delayed surrender to the end of everything. The school would no longer be the same strong institution that she had brought safely through the crisis that had shattered the world. Miss Neary hoped the school would not close, but it was a faint hope . . . and, given the way things were, she could not really blame anyone.

Miss Neary knew that someone had been teaching school in McAndrew continuously since the end of the eighteenth century, ever since the day when a Quaker missionary had opened a school in a three-walled cabin right by Serpent Lake, in order to serve the children of trappers. Miss Neary hated to put an end to a record such as that . . . but she was so tired, so very tired, and there was no one to whom she could pass the burden.

It was time for her to take that final walk. She was just strong enough to manage it, and she needed to do it now, before it was too late. In accordance with custom, she would leave a note expressing her intentions and requesting that no search be made for her body.

Before she left, though, she wanted to take a last look around the house. She had always lived there and had never known another home. The living room was still full of her parents' things. There was, for instance, the old clock on the mantelpiece. It had stopped at seventeen after three on some afternoon about thirty years before, around the time her parents had died, and rewinding it had done no good. She had never noticed the clock ticking, but she missed the sound for many months after it had stopped.

Miss Neary walked slowly around the room, running a finger over some of the many small porcelain figurines her mother had collected during the years before and during her marriage. The little shelves her mother had mounted here and there in the living room were filled with them. She *tsk*'d as her finger came away from one of the shelves slightly dusty, and she suddenly realized that she had not cleaned the room for about three weeks because she had not been feeling well. She suddenly wished that she had managed to dust; she would have liked to have left a cleaner house behind.

Her mother's favorite figurines were kept on shelves hung in the far corner of the room, over the television set. There were little birds and kittens and, here and there, a celebrity: several of the Seven Dwarves, Paul Bunyan, and Bambi. There was also an Eiffel Tower and a set that was Miss Neary's favorite of them all: a sleeping mama beagle with three little puppies nestled against her for warmth. All the dogs had their eyes closed, and their mouths were open in little O's of sleep. Miss Neary picked up one of the puppies and stroked its tiny head with a forefinger for just a moment, and then she carefully put it back with its mother.

Her father's small study was just off the living room. This room was where he had worked at home both before and after the war, and it was from here that he'd run the town from the time of Kingdom Come until his death. One wall of the study was covered with his degrees and citations, including the one for his Silver Star; the opposite wall held framed photographs of her father with famous people. There was, for instance, a picture of her father shaking hands with a grinning Nelson Rockefeller. There was another picture of her father being sworn in by another judge. There was also a group picture of her father with Richard Nixon and some other people, perhaps from some get-together during the 1960 campaign. Miss Neary remembered that her father had sometimes wondered out loud if the Cuban crisis would have erupted into war, or even have arisen at all, if Nixon had won that election instead of the President. Since her father was an honest man, he had never come up with a satisfactory answer.

She sat at her father's desk, took a pencil from the middle drawer, and wrote a note on his yellowed stationery. It did not take her very long at all to say what she felt it necessary to say. She signed it, folded the paper over and placed it under a paperweight.

She rose from the desk and stood there for a moment, taking a last look around the study. She felt her father's presence there. She remembered being five years old and sitting right in that very same chair. Her father had stood behind her, swinging the chair around and around and rocking her back and forth in it, making the chair into a pretend-airplane just like the P-51 fighter he had lately been flying. She had been as happy as she had known how to be, because her daddy was finally home from the war with Japan and he had just finished telling her that he would never, ever have to leave her and Mama again.

But he had, and then Mama had followed him right away. She wished they were with her now, but she guessed she would be seeing them soon enough.

She left the room.

Some people had taken a final friend with them on their last walk in the woods—a razor blade or a rope, say, or even a gun. Whatever they took with them had been lost, because no search was ever made, not even to recover something irreplaceable. Some other people, more considerately, had gone into the woods with nothing except the clothes on their backs. Presumably such persons drowned themselves or jumped from a height—or perhaps they allowed themselves to die from exposure. Miss Neary did not want to take anything with her that would be missed, but neither did she want to make a messy end of things. She considered that she could drown herself in some lake or pond 'way back in the woods, but the idea of actually doing so scared her silly. She was not strong enough to swim for very long, but she might change her mind and struggle at the end, and that simply wouldn't do. The same went for jumping. She wouldn't want the chance to change her mind on the way down.

Miss Neary had already thought of a solution. There was a badly chipped drinking glass in the kitchen cupboard. She had been using the glass for years, always being careful not to cut her lips on the rim. She would take the glass with her. No one would ever miss a nearly unusable drinking glass, and a shard from it would do just as well as a razor blade against the veins in her wrists. They said killing yourself that way was just like going to sleep, once you got over the initial pain of the cuts. They also said that if you cut your wrists, you never bothered to change your mind because you got too foggy and sleepy to think much about it. Miss Neary did not question how people knew all that; she merely derived some small comfort from it.

There was just enough product left in her last jar of Jess Harper's best for a decent-sized drink. It would cut her pain. She might have taken the jar with her into the woods and had her last drink there . . . but the jar was not hers, and it was still serviceable. They would find the jar and the note she'd left and everything else in the house tomorrow, when she did not show up for school, and people would realize that she had disappeared.

Miss Neary tipped the contents of the jar into the chipped glass and drained it dry. She appreciated the glow the product made going down, and her pain receded a little bit. Then she put the glass in her jacket pocket and went to the front door. As she opened it, she suddenly remembered the apple she'd been given at the school. She would not want it to get around that she had not taken it with her. It might hurt the feelings of the child who had taken the trouble to pick it and polish it for her and, given the circumstances, it was the kind of hurt that would last the child a lifetime.

She put the apple in the other pocket of her jacket and left the house without looking back.

CHAPTER 15

RANDY LECLERC CAME HOME EARLY THAT DAY TO find an empty house. School had been only half a day because Miss Neary had unexpectedly sent everyone home at lunch time, and so the student body had taken to the streets of McAndrew in wild celebration. If days off from school were nevertheless filled with work for children, as indeed they were, at least it wasn't schoolwork.

Randy knew his father and brother would be at the store. His mother should have been somewhere around, though. Randy had noticed that his mother had been pretty upset lately. She'd been having some of those nightmares that people said were going around like some disease. Randy himself had not been having any nightmares at all. He'd been having a series of very pleasant dreams about him doing neat stuff like watching TV and playing Darkest Deepest Dungeons or Skeleton Crew on his very own Macintosh IV with the stereo surroundsound and animated desktop, but he had not dreamed last night or the night before. Most of the other kids in school, though, were still having them. They all said the adults in their dreams were real worried about something awful having to do with the Russians.

Randy grabbed an apple from the fruit bowl on the foyer table and bounded up the stairs to the room he shared with his brother. He tossed his schoolbooks and jacket carelessly on his bed. Although Bobby didn't sleep there and might never again, Randy still considered that he shared the bedroom with his brother. He was, therefore, not very surprised to find a note lying on his pillow. The surprise came a moment later.

Randy,

   I got to go now and I am taking Sarah Broom with me. We got married a few minutes ago and so now we are leaving town and finding our own place somewhere else not too far from here I hope. Sarah is here with me now and says to put down that she sends you her love. She says to say so do I. She also says to say that she is not Sarah Broom any more but Sarah LeClerc. She is right.

   We would have told you all this in person but then mom and dad would go rabies if they found us here and I don't need that and neither does Sarah and neither do you either. And they don't either, I mean.

   You are a good guy and so you take care of yourself. I hope I can see you and mom and dad again real soon for a visit. I took something of yours for a souvenir to remember you by. I hope you do not mind. You can have all my stuff I didn't take with me.

                                   —Bob

Written under that was a short addition in a neat hand.

> Hi, Randy—
>   *I'm so happy!!! Hope to see you soon!*
>   *—Your loving sister,*
>   *Sarah xxxo*

Randy read the note another three times before he managed to come up with a reaction other than complete and utter astonishment. *Sarah Broom is sure a better deal than that stupid old Stephanie Crane,* he finally managed, and in that way he discovered that he was happy for his brother—and his new sister, too.

That last thought gave him pause. He now had a sister, of all things, and he found that he liked the idea. Randy suddenly wished he had seen them off. He would have liked to have said goodbye, wished them luck.

It was then that he figured out where his mother must have gone. Bobby surely would not have failed to leave their parents a note, too—not with Sarah there to make him, that is. Randy knew that his brother would have left such a note stuck under the fruit bowl on the foyer table, because that's where he and Bobby always left notes to their parents, and Randy had seen no note. Therefore, his mother had already seen it and gone running off with it to the store.

Randy sighed and grabbed his jacket. There was no sense in waiting for everyone to come home for hell to break loose; he thought he might as well go meet it head-on.

Across town, Jake Garfield was approaching Neary Square. He knew that he must face the music sooner or later, and he wanted to get it over and done with. It was not his style to let the good people of McAndrew come find him. It did not even enter his head to let that happen, no more than it occurred to him to avoid the entire issue by simply sneaking out of town, as the kids had done.

Jake sadly realized that it was likely that the townspeople would kick him out of McAndrew. It was not inconceivable that they might even decide to hang him, although he did not really think that they would. He had, however, upset their world, and he expected to pay a heavy price for having done so.

He wished Prosper would get back from wherever it was he had gone. His partner had been gone now for two days. Prosper had done that kind of thing before without warning Jake, but not often . . . and right then Jake could have used a friend.

He had seen no one else on the streets during most of his long and lonely walk to the square—no one, that is, except for Cy Atkins, who'd been walking patrol on Sixth Street. Jake had given Cy a tentative wave, but Cy had turned his back on him.

Four blocks away from the square, though, it got less lonely. The little Jenkins boy popped out of nowhere, spotted Jake, and ran ahead toward LeClerc's, screeching, "He's coming! Jake's coming!" at the top of his lungs. Jake could hardly believe the volume of which the boy was capable.

Well, LeClerc's was where everyone would be, naturally. Word of the elopement could not have failed to roar through town like a fire through a dry woods in July. Jake had hoped to see Dick and Millie LeClerc alone first, but so be it.

Jake walked on, crossing Neary Square, and saw no one else anywhere. He stopped in front of LeClerc's, took a deep breath, and walked up the front steps and into the store. Heads swung around as the battered screen door creaked open, and silence fell.

As Jake's eyes adjusted to the relative gloom inside the store, he saw Dick and Millie standing behind the counter and a number of people, including Doc, standing in front of it. Even as Jake stood there, three more people entered the store and edged around him to join the people at the counter. The store would be pretty crowded soon.

"Good morning," Jake said softly to all of them. "Dick, Millie, we have to talk."

"It's true, isn't it," Millie said, seeing his face. Her voice shook only a little.

"Yes, it is," Jake said. The folks standing with Dick and Millie murmured and shuffled at that. "I married them a little over two hours ago," he continued, "and I wished them God's love and sent them on their way."

Dick LeClerc's mouth was a thin, white line, and his tone was biting. "Pretty goddamn nervy thing for you to do," he said, "considering you haven't even been in town very long, don't you think?"

"Easy, there, Dick," said Doc. "Let the man speak his piece."

"I'm sorry for your pain," Jake said. "I wish it could have been avoided—but, Dick, they made it very clear to me that they were going to leave anyway. I did what I thought was best for them and for you."

"Sure about that, now?" Dick said. His tone was too casual. "Couldn't even contact us about it?"

"Yes, Dick, I was sure," Jake said calmly. "I strongly suggested that Bobby and Sarah would want to talk to you two and Amanda Broom before they did anything, but neither of them was having any of that. They threatened to run out on me more than once. Bobby said they would leave anyway, whether I married them or not, because they were of age and they were going to go."

"He did?" Dick said. There was the faintest note of grudging approval in his voice, though, and Jake relaxed the tiniest bit. "So what happened?"

"I performed the ceremony, the best way I knew how," Jake said. "Afterward, they asked me for a two-hour head start, and I gave my word on it. At the end of that time, I left my house and headed straight here.''

Dick nodded slowly. "I was beginning to wonder where you were keeping yourself," he said. "I didn't have you pegged for a chickenshit."

"Thanks for that much."

"I began hearing about all this more than an hour ago," Dick continued. "I guess Bobby and Sarah told a few of their friends on their way out of town, and the word spread pretty quickly. Then Millie came in here with a note from Bobby and Sarah, telling what they'd done. So much for keeping it a secret for two hours." His eyes filled. "That's Bobby all over."

"One of the kids ran out to my place to tell me," Doc said, "figuring there'd be some sort of a fight." He held up his bag and grinned. "I brought bandages."

"There won't be any trouble, Doc," Dick said. "This is no time for trouble."

"I wish I knew Sarah better," said Millie. "I hope she's not like her mother—I mean . . .''

"She's a good girl, Millie," Jake said. "A good woman, I mean. She's kind and considerate, and she loves Bobby. They're both good people, and they'll do fine. There's a lot of strength there between them to start with, and it'll grow."

"I wish I could be sure about that," Dick said. "This is such a goddamn surprise."

"Be sure, Dick," Jake said. "It's there, all right."

"But why did they run away?" Millie asked, the tears beginning to fall again. "Why couldn't Bobby talk to us about it? Or Sarah, for that matter? And what about Stephanie Crane?"

"I don't know," said Jake. "All I can tell you is that Bobby and Sarah were in a hurry. I think Sarah was scared her mother might show up and stop them."

"Where were they going?" Dick asked.

"I don't know which way they're heading, or how

far," Jake said. "They wouldn't tell me a thing, although I pressed them on it as far as I thought I could."

"Did they have horses?" Millie asked.

"No, they didn't."

Millie turned to her husband. "Dick, if they're still on foot, we could try to catch up with them. They haven't been gone very long at all, and there's not too many ways they could have headed—"

Dick shook his head. "No," he said slowly. "No, we're not going to chase them. We'll let them go on their way."

Millie was about to say something when the screen door crashed open.

"Amanda," Doc said. "Oh, my."

"My baby!" she wailed, dramatically clasping her hands in front of her ample bosom. *"My baby!"*

"Easy, there, Amanda," a man in the group said. "She ain't dead or anything. She's just married, that's all."

"Might as well be dead," someone else snickered. "Heh."

Amanda's eyes widened as she spotted Jake Garfield. Her wailing stopped in mid-cry and her hands came up with her fingers set like claws. Her teeth were bared. It took three men to grab her and hold her back. Jake stood there passively, willing to accept whatever came his way.

"Not in the store, Amanda," Dick warned. "In fact, not anywhere. Now you calm down and be quiet."

"He ruined my baby!" she screamed, pointing a shaking finger at Jake; the men restraining her were having some trouble maintaining their hold on her. *"I'll kill him, the bastard!"*

"We could use some help here," one of the men holding Amanda said. "This woman's an armful, all right."

"Want some rope?" Doc asked.

"I'll *kill* him!" Amanda cried.

"No, you will not kill him and, no, he didn't ruin anybody," Dick told her. "Jake here performed a wedding ceremony for my son and your daughter— and at no small risk to himself, I'm beginning to see. He didn't ruin Sarah. He made things decent, by anyone's lights—even yours, Amanda, and your particular lamp's been cracked for years."

"Why, Richard LeClerc!" Amanda sputtered, shocked. "I never in my *life*—"

"Now you stop your nonsense, Amanda Broom," Millie interrupted. "The way you're carrying on, I'm beginning to appreciate just why the kids thought they had to leave town."

"He ruined my baby!"

"Oh, be still," Millie said impatiently, waving a hand. She was dry-eyed now. "We've had more than enough from you, Amanda. Why, your daughter's ten times the woman you are. I should have seen it long before this."

"Why, the *nerve*—!"

"Oh, shut up, you stupid twit," Millie said. "Jake, you sure you don't have any idea which way the children went?"

"No, Millie, I really don't."

"Too bad," she said. "I just wish I could get word to them, tell them we're happy for them and invite them to come on back. They belong here with us—"

The door opened again and everyone turned to see Mike Crane and Stephanie walk into the store. Even though she was standing there with her father's arm around her, Stephanie looked very alone.

"I just heard," she said. Then she burst into tears.

Bobby and Sarah LeClerc had cut through the woods south of McAndrew on Logger's Trail, the old dirt road that slashed through the woods west of Serpent

Lake and on through the heart of the Adirondacks. The trail had been carved out of the forest long ago for wagons and trucks, and most of it was still clear enough for hiking. Bobby had it in mind to keep on going until they reached the other end, near the town of Long Lake, forty miles away. He estimated it would take them three leisurely days of walking to do it. After that, he and Sarah would figure out where to go next. They could go anywhere, do anything, be anything. They were free.

Bobby and Sarah were already four hours out, and the terrain had been friendly. Bobby figured they'd already made about six, perhaps seven miles. His knapsack felt as light as a feather. He looked over at Sarah and smiled, and she smiled back. They'd married and run off together in haste, but it felt more and more like the right thing to have done. He tried to imagine Stephanie walking there next to him, matching him stride for stride with that smile, and he couldn't.

He had never felt like this before.

"It's very beautiful out here," Sarah said.

"Yep. Sure is."

"I love the way the sunlight sort of filters through the trees. Don't you?"

"S'nice," Bobby agreed. He spotted a long, mostly flat slab of granite at the top of a rise and hard by the side of the trail. Its surface was about eighteen inches above the floor of the forest; it would make a perfect place for them to rest.

"C'mon," he said, pointing it out to his wife. "We've done pretty well. Time to take a break."

"Okay." They dropped their packs and seated themselves on the rock. Sarah patted her lap in invitation; Bobby stretched out and laid his head down in it. She brushed his hair back with her fingers, and he closed his eyes, relaxed as he knew how to be.

They were both quiet for a while.

"Bob?" she finally said.

"Mmmm?"

She hesitated, and then plunged ahead. "Is it as nice as you thought it might be?"

He opened his eyes and found hers. "Yes," he said. "Every bit."

"I mean us."

"I know."

"Even if we had to run away?"

"Even if we had to run away twice over. Sarah, I was dead wrong about a lot of things. I'm sorry."

"Shhh. It doesn't matter anymore. It's over and done with." She placed a finger against his lips, and he kissed it.

They were both silent for a few minutes, listening to the birds and the rush of the mountain winds in the trees. Then he asked, "Want to camp here for the night?"

"Look at the sun, silly," she said, laughing and playing with his hair. "It's not that much past three."

"Well, we could rest here for a while, anyway," he said. "This looks like a pretty good place to stop."

She looked into his eyes for a long moment. "You know, it really does look like a very nice place," she whispered, as he rose up to kiss her.

Ed, Ben and Connie were sitting in the Gordon kitchen when there suddenly came the sound of frantic barking from just outside the house.

"Is that Eisenhower?" Ed asked. "It doesn't sound like him."

"Ike stays at the Harper place like he was nailed there," Ben said, worried. "If he's come into town, there's real trouble up the road. I'll take a look."

"Wait for me," Ed said, finishing his coffee.

"Me, too," Connie said.

Ben opened the front door of the house to find an Irish setter sitting there. When the dog saw Ben, it began barking again.

"Well, *hello* there, boy!" Ben said, delighted. "My *God*, you're a handsome fella!" He crouched to give the dog a proper greeting and, after a tentative sniff or two, the dog began making loud and deliriously happy doggie sounds. His tail thumped heavily on the porch as he licked and nuzzled Ben's hands.

"Sure it's safe?" Ed wondered.

"This is no wild dog," Ben said as he began scratching the dog behind the ears. "He looks fine. Aren't you, fella? Yes, of *course* you are! Of *course* you're fine! Now, just where did you come from, anyway, eh? I've never seen *you* before, have I? You don't live here in town, *do* you? Say, you're a *handsome* fella!" The dog agreed with that last remark absolutely.

"Whoops, what's that?" Ben said, as his hand found something. "Why, that's a collar, boy! A red one! Wow! Where'd you get a collar, eh? Who gave you a collar? Leather, too! Wow, you must be a *good* dog to rate a leather collar, right? *Good* boy!"

"There's a tag on the collar," Ed said. Then it struck him. "Ben, hold on a minute. He's got a *tag*."

"Jesus, so he does," Ben said, surprised. He grasped it between thumb and forefinger. "Hold still a minute, fella, okay?" he soothed, petting the panting dog's flank with his free hand. "That's a boy, yeah, that's a *good* boy." Ben read the tag.

"What's that thing say on it?" asked Ed.

Ben didn't reply. He simply unclipped the tag from its hook on the collar and handed it to Ed.

"This says he's your dog, Ben," said Ed after a moment. "It says his name's Patrick."

Ben nodded, still petting the dog. "It does indeed," he said. "Not only that, but I recognize him now."

"I do, too, Daddy," Connie said. "He's ours. Yours and Mama's, I mean."

Ed was perplexed. "What?"

"I remember him from last night's dream," Ben said. "He's our dog, all right—mine and my wife's. I got Paddy here from the pound over in Saranac Lake after Connie took an apartment over in Lake Placid a few years back. Paddy helped fill the empty place in the house a little bit." Ben began scratching the setter under his jaw in the exact spot that he knew the dog liked the most.

"The dreams," Ed said slowly. "They're not just dreams, are they?"

"No," Ben said. "No, they're not."

"I guess I knew it already," Ed sighed. "Jesus God."

Close by, over in the next yard, there was the hissing and fussing that marked the bare beginnings of a catfight. Then something plunged like a black cannonball through the thick stand of bushes that separated Ben's property from the next lot over.

"Don't look now, Ben," Ed said, "but a big black cat just ran up behind you and on into the house. It had a collar on, too."

Ben nodded. "It's all right," he said. "That'd be Shadow."

Paddy suddenly *woofed* and headed into the house, and they all followed him. They thought he might be chasing the cat, because that was what they remembered dogs doing, but Paddy headed straight as an arrow for the kitchen, where he immediately began sniffing the floor, especially in front of the counter around the baseboard. After a moment, Paddy began whining softly.

"Must be hungry," Ed observed.

"No," Ben said, his eyes wide. "God help me, I know exactly what it is. He's looking for Martha."

"Oh, Daddy," Connie said softly, her eyes filling. "You're right. Paddy's looking for Mama. She's the one who always feeds him."

They suddenly heard a high-pitched yapping begin

somewhere off in the distance. That dog was soon joined by one a bit closer who had a louder and more piercing bark. Then there came a bark over *here*, and then another one over *there*, then still another, and then another and another, until Ed believed that they might just be able to hear all that barking across the border into Canada.

After more than thirty years, the cats and dogs had come back to McAndrew.

"He's a hound dog," Digger told his son. "He's a beauty, he is."

"Can we keep Reggie?" Justin asked. "Please? Mom says no."

"Well . . ."

Annie frowned. "Dogs got germs."

"*Please*, Mom? He could be a watchdog and help Digger hunt and—"

"Shush, Justin," said Annie. "Like I say, dogs got germs."

"Annie, let's go outside a minute," Digger said. "I need some help with something."

They left the cabin and walked up the path toward the highway. "Where'd he come from?" Digger asked.

"I told you, I don't know," Annie said, exasperated. "All I know is, one minute he isn't there and the next minute he is, and Justin is jumping up and down and calling him Reggie, and the dog is licking him all over and barking and raising Cain. Digger, if that dog makes him even the least little bit sick, I'll kill him dead."

"You're not going to kill that dog."

"I will if he hurts my boy. Be sure of it."

"He won't hurt the boy," Digger said, "and Justin can use the company. You know he can, honey."

"He can't use any company that'll hurt him."

Digger put an arm around her waist as they walked, and she moved closer to him. "I know you're worried about it," he said, "and I don't blame you. But I feel there's nothing bad that can happen here. The dog— Reggie?—Reggie is healthy and happy, and he loves Justin."

"I can tell he loves Justin, all right. The boy loves him right back, too. That's not the problem."

"I also like the idea of there being a dog around here when I'm not," Digger continued. "It'll be that much safer, and it'll put my mind a little more at ease. I still sometimes think of John Meyers prowling around the woods, crazy and murderous."

"It would be safer with a dog around, all right," she admitted. "I won't argue it. But it's taking an awful chance."

"It's a reasonable chance, honey."

They walked on for a moment in silence and reached the edge of the highway. "He's pretty happy about that dog, isn't he?" she finally said, looking somewhere down the road.

"Yes, he is," Digger said. "Happier than I've ever seen him, maybe. Certainly happier than I've seen him in a good long time."

"All right, then," she said only a little grudgingly. "Let's go back to the house and tell him."

He grinned. "That's great," he said. "Truth is, I want the dog, too. He's a friendly cuss, isn't he?"

"I pray the Lord we're not doing the wrong thing, Digger."

"We're not. It can't be wrong to give a poor creature a home. Don't worry about it."

"It's funny, though," she said.

"What is?"

"Those bad dreams I've been having about me and Freddie and the twins—well, the dog's been in them."

"Huh?"

"The dreams," she repeated. "That dog there's been in them all."

* * *

Bobby and Sarah stopped for only an hour or so at the rock. Then they dressed again and, holding hands, continued on their way.

"Lots of birds all of a sudden," Bobby said after walking for a while. "Hear 'em?"

"Hmmm?"

"Birds. Lots of birds." He pointed all around them. "You never hear this many around town. Actually, I never heard this many in the woods before, either."

"Oh, *birds*," she said, smiling that smile. "Sorry. I was off thinking there for a minute."

He laughed. "What were you thinking about?"

"Just things," she said after a pause. "We're really married now, you know."

"We sure are."

They walked on for a bit.

"Uh, Bob?"

"Yeah?"

"This isn't easy to say."

"Try."

"Okay. I know about you and Stephanie."

He frowned. "Everybody knows about me and Stephanie, or at least they think they do. But they don't know everything."

"Tell me about it?"

He shrugged. "What's there to tell?" he said. "Stephanie couldn't have cared less about me. She cared about my father's store a lot, though."

"I see," she said. "That's what I figured."

"You did?"

"Yes," Sarah said. "Stephanie didn't want to be your wife. All she wanted was to be married to you. There's a big difference."

"Yes, there is, isn't there?"

"So what happened?" Sarah asked.

"Uh, we had a really bad fight this morning, and that's when I walked out on her. She couldn't stand me anymore, and I figured I'd put up with more than enough.''

''And that's when you came to me.''

''And that's when I came to you.''

Sarah nodded slowly. ''So you married me because you had a fight with Stephanie.''

''No,'' he said in an unedged way that compelled her to believe him. ''I don't know much, but I know that's wrong. Look, let's sit down and talk for a minute.''

''All right.''

They squatted down on the trail. Bobby picked up a twig and began scratching random designs in the packed soil. Sarah waited patiently for him to begin.

''You know we were making it,'' he finally said.

''Yeah, I guess I did.''

''I really thought once that she and I were going to get married.''

''Everybody thought so,'' Sarah said. ''That's what she was telling all her friends, too. Um, I'm not one of them, but I heard all about it anyway.''

''I was even proving out a house and everything,'' he continued. He began drawing squares and rectangles. ''Look, I was stupid,'' he said. ''I thought her doing it with me meant that she loved me, okay? I really did.''

''But people who love each other do it,'' she said.

''That isn't all they do,'' he replied. ''Anybody can *do* it. Love is what's still going on when you're *not* doing it.''

''I guess I knew that already,'' she said. ''Uh, Bobby? I need you to be completely honest.''

''Okay.''

''Was it good? With me, I mean? Back at the rock?''

He looked up from his doodling. ''Weren't you there?'' he asked her in mock astonishment.

''Well, sure I was—but I don't know how to tell yet if it was any good or not!''

He reached over and, drawing her close to him, hugged her. "It was good," he said. "Believe me."

"Was it better?" she asked in a small voice, her face buried in his shoulder.

"It was much, much better," he said. He had intended only to soothe her, but then he suddenly realized that what he had said was true, and that he meant it. She somehow understood, and she hugged him back hard. "It's much better when you really love the other person, Sarah," he continued. "That's the first thing you've taught me."

She hugged him hard after that. She had loved him for a long time, but loving him had never caused her anything but pain. Now she was discovering for the first time that love could give rise to joy as well. They kissed deeply, lost to the world around them.

That was how it happened that Team Tango took them completely by surprise.

It seemed as if a hundred dogs were barking and howling somewhere outside, but Paddy didn't seem at all bothered by it. He was much too busy thumping his tail on the kitchen floor and panting to care. Shadow didn't seem to be worried, either; the cat was sitting on the counter and grooming herself.

Ed watched her. "If I remember right," he said, "if a cat sits down and washes itself in front of people, it means it feels safe."

"I wish *I* felt safe," said Connie.

There was a knock at the front door. "Mr. Gordon?" came a boy's voice.

"Who's there?" Ben called back.

"It's Randy," the voice said. "Randy LeClerc."

"Hello, son," Ben said. "Come on in. Had your lunch?"

"I'm not hungry, sir, but thank you. Uh, Mr. Gordon, my dad told me to ask you to come into town. There's a crowd gathered at the store, and more people are coming by every minute. Mr. Garfield's in a peck of trouble.''

"Jake's in trouble?" Connie said. "What's happened, Randy?"

"Tell us," Ben said.

The boy did, quickly. "Everything was fine, sort of, about Jake having done the wedding until Stephanie Crane showed up in tears and announced that she had Bobby's baby inside her," he finished. "Then whatever good feeling had built up for Jake fell apart, even though Stephanie swore up and down that Bobby never knew she was pregnant."

"*Is* Stephanie pregnant?" Ben asked.

"Doc says he thinks she may be, from what Stephanie's told him. If we catch a rabbit, he says he'll make sure."

"Doc's guess is good enough for me," Ben said. He frowned. "Damn, I wish Jake had kept his nose out of things."

"Dad!" Connie fumed. "What was Jake supposed to do? Ignore them, for heaven's sake? *They* came to *him* for help! Jake didn't know any more about Stephanie than you did."

"I guess he didn't," Ben sighed. "Sorry, hon, but it *is* big trouble. What do people want to do, Randy?"

"They're talking about throwing Jake out of town."

"At least they don't want to hang him," Ed said wryly.

"Quiet, please, Ed. Randy, what about Prosper?"

"Nobody's seen him today, Mr. Gordon. Some folks think he ran away already."

"Daddy," Connie said, "if Jake goes, I go with him."

"I already knew that, honey," her father said quietly. "I wouldn't expect you to do anything else." He addressed the rest of them. "All right, let's try to get it fixed. Connie, I want you to bring Paddy along; I don't want to leave him alone here, not yet. You can make a leash out of the twine you'll find over there in that drawer under the counter.''

"Why are we bringing the dog along?" Connie asked. "Not that I mind.''

"I don't want to leave him alone here just yet," her father said. "Then there's the other reason.''

"The other reason?" Connie asked.

"Sure," Ben said. "If nothing else works, I plan to sic Paddy on Amanda Broom. That ought to amuse the lynch mob long enough for you and Jake to high-tail it out of town, hand in hand and hearts in mouths, looking for the nearest ice floes to cross.''

"Very funny, Daddy.''

Ben grinned at her expression. "C'mon, kiddo, it ain't that bad," he said, putting his arm around his daughter. "We'll get everything put back the way it was. Don't worry.''

CHAPTER 16

IT WAS A BEAUTIFUL AFTERNOON, AND PRISCILLA Neary was glorying in it. She walked along Logger's Trail at a steady and unhurried pace. She felt only a little tired and not at all out of breath and, oddly enough, free at last. She was even growing a little bit hungry, to her great surprise. She took out her apple and began eating it.

There were birds all over the place. She supposed that she must somehow have frightened them by being here, because one moment the woods had been nearly silent, and then all of a sudden they had exploded with sound. She had not heard such a lovely racket since before the war, when she would take long walks on this same road with her father. *If I'd known that this was where all the birds were hiding,* she thought, *I'd have come to visit long before now.*

Logger's Trail ran for about forty miles and let out at Long Lake, but Miss Neary did not intend to go nearly that far. She merely wanted to find a pleasant spot next to a brook or a stream at a seemly distance from town. She thought she might like to pass into eternity while listening to the sound of clear, clean, rushing water.

She chucked the core of the apple well into the woods and heard it thump against a tree before it fell to the ground. *Maybe an apple tree will grow on that spot someday,* she thought. *That would be nice, wouldn't it?* Then she decided that there wasn't nearly enough sunlight reaching the forest floor for an apple tree to grow properly, if at all, and it disappointed her.

She walked on a bit longer, until her feet started to hurt and her breath began to grow a little short. She stopped at a long, flat rock at the top of a rise and sat down to catch her wind. She closed her eyes for a moment.

There was a small sound, far away—a hollow pop. Then, quickly, there was another. Her eyes snapped open. *What was that?* she wondered. She looked up the trail.

Gunshots? A hunter, perhaps?

Maybe—but something felt very wrong.

Miss Neary suddenly felt that she had to find out what was happening. She rose, brushed the seat of her jeans with her hands, and continued on up the trail, puffing slightly. As she looked down to watch her footing, she suddenly noticed two fresh sets of footprints in the soft dirt. One of them, the larger, had been made by moccasins. The other had been made by sneakers with nearly all the tread worn away. Whoever had left the prints had come from the direction of town.

Another sound came on the wind after a moment. It sounded to Miss Neary like a young girl sobbing. Then the wind shifted away again and the sound became lost to the trees around her.

Miss Neary had heard enough, however. She began

to hurry along the trail, not caring or even noticing how short of breath she had become.

Jake Garfield didn't know what else to do, so after Ben Gordon and Ed Pearson calmed the crowd at LeClerc's and announced that an emergency town meeting would be held that night, he left the store and walked home as quickly as he could. Connie had come by, too, but since Jake had not known what to say to her, he had said nothing.

Those few people he came across on his way home did not deign to notice him. After a while he reciprocated, snubbing others as fully and freely as he himself was being snubbed. He entered his home as utterly alone as he'd ever been out on the road.

Where the hell was Prosper, anyway?

Jake thought he might as well pack his things right then, rather than wait until the last minute. He opened the door of the hallway closet he used to store his few things and retrieved his knapsack. His guitar was in the closet, too, as were some of his newly acquired carpenter's tools—"his" only in the loosest sense, since they were rented from Dick LeClerc and would of course revert to him. Some other things—nails, for example—had been paid for already in hard labor and they were certainly his to take, free and clear. Jake knew that Dick LeClerc had not expected anything from the store to leave town, but Jake was under no obligation to return any purchased item or trade it back. Jake thought he might trade some of the nails and things for road supplies, if Dick would consent to deal with him. He thought Dick might, if for no other reason than Dick had to, as a town officer responsible for safeguarding McAndrew's supply of irreplaceables. Jake planned to go around town soon and collect the small tools he'd rented out himself, such as the special hammer with the screwdrivers hidden in the handle. He wanted to get everything done before the meeting that night.

The meeting. Suddenly angry, Jake ripped his clothing off the wire hangers Connie had arranged them on and tossed them carelessly on the floor in front of the closet. Stooping, he began jamming garments into his knapsack in such a haphazard way that all of them could not possibly fit inside. Then his anger passed, and he found himself fighting back tears.

There was a soft footstep behind him.

"Hi, Wanderin'," Connie said.

"Hi," Jake replied, his voice thick. "I've really blown it, haven't I?"

"What's all this?" she asked him, gesturing at the floor.

"I'm packing," he shrugged. "What else?"

She nodded. "I see," she said. "Does that mean you're giving up without a fight?"

"I'm going to the meeting."

"Then I guess this means you expect to lose."

"I guess it does." He would not look at her.

"Let's see," she said, adopting as pedantic a tone as she could manage. "Two kids come by and ask you, as what amounts to town preacher, to marry them. They say they're going to run away from town whether you marry them or not, so after unsuccessfully arguing against their acting in haste or without their parents knowing about it or giving their consent, you perform the ceremony for them anyway because you're a decent man and, anyway, you like the kids and you don't want to send them away without giving them what they want. Right so far?"

"Right enough. So?"

"You didn't know and even *they* didn't know that there was a baby involved. Nobody knew, but now everybody and his uncle Harry does, and it's all somehow *your* fault for not knowing in the first place. The town's mad at you for getting involved because you're a relative stranger, even though you've suddenly become famous as the fairly adequate consort of the mayor's incredibly attractive daughter."

"Connie—"

"Quiet. The town's leading businessman, in particular, is mad at you for giving him a bastard grandchild. The pregnant girl's father is mad at you for the same thing. The other girl's mother is too mad to do anything but mumble on and on about the seventy-seven ways she's going to kill you. Still right?"

"I suppose."

"You know it," she said. "By the way, my personal favorite is the one where she's going to boil you to death in horse piss. Now listen up, stupid."

"I'm listening."

"My father's the mayor and he's on your side," Connie said. "His best friend's the town archivist *and* my godfather, and he's on your side, too. Dick Le-Clerc is too busy right now thinking about a bastard grandchild to put the grandchild part before the bastard part. He'll get over it soon, though. Dick's no old biddy. He'll wise up. His wife already has."

"Really?"

"Really," Connie said. "What we're seeing here is some of the dumb old ways repeating themselves. Stephanie's father and Sarah's mother think their daughters are ruined for entirely contradictory reasons. Dick is upset mostly because his son didn't say boo before marrying Sarah and leaving town, and he can't understand why Bobby wouldn't talk to him. Millie LeClerc was a young girl once, and so she's been more understanding than any of you men have been about this whole big, stinking mess."

"So what should I have done?" he asked.

"What *I* would have done, you dope! I would have insisted that both Bobby and Sarah approach Millie on the sly to act as a witness to the ceremony, thereby keeping things from getting crazy. Millie would have done it for them, too, and she'd have kept Dick under control afterward. Dick would have then kept everybody *else* under control.''

"I see," he said. "It sounds reasonable—but isn't that twenty-twenty hindsight?"

"No, it isn't," Connie answered, "but I do know these people better than you do. Dammit, I wish I'd been here this morning. None of this would have happened."

"I guess not," Jake said, looking down at his knapsack. "God, I want to stay," he blurted, close to tears again. "I finally found a place in the world with you and with these people, and now I think I've blown it."

"You haven't blown it with me."

"I haven't?"

"Never, my dearest man. We're for keeps."

"Thank you," he said quietly. "I very much needed to hear that."

"We've going to stay here," Connie said firmly. "This town is our home, and we're not going to give it up. Just in case you haven't noticed it, I can be just a little bit stubborn."

"I've noticed it," Jake said.

"I get it from my dad."

Cautiously, Miss Neary continued toward what she believed to be the source of the cry she had heard. She soon reached a spot where the trail had been torn up and trampled. She looked closely at the ground.

There were still those two fresh sets of footprints from the direction of town. It was also clear that something heavy—a dead weight—had been dragged off the trail and into the woods to the right. She walked a few feet farther up the road and found two other sets of footprints heading for the trampled spot. She then looked a little closer. They were not just footprints. They were bootprints.

Miss Neary looked at the place where the weight had been dragged off the trail. It had apparently brought up the rear and so had obscured any other prints going into the woods.

This is very, very bad, Miss Neary told herself. Had someone actually taken a child, or two children? Why would children have come out all this way from town? She thought about matters for a moment, and decided that young children couldn't have put up the kind of fight evidenced in the trampled dirt of the trail. In addition, those footprints from the direction of town were adult-sized, or near enough so as not to matter. That didn't explain the childlike sobbing she'd heard, though—unless it had been the crying of a teenaged girl.

Miss Neary was too upset to worry very much about the details. There was someone in trouble; she was certain of it. After a moment, she reached into the pocket of her jacket and took out the chipped drinking glass. Hoping no one would hear her, she crouched and bashed the glass as quietly as she could against a convenient rock. It broke cleanly, leaving behind a jagged blade thickest at its bottom, where it remained connected to the base of the glass. She took off her jacket and, cutting off a sleeve, wrapped it tightly around the base of the shattered glass. The improvised dagger felt good in her hand.

Miss Neary entered the woods following the imprint of whatever it was that had been dragged off the trail. She still refused to consider that it might have been a body. She watched where she was walking, placing her feet carefully. As she did so, she remembered a time long, long ago when a light step had been a valuable asset in playing Indian—whenever the boys would grudgingly allow the girls to play Indian with them, that is. That hadn't happened very often, and only when most of the boys had been down with the measles or the mumps or something. Miss Neary had been very good at stalking prey and still was, although she hadn't had to do so since the days of the famine.

Whatever had been dragged off the trail had been hauled through the woods as well, no matter what roots or rocks might have been in the way. There were shreds of cloth here and there and, to Miss Neary's distress, streaks of fresh blood.

Miss Neary suddenly heard the deep, almost gentle laughter of a man up ahead. She stopped to listen for a moment and never heard more than the voices of two men. They were talking, but Miss Neary could not quite make out what they were talking about. She moved forward slowly, going through the woods in a path removed from but parallel to the way she had been heading. She no longer needed to follow the path formed by the dragged body; she followed the men's voices instead.

Miss Neary suddenly spotted a clearing about eight feet in front of her. She edged over to a cropping of tall bushes that would screen her from view.

The first thing she saw was Prosper Cross lying on his side on the ground. His arms and legs were tied, and his face was swollen—bruised, too, she thought, but it was hard to tell. There was dried blood on his face and down his shirt. Miss Neary saw murder in his eyes.

Then she noticed that a boy—oh, God, it was Bobby LeClerc!—was also on the ground and sprawled on his side. He was covered with blood, he was not tied, and he was not moving; Miss Neary was terribly afraid that he was dead. She saw that Sarah Broom was sitting on the ground near him, her arms tied behind her. Her clothing was badly torn, and she was bleeding from a cut on her forehead. She looked numb and defeated.

Facing Sarah were two men in uniform. They were sitting on the forest floor about three feet away from her and were talking easily with each other. One of the men was looking through a magazine of some sort; the other was eating something brownish out of a small can. *They look like American Army men,* Miss Neary thought. *My sweet Lord, has the Army come back? But why have they taken Prosper Cross and the children?*

The man who wasn't eating spoke to Sarah. "You'll like the lieutenant," he said in a friendly tone. "And he'll like you, honey. He'll like you a *lot*. He always likes the tight little ones."

Miss Neary grimaced.

"Shit, Russ," the other soldier said around a mouthful of food. "For two cents I'd do her myself. Cutest piece I've seen in quite a while, even if she ain't got much in the way of tits."

"Don't even think about it," Russ advised. "The lieutenant hates sloppy seconds. Remember him raising hell about those twin sisters?"

"Well, her mouth don't count, does it?" Nick said petulantly.

"The lieutenant'll be pissed off, and you know it," Russ said. "He gets first crack, no pun intended."

Nick guffawed at that, and a piece of food fell out of his mouth and onto the ground. He picked it up, blew on it and popped it back into his mouth.

"You cherry, sweetheart?" Russ asked Sarah. "I'll just bet you're cherry."

"You killed my husband," Sarah said dully, looking at the body.

Oh my dear, dear God Above, thought Miss Neary. *Those poor children.*

"Oh, too bad," Russ said, genuinely disappointed. "The lieutenant likes 'em cherry. Well, love, when the rest of the team gets here and we get to wherever it is you're from, maybe we'll find a regular cherry *tree*, huh? We'll shake that cherry tree, all right." Russ began laughing.

The rest of the team? Miss Neary wondered. *How*

many is that? A dozen? More? I've got to get Prosper and Sarah out of here!

"The more I think about it," Nick said, "the more I think the lieutenant won't give a shit about what anybody does in her mouth, particularly as she ain't cherry." He got up slowly. "What do you think, li'l married lady?"

Sarah suddenly looked up at him, fire in her eye. "I think that if you come anywhere near me with that thing," she said evenly, "I'll bite it off."

"Really?" Nick said. He smiled and drew his automatic. "Here's how it's gonna be, girlie. First you'll do me with that smart mouth of yours, and then you'll do my good friend here. You won't say a word about it to the lieutenant about it, neither. You don't do us right, kid, your nigger friend gets it. Got it now, you little bitch? Russ, keep the nigger covered." He reached for his zipper with his free hand.

"Don't you touch that child," Prosper warned.

"Oh, really?" Nick said, laughing. "What's the likes of *you* gonna do about it?"

He will kill me, Miss Neary thought, *but I have to try.* She rushed out from cover and into the clearing as quickly as she could move. Nick barely had time to blink, and to form the beginning of a question about what this ridiculous old bag might be doing here, when Miss Neary got him squarely in the throat with her glass dagger. Nick tried to scream as his life gushed away, but he could find no voice.

It had taken only a second. "Jesus Christ!" Russ cried as he brought his automatic to bear on Miss Neary. She could not reach him in time with the dagger; she simply waited calmly for him to shoot her.

Prosper swung his tied legs as hard as he could, catching Russ behind his knees and sending him to the ground. The man fell heavily, and his gun went flying.

"Miss Neary!" Prosper called. "Don't let him get that gun! Take him quick!"

Miss Neary hurried over and plunged the glass dagger into Russ's chest. He gasped once and died quickly. She left the weapon in him.

"That one there has a proper knife," Prosper said, breathing heavily. "Can you cut us loose?"

"Certainly," Miss Neary said. She wondered if she was in shock, and she supposed that she was, because things seemed just too normal to suit her. She found a very nice hickory-handled hunting knife in a leather scabbard on Russ's belt. It could not have been standard issue; Miss Neary wondered whom Nick had murdered to get it.

Miss Neary went over to Sarah and quickly cut through the rope that bound her. Freed, the girl silently shifted over and nestled against the body of her husband. She did not hug Bobby or hold his hand or cry or do anything but sit closely against him and stare into space without saying a word.

Miss Neary cut Prosper's bonds and then went to look at Bobby. She saw that he had been shot twice in the chest—and at point-blank range, too, judging from the damage that had been done. His body had been slashed and scored deeply in places from being dragged through the woods. The boy's eyes were still open; Miss Neary gently coaxed the lids closed with the tips of her fingers.

Russ's magazine had happened to fall next to Bobby's body. Miss Neary saw now that it was not actually a magazine, but a comic book about someone named Captain Cobalt. She had not seen a comic book in many years, but it looked fairly typical of the genre, as she remembered it. She wondered where Russ had come upon it.

"Prosper?" Miss Neary asked. "How did you wind up here? Who are these people?"

"I was repairin' a fence on the southern end of town

on Saturday morning when these two grabbed me," he said. "They were hunting us—me and Jake, I mean. They wanted information about how many people there are in town, how many weapons they have, that sort of thing. From what I heard them say, there's a whole platoon on its way."

"We've got to get back to town as quickly as possible," Miss Neary said. "We've got to warn everyone."

"Exactly what I was thinkin'," said Prosper. "Is Sarah okay?"

"I can't tell," Miss Neary said. "Sarah? Sarah, darling, can you hear me?"

"Hello, Miss Neary," Sarah said at last.

"Hello, Sarah. Are you hurt, sweetheart? Did they hurt you?"

"Bobby tried to save me," Sarah said quietly. "He saw them first and told me to start running back toward town and I did, as fast as I could, although I didn't want to leave Bobby. I heard the soldiers yelling and cursing. Bobby got in a good lick or two before they shot him. I heard Bobby cry out and fall in the road. Then that one, Russ, ran after me and knocked me down. He was faster than me, I guess. Then they took me here and tied me up, and Nick went back to drag Bobby here. Did you know Bobby and I were married this morning?"

"No, honey. No, I didn't, but I heard you tell this one here, this Russ, that Bobby was your husband."

"He was," Sarah said. "We eloped. Jake Garfield married us." Then she fell silent again.

"Sarah?" Miss Neary said, shaking her by the shoulder. "Sarah, darling? I'm sorry, but we've got to go now. We've got to get back to town and warn everyone just as soon as we can."

With shaking fingers, she nodded and brushed the matted hair back tenderly from her husband's forehead. "All right," she whispered. "I just want to say goodbye."

Ben Gordon took his place front and center. "All right, folks," he called, holding up his arms for quiet. "Thanks for coming. I'd like to get started now."

"Dispense with minutes!" someone shouted.

"Second!"

"Didn't bring 'em anyway," Ed Pearson rumbled from the back. "So there."

"Just like always," someone muttered.

"We want to talk about what's ahead, not what's behind," Ben said. "The minutes are herewith dispensed, er, with. Let's get on right away with new business."

"Let's talk about strange phenomena!" Ed bellowed, as he and Ben had arranged, and there was a roar of agreement. What Jake Garfield had done would not be discussed until later in the meeting, which suited Ben just fine. Delaying the debate would buy some time, and it might even buy Jake some goodwill, if people felt better after talking about the many strange things that were happening.

Ben knew Jake could use all the goodwill he could get. His initial optimism about keeping Jake from being exiled had been quashed by the conversations he'd had with several people whose opinions he trusted. Sentiment was running high against Jake.

Ben looked to where Jake was standing in the back of the church. The mayor saw that everyone had left the busker plenty of room; only Digger Digby had come over to stand with him. It was a dismal sign.

"Unless there's some objection," the mayor said, "the first order of new business is strange phenomena."

Hands went up all around the church. "Meg?" Ben called out. "I see you. Go ahead."

Meg Reilly stood. "The dreams we're all having. What else?"

"What else?" came the piping voice of Kent Trotter. "How about all these cats and dogs, for starters? I've got three cats running around the house all of a sudden, and they do nothing but yammer at me because they want to get fed. They can't even hunt for themselves because they don't have any goddamn claws! Who the hell ever heard of cats without claws?"

"This is a church, Kent," Ben gently chided.

"Yeah, Trotter," Warren McAdoo called out. "You watch your goddamn language, hear me?"

"Look," Tess Jarvis called out. "The whole thing is about these dreams. We've got to discuss that first."

"I agree," Ben said. "Who wants to go first?" There was the sound of a clearing throat. "Doc? Is that you? Do you have something to say?"

"Yes, it is and yes, I do." Doc rose and stood quietly for a moment, thinking. "Friends," he finally began. "Some of you have come to me over the past month or two, complaining of recurring nightmares. While I don't discuss my patients' cases in public, it's fair to tell you that a great many more people have come to see me about similar complaints in the past week. I've been putting it down to—well, let's call it anxiety and stress. I think I should add that I haven't been having any such dreams myself."

Doc walked to the front of the church, talking as he went. "Lacking any other evidence," he continued, "I've held an opinion that this, er, epidemic of bad dreams has continued and grown because one person tells another about his or her dream, and it passes along just like a bug—a measles of the mind, if you will. I never believed any of it could somehow reflect reality."

He paused at the front of the church and turned to face the crowd. "I should say that I didn't believe it until just today," he said.

There was a buzz of discussion in the audience. "Let the doctor continue, please," Ben said, holding up his hands and motioning for quiet. "We'll hash it all out afterward, I promise."

Doc continued. "Some of you will no doubt remember that I used to be a veterinarian—still am, I guess. Anyway, I went around to people's houses on my own and examined some of the cats and dogs that showed up in town today. They are all, without exception, healthy. Many of them have been groomed. They're all carrying good weight. They are also parasite-free, as nearly as I can tell without doing stool tests."

"What are you telling us, Doc?" Ben asked.

Doc sighed. "Only a damn fool would ignore the evidence," he said, "and I hope I'm not a damn fool. If I were, I could insist that all these animals just suddenly wandered in from the mountains for some strange reason, and that they're all young and healthy by some remarkable coincidence. I could even make myself dismiss the collars and identification tags some of the animals were wearing. Well, friends, I'm not a damn fool. Mr. Mayor, put me down on the list with the dreamers."

"Thanks, Doc," Ben said. "No, please don't go back and sit. Stay up here with me, if you would."

"Certainly," Doc said.

"Ed Pearson?" Ben called out.

"Yes, Mr. Mayor?"

"I have an idea, and I need an archivist. If you see one, get him up here, please."

"Coming."

"All right, folks," Ben said, "here's what I want to do. For some time now, some of us have been saying that these dreams are somehow real, that they're like a window on a place we can't otherwise see. The arrival of the animals suggests that this place really exists."

"They come from over there," Emma Reichsback called out. "They *do*!"

"Yes, indeed, Emma," Ben said. "I believe you're right." The mayor held up his hands again for quiet. "So here's what I want to do," he continued. "I want you to start telling the rest of us what you remember from your dreams. Let's try to get a handle on all this. Ed, write everything down; I want to build a list. When we've done that, we'll discuss it further."

Ed produced a pencil and a piece of paper from his shirt pocket. "I'll go first," he said. "I've been dreaming about working in my old newspaper office, except that it's a lot different. For instance, we write on keyboards attached to TV sets, and the words show up on the screen."

"Computers," Del Williams shouted. "Right?"

Suddenly Ed knew it was so. "That's right," he said. "Computers. Thanks, Del." He scribbled a note. "Okay, then. There's news, too. The Russians invaded Western Europe and they were in Amsterdam, but I'm not sure of the details."

"They're in Holland and now they're in Belgium, too," Carl Flannery said. "They're occupying Germany, but the Germans are giving them hell. There's been some sort of ongoing crisis in the Soviet Union, and the government's trying to stay in power."

"Right!" Joe Hermann shouted. "There's a Moslem rebellion going on in the whatchamacallums, the southern republics."

"So the Russians attacked Europe?" Mick Krivak asked. "That doesn't make any sense."

"You having any dreams, Mick?" Stan Maguire called out.

"Nothing special," Mick replied.

"So take it from me, that's what happened," Stan said. "The world's gone crazy."

"Guy on the radio said the Russian attack on Europe was the last gasp of a dying empire, or some such,'' Fannie DeDeaux said. "They're trying to distract their people from their internal problems. The thing is, the Russians might bring everybody else down with 'em. That's what the radio said.''

"Maybe they'll even invade France," said Cecilia Shaw.

"Why would they want to invade France, for Chrissakes?" Mick asked, exasperated. "What would they *do* with it?"

"Beats me," Cecilia said, "but that's the way it is.''

"What are 'tactical nukes?' " Ann Magner asked.

"Can we sort all that out later?" Ben asked. "I think we're getting somewhere with this. Tell me, all you dreamers—what's the name of the President of the United States over there?"

In unison, most of those in the church gave it to him.

"That does it, I guess," Doc said. "They can't all know the same name, not if there's nothing to this.''

"Right," Ben said. "Folks, let's get all the details we can. What else do you remember? Anything, anything at all.''

"Hey, I got something," Clarence Casey said. "There's a kind of spaceship that looks more like an airplane than a capsule or anything. We have 'em and the Russians have 'em, and both kinds look a lot alike. Both countries are launching a few into orbit as part of the crisis. It's like U-2 flights, only a lot higher. We may have to shoot theirs down, and they might have to shoot ours down.''

Martha Gratz spoke up. "I got a name from somewhere," she said. "Sylvester Stallion ring a bell? Or maybe Stephen Stallion? He's a movie star, or was. I saw him in *Rocky V* on the late-night movie just this past Thursday.''

"I've got a watch over there that shows numbers to tell time," Noah Sickels said. "No hands. It has a stopwatch and an alarm in it, too.''

"There's seat belts in cars, just like there used to be on airplanes," Terry Linden said. "And there's health warnings on packs of cigarettes."

"Somebody opened a sushi bar in Lake Placid," Bettina Worthy said. "I tried some on a dare. Now I can't get enough of it."

"Sushi?" Harvey Bell called out. "What's a sushi?"

"Raw fish on cold rice, more or less," Bettina told him. "It's wonderful."

"You actually *ate* that?" Harvey said, amazed.

"I don't know, Harv," Bettina said. "You were the one who told me about it in the first place."

"Can we continue on, folks?" Ben asked. "Art?"

"I've got one," Arthur Leigh said. "Almost all the telephones have little buttons on them instead of dials, and the buttons make music. It's a pretty good idea because you can dial faster and you can even catch yourself when you dial a wrong number. Uh, even though you punch buttons, everybody still calls it dialing."

"I've got Home Box Office," Shirley Clay said, "and I've got a husband, too, but he's not the one I used to have. For those of you who still remember George, rest his soul, the husband I've got over there is a lot better."

"I subscribe to *People* magazine," said Elaine Kirby. "I don't read it, though."

"Speaking of things like that," Ed Pearson said, "I remember that Queen Di visited Washington at the beginning of the year."

"There was a terrible riot in New York," Alan Green said. "People down there went crazy, and I was glad I was here. I mean, I was glad over there that I was here. I mean, I was glad I wasn't in New York City, which I always was, anyway. Glad that I wasn't there, I mean."

"I see," Ben said. "Thank you, Al. Roy?"

"There's a man named Jerry Falwell who's either a preacher or a politician," Roy Libbey told everyone. "I ain't sure. I just saw him on TV last night, though, and he says he's praying night and day for the world to get through this thing. He also says it's a sure sign Jesus is coming."

"I remember something," Tom Mocci said, snapping his fingers. "There's young men and women who dye their hair orange and purple and yellow—not blonde, but bright yellow—and they wear earrings in pierced ears. I mean the men wear 'em, too. Rock 'n roll people, you know?" Tom twirled a finger at the side of his head.

Digger nodded. "What everybody's talking about kinda sounds familiar to me, too," the little man said. "I wish I could remember my dreams better."

"Some people are better at remembering dreams than others, and they always have been," Ed observed. "I never do remember very much about mine, although I remember a little more about them than I used to."

"There's radios so small that you can wear them in your ears," Lisa Blaine said. "That way you can listen to music as loud as you want to as you walk around, but you don't bother anyone else. It's like wearing an orchestra on your head. Pretty neat, huh?"

"I was in the hospital last month," said Clarissa Hanks, "but something called Medicare paid for it."

"Uh, Ben?" Doc said. "As everyone knows, I haven't been having any of these dreams. That goes for a few of us here. We ought to discuss why not."

Ben nodded. "All right, Doc. Anybody have any ideas about that?"

Ed thought about it. "I don't remember dreaming about Doc or even thinking about him," he said. "I suspect that means you never came up here, Doc—or at least we never met. Over there, I mean."

"Does anybody remember dreaming about me?" Doc asked.

It turned out that no one did.

"All right, then," Doc said. "Look, I spent some of my day asking the people whose pets I examined just who and what they'd been dreaming about—if they were dreaming at all, that is, and all of them were. I got enough straight answers to begin drawing some conclusions."

"And they are?" Ben asked.

Doc ticked them off on his fingers. "The first one is that not everyone who's dreaming is dreaming that he or she lives here in McAndrew," he said. "Some folks dream that they're living in other places. I talked to one woman who said she lives all the way out west, in San Francisco."

"That's right," Digger called out. "I remember now. I don't live anywhere near here at all. I live in Boston, just like my pop did."

"Things like that should tell us that dreaming isn't affected by distance," Doc said. "Over there, we are the people we would be if the war had never happened, and many of us left town to go to college or take a job."

"What else, Doc?" asked Ben.

"Just one other thing," Doc said. "It appears to me that people who are dead over there aren't having these dreams. They have no window on the other world. I talked to several people in town who told me that a friend or relative of theirs who wasn't dreaming was known by them to have died over there."

"Uh, yeah," Ben said uncomfortably. "Now that you mention it, that seems right enough to me, Doc— much as it pains me to say so."

It was then that Millie LeClerc started to cry.

"Millie?" Ben called. "What's the matter?"

"I'm sorry, everyone," Dick said, going to his

wife's side. "We've all been under a strain, what with the kids and all—"

"No, no," Millie choked out, waving a hand. "It's not that. It's not that at all. Dick—"

"What is it?" her husband asked, holding her close.

"It's bad," Millie managed. "You and Randy were killed by a drunk driver on the way back from a Cub Scout meeting Saturday night. That's why you don't dream anymore, Dick. That's why Randy doesn't, either. I'm going to have to bury you and my baby over there." She began crying again.

Dick held her more tightly. "Ben," he said, "I'm going to take my wife home now."

At that moment Priscilla Neary, Prosper Cross and Sarah LeClerc burst through the doors of the church. Miss Neary looked around blankly for a moment and then, seeming to realize where she was, relaxed and sank to the floor. Prosper broke her fall.

"Sarah?" Millie said, drying her eyes as she and Dick rushed over to her. "Sarah, darling, what's the matter? Where's Bobby?"

Ed, Ben and Doc hurried over. "Out of the way, everyone," Ben called. "Give the doctor some room, please. Make room for the doctor."

"Priscilla?" Ed said, kneeling next to her. "Pris, take it easy. The doctor's here. Jesus, woman, you should be in bed."

"Ed, go help Ben with Sarah there," Doc said, edging the archivist aside. "I can handle Priscilla. You there—Pete Jenkins! I stashed my bag in the baptismal font right next to you. Get it for me, will you? Sam Fuller! Throw me your jacket. I need yours, too, Will Prince."

Jake rushed over. "Prosper, what's going on? What happened to you? Your face—"

"Big trouble, Jake," his friend said through swollen lips. "They caught me two days ago. Briscom—"

"Briscom?"

Ben Gordon crouched down next to Sarah. "Sarah, what's the matter?" he asked. "What's going on? Where's Bobby?"

Sarah's eyes were almost vacant. "Bobby's dead," she said. "Soldiers killed him."

Millie LeClerc, standing there, gasped. Her husband shut his eyes. "Oh, dear God," Ed breathed.

"What happened, Sarah?" Ben asked, as calmly as he could. "Can you tell us what happened?"

"Well, we got married—"

"We know."

"—and we left town by Logger's Trail, because no one ever goes that way. We ran into the soldiers a few miles from town. Bobby died trying to help me escape. They caught me anyway and took me to where they were keeping Prosper."

"How many soldiers are there?" Ben asked.

"There were two I saw," Sarah replied. "Their names were Russ and Nick. They said they were scouts, and they were waiting for the rest of Team Tango to catch up to them. I don't know how many men there are in a Team Tango."

"Where are Russ and Nick now?" Ben asked.

"Miss Neary killed them," Sarah said. "They were about to hurt me, but she killed them and so they didn't. Hurt me, I mean."

"Good for Miss Neary," Ben said grimly. "Doc, how is she?"

"She's having trouble breathing," Doc said, "and her pulse is—well, I don't like it. I don't know what I can do for her except have her rest for as long as she needs to. I'm going to need a stretcher and a couple of strong backs."

Ben gave orders.

"What were the two soldiers doing there, Sarah?" Ed asked.

"Russ said their squad was looking for Jake and Prosper," Sarah said in a near-mumble. "They knew to come this way. They said the governor wanted them back really bad."

"Ben?" Ed said in a low voice. "Did I hear right?"

"Jesus H. Christ," Ben muttered. *"Get over here, Garfield!"* he barked.

"Right behind you, Ben," Jake said. Prosper moved over to stand by his side.

"Just what the hell is going on?" Ben demanded. "A fine young man's been killed. *Why?* I thought you two said you'd covered your tracks!"

"I thought we had," said Jake.

"Not nearly well enough," Ben said coldly. "Not nearly."

"We had no idea anyone would follow us," Prosper said. "There was no reason for them to. We just wanted out, is all."

"Maybe they just wanted you around, period," Ed guessed. "You'd visited Mount Weather as the President's official guest, and then you'd become the official guest of Governor Briscom. Maybe Briscom thought that gave him a leg up on becoming the next President of the United States. There's a sort of twisted logic there."

"You also left Rensselaer without Briscom's permission and accused of a supposedly treasonable offense," Doc said. "That alone might have been more than enough to set this whole chain of events off. Who knows?"

"This is all my fault," Jake said. "Those soldiers would never have headed this way if it wasn't for me."

"It's my fault, too," Prosper said. "You can't take this one on alone, Jake."

"No," Jake said. "I led and you followed; it's my responsibility, not yours. I picked our route." All the air seemed to go out of him. "Mr. Mayor," he said, "I'm at your disposal."

Ben shook his head slowly. "It doesn't seem to me that either of you are responsible for any of this," he

said, and there was a rumble of agreement from those
standing around them. "It's purely the doing of evil
men."

"This is all very well," Dick Leclerc interrupted,
"but what are we going to do about bringing back my
son's body?"

"We'll bring him home just as soon as we can,
Dick," Ben said.

"I'll go out and get him tonight," Dick said angrily. "Who's with me?"

"No," Ben told him. "No, Dick, you won't. I can't
let you or anyone else do that, much as I'd like to."

"You mean you want to let my son lay out there in
the woods all goddamn night?" Dick grated. "Why
don't you go tell that to his mother?"

Ben looked the storekeeper in the eye. "Dick," he
said, "I can't risk permitting a party to go get your
boy right now. He's beyond our help. I need you here
to help mount the defense of the town. We don't have
very long."

"I won't *be* that long," Dick snapped.

"I also can't tip our hand too early," Ben continued. "If those soldiers spot a party bringing your boy's
body back to town, they'll know instantly that we've
been made aware of what's going on. I want the bastards to think we don't know a goddamn thing. Dick,
I mean it. Don't make me put you under arrest."

Dick glared at Ben for a moment, and then he
sighed. "I guess you would," he said quietly, his
shoulders slumping. "All right, you're still boss. I'll
stick."

"Thanks," Ben said. He put a hand on Dick's
shoulder. "I swear we'll make the sons of bitches pay
for this."

"We damn well better."

"We will." The mayor raised his voice to address
them all. "We need to mount a special patrol," he
said. "Where's Roger Tree?"

"Right here, Mr. Mayor."

"Start picking 'em, Roger. I want us to run a line of sentries around the southern end of town. I also want a couple of scouts to hit Logger's Trail and see what's up."

"We can double the night watch—" Roger began.

"Triple it."

"All right, but it's getting pretty dark out to send a scouting party."

"It'll get darker yet," Ben replied flatly. "Pick."

CHAPTER 17

IT WAS DAWN. TEAM TANGO HAD MARCHED THROUGH the woods all night, giving up the trail so as to avoid any possible trap. Until he knew more, Lieutenant Banks was going to be extremely careful. He had already lost two men on this stupid fucking mission. He'd be damned if he'd lose any more.

They came to a rise. "Stop here," Banks said quietly, and his eight remaining effectives came to a halt. The lieutenant silently handed his rifle to Sergeant Wigg and, in return, the sergeant handed Banks his own pair of field glasses. Crouching, the lieutenant double-timed it up the hill and threw himself flat on the ground as he reached the top.

There was a town down there, all right, and it had people in it. Banks had figured that a populated town had to be close by; the boy they'd found dead at the campsite along with Russ and Nick the Dick hadn't been at all roadworn. Banks put the field glasses to his eyes and gave the place a slow stare. He let the picture build in his mind, allowing his hindbrain to decide on its own if anything was wrong.

The old maps said a little place called McAndrew belonged right on the spot he was looking at—and there it was, big as life and mostly intact. The intelligence boys back at the capital were carrying this entire part of the state on their goddamn population charts as uninhabited due to flu. Well, Banks could see some of the uninhabitants walking around on the streets and going about their early morning routine.

Banks licked his lower lip. It struck him as incredible that the town would have done nothing about fortifying its southern flank. These woods were an obvious avenue of attack. It was Banks' considered opinion that whoever had taken out his people had either come from this town or passed through it afterward, and so they were known to the people there. Banks would find the ones who'd killed his men. He had run more than a few operations like this one before, and usually with fewer men. He knew it wouldn't be long before he would know everything that the people in town knew, no matter how many townies he had to use up.

Banks was certain that the killers, whoever they were, were not the fugitives he was looking for. The footprints on the trail and back at the clearing indicated that whoever had done it had come from the direction of town. The fugitives had been heading this way, too—but they would hardly turn back to kill his men. It didn't make sense.

The lieutenant had himself a pretty fair idea of what had happened back there in the clearing. He knew his people well, and he'd found Nick the Dick with his fly half-open and a pair of cut ropes right next to his body. Nick had found himself some unwilling snatch, the kind he liked best, and despite standing orders he'd tied her up and had been about to do her. Russ had gone along with it, too, the stupid fuck.

Then something had happened, and there had been at least three people in on it—the snatch who'd been tied up, another person who'd also been tied, and someone else who had his hands free. That was the one who'd used the broken glass on his men. Banks also knew that one of the three hadn't been the boy whose body they'd found in the clearing, either. You couldn't drag a body the way they'd dragged that kid through the woods and have him in shape to do much of anything afterward. The kid was almost certainly dead even before he was hauled off the trail.

The broken glass represented a choice of weapon that, as a professional, Banks admired even as he planned his reprisal. Retribution for the deaths was necessary. Whoever had killed his men must pay for it—and not only would the killers pay, but so would as many other people as Banks felt were needed to teach an effective and lasting lesson. Teaching said lesson would make things easier for the next Guard unit to come into this area . . . and it would also help keep the morale of Team Tango right up there where it should be.

Banks was under strict orders from Governor Briscom himself to bring the white busker, Garfield, back to Rensselaer alive and unharmed. There was a conspicuous absence of any orders concerning the nigger traveling with him, though. The governor had said offhandedly that he didn't give a shit what happened to the nigger just as long as he didn't get away to mock him, so Banks had planned on simply putting one in his head upon capture. The deaths of his men had changed those plans, though. Now Banks would personally hang the black bastard from the limb of a convenient tree and laugh in his face as he died. There'd be no quick snap of the neck for him. Banks would put the hangman's knot snugly against the back of the nigger's neck instead of at the side so that the fucker would strangle. Hell, Banks thought he might hang the nigger more than once just for the hell of it. He'd have him taken down and revived a few times. *After all*, Banks thought, *why the fuck not?* He suddenly grinned. As for Garfield, Banks would deal with him on the sly after they got back to Rensselaer. Nobody would be able to tie Banks to it.

The lieutenant continued watching the town through Wigg's field glasses. He saw not the slightest sign of a police force or any other sort of security. No one on the streets was carrying a firearm. Women were working alone in gardens in their front yards. A few people were even walking their dogs. *Jesus*, Banks thought. *They keep dogs. Now when was the last time I saw something like that?* Banks didn't give a shit about dogs except as a food source, but their presence here indicated that there might be lots of other things about McAndrew that were worth knowing. Governor Briscom would just love the report Banks was going to make. Maybe he'd love it enough to jump Banks a couple of grades. Banks would have to do some heavy politicking for that promotion, but do it he would.

First, though, there was a town to take. *That's a stupid bunch of fuckers down there,* he thought. He knew that Team Tango would overwhelm them; it would be his wolves against sheep.

Banks backed down the hill, rising to his feet only when he was out of line-of-sight of the town.

"What'd you see, Lieutenant?" Sergeant Wigg asked him.

"A sitting duck," Banks replied, and some of the men chuckled.

"Will the lieutenant be sending back for reinforcements?" Wigg asked.

Banks looked at the sergeant for a long moment with something bordering on contempt. "Line 'em up, Sergeant," he said at last. "Let's get started—if you think you're up to it."

"Yes, *sir*!" Wigg said, saluting.

* * *

He was sitting quietly in his office, reading quickly through each bulletin and urgent coming into his terminal, trying to keep up with the flow of the news. CNN was playing silently on his desktop television.

There was nothing left to do, really, but wait for someone to push the big button. No, it wasn't a button. He had seen a wire story about how it would be done, and there was no button involved at all. There were calls to be made on gold phones and red phones and even your basic black phones, and there were codes and authorizations, and some people would turn some keys and count backwards to zero, but no one would push a button of any importance at any time during the process.

Most of his staff had stayed at the paper through the night. It was nearly dawn now, and he still had not put the paper to bed. There was really no reason for him to do so. The boss printer in Saranac Lake had not bothered to come in that night, so those few workers who'd shown up for the lobster shift had not even been able to get into the building. He had no way to get the paper printed, short of bringing the boards all the way down to the big plant in Glens Falls. He was willing to do that, but he didn't think he'd ever see the paper come out. Given the way the traffic was, it would take until midafternoon to get the boards down to the big plant. Then the plates would have to be shot and the paper run off and then trucked back up the highway. This morning's paper could not possibly hit the streets until late that night, and he did not think the world had that much time left.

The board for the old front page was still on his desk. Idly, he reread the headlines.

SOVIETS OVERRUN LINE, ENTER FRANCE;
PARIS WARNS OF NUCLEAR RETALIATION

U.S. Puts All Forces on Alert;
Prez Sez Top Reds Flee Moscow

'Missing Pet' Mystery Baffles McAndrew

The headline had just become outdated. He'd dictated a new one to Jim Neumann, who was now setting the type and working on a new layout; the computer ought to have spit it out in a minute or so. He had already told the members of his staff that they could leave whenever they wanted to, and some had, but most had stayed. Even though it was more and more unlikely that today's paper would ever appear, continuing to put one together gave those who stayed something to do besides fret.

The story about all the missing cats and dogs was pretty damn strange, and under any other circumstances it would surely rate the front page, but it suddenly didn't seem very important anymore.

His door opened. It was Jim with the new mechanical for the front page. "Thanks, Jim," he said briefly.

"Never thought I'd have to do a front page like that one," Neumann said. "It's all over now, isn't it?"

"I think so. You want to try to get home?"

Neumann shook his head. "No point to it now. I'd never make it through the traffic."

NUCLEAR WAR IN EUROPE

SOVIETS BOMB TWO FRENCH CITIES
IN RESPONSE TO ATOMIC ATTACK
ON ADVANCING FORCES

Lyon, Cherbourg Destroyed;
Paris Government Vows
'Terrible Revenge'

There was just enough room left on the front page to run portrait shots of the President and his opposite number in the Kremlin. The President would be made to look noble and determined, while the Soviet leader would appear shifty and altogether venial—in other words, he would be made to look like the kind of guy who'd murder your mother in her sleep. Slanted as they were, those pictures were all that Laserphoto had provided him with that morning, and so they were what he would run, if he ever got the chance to run anything. He would have preferred to run pictures of Lyon and Cherbourg, either before or after, but he didn't have any.

"I'll guess I'll go in the back and straighten things up," Jim said.

"Yeah."

He was keeping tabs on his desktop television out of the corner of his eye. He knew that, if anything broke, there would be a big red BULLETIN or something behind the head of the increasingly nervous anchorpeople reading the news, and he would then turn up the sound. The anchors have a right to be nervous, *he thought.* They're all in New York or Washington or Atlanta. Might as well paint big red X's on the tops of their heads, and be done with it.

There was virtually nothing on television except for news and commentary related to the news. Virtually all those cable and direct-satellite services that were not news-oriented, or could not be made so, were off the air. It was possible that the satellites carrying the non-news services had been taken over by the government for the duration of the emergency. If so, no one was reporting it.

He picked up his remote control and began zapping around the dial. Every other channel position seemed to have a journalist or, more likely, a quasi-journalist on it, talking about the crisis. Goombye, *he thought, taking a last look at all those carefully sincere faces hanging under the hundred-dollar haircuts.* Goombye, and rotsa ruck. *He began wiggling his fingers in bye-bye fashion at the newspeople as he dialed past them, and he actually laughed a little.* God, *he thought,* I'm cracking up. *He hummed part of an old Tom Lehrer song he remembered. It was called "We Will All Go Together When We Go"—a cheerfully sick thing about Armageddon. He knew now that they would all, indeed, go together—the Barbie and Ken dolls who read the TV news and a grizzled old newspaperman who watched them even as he despised their success, knowing what it meant to his profession. It didn't matter anymore.*

He zapped back to CNN and watched as Ed Asner, Cardinal Whatsizname of Los Angeles, Meryl Streep, Christopher Reeve, Marlo and Phil, and a young woman who'd been one of the kids on The Cosby Show *stood in front of a bank of microphones to urge peace. He could tell without having to hear them speak that they were urging peace because a huge white silhouette of a dove bearing an olive branch had been painted on the powder-blue drop behind them. It was very Hollywood. He doubted the pleas of all those folks would do any good, but he presumed they all felt a little better for trying. He wiggled his fingers bye-bye at them, too.*

Damn, but he was getting cynical. No, strike that; he'd always been cynical. It was just that he'd had a gun to his head for more than long enough, and he was pretty goddamn tired of it and beginning not to care what the hell happened, just as long as it was over, one way or the other. He'd read often enough that hostages got like that after a while. The hell of it was, he and everybody else in the world had been held hostage by the bomb for more than fifty goddamn years. If he felt fear, it was a fear that was slightly tinged with relief.

CNN was now showing a live feed of a Security Council meeting in progress, and he had absolutely no interest in that. He continued his search around the dial again and stumbled across MTV. The music-video channel seemed to be the only exception to the rule of news on the microwaves this morning, and he found the fact a hugely funny one. He left MTV on, but with the sound still turned down; he simply enjoyed the way the videos looked—all flash and color, with young people who'd turned the volume knobs on the control boards of their lives all the way up. The world might be blown up today, but at least it would be going out not with a whimper, but dancing to the six-quarter oogie-oogie-oogie beat of zock rock.

If there were really aliens out there picking up Earth broadcasts, then when they received today's they would find, in amid all the too-familiar faces telling their final tales of death and destruction, one skinny little finger of a wavelength on which they would see kids in weird clothes and funny-colored hair jumping around and singing and enjoying themselves. It seemed to him that he would much rather have the aliens remember Earth that way. He hoped whoever or whatever might be watching would care to note the fun Earth people were capable of having when they really put their minds to it. He hoped the aliens would give a thought or two to that before they swiveled their pickup antennas to catch signals from some other and perhaps saner planet still capable of sending them.

He wanted desperately to call his wife, but he would not take the chance of waking her. If anything bad happened at dawn, as he expected it might, he wanted her to sleep through it. He thought that Plattsburgh Air Force Base would buy a multiple strike, and that would be more than enough to take care of McAndrew. As much as he wanted to talk to Emma now, he took it as a good sign that she had not called him.

He suddenly hoped with a fierce rush of feeling that Marlo and all the rest of them were right, and that the world might yet be saved. Goddamn it to hell, he had been looking forward all his life to the coming of the year 2000, the big Two-Oh. When he was a kid, he'd often figured out how unbelievably old he'd be when the new century came; it had become a figure as familiar to him as the number over the front door of the house he lived in. Now the bastards were going to cheat him out of his new century, a whole new millennium, just short of the mark. He felt a cold rage, even though there probably wasn't any time left to him for rage.

He soon found out that he was quite right. Just as the clock on the wall came to agree with the small box on the front page of his paper that gave the time of dawn, the electricity went off, and through his office door he heard cries of disappointment and outrage from the production department.

He thought with a sudden and unexpected desperation that it might just possibly be a local power failure of some sort until he absently glanced at his digital watch and saw that the face of it had gone a blank gray. He then picked up the phone, just to check, and found that it, too, was dead.

He knew it would come soon now.

Some of the staff who'd stayed to the end did not live very far away, and he thought they might have just enough time to make it home, if they wanted to and if they could hot-wire the ignitions of their cars, bypassing their now-useless voltage regulators. If anyone wanted to stay at the office, though, he would stay there with them. He would not go home and wake Emma.

There was nothing in his office for him to turn off. The Soviets had done that for him already. He got up from his desk and left his office for what he knew would be the last time. He closed the door behind him, softly humming the Lehrer song to himself slowly, as a dirge.

It was.

* * *

LeClerc's had been designated the command center for what was to come, on the theory that the enemy would first head for Town Hall, in order to find and capture whoever was in charge of things in McAndrew. That would give the people hiding inside LeClerc's the chance to get the drop on the invaders.

That was the theory, anyway.

Ed, Ben and Jake were crouched together behind the front counter, well concealed from any outside view. A dozen other people had hidden themselves deep in the shadows toward the unlighted back of the store.

"Time, Ed," Ben said gently, touching his friend's shoulder. "It's just now dawn."

Ed opened his eyes and, seeing Ben and Jake there, sighed with relief. "Thank God," he said. He sat up and rubbed his eyes. "I guess I can't stay up all night anymore like I used to. How long did I doze?"

"About twenty minutes," Ben said. "Nothing's happened yet."

"What's wrong, Ed?" Jake asked, concerned. "You look terrible."

"Do I?" Ed said, blinking. "Actually, I feel pretty damn relieved. I just had the worst dream yet. It was like I was *there*, guys, and that the place was real as *this* is." Ed slapped the floorboards. "It was starting to happen over there. The war was beginning. All the electrical stuff went kaput at the same time."

"Hmmm? What could do that?" Ben wondered. "Did the Russians bomb the power plants?"

"I don't think so," Ed replied. "Bombing the power plants wouldn't have hurt my watch—but it stopped running, too. I guess they can do something over there to turn off all the electric stuff all at once, even if it's running on batteries." Reflexively, he looked down at his wrist, and then cursed himself for a stupe. "Anyway," he continued, "we've got more than enough on our hands right now."

"Yes, we do," Ben said. "We've got our own war to fight."

"After the war I just saw beginning," Ed said, "this one ought to be a cinch."

"I hope it is," said Jake. "I really do."

"Worried about Prosper?" Ed asked him.

Jake nodded. "Yeah," he admitted. "We've been on the road together for a good long time. I feel responsible for him."

"He'll be fine," Ben reassured him.

"I should be up there with him," Jake said. "We're partners."

"Maybe they won't come today, after all," Ed said hopefully.

"They'll come," the mayor said grimly. "Don't worry about that."

Lieutenant Banks and four of his men walked carefully and watchfully through the neatly kept streets in the southern part of McAndrew. Townies turned to look at them. No one seemed hostile. The only reaction among the townies seemed to be one of mild surprise at seeing strangers, particularly armed and uniformed strangers, walking through their town. That seemed reasonable enough to Banks . . . but his gut was sending him the kind of warning signals that had kept him alive and whole during four years of service in the Guard. He was beginning to think that Wigg might have had an idea back there. Reinforcements would arrive within two weeks—

—and when it got around that he'd asked for help in taking a pathetic dump like this one, he'd have to change his name to Pussy, because that'd be the only name his fellow officers would be calling him by from that moment on. No fucking *thank* you.

"You, there," he called out, pointing at an old man sitting on his porch. "Where's City Hall, Pop?"

"You mean Town Hall?" the old man called back.

"That'll do."

"It's right smack in the center of town," the old man called back. "You can't miss it."

"Okay," Banks said patiently. "How do I get to the center of town?"

The old man smiled and pointed in the direction in which Team Tango was heading. "You're on Sycamore Street," he said. "Stay on it for three more blocks and then turn left. That'll be Spruce Street. Five more blocks and you'll be in Neary Square. That's the center of town. Like I said, you can't miss it. You fellas from the Army?"

"Yes, we are," Banks said.

"Well, nice to see you today," the old man said, nodding and smiling. "Been a while since we've heard from the Army."

Banks signaled his men to continue forward. So far, so good . . . but he couldn't shake that bad feeling.

The five Guardsmen walked on and then turned left onto Spruce Street.

"There it is," Ed said. The black and white war flag was suddenly flying from the pole atop Town Hall. Every man and woman in the store checked his or her weapon again. There came the sharp, metallic sounds of bolts being slammed home.

Ben handed his rifle to Ed. "Take care of this for me," he said.

"Ben," Jake said, "let me do this. Please."

"I said no before, and I meant no," Ben said. "Thanks anyway, son."

"I still think you're crazy," said Ed. "These bastards don't know what the mayor looks like. I'll go instead. The town needs you, Ben."

"No."

"Then let's hit 'em now."

"No," the mayor repeated. "They deserve the

chance to surrender. We give them any less than that, we're as bad as they are.''

"Let me go out there with you, then," Ed said.

"No a third time. This one's on me, my friend." He looked away. "Look, Jake, we haven't talked about this—"

"—and we don't have to," Jake said. "You want me to make sure that Connie's taken care of."

"Yeah—and the dog and the cat, too."

"Don't worry," said Jake.

Ben shifted to address Ed. "And the town."

"Sure," the archivist said. "It's in the bag."

Ben paused. "Thanks for not trying to bullshit me about how I'm going to be around to take care of things myself," he said.

"No problem," Ed returned. "That's what best friends are for."

"See you," Ben said. He got up from the floor, brushed his trousers and, taking a deep breath, opened the door and latched it back so it would stay open. He then went outside into the growing sunlight. Fifty sets of watchful eyes followed him as he walked slowly along the west side of Neary Square.

"Someone's coming out of that LeClerc place, Lieutenant," Sergeant Wigg called out. "It's an old guy. He doesn't seem to be armed."

"Stay alert," Banks ordered. "Wigg, keep him covered."

"Yes, sir."

"You, there," Banks said, pointing his rifle rather casually toward Ben. "Hold it right there, old man. Who are you?"

"My name's Benjamin Gordon," Ben said. "I'm the mayor of McAndrew, the town you happen to be in. And you, lieutenant?"

"My name's Banks, New York National Guard. These are my men."

"What can we do for you, Lieutenant?" Ben said.

"Seen anything of a busker team called Garfield & Cross?" Banks asked. "They were headed this way."

"Matter of fact, we have," Ben said. "They're in our jail right now, awaiting criminal trial on various and sundry charges."

"I see," Banks said, nodding as if what he'd just been told was of great importance. "Our authority is the state government in Rensselaer," he said. "Jake Garfield and Prosper Cross are fugitives from justice. We intend to place them under arrest and transport them back to the capital for trial."

"My," Ben said, blinking. "We had no idea the two of them were escaped criminals."

"They are indeed, and we're here to take them into custody."

"I think we can arrange that," Ben said. "We don't want any trouble."

"Smart."

"You can have them right after our inquiry."

"Inquiry?" Banks asked. "What inquiry?"

"Why, our inquiry into the murder yesterday of one Robert LeClerc, citizen of this town, and the attempted rape of his wife, Sarah Broom LeClerc—"

"That's enough bullshit," Banks said, smiling without humor. He brought his rifle to bear on Ben. "Get 'em up, Mr. Mayor. You're under arrest."

"You freeze right there, motherfuckers!" came a loud voice. It was Dick LeClerc, high up in the belfry of the church. *"Your asses are covered!"*

One of the Guardsmen quickly aimed and fired a shot toward the belfry. That was more than enough to prompt the several score armed men and women hidden on the rooftops around the periphery of Neary Square to start shooting at the Guardsmen.

Ben Gordon dropped to the street and rolled into the gutter; a bullet whined off the sidewalk about six inches from his head. He thought rather absently that the shot must have been fired by one of his own people. If Banks or his men had shot at him, they would not have missed.

Ben watched as two of Banks's men—the sergeant named Wigg and a buck private—were hit simultaneously. They fell next to each other and lay still.

The lieutenant glared fiercely at Ben. Their eyes met, and Ben saw his death in them. The mayor prepared himself as Banks raised his weapon and trained it on him. He was thinking of Martha and how much he missed her as he stared into the black depths of the muzzle of the rifle. He trusted that he would never know what hit him.

Banks flinched as a bullet pinged off the pavement only a foot or so from his right foot.

"Lieutenant!" one of the two remaining Guardsmen cried. "They've got us ranged! What do we do?"

Banks kept his weapon trained on Ben Gordon for another fraction of a second as bullets whistled and pinged all around them. Then the lieutenant suddenly felt a feather-light touch at the collar of his shirt, and the slight tug made up his mind for him. His men were in danger. He must do something about that.

"Rodriguez! Jefferson!" Banks rasped. "Into the park! *Now*!"

Staying low, the three scrambled into Neary Square and took up station in the middle of the park, equidistant from all known points of fire.

The lieutenant looked around him. His situation was not good, but neither was it hopeless. There was a big bandstand on their right that protected them from fire coming from the east side of the square, where Town Hall was. A thick growth of trees protected them from the south. That left them exposed to the north and west, screened to a minor extent by bushes.

"You know what was wrong?" Banks said, almost to himself. "All the fuckers we saw on the way in were *old*. No town's got people who're all that old.

The younger ones were right here, waiting for us. God *damn* it!''

"Lieutenant," Jefferson said, "I can see about four of their people on the roof of that bank building over there."

"So start *firing* at them, asshole!" Banks roared.

"Where'd they get all this fucking ammunition from?" Rodriguez wondered.

"Who fucking *cares*?" Banks yelled. "They grow it on the fucking *trees*, for all I know! Maintain your rate of fire!"

Banks suddenly saw one of the townies on the roof of the bank rise up quickly. It was a woman. Banks thought that perhaps she wanted to shift her position, or maybe it was just that she wanted to relieve a cramp in her leg. Whatever the case, it was the last and biggest mistake she would ever make. The lieutenant aimed carefully, got off a quick shot, and watched without any emotion save satisfaction as the woman was flung backward. He heard cries of outrage come from the roof of the bank. *Too bad*, he thought savagely. *That's part payment for Wigg and Schaefer.*

His thirst for revenge aside, Banks knew full well that killing one or two of these people wouldn't do him or the remaining members of the Team any good. It would just piss off the townies more than they were pissed off already. To win, he must crush them—and to do so, Banks desperately needed more firepower. He was beginning to wonder where it had gone to, when it suddenly arrived.

Without warning, there was a thunderous explosion at the base of the bank building. Shards of glass and wood flew in all directions, and the structure collapsed in upon itself. Banks heard screams coming from the rubble. He smiled tightly as Rodriguez and Jefferson howled with glee.

The other seven members of Team Tango had finally completed their circle around town and had come in from the north . . . and they had brought the bazooka with them.

There was another blast. This one destroyed the empty building next to the bank.

Ben Gordon crawled back to the store and entered it through the open front door. "They've got a bazooka," he told them. "They hit the bank and the building next to it. Heavy damage."

"The bank's gone?" Jake asked.

"Yes," Ben said, suddenly as weary as the world.

"I see," said Jake.

"Did they fire at the church?" someone in the back of the store asked. "Is Dick all right?"

"I think so," Ben said. "He's still shooting at the bastards."

"Who's using the bazooka?" Ed asked. "Aren't they all still ducked down in the square?"

Ben shook his head. "The lieutenant out there held back some of his men—seven of them, from what I could see. They came in from the northern part of town; they didn't go anywhere near the Harper place, or the sentries up there would have warned us. Should have figured on something like this happening, I guess, but we didn't. Anyway, we're in trouble now. The bad guys have got too much going for them."

"So let's do something about it," Ed said.

There was the sound of another explosion, closer this time. "Must have been the dairy," Ed said. "Jesus, I hope everybody got off the roof in time."

Ben ducked his head out the door to take a quick look. He saw two bodies sprawled in the street in front of the wreckage of the dairy. They were not dressed in khaki. "No, they didn't," he said shortly.

"Damn," Ed said. "When is Dick set to begin the second phase?"

"Right about now," Ben said. "You know, about a hundred years ago, I coached Dick in Little League?"

"Do tell."

"Hell of a pitcher, he was." They waited and, a moment later, a fiery streak coursed from the belfry of the church into the street below. The bottle broke and spread fire across a circle about eight feet wide. The blaze quickly turned smoky and began to spread. Flames began licking at the foliage bordering the north side of the square.

"Methanol," Ben said, "and God bless Jess Harper for having cooked up a batch of it last week."

"I hope it's enough," Ed remarked drily.

There was the sound of another bottle breaking, and then there came a scream that did not stop. One of the National Guardsmen, burning, ran blindly toward LeClerc's. Ed fired, bringing him down in a flaming heap. The soldier continued to burn.

"Looks like we may lose some of the older trees in the square," Ed said. "I hope the graves'll be all right."

"I was hoping this'd go down a lot easier," Ben said. He aimed and fired another shot. "Shit," he said. "Missed the bastard."

There was another explosion, followed closely by still another. "The blacksmith shop?" someone in the back guessed.

"I think you're right," Ben said.

"Oh, hell," Jake said.

"You know," Ed observed, "I do believe that a couple of those sons of bitches are headed our way."

"So they are," the mayor said. "I'll take the one on the left."

"Fine with me," Ed replied. The two men fired together, and both soldiers fell. One of them made as if to get up, but then collapsed and lay still.

"I wonder how many of the bastards that leaves?" Ben said.

"Not too many, I hope," Ed said. "Everyone must be about out of bullets."

"I think we've used up the ammunition budget through the year 2250" Ben said.

"Let's hope we won't need any more of it before then," Ed said.

There was another explosion and, again, the sound of shattering glass. "I think that's the smithy again," Ben said. "Dammit, Ed, they're getting too close to the store. We're going to have to go out there and start letting 'em have it at close range. Shooting at 'em from the rooftops isn't doing any good; there's too much distance involved. Our people are out of practice, and I bet you half their gunsights are out of kilter."

"All right," Ed said, "but you're not going alone."

"Glad to have you."

"We're coming, too," one of the men in the back said. The others in the store rumbled their agreement.

Ben looked back and grinned at them. "Okay, then," he said. "Keep up with us if you can, kids."

Carefully, the mayor crawled to the front of the store and, staying near the floor and sticking his head out as far as he dared, he sneaked a look out the front door. A second later, something went *phweet!* off the frame three inches above his head, and he pulled back.

"Seven guys," he reported. "Jesus, they look like they're standing there waiting for a bus. Our people aren't even coming close, and there's no one left on this side of the square except us. We're going to have to take them out ourselves."

"So let's do it," Ed said.

Ben nodded. "Three of you stay here. The rest of us will go out the back way and circle around."

The rate of hostile fire had dropped off considerably since the rest of Team Tango had arrived with the bazooka. Banks could see that the townies had pulled back from their posts on top of the buildings on the east side of the square. That townie bastard up in the church belfry had tossed a brace of Molotovs at them, and he'd managed to nail Chaney with one. With all his men now out of range, however, Banks knew that the fucker in the tower was neutralized; it was just too bad that Tango's bazooka team wasn't in position to nail the son of a bitch. There was still shooting coming from that LeClerc place, but that represented the only current threat to him, Rodriguez and Jefferson, and Banks could see that the bazooka team was readying itself to take out LeClerc's next.

The park was beginning to catch fire on its northern side, but it had quite a ways to go yet before it would reach his position. Indeed, the fire was fast becoming their friend. Anyone shooting at them from the north would find it impossible to take aim through the smoke and heat from the blaze.

Jesus, he'd lost five men in this operation. This little puke of a town had killed half of Team Tango. Unbelievable.

They'd pay.

Ben and the others from LeClerc's carefully picked their way up Second Street, towards Neary Square. They paired off in groups of two or three and hid in doorways along the street. Ben and Ed took up position in the last doorway before Second Street opened out into Pine. Jake and Mike Crane took the doorway across the street from that one.

They all waited, listening as the three men still inside LeClerc's fired their weapons repeatedly and as rapidly as they could. Ben Gordon wondered if the stratagem would fool anyone.

The four soldiers, including two in the bazooka team, cautiously walked along Pine Street, heading for LeClerc's. They crossed Second Street.

"I've got the lead man," Ben whispered to Ed.

"I've got the other," Ed returned.

They were the first to shoot. The volley that followed made sure of the first two soldiers and cut down the other two as well . . . but not before one of the Guardsmen, dying, sprayed the doorway in which Jake and Mike were hiding with automatic fire.

Banks watched his bazooka squad fall. "That's it," he said crisply. "Rodriguez, give me your shirt."

"Huh? Sir?"

"You deaf, asshole? I told you to give me your shirt."

"Uh, yes, sir." Still lying on the ground, Rodriguez fumbled at the buttons of his uniform shirt and took it off. He tossed it over. "Here you go, Lieutenant."

"Jesus, Rodriguez," Banks said, wrinkling his nose. "You stink to Christ, you know that?"

"Yes, sir."

The shirt was stiff with accumulated sweat and grime, but it would do. The lieutenant quickly tied its sleeves to the barrel of his rifle and, holding the weapon near the butt end of the stock, began waving it as high as he could reach from his position flat on the ground.

The townies saw the signal and the head man, the old guy who'd approached Banks at the beginning of all this, called for Banks and his two men to come out into the open with their hands up. They did, and were quickly taken into custody.

The chimes in the church belfry began ringing.

"What the hell—?" Ed cried.

"Keep these prisoners covered!" Ben barked. "Ed, go find out what's going on. I want to know who the hell is ringing the bells, and how the hell is he *doing* it?"

"Right away," Ed said, but he froze in his tracks. The sky suddenly lighted up from horizon to horizon with a bright, pearl-gray radiance. The wind came up, and the entire world seemed to moan.

Dick LeClerc emerged from the church and picked his way over the debris littering the front steps. He was rubbing his ears. "Shit, everybody," he said. "Who turned on the goddamn bells? Damn near broke my eardrums." Then he looked up, and his mouth opened. "I think I'll go find Millie up at the evac zone," he suddenly said, and ran off.

"Jesus," Ben said in wonder. "What *is* it? Some kind of lightning?"

"I know what it is," Ed said. "It's the worlds, Ben. It's time for the worlds, that one and this one, to come together. It's not Kingdom Come, Ben. It's Kingdom Returned."

Annie Digby had remained behind in the cabin with Justin and Reggie, despite her desire to stand by her man at the showdown in town. She had had no choice but to stay with the boy, since she was most reluctant to send him off along with everyone else to the evacuation zone that was up 73 a piece. She and Digger thought the cabin would be safe enough, especially with Reggie there, standing guard.

Since Digger had gone into town, she'd heard a great deal of shooting out McAndrew way, and even some explosions; such sounds carried well in these mountains. She was trying to keep Justin from realizing how worried she was.

The explosions had ended, but they had been followed by—something. What were those sounds coming from town? It sounded as if a giant was banging on a big iron pipe, but it also sounded like music. Annie could not remember ever having heard anything like those sounds before, but for some reason they made her think of God.

The sky suddenly became brighter than Annie could ever remember seeing it before. She wondered how such a thing was possible. Then the wind began a low howling, and she became scared.

Justin seemed happy enough, though. In fact, the boy was sitting at the table, playing with two of his tin soldiers. "Digger's all right," he said reassuringly.

"He is?" Annie asked, wanting to believe him. "How do you know?"

Justin looked at his mother with the most serious expression he had ever worn. "I feel very tied in right now," he said. Annie had no idea what her son might mean by that, but she was convinced by it anyway.

"Would you like something to eat?" she asked, rubbing her hands together. "I think we've got a treat somewhere around here with your name on it."

The boy grinned. "Got two?" he asked.

"Oh, I expect we could manage two," she said, going to the cupboard. There was some rock candy she'd traded for at LeClerc's just the week before. Such a luxury as store-bought candy was evidence of the family's current prosperity. She took two pieces of candy by their strings, closed the cupboard, and put the candy on the table in front of Justin.

Annie suddenly frowned as she heard a long, low, continuous rumble of thunder. She could not place its direction; it seemed to be coming from everywhere at once. She looked out the window. There were no clouds visible; there was just that spooky light all over the sky, but it was beginning to dim now.

Reggie began barking. Annie turned around to find two Justins sitting at the table, each contentedly eating a piece of rock candy. One Justin was watching the other Justin, dressed in pajamas, manipulate a plastic robot that, by pushing and pulling on it here and there, could be converted into what looked like a tank or an armored car. The first Justin was fascinated by the toy and was itching to get at it, but he seemed undisturbed otherwise.

"Hi, Mom," Joey said, turning in his seat. "Your hair's different."

It scared both boys badly when Annie shrieked. Joey was startled into dropping his toy and, catching their mother's fear, both twins began to cry while Reggie danced around madly.

Miss Neary was lying on her couch with her eyes closed. She was weak as a kitten and tired to the bone, but she could not sleep. Ed Pearson had asked her not to leave the house again until they could talk about things, and she had readily agreed. She might have lied, but not to Ed . . . and, to tell the truth, if leaving home to die had cost her soul dearly, then coming back, no matter how needful it had been, had cost her three times as much.

The sound of the fighting over in Neary Square had been more than enough to keep her awake. She fretted about what might have happened. Those Army people had killed Bobby LeClerc, and they'd probably be happy to kill everyone in town. She hated the soldiers for what they had done and, with unaccustomed ferocity, she wished them all dead and gone to God for judgment. She was convinced that the two she'd killed herself were better off dead. They would never kill another child. She'd always thought of herself as a peaceable woman, but no one had ever tried to rape a child right in front of her before. Still, it surprised her to realize that it was she who'd done for those two back in the clearing. It was an aspect of herself she had not known was there. She was, however, glad that it had been

there inside her. It had saved Sarah and Prosper,
and given warning to the town.

She wondered what her father might have thought
about it all. Then she suddenly heard church bells,
and she briefly wondered if she had died. Then her
chest twinged again, and she knew she had not.

It got much brighter outside right then, as if another
sun had come out. She opened her eyes. The sky kept
on getting brighter.

There was something strange going on, and Miss
Neary felt she had to see. She got up and went to the
window, every muscle aching. She pulled the curtain
aside and saw by far the brightest sky she had ever
seen, its blue washed away by a light that was soft on
the eyes and the heart. It was all colors combined,
with the harshnesses filtered out and washed away. It
was a glow more than a light, and it comforted her.
The feeling of security this glowingness gave her felt
very much like when she was a young girl, and she
would sit on her daddy's lap for some solace. She felt
at peace.

There came a long roll of thunder, as if from very
far away and, yet, very near. It came from the sky and
the ground and from inside and outside her soul. It
seemed as if the entire world had turned into low
thunder. As the rumbling ended, the glow began to
disappear.

It was just about then that Miss Neary began hearing, distantly, the excited voices of children.

People were already at work putting out fires and
digging through wreckage for survivors of Team Tango's bazooka attack. They frequently looked up from
their work to watch the sky.

Ed and Ben had joined the bucket brigade that was
helping to put out the brushfire that threatened the
graves of the Nearys. Ben had not yet seen Doc, and

he was getting worried; he wanted to know how Jake and Mike were getting along.

"See that?" Ed said to Ben, pointing here and there in the sky. "It's not just a lot of random light, after all. There's distinct sources for it to the northeast, the south and southwest, and lesser sources east and west of here."

"What does it mean, though?" Ben asked, perplexed.

"I think they're targets," Ed said, pointing along the horizon. "Plattsburgh and Burlington up that way, northeast. Albany and everything else south of here, of course. Syracuse over that way. Even Buffalo, because you just might be able to see the glow from a Buffalo bomb. Bombs, I mean."

"Bombs?" Ben asked, confused. "What are you talking about? Is somebody bombing us?"

"No," Ed said. "We're seeing *their* war—or part of it, anyway. Some of it is leaking through to us, but it's harmless, thank God. Cold light, a little wind, and nothing more. We finally get a break. Thanks to that nap I took before, I know a little bit more about it now."

"You do?" Ben said. "Well, tell *me*, then. Do we have to take shelter, or get ready for blast damage?"

"No," Ed said. "We won't be touched, Ben. That other world is the one where they didn't have Kingdom Come. They got a little lucky and managed to avoid the end for a good long time, but they're sure as hell getting it now—and they're getting it far worse than we ever did. I think that's why you and me and some others were seeing that world in our dreams. We were becoming the same place again. Now, for a couple of minutes, as the bombs begin to fall over there, we *are* the same, or near enough. That'll change quickly, though, as things get worse over there."

"What are you talking about?" Ben asked.

"In our day a missile had just one warhead, and a long-range bomber could carry maybe two big ones," said Ed. "Over there, a missile can have a dozen warheads or more, and there are guided missiles that can sneak in under defensive radar to find you sitting on the pot. Progress."

"Sounds like the kind of progress we could do without."

"You said it," Ed said. "Ben, they have *tens of thousands* of warheads over there. Everything is being hit six ways from Sunday, believe me, and nothing's going to be left on the site of any target but a sea of black glass. I don't think anybody over there is going to live through it. We had our war before we could destroy the whole world. They're able to destroy their world several times over."

Suddenly there was a low rumble from everywhere. It sounded like distant thunder. As it ended, the eerie glow in the sky began fading slowly.

"That's it," Ed said. "It didn't take very long for that other world to get itself into worse shape than ours. We're beginning to move apart now. It's over."

"That's it?" Ben asked. "That's all there is to it?"

"All we're going to get is that little look," Ed said, "and we wouldn't have seen even that much if we hadn't been standing so close by. We were never in any danger, though. It's been like listening to your neighbors across the way having an argument, and they don't even know you're home. No more dreams, Ben."

"I most sincerely hope you're right," the mayor said. "But *why*, Ed? Tell me that. *Why?*"

"I don't know why we've been put through all this, but—"

"Wait a minute," Ben said, pointing down Spruce Street. There was a scared-looking, pajama-clad little girl trotting toward them. She was clutching a rag doll dyed in bright colors the likes of which no one in McAndrew had seen unfaded in many years. "Whose kid is that?"

"I don't know," Ed said.

"There's some more kids coming along right behind her," Ben said. "Jesus! Have we got a mass red alert going here, on top of everything else?"

"No," Ed said slowly, shaking his head. "It's something different. Something . . . grand."

"Mr. Pearson?" came a small voice from behind them. "Aren't you Mr. Pearson?"

Ed looked around. There was a well-dressed and well-fed boy about five years old standing there. "I sure am," Ed said. "Hello there, son."

"Can you help me find my mommy and daddy?" the boy asked. "They were here just a second ago. I didn't go anywhere, but I guess I got lost anyway. Mommy will be mad. I'm not supposed to get lost."

"Where do you live, son?" Ben asked.

"I live at 386 Pine Street," the boy recited. "Do you want my phone number?"

"That's all right," Ed said.

"That house burned in the sixties," Ben muttered. "We lost the whole block that night. Remember?"

"I remember," Ed said. He crouched down. "Son," he asked, "what's your name?"

The boy looked concerned. "You don't know me?" he asked. "I go to the office a lot on Saturday mornings with my daddy. My daddy works for you."

"It's all right, son," Ed said. "This is a game I play with your daddy sometimes."

"Mommy says Daddy could get a better job in the city," the boy said.

"I'm sure he could," Ed said. "What's your name?"

"Jimmy," the boy said, and then he corrected himself. "James Neumann, I mean. James Neumann Junior. I live at 386 Pine Street."

"Okay, Jimmy," Ed said. The name rang not the faintest bell with Ed, but the boy's face seemed a little familiar. Ed supposed that Jimmy looked a great deal like his father . . . or, perhaps, he had seen him come by the office—over there, that is.

"Okay, James Neumann Junior," the old man said, putting out his hand. The boy took it. "First we'll get you something to eat, and then we'll see what else we can do."

"Jesus," Ben breathed. "I get it now."

Ed looked at him. "Congratulations," he said.

Ben nodded. "First it was the woods coming back. Then the crops picked up. Then the game, and the cats and dogs. Now we've got the kids. Everything's been coming in from over there. The Earth's either being restocked, or it's restocking itself. I wonder which?"

"I guess that depends on whether you think it's God or Mother Nature at work," Ed said. "Doesn't really matter, I guess."

"I guess not," Ben said. "Kids popping in from out of thin air. All right, we'll deal with them somehow. What else?"

"Just one thing," Ed said. "These kids are probably popping in all over the place. There are families living up on Route 73 in those condo things—over there, I mean. We need to go round up the kids before they wander off too far, or something worse happens."

"Ben Gordon!" came Doc's voice. "Where are you, Ben?"

The mayor looked around quickly and spotted the doctor. "Over here!" he called, waving. He dropped his arm when he saw the somber expression on Doc's face.

"Jake's fine," Doc said. "Leg wound and a graze alongside his head, and that's all. The graze caused a concussion. He's resting now. Mike Crane's gone, though.''

''Jesus have mercy,'' Ben said, closing his eyes.

''It *is* a mercy,'' Doc said. ''Mike was in pretty tough shape. Cancer.''

''Oh, God,'' Ben said. ''I didn't know.''

''You weren't supposed to,'' Doc said. ''Only Stephanie knew—and Jess, of course, since Jess had to keep him supplied.''

Ben sighed. ''That explains a lot about her and Bobby LeClerc,'' he said.

''There's more,'' Doc continued. ''We lost some on the roof of the bank, but not all. Prosper Cross and the Simpson boys were hurt, but they'll pull through.''

''That's fine, Doc,'' Ben said. ''Well, Stephanie Crane's still up at the evacuation zone with the other childbearing women; I'll go up there to tell her about her dad. I want to speak to Connie, too. First, though, I've got to organize some search teams to find all these kids Ed's talking about.''

''Kids?'' Doc asked. ''What kids? What's going on *now*, Ben? I've been inside the clinic since the attack.''

''I'll handle organizing the search teams,'' Ed said. ''You get along to the evac zone. Ben, you can explain everything to him on the way; there'll still be more than enough for you to do when you get back.''

''Well,'' the mayor said, ''it does appear that I've got a few things to take care of. I'm not sure what I can do about it all, but I'll do something anyway.''

''The first rule of good government,'' Ed observed wryly. ''See you later.''

''G'bye,'' Jimmy called after them, waving. He looked up at Ed trustingly. ''Are we going to find my mommy and daddy now?'' the boy asked, his brown eyes big as saucers. "Why is everything such a big mess? And where's all the cars?"

"Let's get ourselves some breakfast, son," Ed said.

"Okay. Egg McMuffin?"

"No, but I think I know where we can get us some oat waffles instead. Would you like some?"

"Sure," the boy said. "What're oaf wattles?"

CHAPTER 18

TOWN HALL HAD NOT BEEN HIT DURING THE BAT-
tle. Banks and his two surviving men had been taken
there and locked in one of the police cells, and the
three Guardsmen had been cooling their heels for
hours.

There was a wooden bench in the cell, and Banks
had taken it for himself. It was just long enough to
allow him to stretch out comfortably on his back,
gaze at the ceiling and think. Rodriguez and Jefferson were sitting close together on the damp cement
floor in the small amount of space that was not taken
up by the bench, the pedestal of the sink, the toilet,
or the flush bucket. The cell did not have a lamp,
but there was a small barred window to the outside
that let in a sufficient amount of light during the
day.

Banks had already had the powerfully built Jefferson
test the bars in the window and the lock in the door.
Everything proved to be solidly in place. The cell was

secure enough that the mayor had felt free to place
only one guard on duty, while everyone else in town
was busy cleaning up and putting out fires or whatever.

A crowd had slowly gathered in front of Town Hall
over the course of the day as individual townies completed tasks related to the emergency. A whole bunch
had shown up together when the last of the fires around
Neary Square had been put out. Banks had been listening to the low babble of the crowd. It was hostile,
but it also carried a note of restraint. He took it as a
very good sign that, although it had been hours since
his surrender and the townies were pretty pissed at
him—no doubt about *that*!—no one had yet rushed the
jail to hang the prisoners. There was not much Banks
could do against a lynch mob . . . but if one had not
formed by now, it never would. Such a mob could not
form without the heat of anger, and that anger had
since faded into a cold and bitter afternoon of resent-
ment.

It was now getting late in the day, but the prisoners had not yet been fed. When that townie mayor
came around again, Banks would raise hell about
the situation. It would be the first shot in his campaign to take ruthless advantage of every decent
instinct these yokels might have. He needed to create the impression among the townies that he and
his men, not the townies, were the true victims in
this whole affair. Banks needed to convince the
town that he and his men had merely been doing a
hateful job that they'd been ordered to do by some
unseen power far away. He would also attempt to
make them believe that the murder of that kid and
the attempted rape of his wife were acts that he
himself did not condone—and, in any case, Russ
and Nick the Dick had paid for them already.

Banks needed to keep the townies off-balance as

much as he could, if he were going to sell them a line of bullshit that ran so wide and deep. The lieutenant was forced to consider that even if the townies wouldn't lynch him, they might well decide to hang him after a trial.

If Banks could tap-dance around the truth fast enough and keep it up for long enough, it was inevitable that the townies would make a mistake, and it would be at that precise moment that Banks would clear the hell out of this one-ball town and double-time it back to Rensselaer. Then he'd come back with a real force and take care of this McAndrew place once and for all.

Banks considered bringing his two men along with him when he escaped. He then considered that their presence in Rensselaer might tend to draw away some of the credit that he alone deserved for having discovered a fat prize of a town like this. Banks decided his men would be safe enough in the town jail for a while. Probably.

"Rodriguez," Banks said, "get your ass up off the floor and take a look at what's going on out there."

The private did and, as those outside saw his face at the window, the noise outside swelled. "Not much, Lieutenant," he reported. "They got all the fires out. Some of 'em are still dragging shit around—pieces of wood from the buildings and like that."

"I can hear that," Banks said in a bored tone. "What else?"

"There's people milling around outside."

"I can hear that, too. How many?"

"Maybe thirty or forty, sir."

"They look pissed at us?"

"Yes, sir. They sure do."

"Well, don't worry about 'em," Banks said, waving a hand dismissively. "They're just a bunch of pussies. Right?"

"I gotta use the toilet," Jefferson mumbled.

"Not 'til they refill the flusher, boy," said Banks. "I want it kept clean in here."

"But I gotta *go*."

Banks turned his head to glare at Jefferson. "Later," he repeated with contempt. Jefferson fell into a sullen silence. *Just like a nigger to whine like a baby,* Banks thought with contempt.

The lieutenant began humming a tune and kept on at it until the sound of footsteps was heard coming from the front of the building. Banks heard someone say hello to the old fucker they'd assigned as the guard. It was the lieutenant's cue. Banks stood up, crossed his arms, faced the cell bars and assumed a stiffly angry expression.

It was old man Gordon. "I came by to see if you needed anything," he said.

"I'll say we do," Banks snapped. "My men and I haven't been fed since we were captured." He tapped the flush bucket with his foot. "This bucket's empty, and there's no other water supply. My men have been wounded, but their wounds remain untreated."

"Your men are wounded?" Ben asked. "They sure kept it a secret. The doctor's already examined you three for flu and whatever."

"I was gashed," said Rodriguez, holding up his arm. There was a shallow four-inch-long scratch on his forearm. He'd gotten it from diving into the bushes in Neary Square.

"I'll send the doctor by again," Ben said. "I pray he doesn't have to amputate. Anything else, Lieutenant?"

"I demand that you notify my command that we've been taken prisoner," Banks said.

"Why?"

"That's the general procedure for handling prisoners of war, Mr. Mayor."

"You're not prisoners of war," Ben said. "You're suspects in a murder investigation."

"Nonsense," Banks said. "Your own people have told you the three of us weren't even there at the time. You took us captive following battle. Those are the facts. There are rules, Mr. Mayor. Follow them."

"Interesting concept," Ben said, scratching his chin. "Prisoners of war. I'll have to consider that. Um, I'll send some lunch over along with our doctor."

"I gotta go," Jefferson said again.

"I expect I can get that bucket filled, too," Ben said. He called to the man on guard out front. "Asa, I'll need you to fetch Doc. The prisoners will be fine by themselves."

"Right away, Ben," came Asa's voice.

"Oh, and gentlemen?" Ben said, turning back for a moment.

"What?" Banks asked.

"Seems to me that I recall the first duty of a POW was to escape and return to his unit," Ben said. "Is that right?"

"I don't know what you're talking about," Banks snapped.

"I see," Ben said, nodding his head. He left.

Banks frowned. The old man was a little smarter than Banks had thought. It would have been one thing for Gordon to realize that escape was a possibility; it was quite another for him to perceive that escape was Banks's number-one priority. Banks knew he would have to move quickly.

The lieutenant guessed that Gordon would send two or perhaps three men, not including the doctor he mentioned, with the food and water. Banks himself could take as many as three, no matter how prepared they think they might be. Townies like these would instinctively hesitate to hurt him. He didn't suffer from any such inhibition.

"Rodriguez? Jefferson?" he whispered. "Listen up."

"Yes, sir," they said in unison.

"We're getting out of here," Banks said, trying to sound as sincere as he could when he used the plural pronoun. He crouched down to sit next to them on the floor of the cell and kept his voice low; the crowd noise from outside had died down and his voice would be likely to carry to the front, where anyone could be listening. Damn, it *was* chilly down on the floor. It was a wonder Jefferson hadn't pissed his pants.

"They'll be back soon with chow," Banks said. "If we wait any longer, they'll be better prepared. We need them to open that goddamn door. Jefferson, I want you to fake being sick. They won't be as quick to see that you're faking it as they might be with a white man."

"Yes, sir," Jefferson said. "Gut problem, sir?"

"Good enough," Banks said, nodding. "Rodriguez, you make like you're bending over Jefferson. You're concerned, get it? I'll be right there. When I cough, you two go for them."

"What if they have guns, sir?" Rodriguez asked.

That's why you're the ones going for them, Banks said to himself. "You know the drill, Private," Banks said. "At close range, take out the enemy with the hand weapon first. You'll have a split-second before anybody with a rifle can bring it to bear. Also, we're in close quarters here, and these people aren't used to hand-to-hand fighting. We'll do fine. We're Team Tango."

Just then Ben Gordon returned. He was carrying Lieutenant Banks's own automatic rifle.

"Where's lunch?" Banks demanded harshly.

"No lunch, Lieutenant," Ben said. "I wish I could say I was sorry about this, but I'm not. I won't risk the safety of this town."

"So you'll shoot unarmed prisoners?"

"Yes," Ben said. He brought the weapon to bear on Banks and fired through the bars of the cell. The lieutenant crumpled. Then Ben calmly shot the other two, cutting off their screams.

An hour or so later a squad of volunteers was clearing out the holding cell and washing it down. The bodies of the three prisoners were dragged out onto the street. A wagon would be by soon to pick them up and bury them somewhere.

Ed and Ben watched from inside Neary Square. They were standing near the graves of the Judge and his wife.

"I don't like it," Ed Pearson said flatly. "I don't like it even a little bit."

"It was necessary," Ben Gordon said.

"I know it was," Ed said, "and I'd have done the same. I still don't have to like it, though."

Ben nodded. "I don't like it either. I'm not built for murder—but they would have gotten away from us. I knew it, and they knew it. They would have gotten back to that nut case in Rensselaer and told him everything there was to know about us, including the simple fact that we're here. Then they'd have been back with a battalion—a battalion of men like Banks."

"I'm not arguing."

"All I could see was a dozen like Sarah LeClerc raped and maybe murdered—and that just during the first week of occupation."

"So we sneak-attacked them."

"Yes," Ben said slowly. "No 'we' about it, though—and I did sneak 'em, didn't I? I sneaked 'em just like a Russian. Thanks, Ed. Now I feel even guiltier.''

''No,'' Ed said. ''I'm guilty, too, because I approve of what you did. We couldn't afford to wait for a trial and a hanging. That would have taken time, and they might have gotten away.''

Ben looked down at the graves of the Nearys. ''I don't think the Judge would have approved, though,'' he mused. ''I think the Judge would have sat on their chests until a jury came in to give us permission to hang the bastards for murder, and then he would have pulled on the rope himself.''

''Were they really up for murder, Ben?'' Ed asked. ''Sarah did say they weren't anywhere near the clearing when Bobby was killed.''

''I don't mean Bobby,'' Ben said. ''Pris Neary made his killers pay. I mean the deaths of our friends in battle. War's murder, plain and simple. Sometimes you fight a war because you're stuck with it, as we were, but it's war and murder all the same.''

''I think I'd separate the two a little,'' Ed said.

''You can't,'' Ben said flatly. ''It isn't even remotely in the realm of self-defense to kill non-combatants, but most wars had turned into nothing much but a continuing series of murderous actions against civilians even before Kingdom Come—and *that* did such a good job of killing civilians that the whole world has damn near died from it.''

''I won't argue with you about that.''

''It's a peculiarly human thing, war,'' Ben said. ''Some animals kill other kinds of animals for food. Army ants kill each other by instinct; I guess they do it because it keeps down the number of army ants or something. I remember reading once that some kinds of monkeys kill others of their own kind—not to eat 'em or because of instinct or whatever, mind you, but simply because one monkey gets mad at another monkey.''

"Sounds just like people," Ed said.

"It's only a little bit like people," said Ben. "The difference is, monkeys and such kill each other only one at a time. Man's the only creature that kills wholesale.''

"But this puts an end to it," Ed said.

Ben sighed. "It does until someone comes looking for these Guard people, or some bunch of Canadians sends an army down here, or we get hit by bandits, or something. It'll always be something.''

EPILOGUE

THEY BURIED THEIR DEAD AND, WHILE THEY mourned them, the people of McAndrew worked hard, readying their little town for yet another harsh Adirondack winter. Their black and white American war flag remained at half-staff atop Town Hall for a week, and the names of their dead were engraved into a carefully stained and polished oaken plaque that was mounted in Neary Square right next to the Civil War memorial. Ben Gordon designed the plaque and wrote the text. Jake Garfield had been honored to carve it while he recuperated.

OUR HONORED DEAD
IN
THE BATTLE FOR McANDREW

———

Michael Joseph Crane
John Francis Duncan

Clarissa McGonagle Hands
Elaine Ann Kirby
Robert Andrew LeClerc
Roy Jonathan Libbey
Thomas Adrian Mocci
Abner Horatio Palmer
Albert Hugh Wells

———

Let our hallowed dead rest in peace,
knowing that they have purchased for us
with their precious blood
our finest possession: our freedom.

As winter approached, everyone decided it was time for the final town picnic of the year.

The unburned parts of Neary Square were packed. Counting the newly arrived children, there were probably more people sitting on their haunches in the square at that moment than there had been at any time since just after Kingdom Come. Virtually everyone who was not out walking one of the augmented patrols that had been mounted since the attack by Team Tango was at the square.

"Very nice affair," Ben Gordon said. He held up his can of Coca-Cola. "Did you know it took my daughter two hours of searching to find the can opener? It turned out to be up in the attic, in the box with the hand mixer and the blender. Anyway, *salud.*"

Jake Garfield tapped his own can against Ben's. *"Muchas gracias,"* he said, taking a sip of Coke. Then he grimaced.

"Are you all right?" Connie asked.

"Hmmm? Oh, no, it's not the leg, honey." He held up the can. "Ben, tell me something."

"If I can."

"How the heck did you ever manage to drink this Coke stuff?" Jake asked. "I feel like it'll strip the enamel right off my teeth if I even *look* at it for too long. God, it's sweet.''

"That's the whole point," Ed said, taking a gulp. "We did as many unhealthy things as we could think of every day. Drinking this stuff was one of our favorites. Did you know we used to strip accumulated road grime off our automobile windshields with it?''

"Actually," Ben said, "Jake's right. You lose your taste for this stuff if you haven't had it for awhile." He sighed. "I give up. There's just too many holes in my teeth for me to enjoy it much. Anybody want mine?''

"Give it to one of the new kids," Doc suggested.

"That's a good idea," Ben said. "They're used to it." He looked around. "Hey, Ricky!" he called. "Ricky Mahler! Come over here, why don't you?''

Scotty Mahler's new little brother trotted up, and Ben offered him his can of Coke. "Thanks, Mr. Gordon," the boy piped as he grabbed it and ran off.

"He seems pretty happy," Jess Harper observed. "Tell me, are they all doing that well?''

"No, not nearly," Ben said. "We've got plenty of new kids, more than half of them, who don't have a set of natural parents here. Ricky there is one of the lucky ones. He's got the same parents he always had, and he's living in the same house he always did. He's even got the same older brother. That's pretty rare. Other kids come from families that either never lived here at all, or died off between Kingdom Come and now. I think we've done well in placing them, though.''

"You know," Ed mused, "these kids were *there* when the bombs started going off in Plattsburgh and Burlington and those other places. Kids can be awfully practical sometimes. Some of them were pretty glad to find themselves out of it, no matter what. They had atomic explosions going off all around them—not one at a time, like we did, but *all at once*—and it scared them to death. Then, suddenly, they found themselves here, nice and safe. The kids aren't without pain, mind you, but they're working it out.''

Jake grinned. ''Connie and I have already been assigned our two by the committee,'' he reminded them. ''We'll all be together after I marry the town's new head schoolmarm next Saturday.''

''Connie?'' Ed asked. ''Why wait? Why don't you move in right now?''

''It sets a bad example,'' Connie said primly. ''The four of us will be together soon enough.''

''Grandchildren,'' Ben said. ''Never thought I'd see any. God, I'm a happy man. Connie, you and Jake can fill up that house with kids. I won't mind a bit.''

''We have more than enough room for you, too, Ben,'' Jake said, ''and we're not taking no for an answer. We're not letting you stay all by yourself in that big old house.''

''That's right, Daddy,'' Connie said. ''You have no choice.''

''There's always a choice.''

''I'll burn the place down,'' his daughter threatened.

''Okay, so maybe sometimes there's no choice.''

''Take them up on it, Ben,'' Ed said. ''You can't cook and you can't clean.'' He suddenly looked puzzled. ''Say, what *can* you do, anyway?''

''Vegetate,'' Ben said proudly.

''I *knew* it,'' said Ed.

''Hey, look over there,'' Connie said. ''All the LeClercs came out for the picnic. Look, Randy's got his new little stepsisters in tow. Aren't they cute?''

''I hope the girls help ease the pain in losing Bobby,'' Jake said. ''There's certainly enough people in that house of theirs now, what with Randy, the two girls and Sarah and Stephanie, too.''

''There sure are,'' Ben agreed. ''Those folks are doing far more than their share. It was good of them to open their door to Stephanie, wasn't it? With her father gone and all, I mean. They didn't have to do that.''

"I know," Connie said, "but Millie says they feel responsible for their coming grandchild, and I can't blame them. Stephanie told me yesterday she's just happy to have a roof over her head and people around her to help until after the baby's born. Maybe it'll calm her down some, and make her a, uh—''

"Nicer person?" Jake supplied.

"Better said by you than me.''

"Stephanie's not a bad person," Doc said. "She's had some problems, though—and not all of them are of her own making, I might add. Having some security in her life will help her to resolve them.''

"I wonder how Stephanie and Sarah have been getting along, anyway?" Ed wondered. "I haven't been by the LeClercs' place since the funeral.''

"They're all doing just fine, or so I hear," Ben answered. "Stephanie knows she's lucked out. She isn't likely to make trouble, and Sarah's never made trouble for anybody in her life.''

"Was anybody surprised that Sarah moved out of her mother's house when Dick made the offer?" Jess asked. "I haven't heard a word.''

"Nobody with any brains in their head was surprised," Doc said. "Terrible woman, that Amanda.''

Ben lowered his voice to talk to Ed. "You get yourself settled in yet at Pris Neary's?''

"Sure," Ed said, suddenly looking sad. "It won't be long now, but I think she's comfortable enough. Now she's in her own bedroom and surrounded by her things, and she's—well, maybe not happy, but content. I swear, the thought of her going out into the woods to kill herself just makes me nuts. After all that woman's done for this town—''

"She was doing what she thought was needful," Ben said. "She didn't realize we can support her and others like her now. She remembers the famine, Ed. And if she hadn't gone out—''

"I know," Ed replied. "She's one of the bravest women I've ever known."

"Yo! Digger!" Jake called. "Hey, group, it's the Digbys—*all* of them!''

"Hi, everybody," Digger said. He was holding the picnic basket; Annie was holding on to the twins. "Got room for us down there somewhere?"

"Right here, sir," Ben said, scooting over. "It's great to see you all."

Digger smiled. "We finally figured out that if Justin hasn't caught anything from Joey, then he wasn't going to catch anything from anybody else, either. So here we are, and you'll be seeing a lot more of us from now on."

"I'm still a little nervous about this," Annie said, "but I know the twins'll be all right." Suddenly she smiled the smile of a goddess, and it transformed her. "Twins," she said again.

"Say, Ben?" Digger asked. "What was the final count, anyway?"

"Three hundred and forty-three new kids," Ben said.

"That's a lot of children to take care of," Annie said.

"We've got the food now," Ben said. "This year's been so fat for us, we can take care of everybody this winter and even put aside a small surplus. Next year we'll be able to do even better, thanks to the work the older new kids will be doing."

"You heard them bellyaching yet?" Ed said. "They're really quite accomplished at it. 'Who, *me*? *Farm???* Like, you know, *ugh* to the twenty-first *power!*' "

"That'll change," Ben said. "I guarantee it. Um, we've figured out at least some of the rules about why some kids came through and others didn't."

"There were rules?" Digger asked.

"We think so," Ben replied. "Some of them were pretty rough, too. No child older than twelve came over, for instance. We didn't find any children more than half a mile from where McAndrew Road lets out on 73, and we spent three days looking. Joey here is unusual in that he appeared here outside that range, but I think it might be because he's a twin. Then again, it might not have anything to do with that. It makes me nervous that we might have missed some child out there."

Digger thought about it. "I don't think so," he said after a moment. "I think the kids appeared only where people could find them easily. Just a hunch, but it feels right."

"There's more," Ben continued. "No child who was already here came over, so we don't have any, er, duplicates."

"*We're* duplicates," Justin said.

"I'm no duplicate," Joey snapped. "*You* are."

"Not what I meant, son," Ben said. "Hey, don't you two start fighting. Uh, no sickly or disabled children came over, either. Out of nearly three hundred and fifty, odds were that we should have seen at least several."

"How sad," Connie said. "We could have taken care of them."

"Yes, we could have," Ben replied. "Makes you wonder who or what was doing the picking, and why. Anyway, there may have been other rules, but those were the obvious ones. You know what, though? For the first time, I feel like we're going to make it now. I've been wondering if any other towns have had the same things happen."

"There'll always be buskers to ask," Ed said. "We'll know soon enough."

"It's like the story about the Ark," Digger said.

"We were just close enough to that other world for the animals and kids to hop aboard."

"Or be brought aboard," Jake said. "Anyway, we're not the Ark. We're Mount Ararat, where the Ark washed up."

"Who did it all?" Ed asked. "Who brought 'em over here? God?"

Jake shrugged. "No telling," he said. "Whoever or whatever did it, though, maybe this poor old world of His does have a chance now, after all."

"Mr. Garfield, sir," Ben said, "I hate to interrupt your maudlin musings, but it's getting kinda late. When's the show start?"

"Just as soon as Prosper gets here," Jake replied. "I don't know what's keeping him."

"Amanda Broom," Ed snorted.

"Now, Ed," Sammie said, waggling a finger at him.

"Sammie?" Jake suddenly said. "I almost forgot something." He produced a little bundle. "I hear it's your birthday."

"Why, so it is, Jake Garfield," Sammie said, pleased. "What's in here, anyway?" She held the bundle up to her ear and shook it. It made no sound.

"Well, open it," Jake said.

Sammie did, and gasped. It was the Indian doll Jake had brought to McAndrew with him when he and Prosper had arrived, seemingly so long ago. "Oh, Jake!" she said. "I can't take this!"

"Sure you can," Jake said. "You should see the expression on your face. Happy birthday, Sammie." He leaned over and kissed her on the cheek.

"Jake," Sammie said, "I'm leaving my husband for you. Is tonight soon enough?"

"Sure."

"Bye, honey," Jess said affectionately. "It's been grand."

"Excuse me, everybody," Jake said, grabbing his

cane and guitar. "I see my partner has finally arrived. Somebody save me a chicken leg, okay?"

"Will do, you wonderful man," Sammie said.

Jake hobbled over to Prosper. "Hey, baby," Jake called, and then he stopped dead in his tracks.

Prosper was carrying his knapsack.

"Oh, hell, Prosper," Jake said. He saw the news in his friend's eyes. "Oh, *hell*!"

"I'm sorry, Jake," his friend said quietly. "Busking's all I know. I don't know how to be the only black townsman in the Adirondacks. I can't stay here; I got to move on, find a place that's special for me, like this place is for you. I'll winter somewhere else."

"But—Jesus, Prosper! What'll I do without you?"

Prosper tried to smile. "Live happily ever after, man. That's what it says at the end of this book Connie gave me. I read it right out."

"Will you ever come back?"

"I hope so."

Jake sighed. "Just know that you're always welcome in my home. You're my brother, man. Always will be."

"And you're mine," Prosper said. "That'll never change."

Jake's voice was thick. "Uh, look. I hate to point this out, but we've got a show scheduled. One last gig."

Suddenly Prosper grinned. "Sure, man. Wouldn't miss it."

"We'll lay 'em out cold."

Taking the bandstand stairs with care, Jake walked up onto the platform to sustained applause. He was glad that his leg no longer hurt him to stand on, because he would not have wanted to do this particular set of all sets, the last gig of Garfield & Cross, sitting down.

"Folks?" Jake called, holding up his hand for quiet.

"Folks, we're ready to begin the formal part of our program."

"Do tell!" someone shouted, and there was more laughter.

"As you can see," Jake continued, "I have—for one performance and one performance only—taken up the sacred calling once again." He held up his guitar to enthusiastic applause.

"Isn't this like the forty-fifth time you've taken up the calling since you retired from it?" Doc called out, and the crowd laughed.

"The forty-eighth," Jake said, shrugging, "but who's counting? Ladies and gentlemen . . . my partner, my brother, my friend—Prosper Cross."

There was enthusiastic cheering and applause as Prosper mounted the bandstand. He waved and pointed and winked and smiled, smiled, smiled as the crowd cheered and kept on cheering, and soon they all came to see in both of their faces that this was their last show together.

The crowd fell silent.

"How about we do the new song first?" Prosper asked. "That one you remembered from the other side?"

"Yeah, that one," Jake said. "It fits better than ever now."

"Okay, my man. Show time."

"Let's knock 'em dead. One, two, one, two, three *and*—"

They launched into *Here Comes the Sun*.

THE BEST IN SCIENCE FICTION

☐ 54989-9	STARFIRE by Paul Preuss	$3.95
☐ 54990-2		Canada $4.95
☐ 54281-9	DIVINE ENDURANCE by Gwyneth Jones	$3.95
☐ 54282-7		Canada $4.95
☐ 55696-8	THE LANGUAGES OF PAO by Jack Vance	$3.95
☐ 55697-6		Canada $4.95
☐ 54892-2	THE THIRTEENTH MAJESTRAL by Hayford Peirce	$3.95
☐ 54893-0		Canada $4.95
☐ 55425-6	THE CRYSTAL EMPIRE by L. Neil Smith	$4.50
☐ 55426-4		Canada $5.50
☐ 53133-7	THE EDGE OF TOMORROW by Isaac Asimov	$3.95
☐ 53134-5		Canada $4.95
☐ 55800-6	FIRECHILD by Jack Williamson	$3.95
☐ 55801-4		Canada $4.95
☐ 54592-3	TERRY'S UNIVERSE ed. by Beth Meacham	$3.50
☐ 54593-1		Canada $4.50
☐ 53355-0	ENDER'S GAME by Orson Scott Card	$3.95
☐ 53356-9		Canada $4.95
☐ 55413-2	HERITAGE OF FLIGHT by Susan Shwartz	$3.95
☐ 55414-0		Canada $4.95

THE TOR DOUBLES

Two complete short science fiction novels in one volume!